SHAG & BONES:
THE COMPLETE CASES

SHAG & BONES

THE COMPLETE SERIES

RUSSELL BENDER

INTRODUCTION BY
JOHN WOOLEY

ALTUS PRESS

2023

TABLE OF CONTENTS

THE BARD OF DRAGSTRIP HOLLOW

by John Wooley

The producers wanted to do a quickie at the old Charlie Chaplin studios, so they dreamed up this story literally on a couple of weekend afternoons. Russ Bender wrote the script, and he had never written a script in his life—he was an actor— and he had no idea what to do with a creature called a "zombie." In fact, I don't think anyone connected with *Voodoo Woman* had ever read a pulp magazine when they were kids to find out what a zombie was.

> — Paul Blaisdell, quoted in *Paul Blaisdell, Monster Maker* by Randy Palmer (McFarland & Company, Inc., 1997)

THERE'S NO doubt whatsoever that Paul Blaisdell was one of the horror-film greats, crafting wild, weird, and hideously wonderful cinematic creatures whose images are forever imprinted on the psyches of the so-called "monster kids" of the '50s and '60s. But, when it comes to his words about Russell Richard Bender, Jr., the iconic monster maker whiffed so thoroughly that what he said works, in a Bizarro World kind of way, as a perfect epigraph for this book.

Russ (sometimes billed as Russell) Bender was indeed an actor, a ubiquitous supporting player in both movies

Sherry Jackson and Russ Bender (as record-producer Shep Kirby) in
Maury Dexter's 1965 beach-party knockoff, *Wild on the Beach*.

and television from the early 1950s through the late '60s—
one of those performers whose names aren't nearly as well
known as their faces. Like Paul Blaisdell, he was involved
in several of the best-remembered baby-boomer-era horror
pictures, including *It Conquered the World* (1956), *Invasion
of the Saucer Men* (1957), and *Ghost of Dragstrip Hollow*
(1959). In the latter, one of his better-known appearances,
he had a starring role as a magazine writer sent to get the
lowdown on teenage hot-rod culture.

But well before he made his first screen appearance, Russ
Bender was a writer—in real life. In fact, by the time the
movie Blaisdell referenced, 1958's *Voodoo Woman*, came
along, Bender had already scripted one theatrically released
feature, the vest-pocket *film noir A Life at Stake*, Hitting
the screen in 1955, *A Life at Stake* toplined Keith Andes
as a down-and-out homebuilder who'd been shafted by
a partner, and Angela Lansbury—some 30 years before

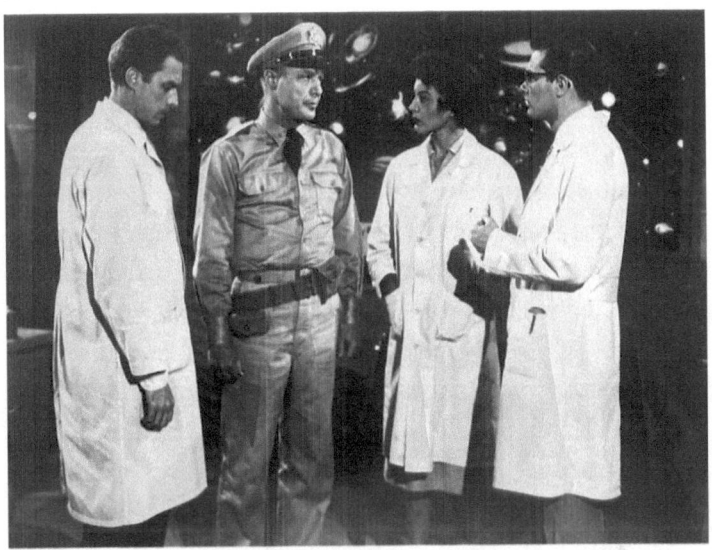

Bender (second from left) lin familiar garb as a military man, with, from
left, Paul Harper, Karen Kadler, and screenwriter-actor Charles B. Griffith
in American International Pictures' *It Conquered the World* (1956).

Murder, She Wrote—as a wickedly effective *femme fatale*.
Bender based his screenplay on a story idea by the picture's
producer, Hank McCune.

McCune, also an actor and writer, and Bender had
worked together on NBC-TV's *Hank McCune Show*,
which ran for one season in 1950–51 (reportedly it was the
first sitcom with a laugh track) and had Bender on board
as a member of its writing staff. The cast included a young
Arkansas native named Maury Dexter, who gets a credit as
dialogue supervisor on *A Life at Stake*. Dexter would drop
acting in favor of producing and directing, becoming one of
the more prolific low-budget-movie makers of the 1960s—
and he'd cast Bender in several of his pictures, including 1965's *Raiders from Beneath the Sea* (in which Bender
played a dipsomaniac who goes along with a scheme to rob
a bank while clad in scuba gear), 1965's *Wild on the Beach*,
the famed 1968 pot film *Maryjane*, and 1968's racial-ten-

sion exploitation drama *The Young Animals*, his final feature, in which he appeared as a high school coach.

At the same time he was working on McCune's TV show, Bender was also writing for the radio drama *Nightbeat*, featuring Frank Lovejoy as a hardboiled reporter for the *Chicago Star*. And those weren't his only early scripting credits. Before he got the assignment to do *Voodoo Woman*, he'd penned episodes of television's *Dangerous Assignment*, *Hollywood Opening Night*, and *The Ray Milland Show*. Post-*Voodoo Woman*, he was a credited writer on a couple of other Dexter-produced-and-directed features, a western from 1961 called *The Purple Hills* and the dope-smuggling drama *Womanhunt* (1962). He even had a substantial part as a deputy marshal in the former. It was one of the more than 50 movie roles, along with several dozen TV appearances, he'd rack up before his 1969 death.

So, yes, Paul Blaisdell was right. Russ Bender *was* an actor.

But some time before his acting career took off, even before he began scripting radio and TV episodes, Russ Bender had been a successful fictioneer, aiming for and hitting pulp-magazine markets ranging from the top-tier *Black Mask* to less prestigious titles, the latter mostly published by A.A. Wyn's Ace Magazines. Along the way, Bender created the babyfaced Shaughnessy "Shag" Roberts and freckle-faced dandy Stanley "Bones" McPherson, the two-fisted team of loan-business operatives whose complete adventures are collected in this book.

Although it's not the intention here to pick on Paul Blaisdell, who only know Bender as an actor and so could be forgiven for his ignorance of Bender's professional writing jobs, it should be noted that—despite the monster-maker's assertions—Russell Bender had not only *read* the pulps; he'd also crafted hundreds of thousands of words for their pages.

Here, then, is the story of how Russ Bender's pulp career began and blossomed, at least for a while, along with the post-World War II career switch—from professional writing to professional acting—that he rather remarkably pulled off.

"WHEN I got out of school," Russ Bender told *San Francisco Examiner* writer Jeanne Miller for a December 6, 1965, feature story, "I began writing detective stories for the pulps. I was only 22 and greatly admired the superb mystery writers, like Raymond Chandler, Dashiell Hammett, and Earle [sic] Stanley Gardner."

Born on January 1, 1910, in New York City, Bender would have been 22 in 1932—one of the darkest years of the Great Depression. Although research has so far failed to turn up the name of his college or the jobs he took before he started hitting the pulps regularly in 1938, we do know that by 1936 he was living in Baltimore (at 2628 North Calvert Street) and had finally managed to crack the pulpwood market. The reason we know this is because, flush with success from his first sale, Bender sent a letter from that city to *Writer's Digest*, which published it in the August 1936 issue.

Wrote Bender:

> I've followed the advice given in several *Digest* articles of selecting one magazine, faithfully studying it, reading every issue, and writing a story specifically for that one magazine.
>
> This advice began to bear fruit when I received not a plain rejection slip, but a letter from the editor commenting on my work. I stuck to my guns—who wouldn't have?—and on Saturday, June 20, a check arrived from *Black Mask* paying for my 15,000-word novelette.

Mary Ellen Kay, Paul Blaisdell in his monster suit, and Tom
Conway in 1957's *Voodoo Woman*, co-written by Bender.

I'll be forever indebted to the market advice and even more
important the instructive articles in the *Digest*. You're doing a
swell job.

The letter bubbles with optimism, and why not? Bender
had just sold a substantial story to the editor (Joseph T.
Shaw, in his waning months at the *Black Mask* helm) of
the top pulp-detective market in the country. Titled "Heat
Target," Bender's novelette came out in October of that
year, a couple of months after the missive ran in *Writer's
Digest*. Certainly, he was on his way.

Except for one thing: He didn't sell another pulp tale for
nearly two years, and then it wasn't to *Black Mask*, but *Ten
Detective Aces*, a lesser pulp published by the above-men-
tioned A.A. Wyn. Certainly, Bender must've submitted his
first Shag & Bones stories, and probably others as well, to
Black Mask. But evidence indicates that Shaw's successor,

Third-billed Russ Bender strikes a pulpish pose in Maury Dexter's
1965 crime-caper film, *Raiders from Beneath the Sea.*

Fanny Ellsworth, wasn't as impressed with the quality of
Bender's prose. By the time he managed to place one with
Ellsworth—the novel-length "Body-Guard to Death,"
which appeared in the October 1938 *Black Mask*—the
Shag & Bones adventures (all narrated by Shag Roberts)
were pretty much established as regular features in *Ten
Detective Aces.*

Although Ellsworth apparently had little interest in
Shag & Bones, Bender had found a taker in Wyn, who ran
Ace Magazines with his wife, Rose. While Ace was not a
top-tier market, and Wyn was notorious for his penuri-
ousness, it was a legitimate outfit whose more successful
publications included the likes of *Secret Agent X*, *Western
Trails*, and, in fact, *Ten Detective Aces.* The latter was such
a big name in the Ace stable that, according to the October 1940 *Writers Digest*, "the rate is a half-cent [a word]

for all [Ace pulps] but *Ten Detective Aces*, which continues to pay one cent."

On the other hand, while *Black Mask's* pay rate began at a penny a word, payment was averaging about a cent and a half during the late '30s. That's according to author and pulp historian John Locke, who's studied the topic of pulp-author earnings at some length. "*Black Mask* in that period," he wrote in recent correspondence, "was less forthcoming about rates, but I think it's fair to say they were a higher-paying market than *TDA*, which is what we'd expect."

Although the difference between a cent and a cent-and-a-half a word doesn't sound like much, it made a lot of difference in those days. A 15,000-word novelette at a cent-and-a-half would net the author $225.00, while the same manuscript would fetch only $150.00 at a penny a word. In those Depression days, that 75-buck difference could buy plenty of groceries and gasoline and pay a month or two's rent to boot.

From 1938 through 1940, Bender sold 18 pulp stories (and maybe more under pseudonyms), including the seven novel-length Shag & Bones numbers collected here, which all originally appeared in *Ten Detective Aces*. During that time, a new Shag & Bones adventure hit the stands every three or four months, with Bender landing several one-off tales as well in *TDA* and other places. He was making a living as a writer, and chances are he felt pretty good about the way things were going.

Then came Pearl Harbor. And, as happened with so many other Americans, Russell Bender's life was upended.

"I had contributed over 2,000,000 words to magazines when the war started," he told the *Examiner's* Miller (in what may have been a slight exaggeration), "and I joined the Army.

"During the war, the pulps really went under because the wood was needed for defense. So when I left the service, the market had collapsed. As a result of my interest in detective stories, I got a job as an actor, working in dramatizations of case files for the Counterintelligence Academy in Baltimore, where student agents were taught the techniques of interrogation. I did these playlets for two years. By then, I was really hooked on acting, and I've been doing it ever since, in the movies, and television and in the theater."

Bender's obituary on the *Find a Grave* website (findagrave.com), written by Lowell Thurgood, characterizes the writing-to-acting transition a bit differently. After the war, wrote Thurgood, Bender "found difficulty in attaining publication of his stories due to a change of taste in marketing and with the use of the G.I. Bill he enrolled at the Actors Studio and chose to embark on a newfound career in acting.

"Upon attaining his degree, he settled in California and began his career as a stand-in for fellow actor Eddie Albert, who later befriended him."

According to Thurgood, Albert pulled some strings and got Bender a screen test, which led to an uncredited bit part as a policeman in the 1952 Loretta Young drama *Paula*. It was the beginning of an acting career that would last right up until Bender's death at age 59; in 1969, the year he left the earth, he could be seen on episodes of three different television series: *Bonanza*, *Petticoat Junction*, and *The Big Valley*.

"Bender, who neither married nor had any children," wrote Thurgood, "died unexpectedly following complications of a non-communicable disease." He then listed orga-

Bender (right, at table in suit and tie), as magazine writer Tom Hendry, digs
the antics of the hot-rod gang in 1959's *Ghost of Dragstrip Hollow*.

nizations Bender supported: the Screen Actors Guild, the
Motion Picture and Television Fund, the Catholic church,
the California State Democratic Committee, the American Red Cross, the Boys & Girls Clubs of America, and
the Writers Guild Foundation, which he helped found.
The obit also notes that Bender was a "prominent" script
writer for the Pasadena Playhouse and a communications
instructor at the University of Southern California.

The *Find a Grave* site's reason given for Bender's leaving
magazine-writing—"a change of taste in marketing"—
seems peculiarly worded. But it likely refers to the dying
postwar pulp market and the paucity of alternatives for
its writers. Bender did sell a handful of tales to late-'40s
pulps, including "The Corpse Strikes Back!", a novel about
a food inspector fighting smugglers of typhoid-contam-
inated butter in Annapolis, Maryland; it was featured on
the cover of the March 1946 *Detective Tales*.

His final pulp credit appears to be a short story in the
June 1949 issue of *10-Story Detective Magazine*—the only

Claudia Barrett and Keith Andes in a scene from Bender's first theatrical-
feature scripting credit, 1955's *A Life at Stake*. The picture's femme fatale, Angela
Lansbury, can be seen with Andes in the art above and beside the title.

one of his post-World War II yarns to come out from his
old Shag & Bones publisher, Ace Magazines.

BY THE time he gave his interview to the *San Francisco Examiner*'s Jeanne Miller, not quite four years before
his death, Bender was well-established as an actor. In fact,
he was in San Francisco to star in a new stage production
called *Once over Nightly*. Called a "sex-and-chatter farce"
by Miller, it would end up running some two years at San
Francisco's On Broadway Theatre.

While Bender told Miller he ultimately chose acting
over writing because, as she put it, "he was somewhat of
an extrovert," he also made it clear to her that he hadn't
entirely turned his back on his former profession.

"I've still found time to write five movies and numerous
television scripts," he said. "But acting is really for me. A
writer's life is a very lonely one. And I'm so outgoing that

I like to find my creative challenges in the interplay with other performers.

"There's all the difference in the world as far as the rewards go, in the two different fields," he added. "If you write a story or a novel, of course, it's satisfying. And if it's well reviewed and people buy the book, there is great gratification. But that all takes time—time to get your work published and time for it to be appreciated."

He compared that to the theater, where "you get your rewards immediately." And, at least for the purposes of this interview, the veteran pulpster felt certain he'd made the right choice.

"For me," he said, "the typewriter will never hold a candle to the boards as a creative outlet."

A FINAL note: The Shag & Bones adventures, like all classic pulp stories, are products of their times, occasionally containing words and scenes that have the potential to upset today's readers. For instance, a few of the stories collected here feature over-the-top racial characterizations and/or violence against women.

Since our purpose in making these tales available once again is to entertain, not offend, we offer the above caveat to those thinking about adding this collection of 85-year-old popular fiction to their libraries.

— John Wooley
Foyil, Oklahoma
2 October 2023

(Big thanks to John Locke, Rob Preston, Glenn Marcum, and Matt Moring for their help with this introduction.)

MURDERERS' REBELLION

Murder is a whirlpool. This one started slowly, but when it gathered impetus, many lives were engulfed in its swirling current. Investigator Shag Roberts wanted no part of it, but he was caught in the maelstrom of too many cross-currents. And now the waters were running over his head—turning crimson red.

CHAPTER I

OVERTURE FOR MURDER

I GOT a fist shoved under my nose on my next to last call, collected six bucks on my last. Ten minutes later, at four twenty-five, I parked my coupé on Bladensburg Road, loafed into the Purple Cat Inn.

Edward, the barman, said: "How's the small-loan business?"

"Okay." I beaded toward a phone booth at the end of the bar, caught a short beer on the way. When I got the office, Janey, our redheaded stenographer, said:

"Not *Shaughnessy* Roberts?"

I'm always kidded about that first name. I said: "The same."

"Just a minute. The boss is busy."

I had just time to push open the door and get Edward to slide me another beer before the boss' voice said:

"Get in here, Roberts."

I came to life. "Get in there! Look. I'm over here every night until six-thirty, working myself to the death, and—"

"Can it. I worked Washington myself once. I'll give six to one you've finished your last call already." I didn't take him up. "But get in here, Shag. All the brass hats are down, from Cromwell up, and there's something about a suicide, a murder, or an accidental death, or something. Get in here."

I said weakly: "Okay."

I hung up and had another beer....

Cromwell, the district supervisor, was a Canadian, a medium-sized man with clear gray eyes, firm muscles in his face, and plenty of restraint about him. He had dignity, but not too much; and he had vigor, which was used quietly. I'd always liked him. The rest of the brass hats weren't so hot, and I passed my opinion along to Bones McPherson, who agreed. My breath reeked with an assortment of breath-killers. Bones held his nose, whispered, "How many did you have—to make you take all that?" and Cromwell said:

"If you'll just stop talking a moment, Mr McPherson, we'll start.... There.... Now, did you fellows know that our district has been fleeced out of six thousand dollars?"

All of us outside men were arranged in an irregular semi-circle in front of the brass hats—the girls were gone—and every one of us looked surprised, even if we weren't. This didn't sound like suicide, murder, or accidental death to me. Cromwell let his gray eyes roam over us

Awkwardly she shoved
out the gun, fired.

for a moment—to let the full import of his news sink in, I suppose—then cleared his throat and went on:

"None of that six thousand dollars was gotten in this office. Altogether, there were twenty loans, each three hundred dollars, and they were spread all over our district— New York, Albany, Newark, Philadelphia, to mention only a few, and the other two Baltimore offices. All the loans were gotten by the same two people, who assumed the names of actual married couples who were away from their homes on vacation trips. We've had handwriting experts verify that by comparing all of the fake signatures. And we've concluded that the man and woman who got the loans knew every in and out of our system in making loans.

"So we've had a lot of trouble, principally placating the people whose names the loans were secured under, and who we insisted should prove the forgery to us. Besides a couple of threatened suits, we've gotten some bad publicity. And that hurts business, naturally. Not that we'll be bothered with the same hoax by the same two people, because an outside man in Philadelphia got an address here in Baltimore on them, and just before we arrived, four hours later, the man was found dead. We think the death was accidental.

"Anyway, we discovered that the woman had been away for several days—and she may have left the man who was found dead, may work the racket with some one else. You see, she doesn't know we're wise to her, or that we even suspect her. And at Mr. Reynolds' suggestion—" he smiled at the Eastern supervisor—"although I insisted on going in the house and stealing the picture myself, we have a photo of her and we'll pass out reproductions.

"Our job now is to locate her before she causes us any more trouble. The point is this, you see: we don't want to prosecute the woman. We don't want to publicize how easy it is to cheat us out of three hundred dollars. We have to find that woman, let her know we're on to her, and scare her so much she'll never try it again. And maybe collect our six thousand. Do I make myself clear?"

EVERYONE LOOKED grave, and he continued: "The reason we're holding the meeting in this office is that we believe that the woman is living somewhere in this office's territory. All of this is, of course, confidential, and none of you shall mention it to anyone outside the company. But, Mr. McPherson—" he levelled a finger at Bones—"we believe the woman is living in your territory. Mr. Roberts—" he switched the finger to me—"we believe we can locate her through her brother, who lives in your territory. We'll pass out reproductions of that picture and everybody can keep their eyes open. Any questions?"

I didn't hear any. The Canuck sat down, the room began to buzz with conversation, the boss got up and began passing out the reproductions. I got up and said: "You said you thought the man's death was accidental. Aren't you sure?"

The room was suddenly quiet again. The boss stopped passing out the pictures; one of the brass hats forgot to light his pipe. I could feel the Eastern supervisor staring at me.

The Canuck gave me one of those soft miles. "No, we're not, Mr. Roberts. Not sure, at all. Why?"

I shrugged.

He said: "If it does turn out that the man was murdered, wouldn't you want to make an investigation?"

I said: "Would you?"

"No."

I knew I'd been right about liking that guy. He was strictly on the level. I said to him: "I wouldn't either, Mr. Cromwell. I don't mind admitting I'd be scared as hell, and I don't mind saying I don't think it'd be fair. We're not getting paid to investigate murders. That's dangerous business, and—"

Cromwell rubbed his straight Canuck nose. "You're right, Mr. Roberts. We all know it's dangerous business, and we're not ordering anybody to go into it. We're asking for volunteers. We mentioned your name and Mr. McPherson's because we believe the woman is in his territory, and we *know* her brother happens to be in yours. But if you want to refuse, it won't go against your record in any way. Not in the slightest. We leave it up to you."

He was quite grave. I thought for a moment, stalled for time, tried to get a clear perspective on the entire mess. And somehow I believed that Canuck. The quiet, reasonable tone of his voice gave me confidence; I was convinced that if I refused, he'd see to it that nothing detrimental would happen to my record. But I knew that something would happen to his opinion of me. Nothing that he'd ever allow himself to show, I was quite sure; but something, just the same. Not contempt, or disgust, exactly; but something with a shade of both.

Why I wanted that guy to like me, I don't know.

I said: "Well, I don't want to, Mr. Cromwell. But I will."

I didn't know what I was getting into....

The murder story broke in the papers the next morning—it developed that the address the man in Philly had gotten was in Towson, which is just outside of Baltimore—and I read the story over bacon and eggs in a cafeteria.

It was pretty interesting. The murdered man's name was James, Francis T. James, and he had lived in Towson all his life. And there wasn't anything shady about his reputation. He was a contractor, in business for himself, and known to everybody as honest, reliable, a man who did good work. Three years ago his wife had died of pneumonia. Two months ago he had turned up with a new wife. Immediately, they'd gone away on a honeymoon. And returned last Saturday... this was Friday. But his new wife had gone away again on Tuesday.

And nobody seemed to know where she'd gone. Also his daughter, Virginia, who'd stayed home while they honeymooned, had disappeared on Thursday. That was the day the man was killed. The reporters waxed eloquent on the mystery.

OVER A second cup of coffee, I studied the mechanics of the murder. It had been cleverly done, I thought. James was found in his living-room, where he was sitting on the sofa apparently cleaning his pistol; and it looked as though the gun had gone off while he was oiling the trigger, and had shot him through the head.

But the detectives, overjoyed at a chance to try the new paraffin test, discovered that James didn't fire the gun. This, however, led to a hell of an argument. Some said if it went off accidentally, what difference did it make whether he had held it—gripped it like anybody would have gripped it, that is—or not? Others said that if the gun went off in his hands, no matter how he was holding it, the paraffin test would show some embedded powder *somewhere*. None of them seemed to know a hell of a lot about it.

An expert was called down from New York, but before he could get here the doubt was settled. It seems that the only fingerprints on the gun were the murdered man's; in explanation, the detectives said the murderer's had been wiped off. Then, according to them, the gun, handled with a rag that had obviously been used in cleaning it, had been put into the murdered man's hand so as to put *his* prints on it In other words, the murderer had planned the entire setup, and James hadn't been cleaning the gun at all.

And the detective's great point was this: there were no prints on the oilcan that was near the body. And the gun had been oiled. So the detectives said the murderer had oiled the gun, wiped his own prints from the oilcan, and either overlooked the importance of putting his victim's prints on the oilcan, or simply forgotten to do it. And they were yelling to the skies that there was a colored boy in the woodpile.

I grinned. I dragged out the reproduction they'd given me of the picture Cromwell had snitched, looked that over. It was surprising how plain and honest the woman looked. She was about forty, I judged, with dark hair and dark eyes and a sweet simple expression. She looked like life had been pretty good to her. In a lower corner was an inscription: *To Jimmie, the best James ever. From Mother.* I frowned, lit a cigarette, put the reproduction back in my pocket.

Bones McPherson drifted in at five of eight. He was tall, skinny, and with a lot of freckles; but his dress was Broadway, and he was neat, well-groomed. He had orange juice and coffee, then leaned over and said:

"I don't like this messing around with murder, and if you refuse, I will. What the hell changed your mind all of a sudden, anyway?"

I said I didn't know.

He crooked a finger at the coffee girl. "Hey, you! More Java! Do your sleeping nights!" Nobody ever accused Bones of being tactful. Then he growled at me: "If you're just showing off in front of the brass hats, I ought to break your neck."

"I don't think that's the case, Bones."

"No, I know it isn't." He dumped three spoons of sugar in his coffee, bellowed for more cream. "No, I know damned well it isn't. But the trouble with you is that you're a good guy who's pretty sensible one minute and screwy as hell the next. I can never figure you out. You know what I thought you were at first?"

I shook my head.

"You won't like it."

"Let me have it anyway."

He said: "See? You're a good guy now. Sensible. You know I won't mean anything by it." He hesitated. "I thought you were a rich man's son."

I laughed. "I rather like that."

"Well, I wouldn't. I wouldn't want any guy to think I was a playboy living on my old man's dough. Every time I ever saw you around, you were dressed up like a million and squiring a different dame." He looked me over. "That damned baby face of yours fools people."

I grinned at him.

He said thoughtfully: "A tough guy with a baby face—that's you, all right And sensible one minute, screwy as hell the next." He wagged his head as if he didn't quite understand.

WE WENT up to the office. The Canuck was there, but none of the brass hats, and when we came in he was sitting behind the boss' desk, toying absently with a letter-opener. And it occurred to me that this was the first time I had seen him when he wasn't actually doing something—either talking quietly to one of the men or looking over one of the office records. He wasn't the kind who wasted time.

He said, "Good morning," to us very gravely, and I noticed a morning paper folded by his elbow. And he kept on sitting there, turning the letter-opener over and over. When we were putting our hats in the coat room, Bones whispered:

"What's eating him?"

I said: "I'll tell you what you do. You spend eighteen years with the company, get to be district supervisor, then have something like this murder business threaten to knock your job out from under you. Who do you think the bigger brass hats are blaming?"

Bones wrinkled his freckled nose. "Cromwell?"

I said, "Not you, you skinny ape," and left him and went to do my daily report. It was fully a half hour later when Cromwell beckoned at Bones and me with a sinewed finger. He led us into a small private office—we call them deal rooms—and closed the door behind us. Blanchard, the boss, was already in there. He's a jolly little man, but explosive as hell, and has a mop of kinky hair and tiny hands and feet. He likes pretty girls around him. He always hires girls with plenty of body; but that doesn't stop him from firing them if they can't do the work. Every time he has a job to fill, Bones and I bet on the number he'll hire and fire. Blanchard winked at me, and I winked back at him.

Cromwell said: "I suppose you've read the morning papers." He was addressing Bones and me. "And you, Mr. Blanchard?"

We all nodded.

"Well, in view of the circumstances—if the woman murdered him—you can see we're up against some one who's pretty clever. Now. When I found out yesterday that the man James was dead, I checked with a few of the larger insurance companies. Luckily, he had a policy with the fourth one Mr. Reynolds and I tried. Five thousand dollars. His beneficiary is his daughter, Virginia, and the policy was taken out six months ago. I talked to the salesman. He knew the family fairly well, had dated the daughter several times. He said that Mrs. James had a brother who worked for the government in Washington.

"It seems that this brother—his name's Alfred Spaulding—had also dated the daughter several times. That's how the salesman happened to hear about him—through the daughter. Spaulding used to come over to Baltimore to see her about twice a week.

"The salesman never met him. He couldn't give me any description, and he couldn't tell me what department of the government Spaulding worked for. So it'll be a fairly tedious job locating him, and it might take one man a lot of time. Therefore, I'm sending both of you over." He looked quickly at Bones and me.

"I want you two to understand thoroughly that we're quite pressed for time. The cops might pick up the same information any day—and we want to get to this woman, Mrs. James, before they do. I think it's quite clear why. If the cops get to her first and indict her for murder—she might have slipped back to Towson and killed the man, you know—it would be highly improbable for us to contact her without getting publicity. On the other hand, with the threat of turning her over to the cops to use as a collection lever, if we get there before they do, we might even collect our six thousand. All of this is taking right much for granted—still, it's a thought."

He stopped, smiled.

Blanchard, worrying about the record of the office as usual, asked: "Will they do any other work?"

"No. Their regular stuff can wait."

I was writing down Spaulding's name. Blanchard strutted over, put his hands on his hips, squared off cockily in front of Bones and me. The boss is your bosom friend until his own record is threatened.

"Now, listen. You two learned the small-loan business under me. I don't want you to call in or come back and say you can't find him."

Cromwell said quietly: "They'll find him."

He sounded as though he was afraid we would.

Outside, when I got my coupé started, Bones looked at me curiously and said: "Say! Don't you think it's funny that none of those screwy loans were gotten in our office?"

I said: "You're damned right I do."

There was plenty about the whole mess that looked funny to me.

CHAPTER II

BOOMERANG RUSE

A **CHECK-UP** on all the government departments is tedious, as Cromwell said; but Bones and I were pretty lucky. We each took a phone booth at Pennsylvania Station, kidded the operators there—who dial your number for you—into getting the personnel branch of each department, then kidded them further into saying: "Here's your party." Then we would say it was Cleveland or Des Moines or St Louis calling, and thus get quicker and more efficient service. There is something imperative about a long distance call. We found an Alfred Spaulding in the government accounting office after only forty minutes in the two booths.

I was on the line. I said: "No, I don't want to talk to him. I want to send him some papers in relation to an insurance claim." Then I thanked the girl, hung up, and hustled Bones out of the station.

We found a parking spot on Eleventh near H, and I said: "I think it'll be safer if we tackle him one at a time. Then if one fails, we won't be stymied; the other guy can try another idea. Besides, two of us might scare him. Got any suggestions?"

"Have you?"

"One." I brought out cigarettes and Bones refused one; he always refused mine. That was one of the good things you could say about him; he certainly wasn't a chiseler. I lit mine, held a match for one of his, said: "It's the old one I pull when I'm looking up any 'skip' with a grown daughter. You know—look cow-eyed, say we're engaged. I'm not bad at it."

"Bragging again."

"But I'm not bad at it. I was engaged once, and the lovely took a powder. I remember how I used to moon around. I want to try it."

"We better call in first."

"The hell with that" I said. "They've probably thought of something they think would be better. Blanchard's always telling you things to do that fit *his* personality. I know what I can do with this baby face."

I got out of the car. Bones walked with me down to G Street, went in a drug store to have a coke and wait. I strolled on, passed the three entrances to the building that are on Eleventh Street, turned around and strolled back again. I was trying to decide which entrance had the most friendly looking guard. Finally I chose one—the guard was a slight fellow with false teeth which he didn't mind showing when he grinned. I walked up to him briskly, went into my song-and-dance.

The guards at the government buildings in Washington *want* to let you in. They don't want to argue; that's a hell of a lot of trouble. I said: "I want to see a friend of mine. I'm just passing through from Cleveland—" That's always enough. Tell them you're from out of town and their faces actually brighten. They consider that a truly legitimate excuse.

This one moved away to call my man downstairs, muttering: "Spaulding, Spaulding…."

I called after him: "The first name's Alfred."

Alfred Spaulding came down in a few minutes. I had no description of him, nor any idea of what he looked like; but the minute he stepped out of the elevator and glanced around the lobby with a puzzled look, I knew it was he. The guard was nearby, so I moved forward, tried to get between Spaulding and the guard so the guard wouldn't see the lack of recognition in Spaulding's face. You can't be too flagrant with those guys.

I said: "Al! Al, you old goat! How you been?"

I was pumping his hand and edging him around a bend in the corridor before he even had a chance to say a word.

When he did have a chance, he jerked his hand away from mine and said: "Have you gone entirely crazy, or is your natural stupidity so great that you can't tell one person from another?" Then: "Who are you? Who do you think you're talking to?"

I said hurriedly: "I'm Virginia James' fiancé, and I'm talking to Alfred Spaulding, her step-mother's brother. Does that make sense?"

He said: "You're what?"

I told him again.

His eyes almost bulged out of his head.

I WAITED then, looked him over. I felt it would be better for me not to force the issue, and I wanted to size him up a little. Somehow, I'd expected a middle-aged businessman, shrewd and brusque. Alfred Spaulding wasn't like that at all. He was young, not over thirty, with a large frame that was carrying at least one hundred and ninety pounds. He wore a brown gabardine suit, beautifully tailored. But he wasn't very neat. The suit needed pressing badly, and I judged his shoes hadn't been shined for a week. You couldn't imagine him wearing a topcoat without turning up the collar.

He was staring at me like he had gone nuts. He asked hoarsely: "Where did you meet Jimmie?"

"Who?"

"Jimmie—Virginia."

I got the connection. I remembered the photo-inscription. I said: "Where did you meet her?"

He boiled. "Now look here! I've had enough of your arrogance and your questions! I've had enough of you! Now, you either tell me what you want or I'll have the guard throw you out!" His voice was ringing through the corridors. "Out! Understand? Out!"

I said docilely: "I hear you."

His neck got positively purple.

"Now, listen," I told him. "I don't want to be thrown out by a guard, and I don't want to offend you." I put the sad, cow-look in my eyes. "But I love Virginia James. I love her better than anything in the world, and I always will love her. And I'm going to find her. She's in trouble and I'm going to find her. If you won't tell me where she is—well, okay, I'll find her anyway. I'll tell the cops you know where she is. I'll tell them, by heaven, and they'll find out from you. Then I'll find out from them. Take your choice."

"Of what?"

"Of telling me or telling the cops."

He stuck his face close to mine and said: "I'm not telling you and I'm not telling the police, either. Perhaps I don't even know. But I'm going to the guard and tell him you lied to him. I'm going to have you thrown out of here."

With that, he circled me quickly and started away, his heels drumming on the tiled floor. I could hear his heavy breathing.

I went after him—fast. I caught him after he'd gone about twenty steps, then edged over in front of him, blocked his way.

I said: "Now listen, Spaulding—listen to reason." I was really bearing down now on that sad, cow-look. "I don't want the cops to know where Jimmie is. Don't forget that I'm in love with her—why should I want the cops to grill her? I want to help her—and I've got the dough to do it. And if mine should run out, I can tap my father's. You listen to me, Spaulding. I don't want the cops to know where she is. Hell—I don't even want to see her. I want to help her, that's all. I want to send word to her that I can even get my father's lawyers—"

I could see that all this stuff was slowly getting him. Curiosity had already replaced most of his anger, and he stopped trying to get by me for a moment, studied me narrowly. I waited. Finally he asked:

"Who's your father?"

I said: "Oh, no, you don't! I'm not getting his name mixed up in this until I know where Jimmie is, know we can help her. Listen. It'll be bad enough dragging it in when we're in a position to accomplish something. The old man would have six fits if it was dragged in otherwise."

Spaulding was still studying me narrowly. All of his anger was gone now, and his eyes were cautious, guarded. He said slowly: "What do you want me to do?"

"I want you to send her a telegram," I said. "I want you to tell her that my old man and I want to help her. I want you to tell her to get in touch with me."

He flared. "Send her a telegram! So you can get the address from the telegraph office!"

I shrugged. "How else can you get in touch with her?"

He said, owlishly: "I can always *write* to her, you know." He looked gleeful then; he thought he had me in the middle.

I said: "Okay. Write to her."

"What?"

"Write to her. I know the post office won't give out addresses. Write to her. Let me give you a note to put in the letter. You can read the note. You can mail the letter. Just let me see you mail it, that's all I ask."

"Why do you want to see me mail it?"

I laughed. "I want to stand close to you so I can see the address. Don't be an idiot. I'll stand a block away. I just want to make sure that Jimmie's going to hear from me."

He said slowly: "Are you actually on the level?"

"Sure, I am."

"But—" He pulled viciously at the lobe of his right ear. "Where did you meet Jimmie? How long—"

I said: "For Pete's sake! Let's not start all that again."

"But I don't understand it."

"Hell," I told him, "neither do I. She didn't tell me about *you*.... Now, look. You going to write the letter now?"

He looked at his strap-watch. "Can't. Got to get back to work."

"When?"

"Well, I'll write it in the office." He was still tugging at the lobe of that ear. "See you down here at twelve sharp. That's my lunch hour."

I said: "Make it the drug store on the corner. The guards might not let me in here again."

"All right."

He turned and went toward the elevators, and I heeled my way outside.

AT TWELVE thirty-six, twenty minutes after Spaulding had gone, I watched the mail truck pull in to the curb across the street from the drug store, and saw the postman climb out and begin unlocking the box. Bones pushed the door open, and I broke into a sprint. I came up to the postman panting, hoping I looked excited, and said:

"Thank heavens I thought I'd missed you!"

The postman looked up and blinked.

I said: "I wrote a letter to my girl, and darned if I can remember whether I put on her old address or her new one." I grinned at him sheepishly.

He began looking through the pile of letters. "What's the name?"

"James. Virginia James."

He pulled a letter from the pile and shoved it toward me. "This it?"

I nodded.

Spaulding had addressed the letter very legibly: *Miss Virginia James, c/o E.F. Rider, Arnold, Md.*

I said: "Whew! All this trouble for nothing. That's right."

The postman was looking over my shoulder. He pushed me suddenly, and screamed: "Look out!"

I don't remember my first reaction. Possibly I ducked; possibly not. But I heard the shot. It cracked out clearly—I'll always hear it—like a solid smash in any ball park. And I heard the slug crash the mail box. It rang metallically, ricocheted. There was the crash of glass next. Some of the fragments nipped the show window of the ladies' shoe shop there on the corner.

Then Bones came loping across the street, yelling: "Come on, Shag! Run!"

I wasn't bewildered. Heaven knows I should have been, but I'm not given to thinking at such moments. I ran. I got ahead of Bones and kept yelling at him: "Damn you! Stretch those legs!"

We went past my car like a couple of Olympic sprinters.

I began to think then. I didn't stop, but swung around, almost dived behind the wheel. Bones piled in beside me. I cut the car around in a sharp U-turn, drew a vicious cussing-out from a swarthy-faced cab driver. At K Street I jumped a red light.

Bones, slightly pale, said: "You're not in Baltimore now. Watch out for these cops."

I nodded. I slowed the car considerably, began obeying most of the traffic laws, alternated with right and left turns for about the next dozen blocks. I was breathing heavily. As I turned into Rhode Island Avenue, and headed out of Washington, I gasped:

"Did—you see the guy who did the shooting?"

Bones shook his head. "The shot came from one of the windows in the accounting office."

"You—sure?"

"Well, I could see everybody who was on the street. None of *them* did it."

I said: "Ugh!" I was just beginning to wonder how close that shot had come to me; just beginning to wonder where I might be now if the postman hadn't shoved me. I fished out a cigarette with one hand. My stomach felt hollow, and when I got the electric lighter hot, got it out of the dashboard, I couldn't get the end of my cigarette on it. I put the lighter back, threw the cigarette away, watched my hands tremble.

Bones said: "I feel like I got St. Vitus' Dance."

"You weren't shot at."

"I feel like that, anyway. Did you get the address?"

I nodded.

Bones said: "I was afraid of that."

He stared out the window, and his face was long and melancholy.

CHAPTER III

SNAKE-EYES

WE ATE lunch in a barbecue on Washington Boulevard, neither of us eating much, and both of us drinking a lot of beer. We hadn't called in yet. I knew the natural reaction the office had to any trouble; it was your fault, no matter what you did; you should have handled the situation better. And I was wondering what they'd say to this, despite the fact that we had the address. Of course, it was our fault, or rather mine, that Spaulding had mailed the letter in that particular box. But I hadn't thought for a moment that the box could be seen from the office windows. To be exact, I hadn't even thought of the windows. But that was carelessness on my part, and the office didn't stand for carelessness.

I said to Bones: "Blanchard'll blast my head off."

"He'll probably fire us both."

"Why you?"

"You told me the scheme, didn't you? I should've thought about the windows, too."

I sighed. Bones was right. We had another bottle of beer apiece, and I went to the end of the bar. There were a pair of phone booths there. I got in one of them, and Bones slipped in the other.

He explained: "To keep some mug from getting in here and hearing what you've got to say."

I closed the doors of my booth tight, gave the operator the number.

Blanchard answered. He said: "Yeah?"

We call in on a private line; that is, the phone book doesn't list the number. I said: "Roberts, Mr. Blanchard. We got the James girl's address."

"You did? Fine!" Blanchard sounded actually pleased. "Fine! Wait a second. Mr. Cromwell wants to talk to you."

I had to wait for quite a long time. Then Cromwell came on and said: "Splendid, Roberts! Where?"

I told him.

He said: "That's really splendid work. How did you get it?"

I told him that, too.

He exclaimed: "Shot at you!"

"Sure as hell he did."

"Hell!"

I waited. I didn't know what to say; the office didn't accept excuses. Then Cromwell's voice came again, cautiously:

"Were either of you hit?"

"No, sir."

"Good." He sounded very relieved.

"Did you get away all right?"

"I think so."

"But you aren't sure?"

I said: "We can't be, Mr. Cromwell. We weren't followed, or stopped by cops, but somebody might have gotten my license number. I don't know whether they did or not."

"I see." He paused. "Well, don't worry about it. If anything comes up, I'll take the responsibility." He paused again. "Do you still want to go on with the investigation?"

My throat felt tight; I couldn't answer. But after I got my throat under control, I hesitated, anyway. I breathed to myself: "Don't be a sucker, Shag. Don't risk your life because you want to help a guy." And I got the economical end in, too. I breathed: "Don't risk your life for peanuts."

But I said aloud, a half second later: "Sure I want to go on with it."

"Does McPherson?" Cromwell asked.

"Sure he does."

"That's splendid!"

I wasn't sure about that. I was so sore with myself by now that I wasn't sure of anything. I said: "Any instructions?"

"Only to be careful. Try not to get shot, or hit on the head with anything. That's dangerous, too."

I said: "Oh, I don't know. Look at Newton. That bum got conked on the head with an apple—and look what *he* got out of it."

Then I lifted my right hand and banged up the receiver.

WHEN I came out of the booth I didn't tell Bones I'd enlisted him for further duty, too. I didn't tell him much of anything. I led him outside, half dragging him by the arm, got behind the wheel and began to drive like a madman. It took me exactly fifty-seven minutes to get to Arnold. That's traveling, in any man's language; we had to double back to Washington, go out the Defense Highway and through Annapolis. Bones said we went by the Naval Academy so fast it looked like a country schoolhouse. And we went by Arnold, too. But Bones couldn't think of any crack for that. Arnold's so small it's in a class by itself.

That's what we thought.

After we'd gone past it three miles before we stopped for directions, we went back and went in the post office for more.

The post office was also a gas station, a grocery, and a package liquor store. The grizzled old man behind the counter said:

"Arnold spreads all over the country, like. We got three rural deliv'ries." He pushed his gold-rimmed spectacles an inch farther down his nose. "Lookin' for somebody?"

I said: "Where's Rider's place? E.F. Rider."

"Oh—*him*." The old fellow made a noise in his throat like he was going to spit, but didn't. "He's a pretty rich feller. Got lots of places. Pretty tight feller, too. Don't give his son no money. You his son?"

Bones leaned on the counter and hee-hawed like a jackass.

We finally got the directions from the old fellow. E.F. Rider, it seemed, owned a large farm on the Magothy River, and used his house there for a summer home. But the farm was only a hobby. He had a pretty large real estate business; and in order to make the farm pay its taxes, he had built several shore bungalows which he rented in the summer. But it was fall now. Only a few of the bungalows were still occupied, and the old fellow wasn't sure exactly which ones.

We didn't inquire about Virginia James or her mother. We took the sand road the old fellow pointed out, stopped at a whitewashed frame house about a mile in from the boulevard.

An old colored woman there gave us directions. "Yas, suh. Dey's in dat dere bungalow what sits out on de point." She lifted a pickaninny by the back of his diapers and carried him squealing to the door. She pointed. "Down dat road, an' turn left. Cain't miss it. Two awful pretty young white womens." She grinned at us toothlessly.

I said: "Two?" That meant Mrs. James was probably with Virginia. "Anybody living with them?"

She laughed aloud and clapped her free hand on her thigh. "Lawsy! Ah doan' know! Dar's strange doin's in dat dar house. Strange doin's!"

"What nature of strange doings?"

She rolled her eyes and said nothing.

I peered at her. I know colored people well enough to know they love to gossip but won't tell anything important. And I guessed she'd gotten all the gossip out of her system.

I went back to the car and kicked life into the motor.

Bones climbed in and said: "What the hell do you think she meant?"

I shrugged. "Your guess, Bones, is as good as mine."

THE HOUSE was a fairly new bungalow. You went back to it along a winding road, just two wheel ruts with grass growing between them. There was a small clearing at the back of the house. The front faced the river, which wasn't very wide here, and the porch was about fifty yards from the water. Everything was very quiet. There was just enough breeze to make ripples on the river, and the autumn leaves rustled faintly in the trees.

I swung the car in a circle around the clearing. Left it head away from the house. If it was necessary to leave here fast, I didn't want to take time to turn around.

Then I noticed a new yellow Eight parked in among the trees.

Behind me, Bones said: "Look! A guy!"

I swung around. The small back porch was no more than a stoop, and on it was a tall, thin man watching us curiously.

We went toward him. He wore white ducks and white buckskin shoes and a very dark blue pullover sweater. He didn't say anything until we were almost up to him. But his eyes followed us all the way—the blackest, meanest-looking pair of eyes that it's ever been my misfortune to see. And what pallor! His skin was as pale as a white perch's belly; and that's pretty damned pale, believe you me. His lips were only a shade darker. They scarcely moved when he spoke; and the booming voice that came out so effortlessly almost drove me back on my heels.

He said: "What the hell do you want?"

I said: "We want to see Mrs. James."

My voice, in comparison, was like a whisper.

He kept staring at us. We were closer now—at the foot of the three porch steps—and I was getting a better look at him. His eyes were what interested me. They were snake-eyes; lidless, lashless.

Then the voice came again: "What do you want to see her about?"

Bones took over then. "Personal business," he snapped, and his green eyes danced. He loved the opportunity of getting nasty.

If it was possible for those lidless eyes to blink, they did. He thought that voice had us buffaloed.

Bones went up a step and said: "We came all the way down here from Baltimore to see her. And we're going to—if we have to get the sheriff."

Bluff is a great thing in the small loan business. Bluff is a great factor in any collections. But bluff meant not a hang to this snake-eyed guy. He roared: "You get the hell off this porch!"

I must have goggled at him. I know I took a step backward: when he let that voice loose it was like thunder. But

Bones went up. He went one step, two, shook his finger in that foghorn's face. He roared back:

"We're here on legitimate business. If Mrs. James is living here, we've got the right to see her. And if you know what's good for you, you'll bring her out!"

The foghorn spat in Bones's face.

I grabbed Bones. He let out a yelp that would have put Tarzan to shame, and I had a hard time holding the skinny devil. Then he began to curse. He'd been to sea—most Baltimore kids have—and he had some of the most magnificent combinations. And by the time I quieted him, Snake-eyes was inside. I heard the lock click on the door.

I let go of Bones and said: "Nice guy."

"Yeah."

"He's slammed the door on us," I added, and grinned.

That happened to be right up our alley. We were pretty damned used to having doors slammed in our faces. Bones rapped: "You take this door. I'll take the front."

I watched him disappear around the side of the house.

I went up on the tiny back porch. I opened the screen door, banged it a few times, beat a fast rat-a-tat-tat on a panel of the wooden door. Bones sounded as though he was kicking the front door. I tried that too, using my heels. Then I beard the sharp, metallic ring of metal against glass. I got out a half-dollar of my own, went to work on the windows.

The racket was terrific. It echoed down the river, reverberated around the coves. Then Bones began yelling: "Oh, Mrs. James! You got company outside!"

A window near me shot up. I saw Snake-eyes's nose pressing against the screen. He bellowed: "Listen, you! There's a sick woman in here!"

Bones bellowed back: "Well, go and tell her she's got company!"

The window slammed down. I kept rapping for a few more seconds, suddenly found my brain at work. Suppose there really was a sick woman in there? I whistled, ran around to Bones and said:

"Hey! Maybe that foghorn's a doctor!"

Bones snarled: "So what?" But he stopped pounding.

I said: "If so, and a woman is sick, they could probably sue the company for about half a million."

Bones looked at me for a moment. Suddenly he yelped: "Let 'em sue! That dirty baboon! I thought you were worrying about the woman."

He went back to his pounding and made the whole window shake.

I put my arms around him, yanked him away.

Snake-eyes appeared at a window about three yards away. Behind him the room was dark, and of course his sweater was dark, and all I could see was a pale face and burning black eyes. And a rifle barrel. It gleamed once, as it caught a ray from the sun; then the muzzle pressed against the screen, bulged that out a little. I froze. Bones—I still had my arms around him—went as rigid as steel. Neither one of us could speak.

CHAPTER IV

BRASS HAT ENIGMA

S NAKE-EYES CLIPPED: "You'll stop that
racket now!"

I felt Bones relax slightly. I relaxed somewhat myself.
I thought Snake-eyes was going to shoot without even
saying such a small thing as boo.

Then Bones made me freeze again. He ripped out, very
contemptuously: "Bah! You ain't got the guts!"

I found my voice somehow. I saw the screen bulge
more, almost imperceptibly, and I got around to speaking,
although my voice sounded queer. It seemed to come from
my toes. I said: "Now, just a minute, mister. We're not going
to argue with a gun. We're down here to see Mrs. James,
not to start a war."

Snake-eyes said: "Well, you're going to start one, if you
don't keep him quiet." If ever a man meant what he said,
the old fog-horn meant that.

I said hastily: "Now look, guy. We're from the National
Finance Corporation, and we're here on legitimate business. We want to see Mrs. James. We haven't told the cops
where she is, and we haven't any intention of doing it. But
if you get funny with that rifle—" I hesitated; it's pretty
difficult to be tough when you're at the wrong end of one of
those things. "But if you don't put up the rifle, we're going

to find a phone and let the cops come down here and see Mrs. James. Get it?"

I guess he got it all right. He thought a moment, then turned and bellowed: "Viola! What the hell does the National Finance Company want to see you about?"

Viola James was one of the most hauntingly attractive women I've ever seen in my life. After Snake-eyes let me in—he wouldn't even consider Bones's joining me—she came into the front room wrapped in a dark-green bathrobe with a tan scarf knotted at her neck, had very black hair. It was bobbed, not too carefully kept, and a few of the strands were light gray. But these were scarcely Noticeable. I judged her to be about twenty-three—it turned out later she was twenty-seven—and she had a very poised, but fragile look. Nothing anaemic about her, though. There was grace and a certain vigor in her slenderness. I think that that's how she packed such a lot of sex appeal into a body that's usually so-so.

She sat on the sofa, her shoulders very erect, and her light green eyes were quite wide and questioning. She said, her voice calmly incredulous: "You want to see me?" There was something about her then that seemed very familiar to me.

Snake-eyes stood beside her, still holding the rifle.

I didn't see any sense in answering the question. I said: "Mrs. James, you and your husband, Francis T. James, got twenty loans from our offices in New York, Philadelphia, and Baltimore—all under assumed names. Now, don't deny it. Our company had checked on you thoroughly, and we know it was you. What we want is six thousand dollars—we won't charge you any interest—and we want it right now."

She looked at me.

I said: "Is that clear?"

She kept on looking at me, and her eyes grew wider, bewildered. "But I—"

I cut her off quickly. "The police are looking for you, Mrs. James. We haven't begun prosecution yet, and we won't start it if you pay the six thousand. But the police are looking for you just the same. We haven't told them where you are."

"You mean—"

"I mean we want our six thousand."

Snake-eyes's voice boomed out: "That's blackmail!"

I shrugged. Since Viola James had entered the room, I'd had my eyes on her. Now I turned them to the foghorn for the first time since she'd come in. I said stubbornly: "We want our six thousand."

BUT HE wasn't looking my way. He had one of his long bony hands on Viola James's shoulder, was shaking her—not hard, but tensely. He said hoarsely: "It is blackmail, Viola—theoretically. But, hell! how'd you get in a mess like that?"

She met his gaze gravely. "You know me, Alex. Francis was so honest, so-o—" she seemed to hesitate—"weak. I—I could make him do things he—hated to do."

Alex slapped her face.

She didn't cringe. Her chin came up a little; she put her hand to her cheek. Otherwise she didn't move. Quite simply she said:

"Please don't, Alex."

He was towering over her, his right hand clenched along his lean thigh.

She looked over at me and said: "I'm sorry."

I guess I'm pretty stupid. I yelled: "For what?"

"For causing a scene."

I swallowed.

Alex took a backward step. His eyes were still on her, furiously—burning as they'd burned at Bones and me. All the tendons in his thin neck were taut. He said: "I guess you'd better pay him the six thousand."

She smiled. "I don't know where I'd get it, Alex. Will you get my bank book for me?"

Alex started out of the room. His face was pinched, flushed—it actually showed a faint color—and then he stopped so quickly he looked like he'd been hit. I blinked, looked around.

There was a girl in the doorway—a black-haired girl whose brown eyes looked enormous in her pale face. But her pallor wasn't scrubbed-looking and natural like the foghorn's. Hers was sickly. Her nightgown peeped out from under the brown robe she must have hastily donned, and which hung loosely over her.

Alex stared at her.

Viola James said: "Jimmie, you shouldn't—"

Jimmie said in a cold, impersonal voice: "Why are the police looking for you, Viola?"

Viola James hesitated. "Why, Jimmie—"

"It's not because of the finance company," Jimmie went on coldly. "I heard what the young man said—they won't prosecute if you pay. Why are the police looking for you?"

"I—"

"Why did you say Dad *was* so weak?"

Alex said tightly, with an effort to sound kind: "Now, now, Jimmie. Now, now, honey. You're sick. You're wrought up. You get back to bed."

Jimmie laughed at him. It was an awful laugh—shrill, with a touch of hysteria in it She cried: "Sick! Who made me sick?" And spinning on Viola, Jimmie screamed suddenly: "You killed him, that's why! You killed him, you—you—" She ran screaming toward Viola.

I bounced from my chair, tackled Alex at the knees. We went down in a corner and I yelled: "Bones! Bones!"

A floor lamp crashed on top of us and a chair tipped over.

Bones came rushing in the front door. I didn't see him; I heard him yelp, "Coming, Shag! Coming!" and heard the pound of his lanky feet outside on the porch. Then I heard the front door to the room slam open. I was hanging on to that rifle with all the strength that was in me. The only other thing I could hear was the pounding of Alex's curses in my ears. He knew some fancy ones, too.

Then Bones leaned over us and said: "Ah! Spit in my face, will you?" He began throwing punches at Alex like a Harry Greb.

Alex let go of the rifle. Self-preservation, I suppose, is still the first law of nature; and I wasn't hurting him, I'm sure of that. He turned on Bones with a snarl. But Bones got in a good right, and Alex sat down on my belly.

I said: "Oomph!" I was holding the rifle at a snappy port arms, and I shoved it out hard, clunked the back of Alex's head with the breech.

He wavered. Bones swung a wide right that caught him above the eye, and he toppled over sideways, not out but stunned. I got to my feet I looked around and was suddenly half stunned myself.

Jimmie was flailing at Viola's face with her tiny fists, and Viola sat taut, motionless, her hands clenched in her lap, taking it Her eyes were closed, her jaws clamped tight.

I said: "Hey!"

Jimmie stopped.

"Your robe," I said. It was half open now, due to her movement.

"Oh."

Jimmie wrapped the robe around her more securely, stared at us defiantly. She had guts, that girl.

I said: "Maybe you'd better get back to bed. Maybe—"

I broke off as I heard the screen door on the porch open. Footsteps pattered across the boards. I looked at Bones, frowned, half raised the rifle. Then the door opened, and Cromwell came in.

He'd hardly put his foot inside before Viola exclaimed: "Charles!"

I looked around quickly. Who in the hell was Charles?

Cromwell said in an extremely quiet voice: "Hello, Viola."

CHAPTER V

GUYS LIKE YOU....

SOMETHING SNAPPED in my brain. Something that seemed to release a catch on a revolving stage and send a whirlpool of facts spinning giddily in front of me. I stabbed a glance at Cromwell.

He stood spraddle-legged, his hands plunged deeply into his topcoat pockets, his chin in against the base of his throat, his eyes like gray ice, soiled and roughened by the wind. I don't think Bones caught anything menacing in his attitude. He exploded, "Why, Mr. Cromwell! How in hell—" and stopped. Jimmie started to say something, too—and stopped. Alex's voice boomed from the floor:

"So you're the sucker she married!"

I said: "What?"

"Viola is this guy Cromwell's wife. Didn't you know that?"

I didn't know it. But, knowing it, a lot was cleared up for me. There was still plenty, however, that I didn't get, and I raised the rifle, levelled it at Cromwell's chest. I wasn't going to take any more chances. But it was funny; I was respectful to him, even then.

I said: "Don't move, Mr. Cromwell."

He looked at Viola James—or rather Viola Cromwell—queerly.

She shrugged and said: "The young man seems to have more sense than you gave anybody in the company credit for."

I scowled at her. It wasn't much of a scowl because privately I was pretty pleased. But then I remembered the business at hand and switched my gaze to Bones. I said: "Get those guns out of his pockets."

"Whose pockets?"

"Who am I pointing this barrel at?"

Bones said incredulously: "Have you gone completely ga-ga?"

"Listen," I told him. "For the sake of something, use your noodle. Or try to. Have you looked at the reproduction of the picture that was passed out to you in the office?"

Bones started. He reached in his inside pocket, dragged out the picture, took one long look at it, then looked at Viola Cromwell.

I said: "Does it look like her?"

He shook his head slowly, wonderingly.

I said: "That reproduction's from a picture of a woman almost forty. Take a closer look at Mrs. Ja—I mean, Mrs. Cromwell."

Bones blinked.

"Recognize her?" I asked.

"Well, there's something familiar—"

"Sure there is," I said. "Something damned familiar. She was the last girl Blanchard hired and fired the first time I won ten bucks from you."

Bones ejaculated: "Well now, I'll be damned!"

"You ought to be. Maybe I ought to, too. I should have known it the first time I laid eyes on her." I tightened up on the rifle a little. "And that clears up why none of those screwy loans were gotten in our office. Blanchard would have recognized the woman as Cromwell's wife." I scowled. "You still don't get it? Listen. Francis James, the guy who was murdered, and Viola here, Cromwell's wife, were the man and woman who got all of those loans. Remember what Cromwell said: 'At Mr. Reynolds's suggestion, although I insisted on going in the house and stealing the picture myself—' Remember? Well, Cromwell had to steal a picture because Reynolds wanted one, and he had to go in the house himself to save his hide. Because if Reynolds had gone in and gotten a picture of Viola, who was posing as James's wife, Blanchard would have recognized her and spilled the beans that she was really Cromwell's wife. Get that?

"And wait. Cromwell went in, all right—and probably planned to say he couldn't find a picture. But he got a lucky break—or so he thought. He found a picture with the inscription, 'To Jimmie, the best James ever. From Mother.' Swell! That was the picture of the first Mrs. James, and she was dead and Cromwell knew it. Let us try to find her until hell freezes over."

THE BEGINNING of what looked like understanding seeped into Bones's eyes. Encouraged, I went on:

"And another thing. How did that outside man in Philly get that address? Where would you look, Bones, if every family you went to see didn't know anybody had used their name, and you didn't even know the right name of the couple who had used theirs? Because don't forget that when Francis James and Viola got those loans, they didn't use the name they were known under in Towson: Mr. and Mrs. James. They *assumed* names of actual couples who were away on vacation trips. And the only addresses that the company knew were those of the couples whose names had been assumed. So where would you look?

"Well, here's what happened: Cromwell planted information with one of the couples whose names had been forged that a Mr. and Mrs. James, who lived in Towson, had used their home in their absence—because the brass hats were pressing Cromwell and he had to do something. So, then, to cover himself, Cromwell told James and Viola what he'd done, and told them to disappear so the company wouldn't find them. Which meant that at least Cromwell had found out who got the bad loans—and found where they lived. Which was probably enough to let him hold his job. Is that clear?"

Viola Cromwell said, "It's terribly clear, and cleverly thought out—but I'm sorry it isn't quite true."

I snapped a glance at her—I wasn't forgetting Cromwell's hands in those pockets—and she was smiling at me gently. I said: "No? Aren't you really Cromwell's wife?"

"Oh, yes."

"And didn't you and Francis James get all those loans from us?"

"Certainly."

"But the rest of it isn't true?"

"Unfortunately, no. Part of it is, though." She seemed brighter, more vivacious than I'd seen her. "The part about Charles telling us to disappear—that's perfectly true. However, I think the trouble is that you're giving Charles credit for entirely too much intelligence. He didn't plant—as you call it—the information. He's rather a careful, efficient man; he wouldn't take such a chance. Not Charles. Taking chances calls for a lot of courage."

Cromwell looked about to choke. He blazed: "Viola!"

She laughed and said: "Now, Charles, you know I love to tease you. Anyway—" addressing me again—"he didn't plant the information. One of the apartments—we had to go to the homes of the people whose names we assumed long enough to let your outside man list the furniture: the company must have its security, you know—one of the apartments was so lovely we spent a few hours there. Francis took off his coat so he could relax while reading the paper. And we were interrupted—it was the son who came in, I think. We had to leave by the fire escape, and poor Francis—" she began to laugh silently, as if she were almost afraid to laugh—"was so much in a hurry he left his suit coat behind." She knuckled her eyes and kept laughing silently.

I said: "You mean the name and address was in his clothes?"

"In his wallet—which he kept in his coat."

"Did you and your husband—Cromwell—plan to get all these loans from the company?"

She nodded. "He planned it. He told me to hire a man to work with me, and I chose Francis. He was the contractor who built our house."

This was getting involved. I took my gaze from Cromwell long enough to look at Bones, saw his eyes looking like flower buds about to pop in spring. Jimmie was staring, too. She sat on the edge of the sofa, her robe hugged tightly around her, not far from Viola. There were deep lines in Cromwell's face, and he hadn't moved. Alex looked balked, nervous.

Viola Cromwell said to me: "It's your turn."

"For what?"

"I love to hear you rationalize. You make Charles out as such an ass."

THAT GUY'S personality had me whipped, I suppose; I know I felt myself flushing. But I had a stronger feeling not to let Viola Cromwell down. I said:

"First, answer me a couple questions. Who is Alex?"

She smiled. "Dr. Alexander Rider. He—or rather his father—owns this house."

"Is that his car outside?"

She nodded.

"But he isn't a real doctor, is he? I mean, isn't he an interne?"

She said: "Please tell me how you knew that."

"I guessed it. Guys don't run around in white ducks and white shoes in the fall—and if he was a full-fledged doctor, he'd have taken the white stuff off. Internes are proud of being internes, and doctors don't want to be mistaken for one."

She looked at Cromwell triumphantly. "See, Charles? And to think he works under you." Then to me: "Please go on."

I was trying to control my flush. "Well, internes are pretty poorly paid, and Alex's father wouldn't give him much money. Now, you don't need to ask me how I knew that, Mrs. Cromwell; the old postmaster said Alex's old man didn't give him any money. So Alex, being poor, and there being a woman in love with him who could lay her hands on money, and give him plenty—"

Alex leaped to his feet "What the hell are you saying?"

I said: "I'm saying that from the way I figure it, seeing Jimmie here like this—that her father figured Viola's influence on Jimmie was not the most desirable thing he'd want for his daughter. And maybe he got sick of the whole business—didn't want Jimmie to be the daughter of a thief. And I'm saying her father got sore, told Mrs. Cromwell to go to hell—and told Cromwell the same thing, refused to disappear. James was going to the cops and confess the whole damned business."

Viola Cromwell's eyes were wide, bright. "And how did you know that?"

I said: "Two and two make four. Alex is poorly paid, but has a new car, yet his dad doesn't give him any dough. The dough must be coming from you. A little while ago Jimmie cried out that she was sick, but who makes her sick? You no doubt made Alex make her sick, drugs or something, and prevailed upon her to come here for a rest. And Alex is seeing to it that she remains. And now with our coming here, and her hearing everything, she suddenly realized that Alex wasn't trying to make her well—"

Viola Cromwell interrupted me. She said: "Alex is keeping her sick so he can experiment, I suppose. That's really amazing!"

"So is the rest of it," I told her.

"What do you mean?"

"That you killed Francis James," I said. "That you slipped up town, shot him, and then tried to make it look like the gun went off accidentally while he was cleaning it. Not because he was going to the cops and confess, either; that didn't mean a damned thing to you. Because you knew as well as I know now—and as well as Cromwell has known all along—that the National Finance Company wouldn't prosecute, wouldn't want the publicity. There was nothing much you had to worry about. And you had to get Jimmie away, because if the police questioned her she might say something that could incriminate you. What you were planning to do with her ultimately, I don't know. But I do know you killed her father."

She was suddenly quite grave—and silent. The others, too, were speechless. My voice sounded loud in my own ears and as I went on the story became even clearer to me.

"You killed Francis James because he was through with you, because you couldn't control him any more. I know your type. You love to lure men on with your frankness, to get them in love with you, then to make them squirm. You pick the kind of men who don't know much about women; they're easy game with flattery. But guys like Alex you fall in love with. Guys who beat you and slam you around. Guys who know just what you are. Guys—"

"Guys like you," she said softly.

I laughed. "Guys like me, hell," I told her. "As long as I'm holding this rifle, it's guys like me. But let me put it down.... Listen. You like to do things ordinary people wouldn't do. You like to be clever. Things can happen to you like they do to ordinary people—but you've taught yourself to take them calmly. You imagine you're above the emotions of ordinary people. Witness the way you let Jimmie beat on you; you sat there and took it like it was all beneath you. But you've got a weakness. Let somebody do something to you that makes you doubt your own power; let somebody do something that makes you doubt your own superiority; let somebody convince you that you're just common like the rest of us.... When you couldn't control a guy as weak as James, it sort of got you, didn't it?"

CHAPTER VI

FINALE—IN BLOOD

S **HE FLEW** at me. She came with her hands clawed, her eyes dilated horribly, her mouth twisted and purplish. I warded her off with the rifle. Bones yelled, "Watch out, Shag!" and suddenly I realized she'd stepped back, was digging into her bathrobe pocket. Her hand came out holding a small, nickeled automatic; she shoved it out awkwardly, fired.

It was practically impossible to miss at that distance. I saw the belch of flame, felt the shock, but peculiarly only in my hands and wrists. The rifle went out of my hands. The barrel struck me under my left jawbone, and the butt fell on my foot. I started forward and tripped. I fell headlong, the rifle tied up in my legs. I guess the gods were with me. There'd have been no rifle breech to stop the second slug. It went through the space where I'd been standing, crashed the wall behind me.

Out of her sight for an instant, I found myself fairly safe there on the floor. She turned toward bigger game; turned with the same savagery that had marked her onslaught on me, only somehow more vindictive. I caught onto it quickly. Her back was to Cromwell—she held him in contempt—and the little, nickeled automatic began spitting flame at Alex.

He cowered. The lidless eyes shrank momentarily, then seemed to burst blackly with horror. I saw a hole in his cheek. I saw another, this one slightly lower. She pumped the other two slugs into his chest, actually knocked him over backwards.

Then she turned, still hot and blazing, and faced Cromwell's guns.

He had them out, all right. Both of them. Big, black thirty-eights, brand new and brightly polished.

I held my breath. He stood there, his fine gray eyes dulled with torture, the firm muscles in his face bunched in ugly rope-twists. She met his gaze defiantly. Her hair was awry, her chin up, her bathrobe half off her shoulder. She made a lovely picture. Too lovely for Cromwell, I suppose. I saw his face soften. It was like an iron bust dissolving over a white flame. She walked into the mouth of his guns, took them both away from him.

I gasped.

I'd forgotten the rifle. I clawed at it now; cleared as I noticed the perspiration dampening her face. She said softly, "Guys like you—" and pointed one of the guns at me.

I got the rifle up somehow. I shot her through the middle twice before she had a chance to fire. But I couldn't watch her die. Suddenly I was very sick.

Not Bones, however. He looked at me, said: "Hold it. Clench your teeth. It'll pass in a minute."

Jimmie asked: "Is she dead?"

Bones frowned, said: "I don't know." He walked over, stood away from the body, craned his neck deferentially. "She looks like it."

I said: "F-feel her."

Cromwell said wearily: "What's the use? She's dead."

We'd all forgotten him. He sat on the floor as if he'd slumped there, his head drooping forward, his back supported by the wall, his legs flopped out straight and absolutely limp. A strong man with a wrecked will.

Bones squinted at him and demanded: "How the hell do you know?"

Cromwell smiled faintly, shrugged. "Roberts is a good shot."

My stomach was feeling better. I said: "Better than you, at any rate. Or were you just trying to scare us? Come to think of it, that mail box was almost ten feet to my left."

The Canuck said: "I was just trying to scare you."

"You followed us, didn't you?"

"Certainly I followed you. I told Blanchard I thought it would be better for me to follow you in case you ran into too serious a jam—and that it was better for your morale if you didn't know about it. When you called in on the private line, Blanchard called me in Washington from another. Then he connected the two lines in the office and we talked."

"I'd guessed that"

"You guessed a lot"

I said: "Where does Spaulding fit in?"

CROMWELL SHRUGGED. "He's Viola's brother, that's all. When Reynolds—the Eastern supervisor—put the pressure on me, I had to have Spaulding looked up, although it didn't worry me. He didn't know anything about the loans."

"How about Alex? Did you know him?"

"I've known about him for quite a long time." Cromwell sighed. "You know I met Viola in Blanchard's office, then happened to run into her in a bar one night We went out together. She was attractive, clever—well, you know, a smart woman can do most anything with a man. I married her. But I didn't find out until much later that she was in love with Alex, had been supporting him with my money. That she married me because she and Alex knew I had money. She went through every cent I had, you know."

"I thought so."

"That's the reason I suggested getting the loans. I needed the money badly. I had notes to meet, bills to pay—you know I couldn't keep my job in this business if my credit went bad."

"I know." I cleared my throat. "But one thing more. How did you know what I was after when I went to the mail box? You hear my conversation with Spaulding?"

He shook his head. "I knew him. I went in and talked to him right after you came out. Knowing you, I knew you had something up your sleeve."

"Oh." I chewed my lip. "But how about the shot? How'd you get away with that?"

"I fired it from an empty washroom, after locking the door."

I said: "Well, well. The plot thickens." I looked at Bones. He was leaning against the wall drinking all the dope in. "Satisfied?" I asked him.

"Nope. Not yet." He moved over in front of me, put his hands on his skinny hips. "Now we've got the murder business cleared up, how about the publicity and the six thousand bucks?"

I said: "Oh." That had slipped my mind.

Jimmie said slowly: "I'll pay the six thousand." She looked from one of us to the other as if to see if we believed her. "I'll pay it. Dad stole it—or rather was a partner in stealing it—and I really think I ought to. I believe he'd want me to." She hesitated. "There's an insurance policy, you know. It goes to me. Five thousand—and it's double indemnity. I'll still get four."

I said: "But Jimmie! After all, it's your dough, and—"

Bones rapped: "Getting soft, Shag?"

I clenched my teeth.

Jimmie said: "I want to pay it. Really I do."

I nodded. It seemed a hell of a thing to me—but if she wanted to, then she wanted to. I looked over at Cromwell. Some of the strength was coming back to his body; he was laboring hard to get to his feet. He finally got there, staggered, leaned against the wall. His smile was directed at me, and he said:

"So you're not all hard-boiled, either—eh, Roberts?"

Out of the corner of my eyes I caught a glimpse of Jimmie. She had the robe hugged tightly around her again. I said doggedly: "I don't see why in hell she should pay and clear your skirts."

Cromwell smiled. Somehow he seemed bright, cheerful. "Oh, she won't clear my skirts.... Now, about the publicity. Hand me the rifle."

"The hell you say."

"Don't be silly. I know what I'm doing."

I handed it to him. He disappeared into the kitchen for a moment, and we heard the sound of water running. He came back polishing the stock with his handkerchief. "Your fingerprints are off now."

I watched him. He went outside, fired the rifle in the air—it was a Winchester repeater—and came back smiling. "In case they make a paraffin test."

I said: "It'll still look screwy. You catch your wife with another man—she shoots *him,* and you shoot her. Then shoot *yourself.* It doesn't add up."

He shrugged. "It'll have to do."

I said: "Oh, no it won't—at all."

Cromwell blinked at me. I stepped in, feinted low with my left, cracked my right on the side of his chin. He slammed up against the wall, sank like a rag doll.

Bones yelled: "What the hell!"

I growled, "Use your head, nincompoop—for something besides to put grease on. We inquired at the post office, didn't we? We got directions from the old colored woman, didn't we? How bad do you think the publicity would be if we sneaked off and the cops got us, anyway?"

Bones scratched his head.

I didn't say anything more. I stood looking down at Cromwell, feeling sorry for the guy, feeling glad too that he'd finally begun to snap out of it. He'd be all right now that his nemesis was gone. He'd lose his job, sure—but the company wouldn't prosecute. He'd be all right—if no more women turned up.

If no more women turned up…. I shrugged. Then I noticed Jimmie James, the robe still tight around her, watching me with a peculiar look in her eyes. She murmured: "Guys like you—"

I turned away quickly. I'd just seen what a woman might do to a fellow. But it was funny; right away, I began pulling for her. I said to myself: "Jimmie's all right. Sure she is." But I wished like hell we had a doctor handy—so he could get right to work on her.

HOST TO DEATH

*Radio was one place where Investigator Shag Roberts
and his partner, Bones McPherson, figured they would
be safe from murderers' lead. But lead is not a fussy
customer—and before they knew it, Shag and Bones
found themselves unwilling hosts to death.*

CHAPTER I

MURDER WITH A FLOURISH

THE BARMAN drew another beer and raked off the foam with a raker that looked like it was solid ivory. He slid it toward me on the black-and-silver bar, then put his elbows on the bar and looked at me quizzically.

"What did you say you were?" he asked.

I said: "Sensations. 'Sensations of the Week.' When we finished cracking a murder case, both of us lit a National Cigarette. Hadn't you heard, Otto? Roberts, that's me, and McPherson, that's my partner. Shag Roberts—Shaughnessy to my mom—and Bones McPherson. Our company thought it was a wonderful idea when National Cigarettes invited us to New York to go on the radio. We didn't understand—but the company did. Great publicity. Shows what fine, noble representatives our company has working for 'em. Do you think we're noble, Otto?"

The barman said: "What I think of you, I ain't saying—I gotta job to hold." He grinned. "But did you say 'murder case'? You cracked a murder case?"

"We split it wide open," I told him slowly. "Took out its insides, and hung them out tied with pink ribbons right in the center of the public square."

His eyes began to bulge. "No!" Then: "You wouldn't kid a guy, fella? You detectives? You—with that baby's pan you got? Now, guy, I can believe so much—"

I said: "Oh, no, not detectives. In a way, maybe. We're—well, investigators. Representatives, the company calls us. We—"

He asked: "You gonna crack any cases while you're in New York?"

I shrugged and drank some beer. "That depends on Dewey," I told him. "Personally, *I* don't know him. But if he needs us...."

The barman grinned crookedly. "Mebbe little Jimmy'll need you."

"What do you mean?"

"Well, according to the gossip columns, he—"

"Oh, that," I said, and made my voice scornful. But I knew what he was talking about. Then he drifted away to wait on another customer, and I picked up my beer and went back to our table.

IT WAS getting pretty late, about seven P.M., and most of the after-business cocktail revelers had gone home. There were only a few couples scattered around. Bones was slumped forward at our table, his arms hanging limp at his sides and his nose mashed pretty flatly into the table-top. You didn't have to look at him twice to tell what was

wrong with him. Drunks look the same whether they're on Broadway or in Baltimore.

I sat down beside him and dragged a folded paper from underneath his chin. It was opened to the gossip column, and I read:

The reason little Jimmy, of National Ciggies, took a sock at Art Lakin, Broadway mystery man, is not solely Baby Dare… Good luck, Jim! Maybe the next time you'll connect… But take a tip and don't try it again in a swank spot… Naughty, naughty. Employers spank.

I scowled and stuck my nose in my beer again.

Jimmy is the little fellow who advertises National Cigarettes. You've seen him, or at least seen his pictures. He introduces their program by blowing reveille on his bugle, and always wears an army officer's uniform, complete with Sam Browne belt and shining boots. Jimmy's a midget. He isn't a dwarf, or just a kid, like a lot of people think. He's just an ordinary guy who never grew tall and who grins at you and says that's his luck. He's that kind of a fellow. He's got a life contract for a job he's nuts about and he'll tell you that's about all a guy could ask for. That, and Baby Dare, for which you can't blame him much. She— But Baby Dare rates a paragraph all to herself.

If you've ever hit any of the better musicals or night spots on Broadway or Fifty-second, then you know her, too. She's not supposed to be long on brains or talent, but she's fixed on pulchritude in a way that brings men right out of their seats. All she ever has is walk-on parts. She walks on and walks off, and that's all she needs to do. The men do the rest. By the time she's finished her encores, your collar's as wet as an oyster, and you wonder what you saw in the blonde that floored you back in Tuscaloosa.

I thought about her and wondered why Art Lakin was a "Broadway mystery man."

Ten minutes later I paid the check, got my arms under Bones' shoulders, and started half carrying him and half dragging him out of the bar. It was our hotel bar and adjoined the lobby. I got him in there some way, got myself a bellhop, and together we hustled Bones into one of the elevators.

The elevator boy looked down his nose at Bones and asked: "He ain't dead, is he?"

I punched Bones, and he stirred.

"Only dead to the world," I said. "It's for his nerves. We're broadcasting tonight."

Up on the fifth floor in the room National Cigarettes was furnishing, we got Bones on one of the twin beds, and I tipped the bellhop and shooed him out. I undressed the skinny lug. But besides the beers, he'd had a few ryes— which I'd steered clear of—and he was getting heavier and heavier, and I wasn't getting any soberer. That last one was beginning to make me woozy. I left Bones on the bed and went down the corridor to Jimmy's room.

I shuffled my feet on the thick carpet trying to shock myself with the electricity, couldn't do it, and knocked hard on Jimmy's door.

The door opened about three inches, and Jimmy peered out. His eyes were just a little above the level of the brass door knob.

"Hello, Shag," he said. His voice sounded funny. Bones and I had been up for a week because of rehearsals, and we'd gotten to know little Jimmy pretty darned well. "How're you hitting 'em?" he asked, and his voice still sounded strange.

I said: "Oh, pretty well, I guess." I told him about Bones. "You couldn't sort of drift down with me and give a guy a hand, could you?"

I thought I noticed him slide his gaze back quickly over his shoulder. He didn't turn his head; his eyes just swiveled sideways in their sockets. "I don't think I c-could," he told me. "I—"

He broke off and I turned around; there were footsteps pattering softly behind me. I hadn't heard them. I found myself looking at Baby Dare, enjoying it naturally and being surprised at her street clothes, not having ever seen her out of a spotlight. Later, I found out she didn't pretend to be a glamour girl. She dressed as one when she hit the night spots, which wasn't so often, and she did this for business purposes. Now she wore low-heel sports shoes, a belted camel's hair coat, and a small Breton sailor with the brim snapped down in front. If she'd had books under her arm, you would have sworn she went to high school.

SHE LOOKED at me and said thoughtfully: "You're Shag Roberts. You're the very tough man with the innocent baby face. Jimmy told me about you." And to Jimmy: "What's wrong, darling? Why all the mystery?"

Jimmy's voice still sounded funny. This time it was like a ham actor registering befuddlement. "Mystery?" he asked, squinting through the crack in the door. "What mystery, honey? I don't know about any mystery."

Baby Dare smiled at me and said: "It was just a trick to get me up in his room—you stick around, Mr. Roberts." She looked back at Jimmy. "Why'd you get a stranger to call me? And now that I'm here, why don't you invite me in?"

Jimmy stammered: "G-get a stranger to call you? W-why, I—"

"Are you dressed?" asked Baby Dare, staring down into his eyes balefully.

"W-why, yes. I got on my uniform. I—"

"Come on," said Baby Dare to me, and pushed open the door.

I've had a lot of shocks in my life, but none of them like that one. The dead man was sitting in a chair in the middle of the room—Jimmy had a suite, and the door opened into the living room—and there was a leaky hole in the center of his forehead, and some of the blood had streamed down over his face.

I almost jumped back out into the corridor. Baby Dare screamed—once. Jimmy, his face a dull sickly tan, pulled her inside and slammed the door behind her. I just stood there, gaping. Baby Dare covered her eyes with her hands. Jimmy leaned his back against the door, looking haggard, breathing heavily.

Nobody spoke for what seemed an age. Finally, Jimmy said: "I didn't do it, honey. You know I didn't do it."

Baby Dare didn't uncover her eyes.

I was beginning to come back to normal. "Who is it?" I asked, but something told me I knew.

"It's Lakin," Jimmy said bitterly. "Art Lakin. Who else could it be?"

I walked past Baby Dare and over to the body. My hunch had been on the nose, all right. But I didn't touch Lakin. I circled him deferentially and began feeling funny down in the stomach. A gun lay on the floor in front of the chair—an automatic equipped with a silencer.

Jimmy must have been looking at it. "It's mine," he said wearily. "Naturally, it is. I would have an automatic with a fixed carriage, so I could have a silencer on it."

I shrugged. "If you didn't use it, you can prove it when the cops give you the nitrate test"

Jimmy said: "I didn't use it. But after the mugs shot Lakin, they put a blank in the gun and forced me to pull the trigger. Put my hand on the gun and held it there."

I stared at him. "They did what? Who?"

Little Jimmy looked up at me and his mouth twisted. He was a good-looking little fellow with a fresher and brighter look in person than his pictures ever showed. "Two mugs," he said. "But who'd ever believe me? Who'd ever believe two guys forced their way in here when I opened the door and calmly walked in the bedroom and got my gun out of my bureau drawer? Who'd ever believe that?

"They had guns, sure. They just came in, one of 'em held a gun on me, and the other went in the bedroom and calmly took mine. And just as calmly came back, made Lakin sit down in that chair, then raised my gun and put a bullet through his forehead. Doesn't it sound screwy? And then what do they do? Put a blank in my gun, put it in my hand, squeeze my hand until it goes off. Nitrate test—huh! Then they take the blank shell out and put the real one back, handling everything with gloves while they're doing it. They put the gun on the floor then, after which comes the proposition.

"One hundred grand they want by two o'clock tonight, or else the cops are tipped, and what alibi do I have? Then they pull down my uniform coat—it's buttoned and locks my arms—pull down my pants and buckle my belt tight around my legs. That's so they won't leave any evidence that they've tied me up. So, then they lock the door and beat it, and it takes me twenty minutes to free myself. By that time, they're out of the hotel, and where am I?"

He paused and wiped some moisture from his lips with his sleeve. "All right, I ask you—where am I?"

I WASN'T through staring at him; I didn't answer right away. I said then, and my voice didn't sound very convinced: "You mean, Jimmy, that two mugs forced—"

"You see?" he broke in disgustedly. "Even you don't believe me."

"Now, Jimmy," I told him, "brace yourself and hold your horses. You said yourself that the whole business sounded screwy, didn't you?" I took a breath. "How long ago did all this happen?"

He sighed and kicked at the rug with a toe of one of his tiny shoes. "Oh, just about half an hour ago, I suppose."

I said: "Well, there's no use asking you if you knew the mugs or not. If you did, I don't know what in the devil you're worrying about. How come Lakin to be here?"

Jimmy kicked at the rug again and didn't look at me. "He said somebody phoned him to come up here at a quarter to seven and collect. I owed him dough. He cheated the pants off of me in a poker game one night." The little fellow scowled at the floor. "I didn't know it until half of Broadway tipped me off about it."

I guess I'm stupid. I asked: "Was the game in Macy's window with floodlights, or did the little birdies spread the news?"

Jimmy looked up sourly. "The news was spread," he told me, "years before I hit this town. Lakin fleeced suckers, and even after they found out about it, collected via the strong-arm route. Only all of my friends had neglected to tell me."

"But you wouldn't pay?" I asked.

Jimmy said: "I told that no good louse that I was just a little guy, but my finger would squeeze a trigger. He didn't try the strong-arm method. He tried embarrassing me in public, every time I was with Baby." Jimmy's face darkened. "He was sweet on her, y'know. He offered her—" The little fellow paused, flushed.

I looked around at Baby Dare. She wore her camel's hair belted loosely; I guess she got tired of men staring at her figure. But I remembered how she looked in a spotlight with about enough on to make a pair of gloves. "I guess he offered her plenty," I said. "Either that or he was a guy who had pretty poor taste. Well—"

Baby Dare took down her hands again long enough to say: "The offer was marriage, if you please, and the money that went with it was plenty. Can't you be a gentleman and get on another subject?"

I grinned. "Oh, sure."

She put her hands back over her eyes and didn't say anything else.

I turned to Jimmy. "Well, what're you going to do?"

He lifted his head and glared at me. "What can I do? I've got to notify the company and see if they'll pay the dough. There's one thing certain: I can't pay it. I don't want them to, but they probably will."

I blinked. "You don't want them to?"

"No," he said firmly, and his bright eyes flashed. "They've been good to me, haven't they? Do you think I like putting them on a spot like this? Oh, I know how they'll take it. They'll pay the dough, pat my shoulder, and tell me to be more careful. They can't do anything else. They spend between three and four million dollars a year for advertising, and what do they advertise—Jimmy and his bugle. If I was up for a murder rap, could they keep on with Jimmy and his bugle? Magazine cuts, placards—they'd even have to change the slogan. So what?

"So I have a life contract, but it has a morality and scandal clause. So they'll pay the dough, keep me until the end of the year probably, and then let me out. They already have three substitutes who can step right into my boots. And the public wouldn't know the difference. They'd probably pay me a bonus to have me say I'd quit, and another Jimmy would go right on blowing that bugle. It's the idea that's valuable to 'em, and they'll pay through the nose to keep using it. But after they've been as good as they have to me, how do you think I feel about getting 'em in a spot like this?"

I said: "Not so good."

"You're derned right I don't. I was making eighteen bucks a week when they picked me up and handed me this job. Eighteen bucks a week—just think of that." He clenched his small fists and his jaw hardened. "I'm going to call McGowan. You better stick around."

McGowan was head of National Cigarettes' radio advertising, and also the director of the radio program. I didn't say anything.

Jimmy walked over to the corner and picked up the phone. "We spend over a million and a half a year for radio advertising alone," he told me. Then he put down the phone and said anxiously: "You better get out, Baby."

"Why?" she asked, not moving her hands.

"Well, you don't want to get mixed up in this. The papers would love that too much." Jimmy frowned, and I noticed that he seemed to be trying to steel himself against something. He added to me: "Couldn't you take her down to your room until I talk to McGowan, Shag?"

I said: "I can when I put a few clothes on Bones, yeah."

"Well, you run down and put some clothes on him and come right back for her."

I went out, and walked down the corridor, wondering why he wanted to get rid of us. That didn't seem to make one whit of sense to me.

KILL CRAZY

SEVERAL COLD wet towels finally got Bones out of his stupor, and he was in the bathroom taking a shower all by himself when I came back from another trip to Jimmy's room with Baby Dare. She sat down by the window and stared moodily out at the dark, and I sat down on the bed and stared pleasantly at her. Bones and I didn't have a suite. I could hear him splashing around in the shower, and then he started one of his bawdy songs, so I went over and stuck my head in the door and said:

"Hey. I got a lady out here."

He was facing the shower and letting the water beat on his head, and he didn't bother to look around. He chuckled and told me: "Don't brag. You couldn't get yourself a lady." But he stopped singing, so I closed the door.

I went back to the bed and sat myself down and stared some more at Baby Dare. All the lights were on in the room, and I could see her pretty plainly. She showed very few signs of nervousness. Occasionally she opened and closed her brown purse, the catch making a metallic click, but on the whole, she simply sat and stared, her feelings pretty well disguised. That is, I judged she had feelings because Jimmy evidently meant plenty to her.

And thinking that way, I couldn't help but admire her; most girls in her shoes would have bordered on hysterics.

I don't like girls who almost tear their hair so whoever is watching will feel sorry for them.

After a while I got to thinking and asked: "Did Jimmy call McGowan while you were there?"

She turned her head around quickly. "No, he didn't. Why?"

I shrugged. "No particular reason. I just wondered."

The door to the bathroom opened, and Bones came out in a faded yellow bathrobe and wooden beach sandals. He had a towel around his neck, and his hair was plastered down and his freckles stood out on his shiny face like brown paint spots on a strip of cellophane. He stopped in the center of the room, looked hard at Baby Dare, then put his hands on his hips, and turned around to me.

"What's this?" he growled. "A daughter you been keeping under cover?"

I grinned. "That's Baby Dare."

Bones snapped: "Who's she?" Then he seemed to remember. "Oh," he said. He turned and looked at her. I hadn't told him about Lakin, so I let him have it gently. He said again: "Oh." And in a moment, with a sly wink at me: "Think I'd kill a guy over her myself."

Baby Dare turned and flared: "Please don't say things like that!"

Bones flushed. None of his ancestors had ever been diplomats, and nobody had ever accused him of having any tact. So, despite his flush, he said bluntly, "Well, I still think I would," and picked up his clothes and went back into the bathroom.

He came out in a few minutes, snappily dressed in a dark double-breasted suit with a light gray pin-stripe that fitted him as closely as molasses fits a pancake. He had on a light-gray shirt and a stiff white collar and a dark knitted tie with tiny red riding-crops woven into it. None of the new styles got ahead of Bones. He got a silk handkerchief from a dresser drawer, tucked it in his breast pocket and demanded:

"Well?"

He was facing the mirror and I was watching him arrange the handkerchief in it. I said: "We're waiting until Jimmy talks to McGowan."

"And then what?"

"Oh, I don't know," I told him. "We might be able to help in some way."

Bones spun around. "And get mixed up in another murder? Not me. I died three thousand deaths in that other business, and all I got for it was a ten-dollar raise. Not me, boy. I been scared enough."

I LOOKED at him and kept back a grin. He hadn't been scared of anything but going on the air since the haunted house of kid days turned out to be a fake. "Don't you like Jimmy?" I asked.

Bones snapped. "Sure, I like Jimmy. He's shown us a swell time and he's a swell egg, but that don't mean I got to go out and stop three or four slugs for him." He planted himself in front of me and dug those long skinny hands into his hips again. "Look, Shag. You're not forgetting you got a noodle, and going screwy on me again, are you?"

I said: "I might try to help Jimmy a little."

Bones turned loose a deep sigh. "There you go. A good guy one minute, and screwy as hell the next." He threw up his hands. "Well, go ahead. Have your fun. But this time, brother, count me out."

I grinned at him broadly and looked over at Baby Dare, who was watching us both like we were a couple of sideshow exhibits. There was a rattle of the door knob, and then a knock. That sequence should have warned me—I'd locked the door.

"That's probably Jimmy now," I said, and got up off the bed. I went over and unlocked the door, as casually as if danger was something I'd never heard of. Then came the shock.

No sooner than I turned the knob, the door slammed open and struck my shoulder. I went reeling backwards, stumbled over a chair, and before I could get my balance, fell into Bones. He held me up. I got my balance again as the door slammed shut, found myself looking at two men who didn't seem familiar. Then I noticed that one of the men had a gun in his hand.

This was all too sudden to scare me, and I was only a little shocked. I rubbed my shoulder ruefully and scowled at the men.

"You sure you got the right room?" I bit off at them. Then I remembered Lakin, and my spine suddenly felt prickly.

The man without the gun began sauntering forward in a manner that looked careless but wasn't, because every step seemed to have purpose to it and his eyes seemed to miss nothing. He was a tall man with a thin, hollow-cheeked face, his complexion grayish and pasty, his clothes cheap and carelessly worn. He had a dirty-gray mustache that was badly in need of trimming. He didn't look so dangerous, but I knew looks didn't tell everything.

The other man was the one who made my spine feel like it needed pruning. He was big, thick, with huge freckled hands that had fingers the size of hot dogs, and yet he carried himself as if he knew how to handle his body. He had a lot more freckles than Bones, a long, hooked nose, and red kinky hair that bristled all over his head.

It was when he pushed back his hat to scratch a pimple at his hair line that I got a glimpse of the bristling red bush. He pulled his hat down again and stuck the gun in his pocket. When he saw we weren't showing any guns, I suppose he figured he didn't need it.

He jerked his thumb at me and said: "You. Over here."

I didn't move because I didn't understand what he wanted.

He snapped nastily: "I said *you*. Over here."

I went back a pace, purely from reflex, and took one hard glance swiftly around the room. Baby Dare sat by the window, her hands in her lap, her eyes huge with surprise, but hardly touched by fear. A body wasn't all that Baby Dare had. She had a heart inside of it stout enough to buck any test.

Then I saw Bones. He stood scowling belligerently at both of our visitors, too completely puzzled yet to say anything. He wasn't far from the gray-faced man, who had stopped sauntering forward and stood looking him up and down. But suddenly Bnes noticed the scrutiny, stiffened and leaned forward.

I said softly: "Careful, Bones. They've got guns."

The redheaded guy went past me in two long strides and stopped as quickly as he had gotten under way. He had quite a lot of grace to his chunky body. He balanced himself lightly on the balls of his feet, whipped a right to Bones' jaw so fast I couldn't follow it. The blow made a peculiar hollow crack.

Bones toppled over stiffly, like a toy soldier falling, his shoulder spilling over a chair, his cheek scraping hard against one of the chair legs. He landed with a dull thump and lay very still. You couldn't even tell he was breathing simply by looking at him.

The gray-faced man said, "Whew," and whistled softly. Somehow I thought he seemed a little worried.

I could feel the muscles in my arms get tense and springy. I said: "You didn't have to do that, you know."

"No!" The redheaded guy turned and lashed out with one of those meaty hands, slapped his fingers flat into my mouth. I tasted blood. "No!" he said again. "What would you rather have me do?"

His voice dripped sarcasm. I wiped some blood from my lips with the back of my hand, said bitterly: "I'd rather have you go down to some nursery and sock a few babies. That looks like it would be more in your line."

The redheaded fellow turned to his partner and said: "I'm gonna take some of the starch outta this wise-cracker."

HE TURNED back to me and got a handful of my shirt and tie. Then he shook me twice and raised his right fist slowly until his forearm was just about parallel to the floor. I saw the punch coming. That big fist shot toward me getting bigger and bigger like a train in a movie comedy that looks like it's coming right out into the audience.

Then my head throbbed like somebody had hit me with a bat. My shoulders struck something, but it didn't seem they hit very hard, and I found myself on the floor with the back of my neck against Baby Dare's ankles. I thought foolishly that *that* wasn't so bad. And I wasn't out. I could see the redheaded guy and the gray-faced man like you see somebody coming toward you in the fog.

Then Baby Dare's ankles moved. I finally realized she was standing up, and I heard her say: "No. You don't want to hit him again. I think maybe you've taught him his lesson."

She was cool, that girl. She had sense enough to humor them.

I pushed myself up to a sitting position, and the fog began to clear away. The redheaded mug stood scowling down at me, and the gray-faced man stood looking at Baby Dare.

The gray-faced man now looked definitely worried. He said: "Maybe she's right, Pinky. Maybe he's learned his lesson."

Pinky growled: "Keep outta this. This happens to be my party." He swung his foot into my ribs, and my breath puffed out of my mouth like I was a blacksmith's bellows. "Get up," he said. "I didn't hit you all that hard."

I retched a little and began to feel sick, and when I tried to raise my arms I didn't have much strength. Pinky reached down and got another handful of shirt, dragged me up and sneered again.

"Give me another wise crack," he said.

I knew this wasn't a good spot for heroics, but I couldn't let the redhead back me down. I got together what was left of my breath and gasped: "Why waste 'em on a thick-headed lug who hasn't laughed since his grandmother died?"

That big fist came up again, in the same manner it had before, the forearm stiff and straight and parallel to the floor, the fist so heavy with meat you couldn't see the knuckles bulge. But I wasn't going to stand there and wait for it again. Somehow the first time I'd expected a bluff; this time I knew what was coming. So I took both my feet off of the floor. My weight made his left arm sag, and I threw my head sharply to one side. But the punch never came. Baby Dare leaped forward, caught Pinky's arm.

She said: "No! No! Not again!"

He wrenched his arm from her roughly and let go of my shirt. I sat down hard. He faced Baby Dare clenching both his fists, and from the way he balanced himself you could tell he used to be a fighter.

The gray-faced man stepped between him and the girl. "Now, Pinky," he said, his mouth working anxiously, "the first thing you know you're going to kill somebody. You know how you get."

Pinky snarled: "Outta my way. I know what I'm doing."

You couldn't help but notice that the gray-faced man turned grayer. He stepped to one side and moistened his lips nervously.

I could feel my stomach get very empty and my mouth get very dry. I put my hands on the floor and got into a crouch, like a football linesman ready to charge.

Pinky stood glaring down his hooked nose at Baby Dare, then got his gun out of his pocket and turned toward me. He didn't aim the gun, but I began to sweat. Out of the corners of my eyes, I saw Bones stir.

The gray-faced man said: "The other one's coming to, Pink."

The redheaded guy turned a little, saw Bones blinking his eyes. Pinky said out of the side of his mouth, "He ain't gonna hurt nobody," and turned back to me. He held the gun loosely down by one of his heavy thighs.

"Look," he said. "You're broadcasting tonight. And after the broadcast, you're blowing town. Understand? Mebbe you ain't planned to blow town tonight, but you're gonna. There's a ten-twenty on the Pennsy that goes right to Baltimore, and that's the train you're gonna make. And you never heard of a guy named Lakin. If any stories get around as to what become of him, we'll know where they come from, and we know where you live."

He lifted the gun where I could see it better, then slipped it very gently into his pocket. He added to Baby Dare: "And as for you, sister, well see you later."

With that he turned around and walked over to the door, and the gray-faced man released a breath and followed him. Bones sat up, still blinking his eyes. I stood up. Baby Dare sat down in the chair again, and the men went out and slammed the door. I leaned against the dresser weakly and tried drawing a lot of air deep into my lungs.

CHAPTER III

MUTINY PAYOFF

IT WAS only about ten minutes later when another knock sounded on the door, and this time I was cautious about the way I opened it. It was Jimmy and McGowan. They came in, and I told them our story and we matched descriptions.

There wasn't any doubt about it; they were the same two mugs who had killed Art Lakin. There had never been any doubt about it in my mind, anyway. But we hadn't called the cops, or the hotel dick. We'd taken a beating, but it was still Jimmy's party. We didn't know yet what he was going to do.

I said from the bed, where I'd seated myself again; "Well, what *are* you going to do?"

McGowan said: "Pay the money. What else can be done?"

He was a man of medium height, dressed in tailored clothes that made Bones' snappiness look a little cheap—he probably paid as much for his shoes as Bones had paid for the double-breasted suit. He had thick curly hair, cropped very close, parted in the middle and with a little gray sprinkled through it. His body was slim but vigorous, and he was deeply tanned. He looked like an aggressive type of business man who probably had three loves—his office, his golf club and his yearly winter trip to Florida.

76

I shrugged. "It's your business. But you've got to hide Lakin's body where the cops won't find it, or else take the slug from Jimmy's gun out of it before you dump it somewhere. And if you hide the body or take the slug out, you're opening yourselves up to plenty of blackmail. When those guys spend their hundred grand, they'll be back looking for more."

McGowan said tightly: "We'll have to take that chance."

"Well," I told him, "it's okay by me. But the banks are closed, and a hundred grand is a lot of cash—if they don't want it that way, they must have escaped from the bughouse. Where are you going to get a hundred grand in cash tonight?"

McGowan frowned. "I can pull some strings and get it. After all, you know, we're a pretty large company."

"And a hundred grand," I said softly, "is a pretty large amount of dough. Or didn't you know?" I looked at Jimmy. He looked very smart in his Sam Browne belt and shining boots, but his small face was clouded anxiously and his bright eyes were worried. "Are you paying off, Jimmy?" I asked.

I caught him glancing quickly, fearfully, at Baby Dare. "N-no," he stammered in a low, choked voice.

McGowan spun on him. "But I thought you—"

I growled: "Suppose you were nuts about a swell girl, and *you* happened to be in Jimmy's shoes? Would you want her to make the payoff and get mixed up in the lousy business, or maybe run a chance of getting a few slugs in her? Would you?"

McGowan spun toward me and goggled.

"Don't ask me how I knew it," I snapped. "It's as plain as that nose in the middle of your face. Jimmy wouldn't talk to you while we were in his room. He didn't want the girl to know the mugs had ordered him that she should make the payoff. Why do you think she got a phone call to come up to Jimmy's room? And in here just a while ago, Pinky said to the girl that he'd see her later. Do you think saving your company a lot of dough is worth putting her in a spot like that?"

McGowan stopped looking dumbstruck and tightened his mouth. His black eyes flashed at me angrily; he probably wasn't used to being bawled out by a young guy he thought beneath him. He said stiffly: "It's not up to the company, Mr. Roberts. It's up to Jimmy. He's the one the police will hold responsible for Lakin's death."

Jimmy took one more quick look over at Baby Dare. I tried to watch him without seeming to; I pretended to fuss with my tie. Jimmy's look wasn't furtive and fearful like his other one had been; I thought I saw a touch of pride in it, a touch of determination. He squared his small shoulders, almost imperceptibly, stiffened his little legs and thrust out his chin. He asked, almost wistfully:

"Do you know, Mr. McGowan, how much I care about *that?*"

I wondered if I caught a flash of sympathy in McGowan's eyes. Evidently I didn't. He snapped:

"I know you're in love with Baby Dare."

"Certainly, I am," Jimmy said, and flushed crimson. But he kept his chin up proudly. "Also, I know how much the company has done for me, and how good they've been to me, and I want to do right by 'em. You would, too— anybody decent would. But I can't ask Baby to make the payoff for me."

Bones said through his teeth: "Maybe Shag and me might make it for you."

I turned and stared at him.

HE PUT his hands on his hips and bellowed: "All right, tell me I'm soft! Tell me I'm just a crack-brained nincompoop who's worse than you are! G'wan, tell me! But you're wrong—get that? You're wrong!" He strode over to me and shook a skinny finger in my face. "I got conked on the chin, didn't I? I want just one chance at that redheaded louse!"

I grinned at him. "But that redheaded louse won't be there."

Bones roared: "Whaddya mean, he won't be there? Where?"

I said: "I don't know exactly where, because I don't know where the payoff is supposed to be made. But wherever it is, the redheaded guy won't be there. Take my word for it. All of us here except Mr. McGowan have gotten a peep at him, and if he was to wait somewhere to pick up the dough, we could simply give his description to the cops and have them pick him up. And he won't be that easy to get."

Bones scowled and rubbed his jaw. "He ain't easy at anything."

"No," I went on ruefully, and lifted a hand and rubbed my own jaw. "If he's clever enough to plan this business like he has, he won't be ass enough to collect the dough himself. Nor will he let that gray-faced guy do the collecting. He'll have somebody there we've never seen—" I broke off and asked Jimmy: "How's the payoff supposed to be worked?"

Jimmy raised his eyes to me darkly. "It's supposed to be made at Henry's Bar at—"

"Where's Henry's Bar?" I cut in.

"It's right across from the hotel here. Right on the corner. You can't miss it."

"Okay," I said. "Go on."

"Well, it's supposed to be made there at eight-thirty," Jimmy told me. "That is, the *first* payment's supposed to be made there. You see—"

I asked: "How much is the first payment?"

"Oh," said Jimmy, moving his shoulders slightly, "only ten thousand. They said they wanted that at eight-thirty as—well, as sort of evidence of good faith. They—"

I growled: "You sure they didn't ask you for your watch as security?" Jimmy looked blank, and I snorted. Bones threw back his head and turned loose a heehaw. Nobody else seemed to think anything was funny. I went on: "Is Ba— is Miss Dare supposed to deliver that ten grand?"

Jimmy nodded. "She's supposed to put the money in an envelope, go there and take a table, and wait for somebody to come up to her and say: 'Lakin sent me.' Then she's supposed to hand the dough over to them. After that, whoever she hands it to is supposed to give her instructions about when and where to deliver the rest of it."

I grinned at Bones. "Sort of secretive and dramatic, huh?" He didn't answer me. I asked McGowan: "Can you get ten grand in time to get it there by eight-thirty?"

McGowan frowned and pulled at the lobe of his ear for a few moments. "I think so."

I said: "Aren't you sure?"

McGowan frowned again and looked at his strap-watch. "It's a quarter to eight," he said. "I can know for certain in twenty minutes."

"Well," I told him, "you better start pulling a few of your strings. You see if you can get the dough, and if you can, phone us here. Then Bones and I will pick it up somewhere and deliver it." I looked around at everybody. "Is that okay?"

For a few moments nobody said anything. McGowan was still looking at his strap-watch, Bones was looking at me, Baby Dare and Jimmy were looking at each other. I braced myself; I had an idea what was coming. Then it came. Baby Dare said:

"If you don't mind, Mr. Roberts, *I'd* rather deliver it. The men want it that way, and I don't want to take any chances. After all, it's the money they want, and if I turn it over to them—"

Jimmy said in a tense, hoarse voice: "No, honey. No."

SHE DIDN'T even look at him; she raised her eyes to me wretchedly. "Can't you see, Mr. Roberts? The men don't know you're going to make the delivery. And there's no way for us to notify them or ask them about it, is there? And suppose that when I don't show up at the bar at eight-thirty, they think we're not going to pay, and phone the police? Don't you see, Mr. Roberts? We can't run that chance. We just—well—"

She paused and bit her lip, her face colorless and tragic.

I took a deep breath. It's hard to be nasty to people like Baby Dare even when you know you have to do it for their own good. But she was right; the guys might call the cops. And I had an idea.

I snapped: "Okay. You go ahead and deliver the money. We've offered to help. You don't want our help. Go ahead. Deliver it. And get out of here. We can keep our mouths shut."

Baby Dare gaped at me.

"Get out!" I roared. I stamped over to the door and flung it open. "Do you want me to write it for you? Get out! We're through!"

McGowan said in amazement: "Then you don't want—"

I snarled: "I don't want you to do anything but get out of here! We're not anything but radio guests. Get out!"

Baby Dare blazed: "Gladly!"

She strode over to me with her eyes flashing, lifted her hand and slapped my face. The slap hurt, but I had to grin. That girl had spirit. But she evidently thought the grin was nothing but sarcasm, because she raised the hand and slapped me again.

I didn't grin this time. I said: "Shame on you—twice on the same cheek."

Her eyes were burning at me furiously. "You're probably right," she told me. "I shouldn't lower myself by touching you." She turned away from me, wrenching herself around, and strode savagely out the door.

I looked after her, knowing I was doing right, but flushing a little in spite of that. Then I turned back and faced the room. McGowan went past me, showing a sneer a mile broad, but little Jimmy hadn't moved. He stood erect, staring at me, as if he couldn't believe what he'd heard.

"Out!" I growled at him through my teeth.

He said, "Shag! Shag!" and looked bewildered. "You—"

He stopped as I started toward him, stood stiffly as I gripped his collar and pants. He didn't even get a chance to struggle. I carried him out the door, put him down, slammed the door and quickly locked it. I was glad his back was to me and I couldn't see his face.

Bones gasped: "Have you gone nuts?"

I grinned and winked at him. "Maybe those mugs are watching our room," I said. "If so, they'll think we're out of it. But we're not, boy. We're only beginning."

Bones' face lighted up. "Then I get a crack at that redheaded guy?"

I said: "I hope so. Somebody ought to."

Bones grinned cheerfully. When he grinned the freckles on his nose overlapped and made it look all brown like a well-turned croquette. "Ah," he said, and licked his knuckles.

"Why that?" I asked.

"Polishing 'em up," he told me, and licked them again.

I laughed at him and tried to think.

CHAPTER IV

THE LADY AND THE KILLER

AFTER ALLOWING a few minutes for our recent visitors to clear out of the corridor, and a few more minutes to get some facts straight in my mind, I sat down at the phone. I got the desk clerk in a moment and said:

"This is Mr. Roberts in five-four-six. I know National Cigarettes reserves this room for their radio guests, and I just bet my partner all the rest of the rooms in this wing are occupied permanently, too. Could you do a guy a favor and check that for me?"

The clerk said: "Certainly, Mr. Roberts. Just a minute." In a few moments he came back on the line chuckling. I'm afraid you lose. All of the rooms are occupied permanently but two. They've been occupied for several months—" he hesitated— "one four and one six, but we can hardly call that permanent. Or can you stretch a point on that and trip your partner up?"

"Trip up that guy?" I asked, and laughed into the phone. "Not that louse." I thanked him and hung up.

Bones growled: "That's right. Call me names. Well?"

I said: "When old Sherlock Holmes looked for something, he always looked in the most obvious place. I thought Pinky and his buddy might have had a room right here in the wing. But I was wrong. Let's go."

84

"To Henry's Bar?" Bones asked.

"Where else?" I said. "Or do you prefer the Ritz?"

It was twenty after eight when Bones and I drifted idly into Henry's Bar and took a table that gave us a good view of the place. It wasn't very crowded. A few men stood at the tong mahogany bar rolling poker dice for drinks. The lacquered booths along the wall opposite us were only about a quarter full.

The tavern was shaped rectangularly. The entrance was on the corner of Broadway and a one-way side street, and at the end of the row of booths a sign read Exit. This was in fancy script on pink ground-glass, and arrows pointed in opposite directions on each side of it—*Men's Lounge* and *Ladies' Lounge*. Baby Dare sat at a table near a large nickel phonograph, bent intently over a long, iced drink.

I said cheerfully: "She's still got the schoolgirl clothes on, lad, but she's still something to look at. McGowan must have laid hands on ten grand, huh?"

Bones was moistening his lips and looking across the room. He blinked his pale-green eyes a few times. He told me: "Yeah, yeah. But take a gander at what I see. Not the same type as Baby Dare, but my, oh, *my!*"

I drank some of the beer a waiter had brought us, then looked around and followed Bones' gaze. "Well!" I said.

This one was curved and slinky with long, aquamarine eyes, and her face was dusky and smooth and looked as soft as water. She had high cheekbones that were rather prominent, and shallow hollows beneath them and bright red lips. She looked cool and poised. She sipped at a drink that was the color of sloe gin, and a dim light near her table glistened on her lacquered nails. They were a deep maroon, slightly darker than the drink, and when she turned and looked at us, I wondered what kept her eyes open. I mean, her lashes really looked that heavy. She lowered them and smiled.

She was only about twelve feet away from us. Bones nudged me and whispered: "Don't tell me that's *me* she's handing the office to!"

I chuckled. "It's a strange world, boy. Anything's possible."

He cracked me in the ribs with his fist, keeping the byplay below table level, and flashed the girl his Sunday-best smile. It looked like that was what she'd been waiting for.

She stood up and, carrying her drink, purse, and gloves, came over and sat down with us, her long eyes watching Bones coolly. I didn't even have a chance to tell him he had other business. The girl took a cigarette from my pack, which I'd tossed out on the table, asked with her eyes for a match, and Bones lit one for her.

SHE TOOK a very slow, deep inhale, blew out the match with the smoke, leaned back and smiled at him very mysteriously.

"Where did we meet?" she asked.

Bones stammered: "In B-Baltimore? At the A-Arundel, or some place?"

"Oh, that's it," she said. "At the Arundel, of course." Her voice sounded like a low musical note. "And your friend?"

I said: I'm not his friend. He's my father." I winced as Bones kicked me under the table. I went on: "We don't look much alike, but heredity isn't everything. You see—"

"Would you like to dance?" the girl asked Bones, shutting me out like a wind that might ruin her complexion.

Bones stammered: "D-dance?" He'd had one girl for ten years and only dreams about others. The tangibility of this one was beginning to frighten him. "Here?" he asked hastily. "To w-what?"

"Haven't you got a nickel?"

"Oh," said Bones, and stared over past Baby Dare at the phonograph.

I knew Baby Dare would see us anyway the first time she looked up from her drink. "Go ahead," I told Bones. "It makes for natural atmosphere."

Bones stood up, still looking pretty undecided, then finally faded away from us, digging in his pocket for the nickel. I looked over at Baby Dare. It seemed a pity to hand her a shock, but we were here now; there was nothing else to do. I scowled, almost forgetting the long-eyed girl. The next thing I knew she'd moved from her chair to Bones', and was sitting beside me, holding her purse in her lap.

I put my eyes on her squarely, not paying any attention to the purse. I said: "Of course, he being the father, he has more dough, but—" I stopped and felt my eyes bulge.

There wasn't any coolness in those aquamarine eyes now. They flashed at me, changing to sea-green and sparkling, and the hand she'd just taken out of her purse was tense and steady. I noticed the gun in it when the short barrel caught light and gleamed. She bent forward a little, keeping the gun out of sight below the table, and whispered nastily:

"Surprised? Or did you think I was going to be sucker enough to let you tail me straight to Pinky?"

I barely breathed. My hands were out on the table, palms down, and when I lifted them, they left dark spots where my palms had touched the cloth. The spots were very damp.

I gasped: "I don't like to remind you, but the safety's still on that gun. Move your thumb and I'll sock you right in your pretty teeth." I sucked in breath. She didn't move. I added quickly: "And it's going to be tough for you to aim after I deliver the sock, too, beautiful. This isn't the sort of spot where I hand out any love taps."

She said in the same nasty voice: "No? And do you think I'd brace you if I didn't have a guy in here covering you?"

The hairs crawled on my neck. But I bluffed it out. I snapped: "No good, my beauty. That's what you'd naturally think *I'd* think. You put the gun away and keep that thumb still while you're doing it."

She still didn't move. I sat with my fingers on the table edge, the biceps of my arms like wires, saw Bones out of the corners of my eyes, saw him drop his nickel in the phonograph. Quite suddenly then, it blared. The girl started at the sound, and I almost leaped out of the chair.

I never knew whether it was the girl's start that made me leap, or the sudden hot piano keys of Fats Waller's music. But I didn't swing at her because we couldn't afford publicity, and she didn't move her thumb, heaven only knows why. Maybe she was too startled; I'm sure I don't know. I sank down again in my chair, sweating; the knuckles of the girl's gunhand looked like tiny ivory balls.

I said through my teeth: "Hell on wheels, beautiful! Let's not go through anything like *that* again!"

That dusky tone of her skin now looked like coffee with plenty of cream in it. She glanced swiftly at Bones and tucked the gun back in her bag.

"It's up to you," she told me, her voice still nasty but a trifle hoarse. "Try to break up the payoff or make any move to follow me, and you'll never even live to get up halfway out of that chair again."

IT WAS then that I noticed that although the gun was in the bag, her hand was in there with it. She was hiding it from Bones; I suppose she'd heard that he was excitable.

I looked toward him again. Baby Dare was on her feet, her hands tightly clenched in front of her, staring whitely at Bones, just as if he'd struck her. Maybe the shock was worse to her than if he *had* struck her. She sank down in her chair, her face suddenly empty, like her horse had been beaten out by a nose at the wire.

But as far as Bones was concerned, she might have been invisible. He went past her without speaking, without even a sidelong glance. He came back to our table, noticed the girl had switched seats, gave me a look that didn't have any love in it. He said:

"So, the infant takes advantage of daddy's absence, huh? But that's okay. You don't have to look *that* guilty." Then he looked at the girl and some of his fright returned. "Well, there's the music," he growled, trying to cover the fright. "Want to dance?"

The full depth of her color hadn't yet come back. Neither did the low beautiful voice quite come off. I think she tried it again, but it came out harshly. "I'm sorry," she told Bones. "I made a mistake. When I first saw you, I thought I knew you, but the moment you stood up, I knew I didn't." She pushed back her chair and rose, still keeping her hand in the large kid purse. "I'm sorry," she said again, and turned and walked away.

Bones gaped after her in amazement then turned and stared at me. He said: "Holy Moses! You didn't try to kiss her right here at the table, did you?"

I snapped: "Shut up, you mutt. Try to use your noodle." Everybody was looking at us. I added: "For cripes sake, sit down!" I didn't care about the people staring; I was watching the girl. Just before she'd gotten up to leave us, Baby Dare had risen, too.

I sat so tensely in the chair my leg muscles began to ache. Apparently Baby Dare was headed for the door marked *Exit,* and even more apparently, the long-eyed girl was following her. And I couldn't see whether or not that hand was still in her purse.

The girl's back was to me; I saw Baby Dare go under the pink ground-glass sign, turn and take the direction of the arrow that pointed to the right. That would take her into the ladies' lounge. The long-eyed girl followed. They both disappeared, and my brain began to whirl giddily.

Was there a guy in the bar really covering Bones and me?

I looked up at Bones. He stood scratching his head and looking after the girl. Then he sighed and sat down. "Oh," he said. "Maybe she'll be back."

My throat felt too tight to say anything.

Bones leaned across the table and growled: "What did you say to her that scared her? Did you tell her I was Bluebeard?" He snorted a little, then looked at me suspiciously. "What's the matter with you? You're as white as a cue ball." He began to turn pale himself. "Shag!" he exclaimed. "What the hell's the matter with you?"

He had half risen from his chair. I stood up quickly, reached over the table, got my hands on his shoulders and shoved him down. We were the center of attraction in the entire bar now. Two waiters hovered around us, looking a little timid, as if they didn't know whether to butt in or not. I didn't pay any attention to them. I kept my eyes on the side entrance, and it felt like nothing happened for a month. I don't know how long it actually was. But then the long-eyed girl appeared at the door, pushed it open, and stepped outside.

I didn't see Baby Dare.

I stabbed a quick glance at Bones. He'd been following my gaze for several moments now, and I knew he'd seen the girl go out the door. I got a grip on myself. Now was the time. I stood up and yelled:

"After her, Bones!"

Then I whirled and faced the room, but heard no shot, saw no guns.

I cursed and said: "She was bluffing, damn her." I ran out the front entrance into the bustle of Broadway.

A MOVIE was playing at the Astor, and the flash of the gigantic sign almost blinded me. The sidewalk was jammed with people. I shouldered my way through them to the curb. The traffic swirled by me. I wasn't worried about getting through, because the traffic blocked the one-way side street. And the traffic on that street had to come this way. If the girl had had a cab waiting for her, I'd see it when it crossed Broadway.

Then the traffic light changed. Cars began to pour from the one-way side street, and I lit out across Broadway as fast as my legs could carry me. There was a cab stand not far from the corner and I had to get one while the girl's cab was still in sight. I really stretched my legs. And it wasn't until I was almost across that I realized my hunch had been on the nose.

A cab flashed by me and I saw the girl inside, her face up to the back window, peering out anxiously. I shoved a guy out of the way who tried to sell me a trick toy, leaped toward the first cab in the line parked near the corner.

It was then that it happened.

Two shots, thundering above the traffic din of Broadway at Times Square, spat flame into the darkness. The slugs crashed the cab window. They didn't miss me more than by the width of a pin. Glass shattered and sprayed, one sliver raking my cheek, leaving a small neat gash that looked like a razor cut. I flopped down on my belly.

Two more shots crashed out, one of them whanging metallically into the engine hood. A big sedan rolled down the street, turned left at the next corner, and I watched its blood-red twin tail-lights vanish into the darkness.

I lay still, trying to get my breath, and a cab hummed by me.

I got to my feet. I knew the worst thing I could do was hang around, because cops would be coming, and cops would ask questions. I looked back at Broadway. Crowds were gathering in the street and on the corners, but they kept their distance respectfully; the sound of gunshots usually causes that.

I slipped around behind the line of cabs, bent down low, and sprinted away from Broadway. People paused and gaped at me, but nobody tried to stop me. At the first corner I turned right, slowed to a walk, ducked in a bar and ordered rye. I was shaking so hard when I lifted the drink that half of it spilled down over my wrist.

I had another one without spilling so much, then went outside and breathed some air. But even after five minutes of that, I was still trembling. I walked in a wide circle of about six blocks and went back to Henry's Bar.

Inside, I ranged the place with my eyes. Bones wasn't there, and neither was Baby Dare.

One of the waiters came running over to me, waving a check. "Twenty cents, sir," he said. "Did you forget?"

I gave him thirty and got my hat and coat. "I thought my partner was going to catch it," I told him.

I looked around slyly. A few of the same customers were still there, and they were staring hard at me. I thought I noticed one of the barmen edge toward the door. I added quickly: "What happened to my partner?" I had an idea that after the shooting outside and our rumpus inside that some busybody might sneak out and tell the cops that something fishy was going on.

The waiter shrugged and moved his hands expressively. "He ran out, too. He ran out the side entrance. But he took his hat and coat."

I growled under my breath, "Catch Bones leaving any clothes behind him." I asked aloud: "Didn't he leave any message?"

The waiter shook his head. "I'm sorry, sir. He didn't. He ran out, and another man ran out after him, and we haven't seen either of them since that moment. Could—"

"What!" I almost yelled. "A man ran out *after* him?"

The waiter gulped and bobbed his head. "Yes, sir. That is, as soon as that gentleman with you ran out, the other gentleman got up and ran out of the same entrance. He didn't pay his check, either. Could you—"

I shoved the waiter to one side. I made that side entrance in four leaps, yanked open the door and stepped out on the street. But nobody was near me. The crowd was all gathered on the other side of Broadway, pressed in now around the bullet-scarred cab.

I clenched my hands and my blood seemed to stop circulating.

"So," I said to myself, "those guys have got Bones, have they?"

I jerked around, made sure no one was tailing me, then walked back to the hotel so grimly I could hardly see.

CHAPTER V

FOOTLIGHT NEWS

HALF AN hour later, exactly at seventeen after nine, I still had the same harsh, choked feeling as I walked through Radio City and went up to the broadcasting studio. I showed a page my artists' pass and went in.

The studio was already crowded. The place held fifteen hundred people—it's the largest studio in the world—and there were only a few of the chairs empty. There was a balcony, too, with regular theatre seats done in red Morocco leather, and that was filled also.

I went back stage, which is literally "side-stage"—the stage is actually a large dais without curtains and you come on in full view of the audience and walk around the curved edge of the dais to the mike. Jimmy was back there, holding the mouthpiece of his bugle up to the light; Baby Dare was also there, watching Jimmy gloomily and still wearing the schoolgirl clothes. She stood up quickly when she saw me, and Jimmy went rigid. I stopped still and we stared at each other.

I growled: "Don't get on your high horse. We were only trying to help you."

With that, I spun around and went back out into the studio, clenching my hands and gritting my teeth.

I walked over to a vacant chair in the front row and sat down. I still had time to think before we went on the air and something told me I needed to do plenty of it. I was wondering about Bones. The only reason I was at the studio was that my company expected me to be there; but if I had had any idea where to look for Bones, I couldn't have been dragged to the studio by four teams of horses.

Then the announcer left the dais and went over to his panel. But my watch said nine twenty-five, which left five minutes. I stood up, still gritting my teeth. My mouth popped open suddenly and I goggled across the studio.

Bones was coming in the door, obviously hurrying. He shoved his pass under the page's nose and began to trot as he started down the aisle. He came up to me and said: "Don't stand there like a yokel in a burlesque house. Come on."

He grabbed my arm and jerked me off balance and I followed him backstage past Jimmy and Baby Dare. Bones didn't even look at them. He led me over in a corner, grabbing one of the radio scripts on the way, shoved it up in front of me and pretended to pore over it. He was breathing hard, but his eyes gleamed happily. One of his skinny hands gripped my arm.

"Look, Shag," he said. "Down in Baltimore, when we cracked that murder case, you were the guy who supplied all the brains. But this time old Bones comes into his own. Do you know what I did?"

I was still too startled to know anything. "What?" I managed to ask.

He grinned and winked. "You yelled for me to go after that dame, and you went out the front. Well, it took me a minute to realize what you were driving at—I hadn't suspected that the dame was there for the dough—so then I ran out the side. And what do you think?

"I saw her get in a cab, wait for the traffic light to change, and I saw Pinky and that gray-faced guy in a big sedan two cars behind her. So, I happened to see an empty cab farther back in the line, so I got in that. I even saw Pinky shoot at you—he had a gun in each fist. I—"

I cocked my head to one side. "But the waiter in the bar," I cut in, "told me a guy followed you outside—"

Bones said, "Oh, *him,*" and waved his hand in disgust. "I grabbed him because I thought he was following me, too, but he was only a guy trying to take advantage of the excitement and run out on his check. You should have heard the hard luck story he gave me. I—"

My cheat felt like a collapsed balloon. "Get back to Pinky," I said, "before I faint."

"Oh. Well—" Bones grinned—"I tailed that sedan to a spot just about two blocks back on the other side of Broadway. You know, the sedan turned left and circled back. Their apartment was over a store on that same one-way side street, just about two blocks from Henry's Bar. Can you imagine that?"

I said: "Wait just a minute."

LEAVING HIM standing there, I walked over to Baby Dare. She sat very still in her chair, her face pale, and looked at me steadily. Jimmy was putting the mouthpiece back into the bugle.

I stopped in front of her. "Whatever you think of me," I said, "please answer me one question. Did the girl you gave the money to make a phone call while she was in the lounge?"

Baby Dare looked questioningly at Jimmy.

Jimmy said in a strained voice: "Answer him, honey. I still think he's okay." Baby Dave raised her eyes to me. "She came in behind me, got in a phone booth, and didn't speak to me until she came out."

"Thanks," I said. "And did she tell where the final payoff was to be made?"

Baby Dare shook her head. "No. She said, 'Lakin sent me,' and I gave her the money, and she said, 'We'll notify you where to deliver the rest.' Then she went out."

I asked: "Was there ten thousand dollars in the envelope?"

Baby Dare nodded thoughtfully. "Yea, there was."

"Thanks again," I told her, and went back to Bones.

Before I could open my mouth, he said:

"Now just a minute, Shag. *I'm* supplying the brains tonight. Why the conference with the streamlined child?"

I shrugged. "Just getting things straight for myself. Pinky and his boy friend didn't plant themselves outside for the payoff. They came on a phone call. But—"

Bones asked: "Do you think Jimmy's got the money on him?"

I said: "What!"

Bones winked and looked smug. "I thought that one would floor you," he told me. "Now get a load of this.

"After I tailed the guys to that apartment, I got to thinking. It seemed to me there was something screwy about all this business. Why had the first payment only been ten grand? Whoever heard of mugs like Pinky wanting a payment as evidence of good faith?

"So, I tried using the brain for a change. What if Pinky and the gray-faced guy were hired on quick notice? Wouldn't it be logical that whoever hired 'em didn't have any ready dough to pay 'em off? So what? So, I figured, that first ten grand was for them alone, to pay them something and keep them happy until the big payoff. Out of that, I figured they were probably due to get another ten grand.

"So, what was the answer? This: Jimmy hired Pinky and the gray-faced guy, and arranged the payments that way to keep 'em happy. Jimmy killed Lakin, then you and Baby Dare broke in on him, and he cooked up that story of the mugs to save his hide. And the idea of the hundred-grand payoff worked two ways. It took suspicion away from Jimmy, and also gave him some dough. He didn't phone McGowan while you two were in the room, did he? You're right he didn't. He faked you into leaving, then phoned those two mugs and got them to bust in on us and make his story look real.

"*Then* he phoned McGowan. And he was even clever enough to pretend the mugs told him that Baby Dare should make the payoff. Why? So he could go through a few heroics about not wanting to put her in danger—which made him look swell to her—and because he knew she wouldn't let us horn in, in case we wanted to. But could I prove that? I figured I could this way."

He paused to catch up on his breathing. Then he went on. "I went around on Broadway, got myself a telegraph boy, and pulled the old telegram gag we pull in the small-loan business. I sent him to the apartment with three tickets for the broadcast that Jimmy gave us to give out to our friends if we wanted to. And I sent a telegram with them. COME TO THE BROADCAST TONIGHT STOP I HAVE REST OF DOUGH. And I told the telegraph boy to say he was given the message and the tickets at room five-fifty in our hotel—Jimmy's room, which the mugs know.

"So the boy delivered the tickets and the message, said it was from room five-fifty in the hotel and beat it. I had him do it that way so the mugs wouldn't stop him and ask a lot of questions. So then I came down here, took myself a seat in the balcony and waited. And sure enough—"Bones paused.

I HAD been so interested in what he was saying, I hadn't noticed the studio grow quiet. I stood bent toward him, trying to stack all of these theories chronologically in my mind, and I didn't notice the orchestra playing the program's theme song until they were almost half way through it.

Then Jimmy's bugle sounded, clear and sharp, and he stepped out on the dais and marched all the way to the mike blowing Reveille. A burst of applause followed. Jimmy's voice came next and he and the announcer pulled a gag. After that the orchestra started a fast swing number, and I turned back to Bones, my arms feeling rigid. Out of the corners of my eyes I could see Baby Dare, who was still sitting down and watching us carefully.

I put out my tongue and wet my lips. "You were saying something," I reminded him.

He nodded. "Yep," he told me. "Sure enough, they showed. The girl—she was in the apartment with them—Pinky and the gray-faced mug. They're all up in the balcony, way over on this side, right in the second row and near a door. And if that doesn't prove Jimmy hired them, what could?"

I took a very deep breath.

Bones sighed and spread his hands. "Ain't it awful," he groaned. "I really liked the guy. I liked him so much I haven't even called the cops." Then his face brightened. "But I supplied the brains, didn't I, boy?" He punched me playfully. "Didn't I?"

My thoughts were whirling and I barely heard him. Distantly, as if actually over a radio turned low, I was aware of the orchestra finishing the swing number and the announcer making the first commercial. I came to life.

I said: "You supplied the brains, all right, but the brains overlooked one little thing. Come on. Let's get out there."

Bones asked sharply: "What little thing?"

"Well," I said, "Who phoned Baby Dare to come to Jimmy's room?" I led Bones over to the edge of the dais. I whispered: "Jimmy didn't. She even had to force her way in."

Bones leaned close to me and gripped my arm. "*You* were there, sap," he whispered back at me. "Jimmy didn't want *you* inside, did he?"

I could feel myself stiffen.

Bones began chuckling softly in my ear. "If I wasn't so afraid of that mike," he said, "I could make the Voice of Experience sound like a kid with the whooping cough. Did you ever bear such brainwork?"

I kicked him savagely on one of his ankle bones. Just then Jimmy announced us and the orchestra blared out a fanfare.

We walked out to our mike with Bones limping a little— we went to one mike and Jimmy stood at another one. The sound-effects man came up with a lot of regalia at another mike. And—well, I don't like to say this—Bones and I got a lot of applause.

Then Jimmy asked a few questions, and I gave out some answers. Bones stood by, squirming a little, already so embarrassed his face was as red as a sunset. After the questions, some actors came up and we did a scene.

Bones had one line: "Come on, Shag! Run!"

He yelled it like he meant to do it right then, and unconsciously I looked up in the balcony. But I couldn't pick Pinky out, although the studio was well lighted, and we weren't blinded by a spotlight. However, I did miss a short line, but with the sound-effects it was hardly noticeable. Yet I gulped, looked at the director, saw him frowning at me. I frowned back. I'd forgotten the director was McGowan. Suddenly I screeched:

"Bones! Did you sign Jimmy's name to that telegram?"

Bones gaped at me and shook his head.

"Then it wasn't Jimmy!" I yelled. "It was *him!*" I pointed wildly at McGowan. "He hired 'em, Bones! *He* hired 'em!"

I'll never forget McGowan. His face turned as white as marble.

CHAPTER VI
PAID OFF IN LEAD

I WENT crazy. I leaped away from the mike, took three long swift strides, slammed McGowan hard with my right hand alongside his left jawbone. I knocked him off the dais and into the first row. Then I froze.

Whether or not the audience thought all of this was a part of the act, I'll never know. But it was real to me—too real. I saw Pinky stand up. I saw guns leap into his big meaty hands like cards appear in a magician's fingers. I saw the guns level. Then Bones was in the air, diving toward me. He tackled me at the hips just as the guns thundered.

The acoustics were marvelous in the studio and there was very little echo. But suddenly half of the audience was thrown into pandemonium. Women screamed. Those sleek silver-backed chairs went over by the hundreds. The mob began to mill wildly toward the exits, piling up on each other like a kid football squad in scrimmage.

I swiveled around on my belly, rolled off Bones. I noticed foolishly that the guy in the control room was literally tearing out his hair.

Then more thunder roared out above me, and a slug kicked splinters from the floor about a foot from my head.

Somehow I hadn't expected Pinky to keep on shooting. I stabbed a glance upward, my blood chilling, saw him with his arms braced on the balcony rail, bringing the two guns to bear once more. Behind him, the red Morocco theater seats had emptied. The exit near him was jammed, and, strangely, nobody was even looking at him. That is, nobody but the gray-faced guy and the long-eyed girl. My glance upward only lasted an instant, but I noticed the gray-faced man's face was ashen, saw the girl pull hastily at Pinky's sleeve.

I'll always believe that saved my life. Flame spurted at me, and noise crowded my ears. But Pinky's shoulder jerked away from the girl's hand and one slug smashed a music stand. The other one actually hit my coat; I've still got the hole to prove it. I spun around on my knees and yelled:

"Bones! Duck backstage!"

We got up and sprinted to cover like mice scampering to their hole.

Oh, I know it wasn't the brave thing to do, but there are times to be brave and times to be sensible. And backstage I stopped suddenly in my tracks.

Jimmy was reaching into his overcoat pocket. He turned and faced us holding his silenced automatic. Baby Dare stood near him, not crying, but with her lip caught savagely between her teeth. She turned as we burst in, and looked at me imploringly.

She said in a strange, terrified voice: "He's going a-after them with his gun. Please d-don't let him, Mr. Roberts."

Jimmy turned and faced me. His face was set so grimly his lips quivered.

Outside in the studio, the noise was still deafening. Chairs were still going over, women were still screaming; there was the pound of feet and cries of panic. I was breathless. It seemed to take me an age to find my voice. When I said:

"I saw her get in a cab, wait for the traffic light to change."

"The gun. Gimme."

Jimmy shook his head defiantly.

I gritted my teeth. "Don't be a ninny!" I almost yelled. "You can't shoot at Pinky! There're people behind him! Suppose you miss?"

Jimmy said very slowly: "I won't miss." Then he turned and ran out the backstage exit, the heavy sound-proof door cushioning shut noiselessly behind him.

I leaped after him, Bones following. We ran wildly up the narrow stairs that climbed to the floor above, came out in a broad corridor that was jammed with fleeing people. I caught sight of Jimmy's uniformed figure ducking through the mob.

He was so small and quick he reached the jammed entrance before we bullied and shouldered our way half that distance. But the entrance was still spewing people, and Jimmy was carried back and knocked sprawling. I flopped on him and wrenched away the gun, and he kicked at me and struggled bitterly.

I said through my teeth: "You've got as much grit per pound as any guy who ever lived. But ease up, will you?"

He suddenly lay still, panting.

I got to my feet. Nobody had stopped to watch the byplay. People were still streaming toward the elevators, but most of them toward the main stairs; the corridors didn't have its acoustics controlled, and the deafening noises echoed weirdly. I slipped over to the edge of the entrance and waited tensely for a small opening.

Then I got it, as a fat woman stumbled and fell to her knees. People went around her and I slid between her and the doorjamb. I was waving the gun unconsciously and a couple of people got out of my way. I burst out into the open with Bones at my elbow, drew up suddenly as I came face to face with that slinky, long-eyed girl.

SHE SCREAMED with a terrific screech. For a fleeting moment our eyes met, then I remembered something and lowered my gaze to her handbag. Her hand was buried in it.

I didn't shoot. I grabbed her wrist with my left hand, yanked hard and twisted. Her small gun went spinning across the balcony. I cuffed her with the wrist of my gun-hand, knocked her sprawling into the balcony seats.

Then I was facing the gray-faced mug and Pinky was below me at the balcony rail. But Pinky's back was to me; he was still looking down at the studio.

I've never faced a moment like that. The gray-faced man had one gun, Pinky had two, and I was standing there with a small-calibered automatic that I'd never even shot before. But the gods of luck must have been on my side; the gray-faced fellow hesitated. He was as startled as I was by the suddenness of the showdown; it took him an instant to gather his wits. Then his gun-arm swung up.

Mine swung down, just before his gun roared. He curled forward like I was seeing him in a slow-motion movie, slid down on the steps at my feet, making not a bit of noise. Or maybe I couldn't hear it because of all the commotion. I remember noticing a little wisp of smoke trailing from the gun I held. It seemed strange at the moment. The gun had no kick, made practically no fuss; I actually had difficulty believing I'd fired it.

Then my head snapped up and I was staring at Pinky. But not at Pinky alone. He was turning, swinging up his two guns, but Bones leaped past me and threw himself forward. He landed with his chest in Pinky's face, wrapped his skinny arms around the red head, and the force of his leap carried them to the balcony rail. They were a mass of arms and legs for a moment. Then there was a yell, a scream—the scream from Pinky—and they went over the rail and dropped out of sight.

I made the rail in four long strides. I looked down, almost afraid to look. They were tangled in a pile of the silver-backed chairs directly below me, and I breathed again when I saw Bones move. He climbed up off of Pinky and stood holding his side. Pinky raised his head and looked befuddled.

Bones made a wry face, pried one of Pinky's guns loose from him calmly, clubbed it, then smacked It hard on Pinky's bristling red bush. The guy went as limp as wet bunting. Bones stood back from him, surveyed his handi-work, looked up at me and grinned broadly.

I grinned back, but the grin froze on my face.

I'd forgotten about McGowan. I caught a glimpse of him just as he disappeared backstage.

But before I had a chance to move, he reappeared. He came backing into the studio, his fists clenched and poised awkwardly, with little Jimmy coming after him, that grim look still on his bright young face. And Jimmy had his fists cocked professionally. He was talking to McGowan, his lips moving in quick jerks; but I was too far away and couldn't hear the words.

Then I saw what had really stopped McGowan. Light gleamed on the blade of a small knife that Jimmy held in one of his clenched hands.

I leaned over the rail and yelled: "Hold everything!"

I spun around, went over to the long-eyed girl, who was half on a theater chair and half off. She was holding her paw and moaning. "You deserve worse," I growled, and jerked her to her feet. It took us about five minutes to get through the crowd and downstairs.

Bones was seated in a silver-backed chair holding one of Pinky's guns in each hand, and covering Pinky and McGowan. Jimmy stood by, Baby Dare near him, and Jimmy still held his knife, a small gold penknife. There were a couple of pages there, too, looking on in awe, and some of the crowd had stopped trying to get away and stood watching from a very safe distance. I pushed the girl in front of Pinky, and went over to McGowan. I snapped:

"The next time don't be so greedy. When you send mugs to scare your radio guests into keeping their mouths shut and getting out of town, don't tell your mugs to tell them to leave *after the broadcast*. Weren't you satisfied to break up tonight's program for a hundred grand?"

McGowan's deeply tanned face began to look yellow.

"And another thing," I went on grimly. "Didn't you stop to think that we'd wonder how those mugs knew that *we* knew about Lakin? You should have used your head a little. Pinky and his friend didn't have a room on our floor, and they weren't in the corridor when I went in Jimmy's room, so how did they know I knew about Lakin? I'll tell you. Jimmy phoned you and told you what had happened, and you phoned the mugs and sent them up. They only lived two blocks from the hotel and got there pretty quick. Didn't you think we'd figure out those things?"

McGOWAN WAS breathing heavily and there was sweat on his forehead. I gave him a disgusted look and spun on the girl.

"All right, beautiful," I said. "You're in this up to your ears. You didn't kill anybody or try to kill anybody, but you're an accessory after the fact, and you're facing an extortion rap. Talk and you'll be sure to clear your trim skirts. Use your noodle, beautiful, and you'll get away with about five years. Come on. Spill it."

The girl was trembling. She looked fearfully at Pinky.

I growled: "He can't hurt you. The law's got him now, and he's going to fry in the chair until he turns a crisp brown. Do you want to do the same thing?"

The girl bit her lip savagely. "B-but—"

"No buts," I cut in. "You save the state the expense of a trial, and they save you from going to the chair. Use that pretty head, beautiful. Did McGowan hire you?"

Suddenly she screamed: "Yes! Yes! He hired me, and Pinky, and Gordon—" She broke off and began to sob bitterly.

I swung back to McGowan. "Maybe," I snapped, "that shows you how you stand. Why did you do it? Just to get the dough? Just cold-bloodedly for a hundred grand?"

McGowan's face was actually yellow now; he was clasping and unclasping his hands in front of him, and the perspiration stood out plainly on his high, tanned forehead. He gasped: "No, no, no! I owed Lakin money. We'd been gambling. He cheated me, and I didn't find it out until Jimmy told me what his methods were. But Lakin threatened to kill me if I didn't pay.

"It was eighteen thousand dollars, and I didn't have that much money. I had to embezzle twelve thousand of it from the company. And Lakin knew that. He blackmailed me, bled me. He said if I could embezzle some I could embezzle more.

"And I could. I'm in charge of all the radio advertising— the company spends a million and a half a year for radio advertising alone. So Lakin kept blackmailing me. I paid him sixty thousand dollars and it had to stop. So I chose this way to stop it, because—" He paused, still clasping and unclasping those hands.

I said: "You had the mugs frame Jimmy, because you knew Jimmy's value to the company and knew they'd pay. Is that it? And because you could put the money they paid back with the company and cover all of that sixty grand you'd embezzled. Right? But you thought you might as well pick up some pin-money while you were at it— about twenty grand—and then Lakin would be dead, your embezzlement covered, and you would have a little extra dough for a nice vacation. Right? Why was the first payment only ten grand? Did the mugs want sort of a retainer's fee?"

McGowan said hoarsely, "Y-yes. They and the girl were to get ten more after all the money was paid."

I asked: "And did you know that the company could get a hundred grand in cash tonight and not have to wait for the banks to open?"

McGowan nodded. "Y-yes."

"And the reason you wanted the money so quick," I went on, "was because you didn't want to give the company a breathing spell? In other words, give them time to hire some investigators to go to work on the case?"

McGowan said again: "Y-yes."

I turned to Bones and growled: "See how stupid we are? We should have reasoned that out. Why, it was all right there in front of us—"

Bones looked up from the guns he was holding. "Who's stupid?" he snapped. "Didn't I figure everything out?"

I grinned. "What you had was straight, except you had the wrong man. But, of course, *that* doesn't matter—not a little thing like that."

Bones scowled and said: "None of your funnybones, now." Suddenly he let out a yelp, and hopped to his feet.

I said: "What's the matter with you?"

He yelled: "What's the matter with me? Look!" He stuck out his leg. One knee of his trousers was ripped wide open from the fall from the balcony. He blazed: "That's what I get! Every time I play around with you, I wind up behind the eight ball!"

He spun on Pinky. "Come on! Don't look startled. Reach in your pocket for some dough!" And then: "Somebody's gonna pay for these pants, you louse, and that somebody's *you!*"

RHAPSODY IN BULLETS

Murder should be private business. Once it starts getting public, wooden overcoats become the vogue. Investigators Roberts and McPherson—Shag and Bones to you—liked murder to be so private that they wouldn't get any part of it. But a beautiful red-gold blonde thought differently, and she plunked them right in the middle of a rhapsody in bullets.

CHAPTER I

SLAUGHTER BAIT
FOR A QUEEN

THE LIMITED stopped in Philly long enough for eleven reporters to pack our drawing room.

We led them out in the narrow passageway—just two poorly paid small-loan company investigators now in the spotlight—and gave them two cheerful statements—one from Bones and one from me. Then we posed for the news photographers, smiling sweetly, cursing under our breath.

I turned back toward the drawing room, still smiling because there were even some candid camera bugs around, still cursing under my breath because I was getting sick of having no privacy.

Bones growled in my ear: "All this fuss, but try to put one of these gushing punks on the nut for a fin."

I said: "If you come back next month, try to see if any of 'em remember you."

Bones grunted. "That would depend on whether or not they lent you the fin."

I scowled at him, and he opened the drawing-room door and went on inside. I was following him when a porter came up and touched my arm.

"Mr. Roberts?" he asked.

I said I was.

He grinned at me, showing a gold eye-tooth, and leaned very close. He was blacker than any onyx you've ever seen. With the whites of his eyes bulging, he whispered: "There's a queen wants to see you, suh—and, by golly, I means a queen."

He jabbed a pink-bottomed forefinger in the direction of the car behind us. "She's a-waitin' just inside the next cah, suh. She says you-all knows her."

I dug out a dime and flipped it up and caught it. "Reporter?"

He grinned again. "No, suh. This is a *lady*. High class."

He said, almost cheerfully:
"I hate you—"

"And she says *I* know her?"

The old darky wiggled his bead from side to side and said: "Aw, g'wan wit' you, Mr. Roberts. You-all's the kind that knows hunderts o' high class ladies."

I gave him an extra dime for that crack, lit myself a cigarette and scowled over it for a few moments. Well, queens were queens, even if they claimed to know me. Reporter or not, there might be fun. I went back along the passage-way—it was rapidly emptying—and opened the door of a car named Narcissus.

The train lurched and began to move. A little dried-up conductor, whistling *The Dipsy Doodle* came in the car behind me and blew his nose. He barely stopped whis-

tling to do it. The queen slid out of a corner and took my arm, smiling up at me and saying:

"Shaughnessy! How nice!"

I looked down at her, then put both hands over my eyes. When I took them away, she was still there. I said: "Honey, you do turn up. Surprise for Bones? Or what?"

JANIE BRANDT laughed. She had a laugh like four or five silver bells and ripples in her eyes like a breeze ruffling green wheat. Bones had been going with her for ten years, and had fought thirty wars to keep her. She told me: "Stanley—" she always called Bones by his full given name—"doesn't know I'm here. I want to talk to you."

She began guiding me along by the arm, looking up at me, still smiling. She wore an emerald hat, styled Chinese coolie fashion, and a few of her red-gold curls peeped out coyly from beneath it. She was a queen, all right. She asked:

"How does it feel to be famous?"

I grinned. "I'll bite. How does it feel?"

She laughed again. "You and your false modesty. You pain me. There was an editorial in one of the morning papers that said the least Baltimore could do was make you and Stanley co-chiefs of the Homicide Squad."

Her eyes became mischievous. "Anyway, if you didn't want to be so famous, you shouldn't have bared the murderer over a nation-wide hook-up. *That* wasn't playing cricket with your dear retiring self.... Well, here we are."

"Where?" I asked.

"My drawing room," she told me brightly. We were in a narrow passageway at the end of the car, and the brass knobs of the three drawing-room doors glittered faintly in the overhead light.

She inclined her head toward the door directly beside us—one with a small F embossed on it in gold. She added: "I'm traveling in class."

I frowned down at her. "Didn't you get on at Philly?"

"Sure," she said. "Why?"

"Why?" I echoed. "And you took a drawing room just to go to Baltimore?"

She didn't seem to be looking at me, and quite suddenly her voice sounded strange. "That's right. It has something to do with Stanley. I'll tell you about it in a minute."

I said: "Well, you don't have to be so nervous about it"

She was gripping her purse very tightly. "I'm not nervous," she told me. She lifted her head and looked at me, and I wondered if her lips were trembling. She added: "Go on in. I'll tell you about it."

I stood looking thoughtfully at her. I guess I was stupid not to smell a rat, but you just don't connect rats with Janie Brandt. She opened the door and stepped aside for me to enter, and I went in mentally scratching my head. I should have known right away that it was funny that she should hold the door open for *me*. But I didn't.

The drawing room was in darkness, and I stopped just inside the door, still a little puzzled, but not too preoccupied to feel for a light switch. I never found it. The door closed between me and Janie Brandt and a pair of arms went around me and pinioned my arms to try side. It all happened so swiftly I didn't get a chance to move. The arms held me like a couple of iron bands, and a pair of hands patted over my pockets. A voice said:

"No rods on him."

The guy who was holding me grunted. Something round and hard poked against my side, and the voice said:

"Not a peep out of you now, Roberts. Be good and you don't get hurt."

I was good, but I wasn't quiet. I said a few unpleasant things about Janie Brandt.

The voice said: "Tch, tch. Just like you were the only guy a dame ever took for a ride."

I had a few unpleasant things to say about that too, but I gritted my teeth and let them go. Already the encircling arms had tightened slightly and lifted me; I was being carried across the room, but the gun stayed in my side.

Then in the next room I was laid flat on the floor and one of the men hovered around me; the muzzle of the gun was now pressed into my breastbone. My ankles were taped together, my wrists pulled behind me and treated likewise. Then a couple of calloused hands started playing around with my face. I pulled my face away from them and said:

"Hey! You don't need to tape my kisser. I won't yell."

The voice said: "Yeah. I bet you went to a grade school that had an honor system."

Tape slapping across my mouth shut off my answer.

Through all of this no lights had been turned on, and I was gradually beginning to be able to see a little in the dark. And there were only two men—at least, only two in the room there with me. Both were tall, and just vague shadows to me, although one was a burly shadow and one was a lean one.

The burly shadow went out the door, making a lot of noise with his heels, and the lean one paused on the threshold, laughing softly. He was the guy who had done all the talking. I recognized his voice when he said:

"Sorry we forgot to leave you a pillow. The very tough man with the baby face oughtn't to be without his beauty sleep."

There's one thing I can't help, and that's my face—and I didn't like his sense of humor.

I lay there and boiled for about five minutes.

I WAS in the bathroom. The hard tile was cold against my hands, and as my eyes became more accustomed to the darkness, I could see the outlines of a shower curtain and the funnel-shaped bulk of a porcelain wash basin.

I risked scuffling sounds as I rolled to the door, then put my ear against it, listened. The train wheel hummed monotonously on.

I lay on my back and tried to think. Nothing about this made any sense, and the more I tried to figure Janie Brandt, the less sense it did make. Tying her up with something shady was like thinking your grandmother had been a Dillinger moll. It just didn't go. I knew Janie Brandt; used to pull her red-gold curls in Sunday School and fight off the whole damned stag line to get four steps with her whenever we had a high-school prom.

And here I was in a spot with a ton of tape across my mouth, and Janie Brandt had literally led me to the slaughter.

I blew some angry breath out of my nose and settled down for a long wait.

Nothing happened for almost half an hour.

The first sound I heard was the click of a lock, and then feet shuffled softly in the next room. I heard the outside door of the drawing room close. There was another dick, and an orange ribbon of light streamed under the door of my prison, the sudden brightness making me blink.

Then I heard voices—hard, angry voices—talking swiftly and passionately, but the words were blurred and indistinct. I couldn't understand them. I was stretching my neck eagerly, putting my ear closer to the door, when I heard a sudden rush of feet, a gasp, heavy breathing, and about five thudding blows that sounded like they were driving into a soft pillow.

Then came one piercing scream. Then silence. Then a heavier and louder thud, like a lifeless body when it lands.

My breathing suddenly became very loud. I clenched my hands and held my breath a few moments, listening carefully. In about five minutes the outside door opened again. Then more voices that I couldn't understand.

After a while, the light switch clicked once more. The ribbon of light disappeared, and I heard footsteps coming toward me, saw the bathroom door swing open. A lean shadow loomed on the threshold. A foot struck my shoulder, and that same voice said:

"Oh. So baby face has turned to eavesdropping."

The shadow knelt beside me. Something warm and sticky splattered on my right cheek, and I could feel it trickle toward my chin.

The voice laughed softly. "That's the blood of a rat on a baby face. There ought to be a moral in that."

I felt my flesh crawl.

The voice went on: "I like you, Roberts. You've cleaned up a couple of murder cases with the odds all against you, and you're a guy who takes advantage of any opportunities that are shoved at you. I like that in a guy. That's the way I am, and I like it in myself. Did you ever kill anybody?"

I made a sputtering noise.

The voice continued: "Well, no matter—but don't think I'm a madman. If I was, I wouldn't squat here and talk like this. I'd shove this ice pick in your throat and that would be the end of it But I'm not mad. I'm just a guy who killed another guy cold-bloodedly and calmly. And I'm telling you I'll kill you just as calmly if you try any of your investigating stunts. Just remember that."

The voice became brisk. "And remember what I said about opportunities. Don't take advantage of this one. Lay off. If you don't you're going to break the heart of your buddy, McPherson, and you're going to die as sure as water's wet. Just keep those things in your mind, and use your head.

"You'll be found here—tell the coppers what you think best. If you can mimic my voice, don't do it—I'll be sure to hear about it if you do. Just use your own judgment—I know that judgment's good. Toodle-oo and happy dreams."

He was gone then before I could bat my eyes—making no more noise than a fly would have made.

I closed my eyes and let myself go limp.

CANAVAN CONNECTS

THE OLD colored porter, after calling, "Bal-tee-mo! Bal-tee-mo!" for almost half a minute, opened the outside door, switched on the lights, looked around, and turned a lovely milk chocolate. My murdering friend had left the bathroom door open. The old darky went out and left the outside door open.

In a few moments, the dried-up conductor came, still whistling *The Dipsy Doodle*, took a better look than the darky, and speeded up his tempo. He closed the door and tried a few bars of *The Martins and The Coys*.

About three minutes later the train slowed to a jarless stop.

A little while after that, I heard a commotion in the corridor. The door opened again and a harness bull came in, followed by two private dicks in gray uniforms. Behind them I saw a crowd with slack jaws and bulging eyes. The harness bull looked around hurriedly, turned a little pink, sat down, and sent one of the private dicks to the phone.

In a little while, two reporters and a news photographer drifted in, stayed long enough to burn. The bull told them no story or pictures until the lieutenant came.

I was still under wraps. My eyes were hating both cop and dick.

The other private dick came back. He closed the door and said: "Headquarters is sending Canavan. The morgue's sending the dead wagon."

The cop looked angry. He bawled: "The dead wagon! You should o' called the ambulance! Don't you know I can't pronounce 'em dead?"

I lifted my feet and kicked the bathroom door.

"See?" snarled the cop. "That one ain't dead." He bent over the broad back of a man who lay face down on the floor. "This one's gotta lot o' blood all over him, but mebbe he ain't, even." He straightened, his face still angry. "A fine spot to put me in, with Canavan coming. With all the lieutenants down at Central, they gotta go and send *him*."

The cop spat He showed an utter disregard for the clean drawing room rug. He added: "Mebbe I'd better undo this live one before that mick gets here…. Ugh! *Canavan!*"

There was a lot of awe in his voice….

Michael Canavan, Homicide Lieutenant, seemed to bring a ton of vitality into the drawing room with him. A lean, conspicuously tall man, he stepped inside, walked to the center of the floor, stood looking around for almost half a minute. Just his presence seemed to charge the air with tension.

He looked at me—I was on the settee, rubbing my stiff legs—said briskly, "Hello, Shag. Mixed up in another one, are you?" then turned away and walked over to the body. He knelt beside it for a full minute, then rose rubbing his hands together, looked again at me, and then nodded to the cop. The cop shuffled his feet, licked his lips and went into his story.

It was nothing but a routine of the set up, a very short story, but the cop made a very poor job of it.

Canavan frowned peevishly and checked it with the private dicks. They were less nervous in front of him, and made a much better job.

They also said that their reason for being there was that my company had hired them. That there was a big crowd at the station to meet Bones and me; that most of the crowd were souvenir-hunting dames who had taken a fancy to the newspaper shots of my face.

They were to guard me from the souvenir hunters, and they seemed to think this was very funny.

But I didn't laugh.

When the door closed behind them, Canavan turned to me.

HIS FACE hadn't changed. His skin was dark, almost swarthy, with that smooth, slick look that denotes a soft, easily controlled beard. Canavan looked young, and was— as lieutenants go. He had a young, vigorous body, lean and straight, which he carried like a West Pointer. His eyes were abnormally clear, very light blue, and looked startling under his heavy black brows. He wore a black fly-front overcoat with a velvet collar, a black derby, a black suit. He always carried black gloves, but never wore them.

Those startling eyes were on me, and I thought they looked friendly. "Give it to me, Shag," he said.

I shrugged and tried to look calm. "There was a dame," I told him. "The train had just stopped at Philly. The old darky porter came up and said she wanted to see me." I shrugged again, more elaborately. "You know I like dames."

Canavan said: "Yes." He had a very precise, clipped way of biting off words. I couldn't tell whether he knew I was nervous or not. He added: "Give me the rest of it."

I stretched my legs and looked down at my ankles. It was difficult to lie into those fanatically clear eyes. I said carelessly, but not too carelessly:

"Well, she brought me to the door here—she was a luscious golden blonde wearing a lot of blue—and we came in and the room was dark. Then somebody grabbed me. A gun was shoved into my ribs, and they taped me up—or rather they carried me in the bathroom before they taped me up. Well, then they went out and left me."

I spread my hands, still not looking at him. "There weren't any lights turned on. I couldn't see them."

"Not even vaguely?"

I kept looking at my ankles. "Well—yes, vaguely. There were two of them. Both were tall and both were big."

"Could the man on the floor here be one of them?"

I raised my eyes. This was a question I could answer honestly. I said: "After they left me, I rolled over to the bathroom door to try to find out why they'd shanghaied me. There wasn't anybody in here—at least, I didn't hear anybody—for almost half an hour. Then two men came in. I could hear the murmur of their voices, but couldn't make out any words.

"Then all at once there was a scuffle, and a sound like a body falling. Maybe the two guys who taped me parted over something. That guy on the floor looks big enough to be one of 'em."

"I see," said Canavan. He slapped his gloves into the palm of his left hand. His face didn't change. He asked bluntly: "How about the blood?"

"You mean on my face?"

Canavan clipped: "Where else would I mean?"

My mouth had begun to feel slightly dry. I said, with almost too much effort at carelessness: "Hell, after the scuffle and the sound that sounded like a body falling, somebody opened the bathroom door and stood looking down at me. The blood dripped on me—either from the guy or from something he was holding in his hands. My guess would be from the murder knife—but that's only my guess."

I hesitated. I gathered some nerve from somewhere and added: "Anyway, you don't have to start getting tough about it."

Canavan smiled tightly. He told me: "What you want to worry about, Shag, is whether or not I do get tough. You shouldn't mind a little thing like a few harsh words." His eyes seemed to get narrow and darker. "You say you didn't know the girl?"

I met his gaze as levelly as I could. "Never saw her before. I don't forget luscious blondes."

"And that's the best you can describe her—a blonde wearing blue?"

I said: "Well, she had blue eyes with a come-hither look in 'em. And she had a body. She—" I steadied myself and asked: "Why don't you ask the darky porter? He saw her, too, you know."

Canavan's heavy brows lifted. I thought his eyes seemed slightly puzzled; he evidently hadn't expected *me* to suggest a check-up. I kept looking at him, kept trying to meet his gaze levelly.

He sent the cop out for the porter, then began to wander around the room, frowning, looking occasionally at the body. I wondered oddly at the moment why he hadn't made any attempt to identify it, why he hadn't even gone through the man's pockets. I didn't know then that Canavan knew the dead man.

In a little while the cop came in with the colored porter. The whites of the old darky's eyes were bulging.

I stood up—fast—and beat Canavan to the punch.

I said: "Sam—it is Sam, isn't it?"

"Yas, suh, Mr. Roberts."

I hurried on: "Lieutenant Canavan wants you to verify the description of that blonde in the blue hat and blue dress that sent you—"

Canavan spun on me and growled: "What the hell are you trying to pull, Shag?"

I looked innocently at him and shrugged my shoulders. I wasn't very much worried about the old darky now. The power of suggestion is pretty strong, and besides, after spending a lifetime being polite to people, it would be a tough job for the old fellow to call me a liar.

I didn't think he would. I just looked at him and waited.

HE STUCK a gnarled finger between his neck and his collar, ran it from the back of his neck to his Adam's apple, then tugged his collar down. He looked at Canavan, then looked at me. Maybe I frowned a little; I didn't like the hesitation. The old darky kept his eyes on me for half a minute, then said:

"You sure 'twas *blue*, Mr. Roberts?"

I tried to grin. "Well, wasn't it?"

Sam went through his collar-tugging act again. "Wal, Mr. Roberts, the lady was blonde and she was a queen, but wa'n't it sort of bluish-*green* she was wearing?"

I scratched my head, as if considering that. I could have wrung his neck for putting so much emphasis on green. I said, trying to make my voice thoughtful: "Now that you mention it, Sam, I think it was. Yeah—a sort of bluish-green." I turned to Canavan. "Satisfied, lieutenant?"

Canavan laughed a trifle nastily without even moving his lips. He said: "The bluish-*green* is enough for now."

His eyes seemed to dig into me, stayed there as the cop led the old darky out. When the door closed, he added: "Maybe you should have been a lawyer, Shag. You're good at leading witnesses." He began to wander around the room again, slapping the gloves in his palm, saying nothing.

After about two minutes of that, he stopped and came over to me. He seemed more thoughtful, but calmer, almost friendly again. He asked:

"And you didn't get a look at the man who opened the bathroom door and stood over you?"

I shook my head. "The lights went off. They were turned on when the two guys came in, but the bathroom door was closed and I couldn't see 'em. Just a little of the light showed under the door. But before the guy opened it, he turned the lights off."

Canavan said: "Oh, he did? How convenient." Some nastiness began to creep back into his voice. He added: "Did he say anything?"

I grinned a little. This was child's play compared with leading the old darky. I said: "Not a peep out of him, lieutenant. Not a peep."

Canavan said softly: "So he came in and stood over you, then went out without speaking. In other words, he came in and went out again for no purpose at all. Either that, or he came in to kill you, and then changed his mind. A nice convenient-acting fellow, the way I see him."

The lieutenant took a step closer to me and put his face close to mine. "Let's have that part again, Shag. The way you just told it, it stinks."

I could feel myself stiffen. I snapped: "Yeah. It does."

"Then let's have it again."

I took a step backward and clenched my hands. I growled: "Well, I might clean it up, but only in tone. The meaning of the words would be the same. Don't tell me you get witnesses to repeat just to improve their diction."

Canavan's nasty laugh came again. "So you're going to dam up, Shag?"

I said: "Listen, lieutenant. The first time I got mixed up in a murder, it was because I thought if I didn't, it would spoil my record with my company. The second time—the last time—I had a lot of false courage from a lot of beer, and I wanted to help out a very swell little guy. This time I haven't any reason. I don't know why I was brought in here—don't know a damned thing, and I'm not going to guess.

"Do you think if I could give you a lead to the killer that he would have left me in here alive? You know better than that. And I'm not going to stick my neck out again and be mixed up in another murder. I'm through with 'em. I've told you what I know, and that lets me out. Take it or leave it."

Canavan said: "So *you're* getting tough?"

I shrugged. "Take it or leave it."

The lieutenant didn't speak for a moment. He took another short step forward, a tight smile on his face, but the smile merely a mask. Behind it those startling eyes had begun to glitter. I noticed his hands clench along his trim, lean thighs.

He said in a low voice: "We always got along, Shag. I remember a couple of years ago when some of the boys under me had loans with your company, and you used to come to me when they got too far behind in their payments. We always got along. You were fresh and I took a lot of lip from you, but it was your job, and anyway the boys had to pay. But this isn't your job—it's mine, and it's murder. This is different. This—"

He broke off and the smile went away entirely. His eyelids narrowed; he seemed to be suspicious. He barked: "You haven't any ideas about cracking this by yourself, have you?"

"Do I look like that big a sap, or are your eyes going back on you?"

I could almost *feel* him stiffen, but he didn't lay a finger on me. He laid his fist instead—I didn't see it coming—and it caught me under the left jawbone, on the side of my neck. I went hurtling backward until the back of my knees hit the settee. Then I sat down. But I didn't get up again. I wasn't fool enough to go into pitched battle with the law.

But I rubbed my neck and said: "If that's your Sunday punch, Canavan, you wouldn't be very hard to take."

He was standing very tall and erect, that smooth skin of his face an angry reddish mahogany, the clear eyes still glittering, his lips still flat against his teeth. Behind him, the harness bull's eyes were popping. I noticed a couple of flies buzz around the dead man, saw one of them go into a power-dive toward a sodden patch of blood.

The room was so quiet you could hear the fly buzz.

Hands hit the passageway door and popped it open, and one of the gray-uniformed dicks stood on the threshold. He didn't come in. He stood looking at Canavan, breathing heavily, looking about to burst with what he had to tell.

Canavan whirled on him.

The dick said: "It looks like you got more business down the way, lieutenant. Roberts' buddy, McPherson, has been pretty badly shot."

I said: *"What!"*

The dick looked at me. He told me blandly: "He stopped a slug, and it looks pretty bad. What's the matter with you guys, anyway? Can't you stay out of trouble? Or doesn't anybody like you but souvenir-hunting dames?"

CHAPTER III

TEN MILLION REASONS

I **SAT** in a huge high-ceilinged room down at Central Police Station and watched Canavan across a large and battered oak desk. He was talking on an old-fashioned upright phone. His voice was clear, concise.

He said: "H'm.... Yes.... Well, how soon can I get to talk to him?... Okay.... I'll be up in twenty minutes."

He hung up the phone, shoved it to one side, pulled one toward him that was on a collapsible arm. He didn't look at me.

He said: "Joe? Bring the Packard.... Yea.... McPherson won't die.... H'm.... No, I'm going up to talk to McPherson now.... H'm.... Yes, right away."

He pushed that phone away from him, still didn't look at me, rocked back in his swivel chair and scratched his bony jaw with a thumbnail. He had taken off the fly-front overcoat, but still wore his black derby. With his eyes on a corner of the ceiling, he said:

"Your buddy's all right. It was just that the kid used a .45 on him. Those slugs'll knock an elephant cold." He touched a spot under his left shoulder socket. "The slug went in there."

I said: "*What* kid?"

Canavan took his eyes from the corner of the ceiling slowly, dropped them down over the wall, over the windows, the floor, and finally to me. The eyes still held a very faint glitter.

Suddenly he banged down on the desk with the flat of his hand. He shouted: "Damn you, Shag! How do you think you're going to get away with it? You can't do this, boy!"

I sat still and looked steadily at him.

He had half risen from his chair. He sank down again, rocked back in the chair and began drumming nervously on the edge of the desk. His lips were pulled back, baring his strong teeth. I could hear his angry breathing very faintly.

"You won't believe me," I said, "no matter how many times I tell you, but I don't know who shanghaied me, I don't know why, nor do I know who shot Bones or why. And you can take me back in the next room and grill me for two more hours—you still won't get any different answer. Why should I hold back on you?"

Canavan growled: "Why should you lead that porter?"

I shrugged. "That's only your opinion. What the hell? Is there enough difference between blue and bluish-green that you should think I'm holding back murder evidence on you?"

I could hear the swivel chair squeak like a few frightened mice as Canavan rocked back and forth in it. His face looked as smooth and hard as a block of glazed brown granite.

I couldn't read Canavan's eyes.

Then he leaned forward slowly, his expression not changing, and asked: "Do you know a young fellow named Christensen Kendall?"

I frowned. "Sure. Why? Who doesn't?"

"Do you know Jane Brandt?"

"Huh?"

Canavan said softly: "So that surprises you, does it?"

MY OWN eyes must have been bulging a little; I remember my mouth hung open. I sat back in the chair very slowly, made a few meaningless motions with my hands. I wanted to stand up and yell and find out what the hell he was driving at. I didn't. I got a grin on my face somehow and said:

"Huh? Sure, it surprises me. Janie Brandt happens to be Bones' girl."

"Not really?"

I growled: "Have your fun. Yeah. Really. They've only been running around together for ten measly little years."

Canavan's head jerked forward, and he asked bluntly: "Then how long has she been engaged to the Kendall kid?"

I could only goggle at him. Those startling eyes of his were fastened on me, but if he figured my surprise wouldn't be genuine he bet the wrong horse. I almost passed out from the shock. I said: "Why, hell, lieutenant, you're just plain nuts. Janie Brandt wouldn't look at Kendall through an audioscope, even for a laugh."

I was still goggling. "He used to hang around her, sure. Everybody knew he carried a heavy torch for her; the boys used to treat it as one of those standing jokes. But Kendall and Janie—engaged?" I looked suspiciously at him. "What're you trying to hand me? Give me one reason for it."

Canavan said: "I'll give you ten million reasons."

I blew out some breath. "Then hand them over, but not one at a time. Just pick out the high spots, say one in every two million."

Canavan said softly: "I can do better than that I can give it to you in one lump. Here." He leaned slightly forward. "The Kendall lad's mother just died and left him ten million bucks."

I yelled: "How much?"

"A cool ten million bananas, but left in trust. He gets it in two years, when he's twenty-five, if he's been married two years. Which means he'd have to marry by his birthday next Wednesday. That's four days."

I asked quickly: "And if he hasn't been married two years?"

'Then he doesn't get it until he's thirty. I suppose his mother figured two years of married life might sober him. Anyway, she figured it would do as much to make a man out of him as seven years of batting around."

I gasped: "And he's engaged to Janie?"

Canavan tapped on the edge of the desk with a long forefinger. "Not *is*, Shag, *was*. Kendall caught Miss Brandt in the drawing room with your buddy, McPherson, and when McPherson got tough and punched him, the kid drew a .45 and let him have it," I wondered if I caught a wisp of a smile in Canavan's clear eyes. He added: "It seems Kendall made a few cracks about the girl that McPherson wouldn't take."

I was limp. I managed to ask: "S-such as?"

"Well, they were pretty nasty cracks, the nicest one accusing the girl of having hooks out for the ten million. McPherson got tough on that one. He punched the kid, the kid came up with a gun, and let go a few real nasty gems. So McPherson waded into the gun." Canavan looked obliquely at me. "Then the kid shot him and disappeared."

I said: "Huh?"

"Disappeared. Clean as a whistle. But we'll get him." Canavan rubbed his chin. "The Brandt girl gave us all the dope we have. We just let her go." He looked at me shrewdly out of the tops of his clear eyes. "Do you happen to know the name of the dead man?"

I shook my head. "I didn't even get a good look at him."

"It was Rentner—Sam Rentner," Canavan said, "but there were none of his fingerprints around any place. In fact, no prints at all except yours in the bathroom, and some of the colored porter's. The rest were too old or too smudged to do us any good. And the drawing room was in the name of Smith."

"So?"

"John Smith."

"Oh." I looked at the floor. "Maybe that girl was Pocahontas."

Canavan said softly: "Nothing stops that flow of lip, does it, Shag?"

HE WALKED over to the closet and got his velvet-collared overcoat. When he came back, nothing about his expression had changed. "It's this way, Shag. Rentner was a lone-wolf private dick, too cheap even to have an office, too crooked to hold down a job with an agency. Just a rotten chiseler, making a buck any way he could.

"And if the Kendall kid would happen to kick off, that ten million would revert to his father's estate. You see, his dad's still living—it was his mother, like I've told you, who left him the dough." He paused, evidently to let that sink in. "Do you get any connection?"

I said: "Not if the ten million reverts to the estate even if the kid is married, no."

"Well, it doesn't."

"You mean that if the Kendall kid is married when he kicks off, the ten million goes to his wife?"

Canavan said dryly: "I'm glad you finally got it. Yes. That happens to be the angle."

I grinned. "Now who's handing out the cute lip, lieutenant? Or is my company actually contaminating you?" I made my grin broader. "Anyway, I don't get any connection, even with that information. The whole thing's just a lousy muddle to me."

Canavan said slowly: "It's lousy, all right" He took off his derby and ran his finger around the sweat-band. Then he pointed the derby at me, and his eyes grew cold and his voice spaced his words.

"If you're holding back, I'm going to pull you in and book you, and I don't mean for disturbing the peace. The Brandt girl wore a *green* hat without any blue in it, and if it develops that she was the girl who sent that porter for you, it's going to be a pretty serious thing. She *said* she wasn't."

He hesitated. "You know, Shag, sometimes we can even get compounding a felony out of concealing evidence on a murder. That goes for both you and the Brandt girl. Am I clear?"

I said grimly: "You don't need to draw a diagram."

He stood tall, poised, straight as a rifle barrel, a hard man but with plenty of judicial tolerance. He looked directly at me for a long moment, and then I could tell that if I deserved a break, he was the guy who would give it to me. But I knew if I didn't deserve one, and if he found me out, that all hell and high water couldn't keep him from cracking down on me.

I scowled and shifted my feet uncomfortably.

Canavan turned around and walked over to the door. I started for it, trying to look casual, and he said:

"I'm telling you again, Shag, I like you, boy, and if you want to change your mind, just stop and do it now. Once you go out of here, it's going to be too late."

I just kept on walking and looked at him out of my eye-corners. He didn't speak again. I didn't, either. My throat felt too tight for it, and when I got outside, I stopped on the sidewalk and looked at my hands.

The palms looked shiny with moisture, and even my arms were trembling.

There seemed to be a lot of people liking me that night. Yeah—liking to cut my throat in a very friendly way....

I took a cab at the corner of Fallsway and Fayette, and we hadn't gone over a dozen blocks when the driver slid back the window and said:

"There's a car been on our tail ever since you climbed in. It don't mean nothing to me, but I kinda thought I oughta tell you."

I sat up straight I didn't turn.

The driver chuckled and added: "Me, I was borned and raised in this section, mister, and I like to tool this wagon. Now, if you'd kinda like to have some fun...."

I said quickly: "Don't lose 'em."

The driver sounded disappointed. "Oh, you like company, huh?"

"Not particularly," I said. "Maybe we'll get rid of 'em later." I thought for a moment. "You drive up to Morley's Bar on Charles Street now." I gave him the address. "And when we get there, take a peak in your rearview mirror at that car behind us, and tell me how far back it parks. Then wait for me."

"Yeah. With the motor running?"

"Save your gas," I said, "and make the stop look natural."

I sat back, pressed myself pretty far over in one corner, and risked a peep through the back window after taking off my hat. The car was about two blocks back. I put my hat on again and tried to think. I figured that either Canavan was having me tailed, or my murdering friend was keeping a close watch on me. I hoped it was my murdering friend. I had an idea and sat and wondered if I should try it all the way up to Morley's bar.

The driver parked in front of Morley's, slid back the glass again, and said:

"They turned the corner, mister. Probably playing smart."

I said: "An old trick. They'll turn around, park out of sight, get out and keep an eye on us on foot"

I got out of the cab without looking down the street behind us, kept myself looking casual, and went into Morley's. It isn't a very large place. It's just one of those neat clean, friendly little bars that draws the drinkers in the neighborhood like sugar draws flies.

I got half way to the door marked MEN before some of the boys at the bar glanced around and recognized me.

I waved my hand and kept going, fast, so as not to be bothered with a bevy of questions. I pushed through the marked door, stepped down one step to concrete, trotted across a small back yard and into a narrow alley. The alley was very dimly lighted, and fog was thick in it, like smoke. I sprinted down to the street where the car had turned, inched my head around the corner, just one inch at a time.

THERE WAS a long, sleek sedan, the lights turned on, parked about fifteen yards from Charles Street, and well out of sight of my cab. The motor was throbbing gently, but the sedan was empty.

A tall, lean man wearing a belted camel's-hair topcoat loafed, too casually, in front of the sedan at the corner.

I wished I had a gun.

But I hadn't. I memorized the license number and sprinted back to Morley's.

I got in a phone booth at the end of the bar and called the Northeastern Police Station. I got a cop on the night trick who used to owe our company money, and who had had a lot of trouble paying it because he had too many wives.

That was a little secret we kept diplomatically between us.

He gave me this:

The license number belonged to a four-door sedan that was owned by an Edward Monnett who lived in the Northern Arms Apartments. It seemed that Edward Monnett owned a detective agency which was small but competent, not very well known, but reliable.

I whistled softly. That made a little sense.

I had him check the stolen-car list thoroughly, and make sure Monnett's wasn't on it.

Monnett's sedan wasn't on it I tried a call to his apartment just to check a little further, but evidently no one was there to answer his phone, either. This was beginning to hold together. I called the Kendall house, but again got no answer.

The big Postal clock over the hand-carved back-bar had its hands pointing at three minutes to twelve. I couldn't stay in the bar too long. If Monnett knew anything about me at all, he'd know I wasn't a guy who let cab bills run up for nothing.

I put through a hurried call to Union Memorial Hospital, got a sudden shock, and gripped the phone. Bones had been treated and moved, on the advice of his physician—and his physician was Dr. David Brandt. You guessed it—Dr. Brandt was Janie's father. Bones had been moved to the doctor's home.

I slid out of the booth, ignored a lot of friendly questions, bought myself a case of beer, and went out carrying it. My cab was still parked at the curb. The beer was something Monnett could see me carrying, something he might believe I actually went in for.

I told the driver nothing in a grim, tight-lipped way, heaved in my case of brew, and climbed in after it. We hadn't gone a block before lights were again behind us. I scratched my ear and did some angry thinking. The sedan stayed in our wake all the way to my apartment, turned a corner again when we slowed and stopped.

My phone began ringing when I hit the third-floor landing, was still ringing when I keyed open my door. I put down the case of beer, crossed to the large bay-window noiselessly, got the phone off its stand and sat down in the dark on the window-seat. It kept ringing while I held it and looked down at the street. The street was deserted. The lights were dim through the fog.

I uncradled the phone and said: "Yes?"

It was the voice—the voice of my murdering friend. "Is this Roberts?" it asked.

I said softly: "I can recognize your voice."

If the owner of the voice was Monnett, then Monnett had a nice gentle laugh. He let it bubble for a moment then said: "I just wanted to find out how you made out with Canavan. Good?"

"So you were the guy who followed me," I said.

"Oh, you know?"

I didn't say anything.

The voice went on: "You're a smart boy, Roberts. You know your way around. I was wondering about that case of beer. Pretty thirsty, aren't you?"

"I like beer," I said.

"And you probably like living," he told me. "Most of us do. It's one of those nice little stimulants that we can't do without."

The line went dead as I started to answer, and somewhere nearby a floor board creaked dismally. I sat motionless on the window-seat still holding the phone.

My eyes tried to look everywhere at once.

I couldn't see much. I'd left the door open just about six inches, and yellow light streamed in, touched the tops of my beer bottles. Then another floor board creaked. And it was inside my apartment not out in the hall. I drew my legs up under me, hunkered my weight on my heels.

Against the window, silhouetted clearly, the target I was making was an assassin's dream.

CHAPTER IV

GUN-READY

A **GIRL'S** voice gasped: "Shaughnessy? Is that you, Shaughnessy?"

I sank down limply on the seat and groaned.

In a little while, I said: "The lights, Janie, the lights. All of this owl's paradise is no fun for me."

I heard a key twist in the lock of the ancient oak door to my bedroom, and light funneled in rapidly as the door swung open. My apartment is a garret, Colonial, not Bohemian, and such things as transoms would be a sacrilege and a sin.

Janie Brandt came in and switched on the lights.

I stretched my legs out and sighed, cradled the phone. I just sat there and looked blankly at her.

She was wearing an emerald-green skirt and a white pongee blouse, and a small rhinestone clip instead of a tie. The clip was almost heart-shaped, the tail of it slightly curved. She looked at me with sad, tired eyes that no longer had any ripples in them.

She said: "Stanley's here."

I bounced off the window-seat, *"Huh?"*

Her lips parted in a faint, apologetic smile. "Dad said we should bring him here. I don't know why."

Just inside the door to my bedroom there were the sounds of steps, and then a short, heavy-set man, about forty-five or fifty, came in the room and walked over to me. He looked nervous and worried, and his broad face was deeply etched with lines. I knew Dr. Brandt. He always looked worried. But he had a double order of worry now. His thin lips worked like he was tasting something bitter, and a nerve twitched just under the corner of his left eye.

He stood staring at me, but didn't say anything.

I scowled and said flatly: "Suppose you tell me."

That nerve under his eye twitched faster. "What?"

"Suppose you tell me," I said, "why Janie was a come-on girl, and why she lied to Canavan about seeing me, just like I lied. Suppose you tell me why you brought Bones up here. I'd like to know those things. I'd like to know why one guy is threatening to kill me, and why Canavan is threatening to lock me up and eat the key. I'm funny that way. I like to know those kind of things."

Dr. Brandt said: "Don't get nasty."

"Don't get *nasty?*" I was keeping my voice low, but that time I almost yelled. I poked him in the chest with a forefinger. "Listen, Dr. Brandt. In the last couple of months, I've been playing around a lot with Death, and the old Grim Reaper is beginning to get on my nerves. Try playing around with it yourself sometime. It's no picnic. Now there's a cold-blooded guy watching me, just waiting for me to stick my neck out, and Canavan is on that neck, doing his best to get me to stick it out."

I poked his chest a little harder. "Which leaves me where? I won't tell you; there's a lady here. But if you think I'm being nasty, just guess how I'll be if you don't tell me things." I really poked his chest. "Chris Kendall's mother died and left him ten million bucks. Janie decided maybe she ought to marry him. It's that simple. Go on from there."

Suddenly Janie screeched. She wasn't looking at me. The back of her hand flew to her mouth, and she stared past me, stared toward the bedroom in horror.

BONES LEANED in the threshold of the door, a pair of my best striped pajamas hanging loosely on his skinny frame, his left arm in a big sling, the shoulder lumpy with bandages. He was pale as white sand, and the freckles on his face stood out. He looked at Janie for a long time, didn't say anything to her.

He said to me: "Hello, boy."

I nodded. "Hi, son."

He didn't try to come through the door. He looked like he couldn't, like a good wind would blow him over. There was a grim, tight bitterness around his mouth.

In a little while, he asked: "What was that again, Shag? What was that about Kendall?"

I'd never seen him bitter in a deep, sad way. He was the kind of guy who fought and asked questions afterward; the kind of guy who took his medicine standing up and snarling.

I didn't say anything.

He grinned at me a little whitely and said: "Now ain't this a hell of a thing? My own buddy dummies up on me—afraid he'll say something that'll get to me. Sure it will, Shag. Boy, it'll hurt something awful. It just did." He looked at Janie. "Didn't it, honey?"

Janie had her hands pressed tightly over her eyes. She took them away, looked at him, but didn't put them back. There were some tears on her cheeks. But she lifted her chin proudly and looked at her father. I caught on then.

There was something *she* was going to tell Bones, even if her father wouldn't.

But her dad must have caught on, too. He evidently figured it would sound better coming from him. He coughed, shuffled his feet nervously, but didn't look at Bones. He said: "Janie did it for me, Stan." His voice was much too loud.

Bones didn't change his white little grin.

Dr. Brandt seemed to be studying the design of my rug. The way he kept looking at it, it must have taken a lot of study. He went on: "I'm broke, Stan. I gambled. I went through all my money—and my wife's entire estate. Hers was forty thousand. I wanted to put it back before she found it out. The shock of knowing I'd lost it would probably kill her. I asked Janie to help me by marrying young Kendall." He hesitated. He rubbed his palms on the legs of his trousers.

"Keep right on," I said softly.

He didn't look at me, either. He added: "Well, Chris has diabetes, but he won't take care of himself. He won't live over three more years. And he had asked Janie to marry him when he was left his money. She refused. She's in love with Stan. But when I told her what she could do for me, she thought it over and changed her mind." Then he looked up—but at me, not Bones. "And that's the reason. It's the only one."

"Aren't you Chris' doctor?" I asked.

My rug must have fascinated him. He began studying it again. "Yes. I've been his doctor for quite some time."

"And doesn't Chris' old man," I went on, "know that if the kid doesn't take his diabetes seriously that he won't live for three more years?"

"Yes. Mr. Kendall definitely knows that."

I growled at him suddenly: "Then how much did old man Kendall pay you and Janie for letting Chris catch her in our drawing room with Bones?"

The doctor didn't exactly start with any small, sudden jerk; his sad eyes lighted up, blinked, then dulled and became sullen. He just stared at me. The stare said plainly that he'd like to have me by the throat.

I glanced quickly at Bones. His jaw was slack.

Janie Brandt sat down in one of my upholstered chairs and promptly stood up again. Her eyes were very wide and very green and very filled with wonderment.

I was polite to her. I asked softly: "How much, Janie?"

She burst out: "How did you *know?*"

I moved my shoulders. "It's the only thing that hangs together—the one right angle. You lured me away. Why? So you and Bones could be alone, because it would be more effective if Chris found you that way. But the reason you let yourself get engaged to Chris in the first place was because your dad needed money. All right. You probably wouldn't change your mind then, unless your dad *got* his money. And who would give it to him?

"Why, old man Kendall. If Chris isn't married two years by the time he's twenty-five—which means he'd have to marry this week—then he doesn't get his ten million until he's thirty. By that time—not watching his diabetes— he'll have been under the sod about four years. And the ten million will revert to the estate, which will mean to old man Kendall. Why, the old codger ought to be willing to pay a couple hundred grand to get himself a cool ten million."

Janie hadn't even begun to lose her surprise. Her eyes were still wide and very green. She gasped: "Just a hundred thousand. It—it was all he offered."

"You got hooked," I said.

DR. BRANDT'S eyes were still fastened sullenly on me. Now he was looking at my throat. I didn't like it. Bones didn't seem to have liked anything he'd heard. He had lost his paleness and turned a little yellow. He kept looking at Janie and moistening his lips. In a little while, Janie turned and looked at him.

Suddenly she screamed: "Stanley!... Oh, my heavens!... I didn't realize...." She ran toward him. He turned without speaking and leaned heavily against the door-jamb, and she threw her arms around his back. "Stanley!... Stanley!... Listen to me!... Listen...."

He didn't move. She slid to the floor at his heels, keeping her arms around him; her arms slid down until they were around the calves of his thin legs. She began to sob, bitterly and brokenly.

Dr. Brandt started toward them and I reached out and collared him. I jerked him around and shook him a little.

My telephone rang.

I turned him loose and opened my right fist. It had been clenched so tightly that the knuckles felt stiff. I backed to the window-seat, keeping my eyes on him, dragged the phone off the stand and put it in my lap again.

I lifted the business half and said quietly: "Yes?"

It was Canavan. Somehow I'd known it would be he. His voice was brisk and had a hard ring to it. He said:

"It seems that you and McPherson are the best copy since Zioncheck. Washington put out an extra on you."

I kept my eyes on Dr. Brandt. Over at the bedroom door, Janie still sobbed bitterly.

Canavan pressed on: "Well, anyway, one of the conductors on your train saw one of the extras there. That's the end of the train's run. He just phoned over here about a girl in a *green* hat."

I felt myself grow oddly cold.

Canavan added: "Just as the train was leaving Philly, he stepped in a car and this girl spoke to you. She called you Shaughnessy, your full first name. And she had red-gold hair and was quite a beaut. The conductor said he remembered it because that name was odd, and because the girl *was* such a beaut. Doesn't the Brandt girl call you and McPherson by your full first names?"

I didn't say anything. I couldn't if I'd wanted to.

Canavan asked: "How soon can you get down here?"

I looked out at the street. A gust of wind hit my windows and rattled them, and the tops of the trees stirred very gently. The fog had cleared, but the street lamps seemed dimmer. I rubbed my eyes with the knuckles of my left hand.

I said softly: "If I don't come down, do you put me on the air?"

There was a slight pause. Then Canavan said: "Don't be a fool, Shag." His voice sounded irritable and worried.

I kept looking out at the street and slowly broke the connection with my forefinger. I didn't say anything else. I got up and went into the bedroom, squeezing past Bones and Janie Brandt, opened my dresser drawer and got out my gun. It's an old gun. A Smith & Wesson .32 that my father left me when he died.

When I started out of the bedroom, Bones blocked the door.

I stopped, and we looked at each other. At Bones' heels, Janie Brandt had stopped sobbing, and she looked at both of us. In the center of the floor, Doctor Brandt stood and seemed to stare at nothing.

He looked haggard and very, very tired.

Bones asked gently: "Where to, boy?"

We kept looking at each other. I said: "I've got to clean it up now, or Canavan'll clean me up. I've got to."

He grinned a little. "I'll go along."

"You can't even walk," I said.

"Then you'll carry me."

His grin got broad and almost cheerful. He turned slowly, looked down at Janie, watched her stand up beside him, stare at him wretchedly. Then he closed the door between them and began taking off my striped pajamas. He didn't say anything about her at all. He added: "I'm going with you, boy. You need my brains."

I didn't feel like arguing. I began very grimly to load my little gun.

CHAPTER V
DEATH TREADS SOFTLY

TWO ROWS of boxwood hedge as high as my shoulders lined the flagstone walk into the Kendall home. The walk was at least a hundred feet long. Bones and I went up it with him leaning against my shoulder, neither of us talking and me doing a lot of thinking.

So far I hadn't made too many mistakes. I should have known something was wrong the moment Janie said she had a drawing room, and I should have laid everything I knew nicely in Canavan's lap. But I hadn't. That was two mistakes. My third one was underrating my murdering friend.

I didn't think he'd still be tailing me.

Bones and I had just reached the foot of the four broad, semi-circular porch steps when gunfire hammered into the night behind us. There were just two shots. One of them was close to my left shoulder and chipped marble from the white steps. The other one was high, bounced off one of the big white porch columns. By that time I had my nose down on the flagstone walk, and had dragged Bones down on top of me.

I tied myself into a pretzel getting out my little gun, swiveled around on my stomach and looked down the walk. But it was empty. There was some moonlight, and it lighted my coupé far away at the curb. But there were no other cars. Across the street a window banged up and a woman in a boudoir cap put her head out. In a little while, the window banged down again. The rest of the neighborhood just wasn't curious.

I treated my lungs to a bit of normal breathing, then crawled to the east row of boxwood and poked my head around it. I didn't see anybody. I crawled over to the west row, scowling a little, poked my head around that side, and still didn't see anybody. My murdering friend was being nice and cagy. I wondered how far down in the hedge he had hidden himself.

I crawled back to Bones. "Our buddy is cooling his heels in ambush," I whispered. "It looks like it's either him or us."

Bones groaned.

"You hit?" I asked anxiously.

He was lying on his right side and the moon gave just enough light to see him wince. He whispered back: "No. It's my shoulder. When you pulled me down, it must have opened."

I put my left hand down to crawl closer to him, and my palm splattered into something warm and wet. I didn't need to look at it to know what it was. I pulled myself closer and saw that the shoulder of his gray coat was almost all dark with the blood. Then I touched his bandage. It was almost off.

I looked down at him and bit hard into my lower lip. It was my fault. I shouldn't have let him come. He hadn't been in any condition to help anybody.

Then I noticed he was grinning at me just a little. He said: "I know. You're calling yourself a heel. Don't do it, boy. I wouldn't've let you come without me." His grin had begun to fade.

I kept biting hard into my lower lip.

He kept looking at me. He said presently: "You know, Shag, I'd hate to die without seeing Janie again and telling her things are all right."

Then he closed his eyes and lay very still.

I bit down so hard on my lower lip that a little blood gushed, touched my tongue. I thought Bones was dead. But then he stirred. I felt his pulse. It beat faintly.

Now I had to kill a man. That was the only chance I had to get Bones to a doctor.

I TOOK one long hard look at the Kendall home. There hadn't been any lights in it when we had come up the walk, but I thought maybe there would be some now. There weren't. The house was big and square and dark and silent and the roof stood out against the sky. I had made another mistake. Neither old man Kendall nor his kid were home.

I fired my little gun twice into the ground.

Presently that window across the street banged up again. I waited until I saw the boudoir cap.

Then I yelled: "Call the police! A man's been murdered!"

The window banged down so quickly the sound of it startled me.

I twisted my face into a hard, sour grin. That would fix my murdering friend. He couldn't just stay in ambush until the cops came, because he had no way of knowing he *hadn't* killed Bones. He was sunk, my murdering friend. If he ran, he would make a target you could even paste with a snowball, and if he didn't run, he would have to stalk *me*. Then, if he got me, he could get away nicely. *If* he got me. I didn't think he would. Being stalked had all the odds.

That's what he would naturally think *I'd* think. I went forward, inching along on my belly.

I heard the first sound after I'd gone about six yards, and it was so close I almost dropped my gun. A head poked out of the boxwood not over ten feet in front of me, and my first shot probably missed it a quarter of a mile. I think I shot almost straight into the air.

Then a tongue of red and blue flame, like synthetic fire from a toy gun, forked at me, flaring brightly in the darkness. But there was nothing synthetic about the report. It boomed in my ears like a salute to the President, and some dirt pyramided just under my chin. I leveled my little gun and squeezed the trigger.

It was either him or me, and it turned out to be him. He fell heavily out of the boxwood, landing on his face, and for a long time I didn't move. But neither did he. Windows began to bang up all along the block.

I got out my handkerchief, mopped my face and looked over the situation. The neighborhood was finally awake. Some porch lights came on, a lot of windows lighted up, and one old guy on a cane even came out on his steps. But the Kendall house remained dark and silent. I kept in the shelter of the hedge and went over to my murdering friend.

Looking down at the result of my shooting, I saw that my bullet had gone in just above the right eye. I knelt down and touched the guy's pulse, except that there wasn't any pulse, and I had guessed there wouldn't be. He was dead, all right—and my eyes were bulging out of their sockets. I hadn't killed my murdering friend. I had killed Dr. David Brandt.

I was so weak from the shock of seeing the doctor that I just stood and gawked for maybe half a minute. It seemed like every time I got mixed up in a murder, I ran into something crazier and goofier. Dr. Brandt taking shots at me just didn't make any sense at all.

Then the faint wail of a siren, far in the distance, brought me to my senses and reminded me of Bones.

I turned and sprinted back to him, knelt, and hastily felt his pulse. It was about the same. I put him on my shoulder and ran down to my coupé. The siren wailed again, still in the distance, but closer. I got Bones in the car and got my motor going.

As I roared out of the neighborhood, without turning on my lights, the old man on the porch shook his cane at me violently. Then a shotgun blazed from somebody's third floor. I wondered if it was the woman in the boudoir cap.

I put my accelerator flat on the floor, and took the next corner on about half a wheel. I didn't care if it was Miss Boudoir Cap. I didn't care who it was. All I cared about was that somebody had missed my tires. I hoped the shotgun had kicked his chin.

A YOUNG interne came into the waiting room of the accident ward, where I sat staring at a cold brown linoleum floor, turning my fifth cigarette around in my fingers.

"He'll be all right," he said. "At first I thought we'd need a transfusion. What time did you say Dr. Brandt would be here?"

"In about an hour," I told him. "He was held up." I kept staring at the cold floor, at the long brass strips that fastened together its sections.

The interne asked pleasantly: "What happened to McPherson?"

I was glad nobody in the hospital sat up listening to police calls. I said: "We thought he was strong enough to walk. He fell down the steps." I mashed out my cigarette in a tray. "He said he was strong enough."

The interne grinned. "He would. He was quite a tough baby when he was here the first time. He wanted to get up." He looked at me with young, bright eyes. "Say! That Lieutenant Canavan was sore as a boil." He whistled. "Did he raise hell!"

I lifted my gaze slowly. "Yeah? About what?"

The interne made his grin broader. "He hadn't questioned McPherson, and Dr. Brandt moved him before he had a chance to. Just wait till that Canavan sees Dr. Brandt!"

I bit into my lip. I seemed to be doing a lot of that sort of thing. "Yeah," I said grimly. "I almost wish I could hang around for it. That'll really be one for the book."

I stood staring at him steadily, then shrugged my shoulders, heeled my way past him and went outside. I didn't think he had smelled a rat. If he had, he still had to take care of Bones, and there was nothing he could tell Canavan that would do me any harm.

Right now I was wanted for concealing evidence on a murder, which was too easily compounding a felony, and probably for another killing which Canavan would swear was a murder. No interne on earth could add anything to that. I was glad Bones hadn't needed a transfusion.

Ten minutes later I found a telegraph office....

The Northern Arms Apartments had a long rectangular lobby with somber, high-backed chairs, thick rugs, sand-filled urns, and a large desk. A pale-looking medical student, working at night, was catching up on his lessons behind the desk. He merely gave me a glance. I went into an elevator, shook a big colored boy who was asleep on a stool.

He came out of it swinging his long arms.

I stepped back and said: "Fifth. Or has Mr. Monnett moved?"

I didn't want to go to the desk. I'd left orders for my telegram to be delivered in half an hour, and the desk was where the telegraph boy would ask. Monnett might suspect a trick and ask a lot of questions; and if somebody else had asked for him, he might not let the boy come up. It was a personal telegram. Monnett would have to sign for it.

The colored boy blinked and said: "Huh, boss? Oh, Mr. Monnett, he at six-oh-four. Always been there."

I rode up to the sixth floor and waited for the telegraph boy.

He came in a little while, a slender little fellow with a short, brisk walk. He didn't even look at me. I pushed my shoulder off the wall and sauntered after him, probably looking as casual as an expectant father on his first-born. My right hand was in my coat pocket, and my little gun felt slippery. I had loaded it again, but I hoped I wouldn't have to use it.

The telegraph boy practiced the Morse code with a triangular brass knocker.

I had timed my little game fairly well. The boy stood back from the door, continuing his Morse code practice with his toe, and I came up behind him as the door swung open. Monnett had heard about the boy from downstairs; he wasn't expecting me. I sauntered right into his face, just poking my coat pocket out suggestively.

I said: "Hello, Mr. Monnett." My voice didn't sound like my voice.

Monnett didn't say anything. His face turned a little sallow.

I went in, keeping my hand in my pocket, slid back along the wall where the telegraph boy couldn't see me. I didn't take my gun out of my pocket. Monnett was wearing a maroon cocktail jacket; I didn't think he would have a gun under it. I didn't think old man Kendall had even ever carried a gun. He stood up out of a big blue leather chair, put down a highball glass, and stared fixedly at me.

Monnett's hand shook as he signed for the telegram.

He tipped the boy, closed the door, and I said softly: "You don't need to open it. It's just an April Fool's joke of mine."

He leaned against the door and slowly tore the telegram into bits.

MY VOICE still didn't sound quite like my voice. I wasn't a gunman, didn't even like the masquerade.

Old man Kendall said deeply, gruffly: "I suppose you're Roberts." But he didn't look at me. His eyes were trying to wither Monnett.

I merely nodded. I'd never met the old man. He owned a string of good horses, and I'd seen him at Pimlico and Bowie.

He was about medium height, slender, with snow-white hair as soft and fine as cotton. Monnett wasn't paying any attention to his withering look. He was tall, lean on the spare, angular side, and his black eyes kept going restlessly from my head to my toes. I stayed against the wall and looked hard at him.

I said: "I can come to the point. I'm here because Canavan's after me for concealing evidence on Rentner's murder, and also for killing Dr. Brandt. You two guys are going to tell Canavan why I killed him. Or don't you think you are?"

Old man Kendall picked up his highball glass, tilted it, and drained it in a gulp. He poured himself a stiff jolt of bourbon and tossed that off. He looked like I'd asked him if it was raining outside.

He asked me: "*Why* did you kill Dr. Brandt?" He leaned over to the little coffee table and poured himself another jolt of bourbon.

I growled: "Don't be funny. Dr. Brandt tried to kill me because I was going to see you, because you could tell me enough to make me know that he killed Rentner. You hired Monnett to break up Janie's marriage to Chris, and Monnett, trying not to spoil the nice reputable name his agency's got, hired Rentner for all the contacts and dirty work. But Rentner double-crossed you and Monnett, and promptly teamed up with Dr. Brandt. What did they do? Jack the hundred grand price you offered Janie?"

Old man Kendall tossed off the shot of bourbon he'd just poured. He poured himself another one, about four fingers. Then he looked at me without touching it. "They wanted another hundred thousand," he snapped.

"And you gave it to them?"

The old man moistened his lips and looked at the bourbon. But he still didn't touch it "Ten million," he said, his voice nasty, "is worth two hundred thousand any day."

"Oh, I wouldn't argue about that," I told him. "Ten million is even worth *three* hundred grand…. Did you know Rentner and Dr. Brandt had teamed up to jack the price on you?"

The old man grabbed up the bourbon, like he just couldn't stand watching it any more, and tossed off the four fingers. I wondered if he gargled with it in the mornings. He said, still nasty, but smacking his lips pleasantly: "Of course, I knew it"

"But you paid, anyway." I didn't make it a question; it was merely a primer. "You paid through the nose rather than make a fuss."

The old man stopped looking at the bourbon bottle long enough for his bright eyes to hate me. He snapped, even nastier: "That'll be enough out of you, young man."

I growled: "This is the little baby that's giving out the orders, grandpa." I shoved out the pocket of my coat a little more. He got the idea, and I hoped he didn't like it. I knew his type. He was the kind that never paid his servants, but always made sure his horses had their oats.

Damned if he didn't pour himself another jolt of bourbon.

I said: "All right, you knew Dr. Brandt and Rentner were robbing you. But you didn't care—the ten million was worth two hundred grand. And Dr. Brandt knew that you knew he was teamed up with Rentner. So he tried to kill me to keep me from finding it out. Are we clear on that point?"

Monnett put in slowly: "What are you after, Roberts?"

It was that voice—the voice of my murdering friend. I turned my head and grinned sourly at him.

"You're a smart guy, you are, Monnett," I said, "only the next time you try to buffalo me, leave out that stuff about the madman. That's kid stuff. That, and dropping that blood on my face. And the nice cold-blooded way you said you'd knock me off, *too*. Hell, there was a big scuffle and a lot of angry talk before I heard the body fall. The idea was good, making the threat seem straight from the killer, but the way you tried to put it over wouldn't have fooled a kindergarten.

"You thought it was a nice way to keep me out of the mess, didn't you? Brother, I'd have been after you as soon as the tape came off if it hadn't been for me wondering why

Janie Brandt turned me over to you." I snorted. "I didn't want to get her in trouble.... Do I make myself plain?"

MONNETT'S PALE face began to look wooden. Faint pink spots appeared high on his cheeks. "All right," he snapped. "What of it?"

I shrugged. "Only this. The way you planned to break up Janie and Chris didn't include a murder, and didn't include Chris pulling a gun on Bones. That was Chris' idea. You shanghaied me so Janie and Bones would be alone, because Chris finding them that way would be more effective. I don't think you even intended for Chris to go *in* the drawing room—being afraid that there might be some rumpus.

"What you wanted was for Chris to see them come *out* of the drawing room, which you could easily have arranged if things broke right. You probably didn't even want Bones to see Chris, because Janie didn't want Bones to know that she had even considered marrying Chris. Bones would have heard of the engagement later, but then Janie could have laughed it off as a rumor.

"Then you would turn me loose, and what could I do? Say I'd been shanghaied—shanghaied for what? Or Janie could have explained the whole business to me on the sly. I'd have kept my mouth shut for Bones' sake, which she'd know and certainly tell you when you made up your plan." I snorted again. "Am I clear on that score?"

Monnett said tersely: "Again, what of it?"

I peered at him. His face still had a hard, wooden look, and nothing about him seemed to be friendly. I stabbed a glance at the old man. He was sitting comfortably, watching us, looking sober as Carrie Nation, although the bourbon bottle had gone down a few more inches. I wondered if he had a steam boiler for a stomach.

I said: "You can bring your bottle along, grandpa." He disliked the name so much I couldn't help using it. "We're going to take a little trip down to headquarters and have a talk with Canavan. I'm not going to start taking my daily walk in an exercise yard just because of you guys."

Monnett said: "No. You're not going to take any daily walks." His voice had that gentle softness it had had over the phone, a softness that I didn't quite like.

Then the doorbell rang. My eyes shot sideways to Monnett, dug into him.

He seemed startled, puzzled, like maybe the ring was a real surprise. His eyes got hard and opaque, and he called softly: "Who's out there?"

A voice answered: "Chris Kendall."

I said to Monnett: "Open up for him."

The private dick turned his hard, opaque stare on me for a moment, looked like he thought I was nuts, but then opened up. Chris Kendall came in and closed the door behind him. He was a slightly built youngster, very good-looking in a weak, soft-eyed way; his forehead was rather low but broad; his hair light brown and very curly; his lips very red and full, and as soft as a young girl's. His chin was pointed, and due to the broad forehead, his head had a triangular, immature look. He looked like a flower with nice possibilities that some crackpot had spoiled by too much attention.

Right now he looked like he hadn't had any of that attention for days. His face was sallow; his usually soft eyes were bright and feverish; he didn't seem to know what to do with his hands. He kept moving them around like they itched him, or tickled him. His soft lips quivered, and I heard his teeth chatter. He looked at me, at Monnett, and then very brightly at his father. He seemed to grow cheerful. He said, almost cheerfully:

"I hate you, I hate you, I hate you, I hate you."

Then he pulled a gun out of his pocket and shot his father in the belly.

CHAPTER VI

TOO MANY KILLINGS

I **DON'T** know why I did it, but I kept looking at the old man. His torso seemingly pinned by the bullet to the back of the chair for a moment, he looked like a fighter who had been suddenly paralyzed by a low blow.

Then he put his hands down on his belly. His legs flapped bonelessly, like a rag doll's legs, and his tongue popped into sight between lips that had gone dry. A little half humorous light appeared in his blue eyes. He looked wistfully at the bourbon bottle he could no longer reach.

He said musingly: "You were always a treacherous brat, Christensen—always a treacherous brat."

He died very quietly, his eyes a little humorous even in death.

Then the kid saw the eyes, and their expression seemed to irritate him. He scowled and looked surly, as though he had been cheated.

That was when I should have pulled my gun. But I didn't. I almost forgot I had a gun; it was that lip of mine that came first. I yelped at Chris:

"That's tough, kid. Maybe you should've told him to get down and beg. He might've done it if you'd given him the chance."

The kid turned on me, still surly, still scowling.

He was just inside the door, about two feet in front of it, and suddenly it slammed open, driving hard against his right shoulder. He went stumbling to his left, trying hard to get his balance, tripped over an ottoman and fell sprawling on his left side. His big gun, held loosely, kicked out of his hand as it went off. The bullet thudded into the wall about a foot over my head, and the gun went spinning over the thick carpet until it hit old man Kendall's feet.

Another bullet kissed the wall about an inch from my left shoulder.

My gun was half out of my pocket; I had finally remembered I had it. I saw Monnett dimly, standing by a desk over against the wall; the desk drawer was open, and he had a big blue gun in his hand. I thought at the time that gunplay was a sap's move for him. Then I got it. I was drawing a gun; he could claim self-defense. I was the only witness left against him now that the old man was dead, too.

I stopped trying to draw my gun and shoved my hands up in the air.

It was then that I saw Canavan. He stood in the doorway, a Police Positive in his right hand, drawing a deliberate bead on Monnett's thin chest. But that wasn't right; that wasn't the way I wanted it. If he killed my only remaining witness, I'd probably be behind bars until I rotted. I took one long jump forward and brought both my hands down on his gun-arm.

Monnett's second bullet kicked a lot of splinters from the door jamb.

I yelled: "Hey! Hey! Nobody's shooting at you!"

Canavan yelled at me: "Lay off, Shag! Lay *off!*"

I had my hands gripping Canavan's gun-wrist; I knocked his gun against my knee and it thudded to the floor. I didn't pay any attention when he kept on yelling. If there was no more killing, I had an out, and my one-track mind at that point wasn't taking suggestions. This was my last chance and nobody was going to spoil it. I didn't think at the time that Monnett had another excuse to shoot. I didn't realize that he could blaze away and afterward claim he was helping Canavan.

His third bullet nipped a small hunk out of my right leg.

I let out a yelp, let go of Canavan, and threw myself face down on Monnett's rug. His gun didn't stop blazing. I counted two shots before I could drag out my little gun, then rolled to one side and snapped a shot at his shoulder. I hit a picture of a bulldog about a yard to his right. One more roll got me over behind a big blue leather davenport.

Then the shooting stopped. I looked around. The Kendall kid was getting up from where he'd fallen, and Canavan stood in the doorway looking down helplessly at his gun. I couldn't see Monnett. But from the way Canavan was standing, it was a good bet that the private dick had his gun trained on him.

I began inching myself toward the end of the davenport.

Canavan said suddenly: "No, Shag. No."

My back was to Canavan; I was crawling toward the far end. I stopped crawling and looked over my shoulder.

Canavan said: "Don't risk it boy. You're in the clear. The Brandt girl came to me and told me everything."

I growled: "You wouldn't kid me, would you?"

Canavan shook his head slowly, and looked at Monnett. The lieutenant's eyes were hard, glittering, narrowed down, and he didn't look at me when he went on talking. He said:

"I wouldn't kid you, Shag. And I don't blame you for not telling me the Brandt girl was the one who lured you. Maybe I would have done the same thing if that girl was going to marry *my* buddy."

I said: "Maybe you would if that buddy had saved your life a couple of times."

"Yes. Maybe I would, Shag. Maybe I would."

HE WAS still standing in the doorway, still looking at Monnett, and for the first time I noticed a lot of commotion in the corridor. I think it was the first time any of us noticed it. The Northern Arms Apartments was awake, and people were getting curious. They probably wondered if the Spanish Civil War was being fought on their sixth floor.

There were a lot of doors opening and closing, and a lot of excited voices. But I didn't see anybody appear behind Canavan.

Canavan kept looking hard at Monnett. The lieutenant said: "The Brandt girl happened to tell me your angle, too. Her father confessed to her that he and Rentner—without telling her—had jacked the price on you and Mr. Kendall to two hundred grand. And Dr. Brandt confessed to her that he killed Rentner because Rentner double-crossed him, and was only going to give him twenty thousand of the entire two hundred thousand.

"The doctor had suspected he might be double-crossed, and had taken along an ice-pick just in case he was. But you had only paid half of the money to Rentner at the time the doctor killed him, so the doctor waited in the drawing room for you to come with the rest. What happened when you got there, I don't know."

I snapped grimly: "I do, lieutenant."

Canavan looked quickly at me.

I met his gaze, still looking over my shoulder. I said: "Don't look at me like I'm touched in the head. Listen. Dr. Brandt waited for Monnett to get the other hundred grand. But I was tied up in the bathroom. All right. With a murdered man out in the other room, you coppers would naturally grill me until my ears rang. And Janie Brandt had lured me to the drawing room. So if I told you coppers that *she* had tricked me into coming there, you would grill *her* to find out *why*. And if she told you the plot to break up her and Chris, you would question Dr. Brandt because he was in the plot.

"So naturally, Dr. Brandt being the murderer and not wanting to be questioned, he had to have some way to shut me up. But he wouldn't kill me—he wasn't that cold-blooded a guy. And he couldn't talk to me himself, to try to scare me into keeping quiet, because I knew him, knew his voice. So when Monnett came in, he got Monnett to talk to me. Don't you see, lieutenant? He had to wait for Monnett in order to get the second hundred grand, so Monnett knew the doctor killed Rentner, but the doctor knew he wouldn't talk.

"Why should he talk—with a fat slice of the ten million bucks coming to him if he didn't? Because if he did talk, the plot to break up Janie and Chris would come out, and any law court in the country would have broken that will for Chris with that plot in front of 'em for evidence. Get it? Any court would break the will so the money *wouldn't* revert to old man Kendall, and so the old man *couldn't* have gotten any of the ten million, which meant Monnett couldn't, too."

I snorted. "So Dr. Brandt got Monnett to talk to me— they got together *after* the murder. And Monnett talked to me—even telling me if I talked I'd break Bones' heart. Which makes Monnett an accessory after the fact.... Why don't you ask him about it?"

I heard Monnett say softly: "All on theory and no proof? Grow up, Roberts."

I grinned. I said: "You'll wish you had a chance to grow up when you feel that hangman's noose tickling your chin. Listen, guy. Even Chris knew you and Dr. Brandt were on the train." I looked up at the kid and made my grin broader. "Didn't you, Chris?"

The boy's eyes popped at me. I guess the way I'd reconstructed the mess really surprised him. "Why, sure," he said.

He was standing about a yard away from me, looking down, and I reached out suddenly and grabbed his ankle. He looked bewildered, struggled for a moment But then I upset him. I put my gun down long enough to reach out with both hands, get a grip on him, and drag him in close to me. That put him behind the davenport, too.

I picked up my gun again and said gently: "Now just lay still, my friend. You're where Monnett can't shoot you." I grinned again. "So just tell us why you disappeared after you shot Bones. In other words, tell us who told you that Bones was going to die. Didn't Dr. Brandt make you think you were a murderer?"

Canavan said: *"What?"*

I growled: "Nobody expected Chris to lose his head and shoot Bones. That's what threw Dr. Brandt's plans in a stew. You see, Janie loves Bones. His being shot would throw her in a panic; and *she* knew her father was on the train. After all, he was to collect the payoff money—which Janie still thought then was one hundred grand. And after Bones was shot, she'd either send for him, or send Chris for him." I looked questioningly at the kid.

He gasped: "She s-sent me. I—I didn't w-want to kill anybody. I was s-sorry afterward. I lost my head."

"Just keep right on talking," I snapped at him.

"Well—" his soft girlish lips twitched—"Janie sent me to a compartment where Dr. Brandt was. Mr. Monnett was with him. They went down to l-look at McPherson, then came back and t-told me he would die. Only they didn't really examine McPherson, but I didn't know they were lying to me then. There was too m-much crowd, and the doctor didn't want to be recognized or get mixed up in the trouble. And they offered to hide me. They sneaked me off the train and t-took me to Dr. Brandt's house. They locked m-me—down in the cellar."

"Without any insulin for your diabetes," I put in.

He stared blankly at me. "Y-yes," he said. He still looked like I was really giving him surprises. "Y-yes. They didn't give me any."

I just nodded at him and then looked quickly at Canavan. We were in a spot, all right. I was slowly piling up the proof on Monnett, and Monnett was the guy who had his gun on the room. But Canavan didn't seem to mind. His startling eyes were like chips of blue stone, boring hard across the room in Monnett's direction. I wondered oddly if those blue eyes were looking directly into Monnett's, or just staring into the muzzle of the big heavy gun.

I laid long odds to myself that it was eye to eye.

THEN I moistened my lips. After all, if Canavan didn't mind being on the spot, it wasn't up to me to kick. I *had* my gun. I braced myself, said:

"Well, there you are, lieutenant. Dr. Brandt and Monnett were together in a *compartment,* and after Dr. Brandt had killed Rentner in the drawing room, and after Monnett had come to the drawing room to pay the second hundred grand. Don't you see it now? Monnett talked to me to try to scare me into silence, and that made Dr. Brandt and Monnett partners in crime. So then they went to the compartment together, and then Chris arrived there with the news that he'd shot Bones. Get it?

"Chris' news was just about disastrous to them. With Bones shot and me tied up in the drawing room with Rentner, you coppers would naturally think that both of us had been manhandled for the same reason. And with Janie in with Bones when he was shot, you would naturally question *her*. So Dr. Brandt and Monnett tried another scheme to save their hides. This: Dr. Brandt confessed to Janie that he and Rentner had jacked the price to two hundred grand, and that he had killed Rentner because Rentner tried to double-cross him.

"All right. Janie is a nice girl—and nice girls will always protect their fathers. So Dr. Brandt and Monnett were safe as far as she was concerned. But—here they got *too* smart—Chris had now seen them and knew they were on the train, and it was very advisable to get rid of him. So they tried the proverbial killing two birds with one little stone, and made Chris think he'd killed Bones, and took him— he thinking they were hiding him—out to Dr. Brandt's house and locked him in the cellar." I turned and looked at Chris. "Where was Mrs. Brandt?"

The boy's soft eyes were still popping at me. He gulped, stammered: "She's—she's been away. Been away a m-month."

I looked back at Canavan and said: "Well, there's everything. Chris was going to be kept down in that cellar without his insulin until his diabetes put him in a coma. That was the two-birds-with-one-stone idea. Diabetics go into comas before they die of it, you know. Then they were going to plant him some place where it would look like he had been hiding—it would be natural for him to hide after shooting Bones—and where it would look like he died simply because he didn't have his insulin.

"And that would have left the ten million to old man Kendall; Monnett would have gotten a young fortune from it and probably given half to the doctor. Don't you see *now*, lieutenant? Dr. Brandt moved Bones to my apartment— Bones has a key—before you had a chance to question him, because the doctor didn't know what kind of a cock-and-bull story I'd given you, and he wanted whatever it was to hold, wanted Bones and me to get together on it.

"But then that conductor called from Washington and you forced my hand. I went out to see old man Kendall. Dr. Brandt followed me, then shot at me because he was afraid I'd find out the whole business. And I killed him— in self-defense. I suppose you know that."

For the first time in a full minute, Canavan looked away from Monnett. The lieutenant's face was a hard mask, and there were tiny knots at the tips of his jawbones. He said very softly:

"The hospital phoned headquarters that McPherson was back. I talked to him. Yes, I know that."

I was still on my stomach behind the davenport, still looking over my shoulder. The Kendall kid was lying beside me, and I knew Monnett still had the big blue gun on Canavan. I could hear Monnett breathe. In the background, behind his breathing, there was a distant hum of voices in the corridor, very low and hushed. I scowled a little. My leg felt warm and sticky from where the slug had nipped me.

I looked at Canavan and growled: "Well, there's the crop. You've got the rest of the answers. Janie's given 'em to you. If you're still doubtful, hand 'em out to me. We'll see just how they fit."

The lieutenant's face was still merely a hard, set mask. I couldn't read anything in it. I didn't know if he'd give out the rest of the answers or not but whatever he did, it was all right with me. After all, Monnett's gun was still on *him,* and it was his party; Monnett was the guy he wanted. There was enough evidence now—if it fitted with what Janie had told Canavan—to make the private dick swing. The worst part of the whole business was that Monnett had just heard it.

That wouldn't make him very easy to take.

BUT CANAVAN gave no sign he was aware of that. I thought I caught the shadow of a grim smile lingering round his mouth corners.

He said softly: "I'll give you the answers, Shag. They seem to fit all right" He didn't even look over at Monnett. He added: "You see, when Dr. Brandt confessed to Janie, he didn't tell her everything. He only told her the principal things—that he'd killed Rentner and that he had jacked the price.... Anyway, after you and McPherson left your apartment, Dr. Brandt started to follow you. But the Brandt girl guessed he was going to try to kill you.

"She played smart, and instead of trying to stop him, sympathized with him, and he told her about young Kendall. She hadn't known her father had locked him in the cellar. The doctor still didn't tell her that he had a new partner."

The lieutenant glanced swiftly at Monnett and went on: "So when she found out about young Kendall, she thought she had a way to help you. She went to her house and told him the whole story. She even got his gun from where her father had put it, and handed it over to him so he'd believe her. She wanted him to come to us and tell us everything. She was so ashamed of herself she was going to run away."

The lieutenant glanced again at Monnett, hard. I didn't hear Monnett say anything. Canavan went on once more:

"But young Kendall only wanted to go gunning for his father." The lieutenant paused and looked at old man Kendall's body. "So he left, did just that, and Miss Brandt got in touch with headquarters and finally saw me. I found one of Edward Monnett's business cards on Dr. Brandt's body in an envelope inside his coat lining that had two hundred thousand dollars in it. It was a good hunch, and so I came here." For the third time, he paused, glanced swiftly at Monnett.

I got it then. Canavan was showing me Janie's story fitted, but was also stalling. Stalling until somebody out in that corridor got sense enough to run outside and get a cop.

Then I heard Monnett say, in the soft voice I didn't like: "Just move out of the doorway, copper. Just do that and tell Roberts to toss away his gun. Tell him to toss it out where I can see it. Just do that, copper, and make it fast."

But Canavan didn't move. He just stood looking at Monnett, then looked at me. He smiled a little, very grimly. He was telling me that if I hadn't knocked away his gun, he wouldn't be standing there in this nice tough spot. But he wasn't bitter about it. He didn't blame me at all. It was only a mild rebuke.

Guys like that are odds on for my money. I started to toss out my gun before I busted out in tears.

Canavan saw me move, yelled: "Don't be a sucker, Shag! He'd mow us all down!"

I was startled. My hand stopped in mid-air.

Monnett's voice tore out without softness. He clipped in a harsh, biting tone: "Keep your trap shut, copper! I'll let you have it!"

Canavan's face was a little white. He stood with his hands clenched down by his thighs, bent over just a little, only from the waist. His light eyes burned frantically at me.

"Damn you, Shag! Don't let me down! Don't go soft on me just when I need you!"

Monnett said: "Copper!"

I saw Canavan turn.

I scrambled to my knees wildly and yelled: "For cripes' sake, Monnett! I'll toss my gun out!"

Then, beside me and a little behind me, the Kendall kid suddenly went crazy. He reached up, clawed at my gun-arm, got hold of my gun. His face was the color of gray stone. He bit at me, kept sinking his knees in my kidneys, yelled at me like an Iroquois. His breath was warm and heavy on my neck. I twisted my torso, not getting off my knees, pulled my gun away from him and swatted him with the barrel.

He snapped back as if he had a spring inside of him. I saw his head bounce on the thick carpet, rock a little, and then a thin stream of dark blood began to ooze from a cheekbone. I got down again behind the davenport just as Monnett fired at me.

THAT SLUG cut through the back of the davenport like it was so much tissue paper, hit the bourbon bottle on the little coffee table and sprinkled the room with old man Kendall's private stock. The place began to smell like a distillery with a free tap. Then we had silence.

I sniffed at the bourbon, looked at Canavan, saw him gaping at me, and looked at the kid. He was groaning and pushing himself up. He had more beads of whisky on his nose alone than he had drops of blood on his cheek where I'd swatted him.

And I hadn't knocked the craziness out of him.

He sat up and yelled at me: "You fool! If you throw your gun away, he'll kill us all!"

I was making myself small, and keeping down low behind the davenport I didn't bother to answer the kid.

He took one look at me, and then seemed to grow calm. As I watched him, he began to grow *too* calm, like the pool-room sharks when the hick comes in. A little craftiness got into his soft eyes. He was pretty far away from the daven-port now, not over a foot away from his old man's body. I'd forgotten that the kid's own gun was at his old man's feet. The kid suddenly leaned backward and swooped it up.

That was nothing in the world but a practical suicide. Monnett's big gun boomed, and the kid went backward; one slender hand gripped his gun, the other one clawed at his throat. It wasn't nice crouching there watching him die. He twitched a lot and lived for quite a while, trying to get up, and with blood gushing from his mouth. My stomach turned over and I could barely hold it down.

Then Monnett clipped hoarsely: "Toss it out now, Roberts, or just don't bother."

I swallowed and looked down at my trousers. The right leg of them was dark from my blood, and I didn't want to watch any more deaths. But then I looked at Canavan. He smiled gently at me. He said in a warm voice:

"Don't do it, boy. You can take him. When he gives it to me, just lean out and let him have it."

I gritted my teeth; that settled things for me. I wasn't going to let a guy like that down.

I just stood up, in the middle of the davenport.

Monnett seemed five miles away, across an ocean of floor, only his big blue gun seemed very close to me. Canavan yelled. I heard that yell, and maybe I'll always hear it, even wake up in dreams with it ringing in my ears. But it drew Monnett's eyes; that was the trick.

When the eyes came back to me, I had my little gun up, and the barrel was looking at him and I was looking down the barrel. His whole body jerked toward me, in an awkward motion. I shot him twice in the chest and stood looking down at him.

I gulped, swallowed, and as I stood there swallowing, Canavan came up and touched my arm.

Canavan looked down at Monnett, too. He said softly: "Some shooting, boy. Maybe the papers didn't overrate you."

He had his gun in his hand and he knelt beside the body, held the cylinder very close to the open mouth. But no moisture got on it. He stood up and added, still more softly: "Some shooting, boy. I'll bet he was dead before he hit the floor."

I was still swallowing, very hard now. I gulped, managed to mumble: "It was j-just luck, lieutenant. I've always been lucky."

IT WAS almost three hours later when Canavan stood in the hospital corridor with me, and the nurse came out of Bones' room and stood holding the door open for us. She looked at us wistfully, and stood aside for us to see in. She smiled and asked softly:

"Do you want to go in now?"

Inside the room Janie Brandt sat on the edge of Bones' bed, and the gray light of dawn at the windows played on her red-gold hair.

I looked at Canavan and grinned. "Well?"

He grinned back at me.

Then when the nurse closed the door softly and went catlike down the corridor, we turned away from the room and went down to the street.

The plots of grass in the middle of Thirty-third Street smelled fresh and earthy in the crisp morning air.

We walked across the plots, with our heels sinking in, stood across the street and tried to guess which was Bones' window.

Canavan growled: "You're not lucky, Shag. It's just that McPherson has so much luck, a lot of it overflows and goes to his buddy."

And I growled: "Well, that shows I'm lucky, doesn't it? Lucky to have old Bones as a buddy?"

A CORPSE AT LARGE

As soon as they landed in town—Messrs. Roberts and McPherson—they looked like a walking morgue, the way the corpses started turning up on their heels. But maybe it was easier that way. For those merry musketeers of murder—Shag and Bones to you—were selected as the piece de resistance of the corpse heap.

CHAPTER I

MONEY SPELLS MURDER

HE WAS pressed back against the trunk of a huge
locust tree, his thin body motionless, his hat brim
pulled down obliquely over pale, blood-shot eyes when I
noticed him. Bones and I had just gotten out of my coupé,
and were standing looking around in the moonlight. I told
Bones to wait, and walked over to the man.

But he stayed motionless. He wore a dirty white linen
suit that might never have been pressed, and a dirty white
Panama that might never have been white. His eyes didn't
seem to see anything of me but my throat. I looked back
hard at him and asked:

"Could you tell me which of these mansions around here
Katherine Kraft lives in?"

His eyes seemed to jump at me, but nothing else about
him moved at all. He said in a surprisingly cultured voice:
"I'm very sorry. I do not know Miss Katherine Kraft."

I thanked him and turned away.

When I got back to Bones, I whispered: "Do you notice
anything funny about that guy?"

Bones screwed up his freckled face and glared at me.
He's one of the crack investigators in the small-loan business, and our company usually puts us both on the same
job. He whispered back nastily:

"Outside of having a bulge under his left arm that might be a baby howitzer, no, not a damned thing. Do you notice anything funny about me?"

I grinned. "Oh, you look all right."

Bones leered at me. "If you see my skin hop off and take it on the lam, don't say I didn't warn you. That nasty-eyed ghost of walking death has given me a lousy case of the creeps."

I took a quick glance back at the man to try to see if he'd overheard us. But he hadn't seemed to; he kept on being motionless. I shrugged and led Bones across the street.

We went up a long flagstone walk to a porch almost big enough for a couple of tennis courts. All of the houses in the block looked like they were built for families in the Canadian Baby Derby.

I dug into the bell.

A beautifully groomed and snooty butler told us Miss Katherine Kraft lived next door.

When the door slammed in our faces, I grinned and looked at Bones. He grinned back at me. Then we both looked across the street.

There was nobody leaning against the trunk of the big locust tree.

I whistled softly. "Now you see him, and now you don't."

Bones didn't say anything. He made a growling noise.

KATHERINE KRAFT, answering her door herself, wore dark green gabardine slacks, a light green military blouse and green toeless beach sandals. She leaned indolently in the doorway and looked us over. The sleeves of the blouse were rolled up, showing soft milk-white arms, and in spite of her outfit, you didn't miss any of her curves. She had enough to make a big-league hurler jealous. Your grandfather would have kicked three holes in his buggy if she had showed him an ankle.

I closed my eyes for a moment, then wrenched them open, but Katherine Kraft was still leaning indolently in the doorway. I hadn't known they made women who were all-woman any more. I dug out a card and said:

"Misters Shaughnessy Roberts and Stanley McPherson. We're representatives of National Finance."

Katherine Kraft inspected my card, handed it back to me, then led us into a huge living room and found us chairs. In the brightness of the light inside, she was even more impressive. But she was not pretty. Her eyes—a light vivid green that blended with her clothes (she even used green cherries in Manhattans)—were set too close together and her nose was too long. Yet her face was the same soft milk-white as her arms, and her hair was a rich red-brown that fell carelessly over her forehead.

She sat down on a green settee near a Filipino chow-bench and picked up a gin drink. I noticed a man's light-weight summer felt on the edge of the chow-bench.

I looked at Katherine Kraft and said: "I suppose we might as well get down to business."

She nodded without speaking and looked at me attentively.

I looked at the man's hat again, peeped around to make sure he wasn't in a corner, didn't see him, and went into my act. I said: "Miss Kraft, just about seven weeks ago your sister, Margaret, got a loan in our office. Since then we haven't seen her. Three days after she got the loan, she skipped out of Baltimore and didn't leave any address. We got a tip she was down here in Brighton City. In fact, we got a tip that she was living with you. So we came down."

I shrugged and spread my hands. "If she's here, we'd like to see her. We want our money."

Katherine Kraft said evenly: "Everybody wants money."

I stared at her.

She took another sip of her drink and added: "If you think Marge is in this house you're dippy as half a dozen loons."

A door in the far corner of the big living room opened and a tall black-haired man came into the room. He was dressed like a movie star making a personal appearance. His gray double-breasted suit fitted him very snugly at his narrow waist and his trousers had a crease sharp enough to cut a whisker. His thick curly hair looked like it had been lacquered. He was a little taller than I—which made him over six feet one—and he had heavy, solid shoulders and big, faultlessly kept hands. He looked like a guy who spent most of his mornings in a barber chair.

He was carrying one of those gin drinks, and his eyes settled on me.

I stayed in my chair impolitely. I didn't like his stare.

But the guy kept looking at me. He said: "Collectors, Kitty?"

Katherine Kraft explained briefly. "Finance company investigators. They think Marge is here."

The man's black eyes got narrow and darker. He kept his gaze on me and jerked a thumb toward the door. He said: "You better beat it, fella. She isn't here."

I LOOKED at him, but didn't move. I was trying to figure just who he was. "Well, thanks," I said, "for all the help." I wiggled a finger at him. "But we got a tip—and the tip said she *was* here. Look. Aren't you Wes Hearn?"

The guy said: "What?"

I grinned a little. "This is the third day we've been in Brighton City, friend. We had other work besides finding Margaret Kraft." I wiggled my finger again. "In other words, since we've been working around, we've kept our ears open and picked up some nice gossip. Like this: Everybody in town seems to know you boss every horse joint where a guy can bet anything over a buck. What's the answer?"

The guy said coldly: "What're you driving at?"

I moved my shoulders. "Well, there's a dog track in town here that's been running about three months, and your take on the horse joints has dropped to practically minus nothing. Guys tell me they'd rather bet on the whippets and watch them run for their money than sit in a back room and get horse results over a radio. But Miss Katherine Kraft here owns and runs eleven dogs. She's made a young fortune since the dog track's been open—but lately you've been running here to see her every night."

I looked squarely at him. "That doesn't make any sense to me."

"Doesn't it?"

"Brother, not a dram of sense—unless you're trying to get her to stop running her dogs, and trying to close that dog track some way... Look." I grinned. "We know Margaret Kraft left this town fast. She must've—when she moved in a furnished apartment in Baltimore, she only had a small overnight bag. And how do we know she didn't leave fast because of some trouble between your horse joints and that dog track?

"You see," I finished, "we know Margaret Kraft lived here before she came to Baltimore. This was the house where she left all her clothes."

Hearn said nastily: "In what drawer?"

"Be funny," I growled at him, "but use better cracks. Listen, friend. A little more gossip: There's a guy named Paul Geisler who's running the dog track, but people say he doesn't really own it. People also say that Paul Geisler is carrying a big torch for Kitty Kraft. In fact, gossipers tell me that Paul Geisler is the guy who bought Kitty Kraft her dogs. They—"

Katherine Kraft banged her drink down hard on the chow-bench. Some of it slopped over, but she didn't seem to notice. She sat quite still, her eyes dilated and mean, and stared at me as if I had come to dump the garbage. She snapped:

"Paul Geisler wouldn't buy his grandmother a postage stamp. Don't get the idea he ever gave anybody anything."

I grinned at her. "He's plenty tight and strictly out for the dough, huh?"

"Strictly," she snapped.

I said: "Well, nobody talked about your generosity, either."

Katherine Kraft's eyes stayed small and mean. "I like money," she told me. "And when I get it, I hang on to it. That's my business. A girl's got to protect herself."

"From who?" I asked.

Katherine Kraft turned to Hearn and said: "Are you going to throw 'em out, Wes, or shall I call the cops?"

I kept my grin and leaned back in my chair. To my right, Bones was sitting forward, his bony elbows on his knees, his green eyes staring angrily at Katherine Kraft's green ones. Bones' face was a little pale beneath his freckles. He stuck out his chin and bellowed:

"The cops? Do you want *me* to call 'em for you?"

Katherine Kraft looked startled.

Bones stood up and shoved a long freckled finger at her. Tact is something he isn't quite familiar with, and he's also excitable, which makes a nice combination. He growled:

"Look, lady. Dog tracks are illegal in this jerkwater town. And you own dogs—we can prove you run 'em. Go ahead—call the cops. We're only here on business."

"And on legitimate business," I put in, still grinning.

Katherine Kraft's face was hard to read. Her eyes were still mean and mad, like she'd enjoy cracking our heads together, but there was only a slight pinch of irritation around her mouth. She looked for a moment at Bones, and then at Wesley Hearn. Slowly the meanness left her eyes, and I thought they began to look crafty.

She said: "You better beat it, Wes. I'll take care of them."

HEARN SEEMED to be studying her for a moment. His black eyes held a very faint glitter, and there was a slightly contemptuous twist to his mouth. He put down his gin drink and picked up his hat from the chow-bench, saying: "She'll sell you anything she knows if you've got some dough."

Then he turned and hoofed it out. His heels made noise in the hall, and we heard the door slam.

I sat and looked blandly at Katherine Kraft.

She was giving the living room door a black, murderous look. She said low in her throat: "I hate that guy." After a moment, she took a long drink from her glass and banged it down, hard. Some more of it slopped out and wet some cigarettes, but she still didn't seem to notice.

Her gaze came over to me and she inclined her head toward a far door. "Talk to you, handsome?"

I grinned. "Talk ahead."

"In there," she said. She kept her head inclined toward the door.

I turned my own head far enough to wink at Bones without her seeing it, then got up and let her lead me into a large green-and-white kitchen. She hadn't brought her drink along. She went to the kitchen shelves, opened their frosted glass doors, and I saw about two dozen bright labels announcing the same brand of gin. She took down a bottle that was open and got a lemon from the refrigerator.

"Drink?" she said.

"I'm working tonight."

She hacked the lemon in half and waved the stainless steel knife at me. "I wouldn't be cheap enough to snitch on you, handsome."

I grinned. "I'm still working. The two don't fit."

She shrugged her shoulders, saying, "Well, it's your loss," and poured herself out a quarter of a tumbler of the gin. Then she poured some salt in the crevice next to the joint of her thumb. She added: "A Swiss-hitch, handsome. Awful easy to take."

She tossed the salt into her open mouth with a backward flip of her wrist, followed it up with the gin, and then swallowed quite easily. She wound up biting into the lemon and looking like she'd taken nothing but water. "You ought to try it some time," she told me.

I said: "I call it a switch-hitch. Let's talk about Margaret."

Katherine Kraft lifted her eyes to me and laughed. "So you did some drinking during the great dry era, too?" She was standing in front of me, and not far away. With the nastiness gone out of her eyes, she looked like four different people.

I shifted my feet and tried not to stare at her.

She took a step closer. "What's the matter?"

"Nothing," I said. I shivered a little. The light was brighter in the kitchen than it had been in the living room, and you forgot her close-set eyes and long nose in the beauty of her coloring. She took another step closer, and I shivered a little more. She asked softly: "Has Margaret been murdered?"

I said: "Huh?"

She waved a hand. "Don't stall. I know you, Shag Roberts. I read the papers. You're the very tough man with the baby face, and you and your partner have cracked three murder cases. That name Shaughnessy threw me off for a little while. Has Margaret really been murdered?"

I was gawking at her. I gasped: "Not that I know of."

"You sure?"

I said: "How do I know when I don't know where she is?"

Katherine Kraft took one more step toward me. That put her right up against we, and slowly she raised her eyes. Her lips came up with them, and I tried not to notice. She whispered:

"How much would it be worth to you for me to tell you where she is?"

I didn't move. My palms felt moist.

She said: "A hundred dollars? Fifty of it now?"

I put my fingers against the base of her throat and pushed her away. My mouth was dry and my stomach felt cold. I said: "Save it, sister. I'm not putting out a penny."

Just then there was the sound of a shot outside on the porch.

CHAPTER II

MORGUE STEPS

KATHERINE KRAFT took one swift step backward and brushed the hair absently off her forehead. Her vivid green eyes were wide and unblinking. Her teeth were gritted tightly together, and her hands were small balls at her side.

She said through her gritted teeth: "If you were lying to me...."

I simply gaped at her.

She picked up the stainless steel knife from the kitchen table. Her green eyes were still wide, unblinking, but growing furious. She waved the knife at me and her gaze settled on my throat. "If you were tricking me into admitting I know where Marge is—"

I weaved my body forward and caught the hand that held the knife. I hadn't quite lost my gape, but I felt it was time to move. I forced her arm down and back until I had It behind her.

Then she went crazy. Her skin grew blotched and faintly purple; she kicked wildly at my shins, and her breath hissed hotly through her teeth. I tried to twist her wrist and she sank her teeth Into my shoulder. Trying to hold her was like trying to hold a python with the itch.

195

I put both arms around her and threw her down on the kitchen floor. I sat down on top of her and gripped her knife-wrist with both hands. I almost wished I had the same grip on her throat.

Then the swinging door of the kitchen popped open and Bones stood and stared at us. I kept my grip on Katherine Kraft's wrist. I growled:

"Don't stand there and gawk like an oaf, ninny. I wasn't trying to kiss her. Chuck some water in her face."

Bones said: "Yeah?"

I snapped: "Yeah. And if you don't get that skinny frame moving, I'll twist it into enough pretzels to go into the business. Get going."

Bones grinned at me. He said: "You always had a rough technique, boy." He went over to the kitchen sink, drew a glass of water, came back and stood over us, his freckled face still grinning. He added: "Maybe I ought to chuck half of it in *your* face. You look just about as sore as she does."

But he chucked it all, and then another glass, in Katherine Kraft's face, and she sputtered and relaxed, and I took the knife away from her. I stood up and she sat up on the floor. The knot of the green scarf at her throat had been twisted up on her shoulder, and her hair seemed to be all down on her forehead. I got down a dish towel and tossed it at her. Bones was clucking his tongue and looking at me reproachfully.

I said: "Damn you. When we heard the shot, she went crazy. She thinks her sister's been murdered and we're trying to crack the case." I got out a handkerchief and mopped my face. "She recognized us, ninny. What was the shot?"

Bones was watching Katherine Kraft wipe water from her face. He said: "What was the matter with her?"

I growled: "Didn't I just tell you? When she gets sore, she goes into a tantrum. One of these days she'll never get out of one of 'em and wind up stark, raving mad." I scowled. "What about that shot?"

Bones said: "Oh, that." He spoke still looking curiously at Katherine Kraft as if he'd hardly heard me. Then he looked up at me and grinned. "How do I know? I beard it like you did, and ran to the window. There's a guy lying outside on the porch."

I said: "A guy?"

"Sure. What'd you expect—Margaret Kraft? This guy's lying half on the top step and half on the porch, and doesn't seem to be moving more than a thousandth of an inch at a time. In other words, I haven't seen him jelly a muscle. You want to go out and look?"

I growled: "Do you?"

Bones snorted. "I should stick *my* neck out. I don't see any killers hanging around outside, but maybe that guy on the porch didn't see any, and look what *he* got. Not me, son. You're the screwy fellow around here. You see if you can help him."

I GAVE him a look that would have soured a jar of cream, poked open the swinging door, and went out into the hall. At the front door, I opened it about a foot and peeped through the crack made at the hinges.

The man, dressed in a neat white drill suit with a fancy pleated back, was still lying half on the top step and half on the porch. I didn't see any part of him move. There was a small dark spot just under his left shoulder.

I said half aloud: "Somebody in this burg knows which way they're shooting." I tried ranging the street with my eyes as much as that tiny crack permitted.

There was nobody leaning against the big locust tree. The pavements were empty, and there weren't any parked cars but mine. All I could see was a quiet macadam street with a white stripe down the middle, and a lot of moonlight making bright patterns through the trees.

Footsteps pattered behind me, and Katherine Kraft touched my arm.

I turned around slowly and peered down at her. She wasn't showing any remorse or apology or any guilt in her green eyes. She merely looked back at me and smiled a little. I was still wondering whether or not she *would* have knifed me.

She said softly: "Give a friend a gander. If he was on my porch, I ought to know him."

I noticed Bones leaning against the wall at the end of the corridor. He looked composed and amused, and was smoking idly, watching us.

I stepped away from the door and Kitty Kraft took my place. Light from a green shaded wall-lamp played softly on her hair.

She turned suddenly, and I thought she looked slightly pale. Her eyes were wide again, and unblinking, and once more they began to stare at me. At that moment the house was so quiet, you could have heard a fly yawn. She said huskily: "It's Paul Geisler.... Heavens! Who'd want to kill him?"

I stared hard at her and tried to read her face. I couldn't tell whether she was trying to bluff us or not. I said slowly: "The Geisler who runs the dog track? The guy I still think bought you your dogs?"

She nodded absently. "Yes," she almost whispered.

I growled: "We wouldn't be running into Wes Hearn's war to try to close that dog track, would we?"

Kitty Kraft started. Her gaze came up to me quickly. "What do you mean?"

"Mean?" I snapped at her. "A few minutes ago you just told us you hated Hearn, Yet he's been running here to see you lately. Why would—"

She blazed: "I hate *him!* He *goes* for me!"

"Oh," I said. "Is that—"

I broke off and stared at her. My spine suddenly felt cold.

At that moment, the telephone rang.

But I didn't pay any attention to the phone. In the kitchen there was a faint sound, like a suppressed curse, then a clatter like a load of scrap iron on a roof. I must have stood stock-still for almost ten seconds. Then, working with the same intelligence that'll make a baby crawl into a blast furnace, I shoved Kitty to one side and legged it toward the kitchen.

It took me about ten good strides to reach that swinging door. I was hardly through it—still standing straight up and sprinting—when a bullet kissed the wall about a foot above my head.

I took one more long stride and dived forward on my belly. I landed near the row of shelves alongside the kitchen table, my nose pressed into the linoleum, my body stiffer than a fried fish. I got a glimpse of a pair of pale, bloodshot eyes measuring me coolly over the barrel of a big blued-steel pistol.

I don't even remember having time to be scared. I was jerking at the leg of the kitchen table, trying to tip it over in front of me, when Bones came storming through the door. I would have liked to have seen his face, but I only heard him.

His lanky feet pounded across the linoleum; he yelled like a Comanche, and that drew those pale, bloodshot eyes.

I saw the barrel of the pistol swing quickly away from me. I noticed the dirty white linen suit and dirty white Panama behind it.

BY THIS time I had the kitchen table tipped over at a pretty steep angle, and there was a sudden rain of gin bottles down on my neck. They were Katherine Kraft's gin bottles—the cause of the big original clatter when they'd tumbled from their shelf to the porcelain-top table.

But I didn't realize it then; I just grabbed one. All the noise they were making drew those pale eyes my way again.

I didn't have time to sit up; I pushed my bottle at him like a basketball. It didn't go hard—it looked like a feather floating—but it did get to his chest and knock him a little off balance. That gave me a chance to grab another one and sit up. But before I could throw it, Mr. Pale Eyes had faded out of the kitchen door.

I heaved up to my feet and reached it in time to see him sprinting across the back yard, his coat-tail out so nice and flat behind him that he might have been a sailfish. I stopped and glanced back at Bones.

He was getting up from the kitchen floor—he'd dropped a few feet from where I'd been—and I yelled at him to follow me, and jumped off the back porch. I was still using that same brand of intelligence that makes the kiddies love the furnaces. I got through the back gate and into the narrow alley as he whisked around a corner.

I took a few deep breaths, and made that corner in three seconds flat. This time Mr. Pale Eyes was hopping into a car. I got about thirty yards from it before it roared away from the curb, then stopped and watched its twin tail-lights disappear into the darkness.

I sat down on the curb and tried pulling some air into my lungs. I was really working hard at it when Bones came sprinting out of the alley.

He stopped at the curb, then saw me half way up the block, and came charging up to me, his own breath wheezing. When he saw I was all right, he sank down wearily beside me. We sat and panted at each other like a couple of dogs for almost half a minute.

Finally I got a little breath into me. I said: "He had—a car. Got away. Couldn't—see the number."

Bones nodded. "Plant—I guess."

I said: "Yeah. And what about Katherine Kraft's phone ringing?"

Bones scowled. "I don't know. Anyway, the whole damned thing is just too pat A shot in front—then he slips in the back. Think so?"

I said again: "Yeah."

"Me, too. He must've been fiddling around in all those gin bottles. Left the car out here because he knew he'd come out the back. What's the answer?"

I shook my head. "Couldn't guess."

Bones said: "Maybe he just went in for a drink."

I scowled at him but didn't say anything, and started looking around to find the effects of our war. We were on a different street, but still in a big-time neighborhood. All the houses sat back in nice huge lawns, and none of the occupants seemed curious about any shots. The street was quiet as a Quaker town on Sunday afternoon.

I grinned at Bones. "Maybe an earthquake would shake 'em up a little."

He snorted. "It might be different around in front of that Kraft woman's house."

We got up, lit ourselves cigarettes, walked to the corner and took ganders up and down the street. There was still a lot of bright moonlight and big bucketfuls of quiet. My coupé was still parked across the street from Katherine Kraft's house, and we couldn't see anybody parading on the sidewalks.

We crossed the street to try to see Katherine Kraft's porch. It was hidden from us by a row of big sycamores along the curb and a lot of overhanging locust trees that grew on the front lawn. But there was a big car parked in front of the house that we hadn't been able to see from the other side.

I reached out and grabbed Bones' arm. The car was parked without lights, and didn't look like a prowl car. I breathed: "Visitors."

Bones licked his lips. "Ah…."

WE DROPPED our cigarettes and stepped on them, grinned at each other, then found nice protective tree trunks about five yards apart. We poked our heads around and watched for maybe thirty seconds. Nothing seemed to be happening, and I didn't like just standing around.

I stage-whispered to Bones: "I'm going up and catch a look at that license number. You stay here and cool your heels."

I waved a hand to him and slipped across the street.

That row of sycamores gave me plenty of protection, and I sneaked from tree trunk to tree trunk until I could see the license number. Then I memorized it and started back by the same route.

When I had gone about five trunks and was starting on my sixth, a man came down Katherine Kraft's walk and climbed into the car. I hopped back to that fifth trunk and shoved out my nose. The car purred softly out of the block without showing any lights.

I hadn't been able to see much of the man.

I whistled a little and ran back to Bones. He was leaning against the tree, looking sourly at me.

I scowled. "It was too dark to get a gander at the man," I said. "But I got the license number. Think we can check it?"

Bones scowled back at me and moved his skinny shoulders. "The devil knows what you can and can't do in this jerkwater town."

I laughed at him, and we walked across the street, moved cautiously up the pavement to Katherine Kraft's long walk. The big locust trees in the front lawn still hid the porch from us. We were halfway to the house when Bones gripped my arm.

He leaned in close to me. "That's funny."

"What?"

"No lights in the house."

I frowned, and we moved on slowly. All the windows in the house were dark, and even the green light in the hallway no longer showed. I couldn't figure it, and I didn't like it. Fireflies were winking against the big dark trees.

We reached the porch steps, still watching the house, then stopped and gaped at what lay in front of us. Maybe our eyes almost bulged out; I don't know. The body of the man still lay where it had fallen, but there was another body beside it and this one didn't wear pants. This one was a girl in a blue dress with marks on her throat, and glassy vacuous eyes that were mercilessly open.

This was Margaret Kraft and somebody had strangled her, and Bones was passing his hand over his eyes as if he couldn't quite believe it.

I managed to gasp: "Yeah. It's Margaret."

He yelled: "What are these porch steps—the city morgue?"

CHAPTER III

HARD COMPANY

I **HAD** a nightmare that night in which it rained bodies and gin bottles, and in the morning I felt like a mountain climber who'd slept hanging by his chin. I got out of bed slowly and gently held my head. There was a note on the writing desk from Bones saying he'd gone out for a little work, and a morning paper lay beside it with headlines tall and black as Zouave general.

I picked up the paper and sat down heavily on the bed. I couldn't have taken a shock like that standing up even if I'd had my breakfast. I read:

BODIES OF MAN AND WOMAN
FOUND IN VACANT LOT
MAN SHOT; WOMAN STRANGLED

I screwed my eyes tight, let that bang around in my brain, then opened them again and stared at the pretty hotel wallpaper. Bones and I had left that neighborhood two minutes after we saw the bodies, and we hadn't tipped the cops because we just didn't want to get mixed up in the two murders. But here was something else screwy, and I couldn't figure it.

I started to light a cigarette, remembered they made me dizzy before breakfast, stuck it economically back in the pack, and slowly read the story. There wasn't much to it that the headlines didn't tell.

The bodies had been found by a milkman at four o'clock that morning, and nobody had heard any shots or could throw any other light on the situation. The cops believed the bodies had been dumped in the lot, and the rest was the usual police handout. The boys were investigating, and promised a very early solution.

I had chicken livers sent up—we had an expense account—and was just finishing my coffee when Bones came back. He was wearing a neat double-breasted brown gabardine suit, and a maroon tie with a gold tie-pin snug under the knot. He looked fresh and very clear-eyed—nothing worried Bones.

He grinned at me after closing the door and said: "What do they do in this jerkwater burg—play drop the handkerchief with bodies?"

I scowled at him over the coffee cup. "Don't tell me they found Katherine Kraft's, too."

He shook his head. "Nix." He walked over to my twin bed, sat down, and stretched his skinny legs. "But if the cops talk to her and she tells them we were at her house, they'll probably toss us in the bastille and throw the key away."

He grinned again. "And they'll talk to her, all right. We were bright boys."

I put down the coffee cup. "Bright boys about what?"

"About not reporting those two bodies to the cops, my son."

I laughed. "Oh, that." I reached for the coffee cup again, and then stopped my hand in mid-air. I looked up obliquely at him. "What do you mean they'll talk to her?"

Bones snorted. "She's Margaret Kraft's sister, isn't she? Wouldn't they naturally question her?"

I said: "Do they know where she scrammed to last night?"

Bones grinned at me. "Ah..." he said. His green eyes looked merry. "Listen, boy. Here's one bright guy who doesn't think she *did* scram."

He thumbed his chest. "I called out there on the phone this morning, and her voice was the one that answered it. So I just hung up without speaking and did a little thinking. Maybe we *thought* she had scrammed just because the lights were out. Maybe she was there all the time and just doused the lights to make us think she'd scrammed."

I growled: "Why?"

He waved a hand. "That's one for you to answer."

I scowled a little and stared thoughtfully at him. Katherine Kraft trying to trick us didn't make much sense to me. I said: "Well, you think up an answer. I'm tired.... Look. We've landed right in the middle of Wes Hearn's little war to try to close that lousy dog track. That's the McCoy—the one right answer.

"And don't think he's been going to see Kitty Kraft just because he carries the torch for her. She hates him, and she used to keep him away. But now she's letting him come, and for one simple reason. He's trying to buy the information about who owns that dog track and she's holding out for plenty of dough for it. Catch on?"

Bones looked hurt. He said in a sad sing-song voice: "I have something in my hand from a lady in the third row, O Swami. She'd like to know if her husband's off the booze. Could—"

I growled: "Don't be a clown. You're not in an act.... Look, son. All we've got to find out is who moved the bodies from Katherine Kraft's porch, who put Margaret's body *on* that porch, and why. Then we'll have the case all solved." I snorted. "Then we'll have our pictures in the paper again."

Bones grinned. "And you'll be run ragged by girlies wanting locks of your hair for souvenirs." He paused and his face lighted up. "Hey! Maybe we can even collect our dough."

"Yeah," I said. "I'd sort of forgotten that. We still work for a loan company, don't we?"

BONES WAS grinning broadly and I was muttering under my breath when a light furtive knock sounded on our door. Bones got up and crossed the room. He put his freckled hand on the knob and frowned over his shoulder at me.

Still frowning, he called softly: "Who's out there?"

There was a short pause. Some colored hucksters down in the alley were yelling their heads off selling watermelon. A very hushed, guarded voice said:

"My name's Reynal Patterson. It mean anything to you?"

Bones kept his frown, his eyes now questioning me.

I whispered: "Wait a minute." I bounced out of my chair, yanked open a dresser drawer, got out my little .32, and went over to the bed. I sat down on the edge and put the .32 under the pillow. I kept my right hand under the pillow with it, played with the safety with my thumb. I added:

"Go ahead. Bring him in. But if it's our nasty-eyed boy friend, just you duck."

Bones' face tightened but he turned the knob, opened the door quickly, and then stepped back. The man on the threshold was not our nasty-eyed friend. This man was of medium height and lean and flat-muscled, and wore clothes that smacked of snooty, exclusive clubs.

He came into the room and just stood arrogantly and peered at us. His mouth was thin and cruel; he didn't look like he'd ever had much fun; and light from our windows glittered on his rimless glasses. I wondered how often he browbeat his servants and kicked little puppies out of his path.

He said in that same hushed, guarded voice: "Roberts and McPherson?"

Bones winked at me. "McPherson and Roberts."

"I see," the guy said. He frowned darkly. I made him for about as much sense of humor as a crippled duck.

He took off a Panama that must have cost him twenty-five bucks and placed it upside down on the glass top of the writing-desk. Then he sat down in the chair I'd vacated and hitched up the legs of his trousers. That showed us black silk nocks with fancy ivory clocks.

He leaned forward and tapped his fingertips together. He couldn't have been a day over thirty, but he had the habits and nervous mannerisms of an ill-tempered guy of fifty with the gout. He said, not changing that careful voice:

"I'd like to talk to you. I'm here from Miss Katherine Kraft."

I don't think I started or showed any signs of surprise. Over by the door, Bones' eyes widened just a very little. I said: "You mean you don't want us to tell the cops that she moved a couple of bodies last night?"

That got to him. He didn't start, or make any floozy movements at all, but he sat so still he might have been petrified. Out in the alley, the colored hucksters were still yelling their heads off about watermelon. The guy said:

"I don't quite follow you."

I grinned a little. I said: "The police commissioner in this town is old Tucker Patterson. He's got a son named Reynal who's pretty strong politically himself. Reynal's friendly with Katherine Kraft." I made my grin broader. "Hi, there, Reynal."

For the first time in a full fifteen seconds, Reynal Patterson managed to move. He tapped his fingertips together again. Otherwise he was still the petrified fossil, and I couldn't tell how he was taking my guess. He said slowly: "Sorry. Afraid I don't quite follow you yet."

I made myself more comfortable against the foot of the bed. I was worried a little, but not too much. I growled:

"Look, fella. You're here from Katherine Kraft. She sent you for one reason. We know the bodies of Paul Geisler and her sister were on her porch last night, and we know the bodies were found this morning in a lot. She sent you here to ask us to keep quiet about that porch angle. Now didn't she—or are you going to keep stalling around?"

I couldn't see Reynal Patterson's eyes. The light from the windows still glittered on his glasses. He hitched up his trousers again and frowned slightly at the floor.

He said quietly: "Aren't you being just a little presumptuous?"

Bones said: "A little *what?*"

Reynal Patterson didn't look up. He said slowly: "I mean, taking a little too much for granted?"

I stared at the guy. "Look," I said. "You're a friend of Katherine Kraft's. Last night when Paul Geisler was shot on her porch, she wanted to get rid of the body—she didn't want her name mixed up in the murder. So she called you. You were the guy to move the body because you've got plenty of pull. So when we ran out to chase a guy who was in her kitchen, she phoned you, and you told her you'd be over. Then she doused her lights to make us think she'd scrammed."

I spun around and jabbed a finger at Bones. "Call the cops, son. This guy's an accessory after the fact. We'll turn him in and get out of this town."

REYNAL PATTERSON knew some beautiful cuss words. They sputtered over his lips like angry hornets, most of them so close together they weren't quite plain. But I laughed at him. I would have bet all the cartridges and bayonets in Europe that he had moved those bodies now.

Then he came out of the chair, his face blotched and furious, and Bones stepped in and grabbed him, gripped his elbows from behind. I didn't take out my gun; I just sat and watched. I didn't think Bones would have trouble handling him.

Reynal Patterson bent forward from his hips, pulling Bones forward, then snapped erect and broke Bones' grip. I sat there and gaped at Patterson. He spun, weaved under Bones' long arms, straightened and butted him squarely on the chin.

Bones staggered, took a long time to fall down. His legs collapsed slowly, like boneless legs, and his skinny body sank down, then keeled over gently. He didn't make any more noise than a couple of atoms colliding in the air.

The Patterson guy swung toward me.

I bounced off the bed, leaving my little gun behind, feinted high with my left and pulled up Patterson's guard. I hooked my right into his chest, trying hard for his solar plexus, missed by a few inches and caught him under the heart. He went back on his heels, and I hooked my left into his stomach. He doubled forward like he had a spring in him—and then we had company.

The door of our room came open slowly and a tall thick-set man stood on the threshold. I didn't have to look twice to know he was used to authority. He had shaggy gray brows and fine gray eyes, and his carriage was erect and vigorous without being stiff. He might have been any age between forty-five and sixty.

His eyes grew bright with surprise, and he stood and stared at us.

I was a little excited. I growled: "Tickets for this fight are downstairs on the mezzanine. Don't you read the papers?"

The fine gray eyes blinked at me. "What was that?"

"Skip it," I said. I stepped away from Reynal Patterson. I was scowling; I didn't like the interruption.

Reynal Patterson was looking hard at me. He had his lean brown hands pressed tightly against his diaphragm, and his face was the color of cold dry ash. He made noises like an air-pump, tried to get his breath. Then his glance strayed slowly past me, settled on the man in the doorway.

Reynal's face grew a little yellow and sallow.

The thick-set man came inside slowly, but did not bother to close the door. His face was tightly set, showing deep clefts obliquely above his mouth corners, and his lips were a thin, implacable line. He said, moving nothing in his face but his lips:

"The more I see of you, Reynal, the more I despise you. I think I understand quite a lot now."

I growled: "Lay off the riddles. Understand what?"

Those fine gray eyes moved slowly in their sockets. They looked oddly at me and glittered a little. "Are you Roberts?"

I said I was.

The thick-set man pointed down at Bones. "And he's McPherson?"

I said he was.

The thick-set man frowned very slightly. He said, still moving nothing but his lips: "I'm Tucker Patterson, Police Commissioner."

I must have started, but I don't remember it. I stared a little, blinked a little, got out my handkerchief and mopped my face. We were having too many visitors from the Patterson family. I growled:

"*Your* dad isn't coming too, is he?"

Then we had a little more company.

I saw the nasty eyes beneath the dirty white Panama as I looked at Tucker Patterson after my crack. The man stood in the open doorway, still in his white linen suit, the knees baggy and dirty, the coat pockets bulging with his hands. I didn't need to look twice to know that his hands had things in them. Both pockets had peaks in the dirty linen, and one of them pointed at me.

CHAPTER IV

SKRONTCH POINTS A GUN

I STOOD very still, the back of my neck feeling cold, remembering that this guy had probably shot Paul Geisler cold-bloodedly from behind, and remembering how quickly he'd shot at me when I barged into Kitty Kraft's kitchen. Besides, I was a good ten feet from my twin bed, and I couldn't remember if I'd left the safety on my little gun on or off. So I just stood and made sure nothing about me moved.

The nasty-eyed guy came inside slowly, then closed the door and leaned against it. He kept both of those peaks in his pocket pointing very steadily at me.

I let my eyes swivel around just a little. Over near the writing-desk, Bones was slowly sitting up, shaking the stupor out of his green eyes and trying to get his bearings. Near him, Reynal Patterson still held his diaphragm and did not move. In front of me, old Tucker Patterson was looking over one of his broad thick shoulders, his face quite cool and composed, like he was watching an infield single by the visiting team when the home club was fourteen runs ahead.

The nasty-eyed guy said in his cultured voice: "Why, Tucker, imagine seeing *you*."

I was watching old Tucker Patterson pretty closely, and nothing about his face seemed to change. He said casually: "Hello, Skrontch." But I noticed that he kept his eyes on Skrontch's pockets, and took elaborate care that he did not move.

Bones climbed to his feet slowly.

I took one quick glance in his direction and the back of my neck got cold as a glacier. Bones' face was growing tight and rebellious. All of the stupor had left his eyes, and they were staring sultrily at our nasty-eyed friend. I said quickly:

"He's holding the top cards, son. For cripes sake let him play the hand."

Bones just said nastily: "If he can."

I took another quick look at the nasty-eyed Skrontch. He was still leaning against the door, showing a small and humorless grin. All of his front teeth were broken off and looked jagged, almost like splinters of old slate that had been weathered black. He said brightly, running his tongue over the dark teeth:

"I could play this hand with my eyes closed tight."

Nobody said anything, and Skrontch added more brightly: "You won't object to *how* I play it, either, will you, Tucker, old boy? How would it be to have the story spread around that our police commissioner bought Miss Katherine Kraft her whippets? Wouldn't that be nice? A nice illegal dog track, and you buying dogs? Tch, tch.

"And as for our two friends"—he looked at Bones and me—"you'd like to go back to Baltimore still beautiful and whole, wouldn't you?" He wiggled the peaks in his pockets at us. "Well, wouldn't you?"

Bones growled: "Would we?"

"I think so, my freckled friend."

I was staring a little, and maybe gaping a little, looking hard at old Tucker Patterson. I didn't say anything. I was wondering why he'd bought Kitty Kraft her whippets, and wondering if he was the dog-track owner. The whole business seemed to be making less and less sense. I couldn't even figure why Skrontch had visited us.

I wiped some perspiration off my forehead without drawing a shot, and screwed my eyes around until I could see Reynal Patterson.

He had stopped holding his diaphragm and stood erect. His face was slightly pale, and his cruel mouth twisted arrogantly. For the first time his back was to the windows and no light glittered on his glasses, and I could see his cold pale eyes staring hard across the room. His gaze seemed to be fastened on Skrontch.

But Skrontch was still showing his dark broken teeth to Bones. And Bones was saying: "What you think don't mean a damned thing to us, guy."

I started a little and clenched my hands and got my leg muscles ready to move me fast. Bones' jaw was jutting out slightly. He stood with his fists clenched and his eyes bright and gleaming, and then he even lifted his right fist and licked his knuckles. That meant he'd cleared his decks for action. He actually looked a little happy about it.

Skrontch said: "Damned if you're not tough, at that."

TWO BIG blue guns came out of his coat pockets so quickly you hardly even saw him move. But he kept leaning casually against our door and looked as calm as if he'd pulled a handkerchief. He showed his broken teeth to Bones again and jiggled the barrels of the big guns at him.

He said pleasantly: "You're tough, but you're not a fool. I'm up here on a kidnaping job." He poked the barrel of one gun quickly at Reynal Patterson. "Come along, my friend. We don't want any gun-play."

I was still standing with my leg muscles tense, and I looked quickly at the younger Patterson. His face didn't change. He looked levelly at Skrontch and then at me, and his cold eyes began to glitter. He picked up his expensive Panama and clapped it on his well-groomed head.

He said to me: "It's a damned shame you thought you were so smart."

I said: "Huh?"

"If you'd have let me have my say before you started all those accusations, all of us around here would be a damned sight better off."

I looked at Skrontch. "Maybe you would, Reynal."

Reynal Patterson's cold eyes kept glittering at me. "So would you, man. Take my word for it. If Hearn thinks you know who owns that dog track, he'll be after you, too— mark my words. I'm only one person he's going to torture in his effort to find out who owns that track."

I snapped: "Like he tortured Margaret Kraft?"

Reynal's eyes still didn't change. He said coldly: "He only threatened Margaret with torture."

I moved my shoulders. "And then she lammed out of town?"

The younger Patterson frowned irritably at me. He said: "Of course, she did. And I don't blame her. Any young girl would have been half scared to death."

Bones growled: "I wouldn't've. Not of this Skrontch guy. Don't tell me he *works* for Hearn."

Reynal Patterson's thin mouth twisted contemptuously. It was an expression that looked as natural on his arrogant face as a smear of jam on a baby's cheek. His cold eyes began to glitter again. He said coldly: "Tell them, dad."

Old Tucker Patterson merely moved a thick shoulder. He said: "Skrontch's worked for Hearn for the last three years."

Reynal Patterson's thin mouth twisted a little more, and he walked slowly across the room and Skrontch opened the door. I stared at old Tucker Patterson. His son was being kidnaped right under his nose, and he didn't look like he was going to do any more about it than if he was going out to lunch. I shuffled my feet and clenched my hands. I rapped:

"What kind of a burg is this town, anyway? What the hell kind of families do they raise down here? Is the water around here thicker than the blood?"

Old Tucker Patterson didn't move for a moment. When he turned, it was very deliberately, and his fine gray eyes seemed to bore into me. Then I saw something. Behind the clear gray color there was something dark and shadowed, like pain was twisting through his brain behind those eyes. And his mouth was very faintly lined at the corners; there was hardness along the stubborn line of his large thick jaw.

He said slowly: "Some of our children seem to have that viewpoint. Heaven knows we didn't instill it in them."

I saw Reynal Patterson stop almost at the door—stop as though he'd rammed a wall. He turned swiftly, and his hands were clenched. Once more I couldn't see his eyes; light from our windows had caught his glasses.

He said in a tight, very strained voice: "No, you didn't instill it in me. You simply had one filthy love affair after another and drove my mother straight to her grave. You didn't instill anything in me—except a hatred for you and your weakness for women. Why, you stayed away for weeks at a time, just—"

Bones yelled: "The gun, Shag! We can take him!"

I might have known that the skinny stiff hadn't licked his knuckles for nothing. Skrontch was standing in the doorway with Reynal Patterson in front of him, and Bones charged across the room and drove his head into Reynal's belly.

Reynal's glasses leaped up high on his forehead and his body was driven backward into Skrontch. I spun around and dived for the bed. I got the pillow in my left hand and my little gun in my right, then spun around again and tried to cover the room. But I was too late. Skrontch hadn't been knocked off his feet and he staggered in behind Reynal and swung a long arm around him.

One of his big gun barrels whipped Bones across the cheek. Bones stumbled backward but didn't fall, and Skrontch put an arm around Reynal and hauled him out into the corridor. Then one of those big blue guns levelled at me.

I ALREADY had my little gun up, and I fired but didn't aim at Skrontch. Reynal was still in front of him and I didn't have much target. I fired at the door, kicked loose lots of splinters—and I think that spoiled Skrontch's aim. It's a whole lot different shooting when you think somebody's shooting at you. His bullet nipped a window behind me, and the colored hucksters stopped yelling about watermelon.

Then old Tucker Patterson leaped forward, grabbed my gun-wrist, and clung to it as if it was his last two bucks.

He breathed hoarsely: "You'll hit Reynal, you fool."

I'll bet my eyes bulged about forty inches, but then I snarled at him like a few battalions of wild men. I twisted my arm and tried to pull loose. Bones charged into both of us and keeled us over on the bed—afterwards he said to put us out of Skrontch's line of fire. But Skrontch didn't make any more attempts to fire. When I wriggled out of the mass of arms and legs, there was nobody at all standing in our doorway.

I hopped to my feet and slammed out into the corridor. There were plenty of people there, but no Skrontch or Reynal; most of the people were peeping out through cracks in their doors. A lot of them ducked back at sight of my gun. But a tall, stately blonde wrapped in a pale blue negligee leaned casually in her doorway and looked me over.

She said in an offhand manner: "They took the automatic elevator, handsome. What's the matter? They steal your toothbrush?"

I scowled at her and started for the stairs. A lot of the heads poked out again, and I shoved the gun in my pocket and began to sprint. I took the stairs three at a time. I must have looked like a wild man when I hit the lobby—even the salesmen at the slot machines stopped playing to stare. I reached the street in time to see a car whisk around a corner, then spun around and buttonholed the big darky doorman.

He was wearing a uniform that would have shamed a czar. The whites of his eyes bulged and his mouth hung open. He said: "Huh?"

I growled: "I haven't asked you anything yet." I scowled and described Skrontch. "You see a guy like that with another guy with glasses?"

He just gulped at me. "Huh?"

I said: "Don't you know anything else?"

"Huh?"

A newsboy standing by said excitedly: "Jeeze, mister! Two guys like that just left in a car. Aw, jeeze!"

I thanked him, dug out a dime and flipped it, and stalked back into the ornate lobby. The salesmen had almost abandoned the slot machines. They were in small groups, whispering low but furiously, rubbernecking at me. I didn't pay any attention to them.

I noticed that the redhead on the switchboard was yelling in her headset for cops, and that the desk clerk was chewing nervously on a freshly dipped pen nib. I went hard-heeled to the automatic elevator, pressed my floor button, and shot up fast.

Our corridor was choked with a lot of people, and my casual blonde was still at her post. She waved indolently at me. I scowled at her again, pushed my way through the crowd, found the door of our room closed, and promptly pushed it open. I found myself with Bones, old Tucker Patterson, the hotel manager and the house dick. I closed the door behind me and looked sharply at Bones.

He was sitting on the bed, gently rubbing his cheek and jaw. "They get away?"

"Yeah," I said.

Old Tucker Patterson looked blandly at me. He said slowly: "I'd rather you didn't give any details, Roberts. This has been private police business, and—well, we want to keep it private."

I stared at him but didn't say anything. If he wanted us to keep quiet because Skrontch had threatened to squeal on his dog-buying, there didn't seem to be much that I could say. So I nodded and went over to the bed. Bones and I sat and waited while he mollified the manager and the house dick, kept our seats when he ushered them out.

OLD TUCKER PATTERSON turned from the door and just looked at us. His clear gray eyes had that shadow again back of them, and I thought his cheeks sagged a little. But the large thick jaw was square and set. He said slowly: "I suppose you'd like to know why I came here."

Bones bounced off the bed like a snake had bitten him. I didn't even get a chance to stop him. He yelled: "*Like* to know?" His lack of tact stuck out all over him like bristles. His skin was red and angry under the freckles. He roared: "Just try to get out without telling us, guy!"

I grabbed him and pulled him back on the bed. He was breathing like a mad elephant. I said: "Whoa, son." I looked at Tucker Patterson. He was flushing and clenching his huge gnarled fists.

I got Bones quieted and told old Tucker: "Just go ahead. We're calm now. We're listening."

The old fellow didn't even look at Bones. His big hands were still clenched, his face still flushing slightly, and he kept his gaze squarely on me. He said slowly: "Katherine Kraft sent me here."

I know I started. I yelled: "You, too?"

He blinked his gray eyes. "Me—*too?*"

Right then I thought I caught on. I laughed a little. I said: "You were sent here by her to tell us to keep quiet about the bodies, weren't you? About the bodies being on her porch?"

He nodded slowly. "Ye-es."

I said: "Well, so was Reynal."

He put his large head to one side. "What?"

I stared at him. "Look," I growled. "Either you're lying or Reynal was lying. Katherine Kraft wouldn't send both of you here. Now, which is it?"

Old Tucker Patterson slowly clenched his fists again. He said in a very level voice: "Miss Katherine Kraft telephoned me last night. She told me that Geisler had been shot, and if I didn't keep her name out of the murder that she'd make it public that I bought her litter of dogs for her. So I went over to move the body. But when I got there, she and Reynal were just arriving—she said that Reynal had phoned her and asked her to meet him on the corner.

"But I don't know why Reynal met her on the corner. I don't know how Margaret Kraft's body got on the porch steps, and neither Katherine nor Reynal seemed to know, either. As far as I could see, both of them were almost shocked out of their wits when they saw Margaret. All I know is that Reynal was engaged to Margaret, and that he and I moved both bodies to a vacant lot. Then Katherine told me to be sure to come down and see you two fellows."

I growled: "What corner did Reynal meet Kitty Kraft on?"

"What?... Oh." He frowned at me. He named one of the northern corners. Bones and I had been on one to the south.

I looked at Bones. I snapped: "Well, let's go."

"Where?" Bones asked.

"To Kitty Kraft's, dope—not the aquarium." I spun on old Tucker. "And you're going with us."

He said: "What?"

I growled: "Don't they make police commissioners take hearing tests around here? You're going with us, and don't think you're not. Seeing as what we're liable to run into, a police commissioner might come in pretty handy."

CHAPTER V

DEATH STALKS SILENTLY

THE BIG locust trees, shaped like gigantic mush-rooms, shaded Katherine Kraft's neatly kept lawn and porch. I paused on the porch steps and shuddered a little. Both the steps and porch were blocked from the neighbors' sight by clusters of the trees at both porch ends. I frowned at Bones, tried to think, and let old Tucker Patterson ring the brightly furbished bell. Again there were no parked cars on the street but mine.

Katherine Kraft, dressed in an emerald housecoat with soft golden stripes, opened the door a few inches and looked out at us. We evidently weren't quite who she was expecting. Her lips were framed as if her speech was rehearsed, but when she saw us, her face went to pieces. I think she was ready to slam the door.

But my foot sliding in stopped that idea, and my torso following it made her draw back. I took another step, and that put me in the hall. I held the door open for Bones and old Tucker Patterson.

They came in, and I said: "It's a very pleasant and surpris-ing morning, isn't it, Miss Kraft?"

Her close-set eyes, bright and shiny, settled on my chin and wished I would rot.

With his white linen suit now so dirty it might have been a baggy pepper-and-salt tweed, Skrontch slid quietly into the doorway to the living room, leaned there, and showed us his broken teeth. I remember blinking, then staying carefully still.

His thin hands were again in pockets that had sharp sinister peaks, and his tongue was running back and forth slowly, licking his teeth. His nasty eyes were shadowed by the bannister of the stairs. He said mockingly:

"A very pleasant and surprising morning to *you*."

I had a little lip for that, but choked it back, slid my eyes around and studied Katherine Kraft. She still looked as mean as an old-fashioned melodrammer villain. Then Skrontch stepped out of the doorway, made gestures at us, and we filed quietly into the living room and looked around.

Reynal Patterson hitched up the legs of his carefully pressed trousers, adjusted his glasses arrogantly, but otherwise didn't move. He was on the settee beside the chow-bench and didn't show any signs of being tortured. Katherine Kraft—still looking mean—sat down beside him and glared at me. Skrontch came through the doorway and wiggled the peaks in his pockets at us.

"Have seats, won't you?"

"So nice of you," I said. "Where's Hearn?"

He showed his dark broken teeth again. "Oh, he'll be here, my pretty friend.... Also, I think you've had that little gun of yours just about long enough. You wouldn't mind standing for one more little moment, would you?"

I scowled at him but didn't say anything, stood still, and let his thin hands frisk me. He got out my little gun and dropped it into a hip pocket. Then he frisked old Tucker and Bones, found no guns on them, went back to the door, and leaned casually against the wall. He kept running his tongue over his teeth, and looked slightly amused.

Katherine Kraft kept her green eyes on me.

I looked hard at her. I grinned a little and said: "Look, lady. We know you met Reynal last night on a corner. We know he phoned you, and asked you to meet him there. You didn't turn your lights off when you went to meet him, did you?"

Katherine Kraft's eyes blinked once, then stared at me. Very slowly, they began to grow nasty. She snapped: "Yes, I did. What's it to you?"

I moved my shoulders, but kept my grin. "Nothing," I said. "Bones and I came back, found the lights off, and Margaret's body was on the steps then. But before we came up and saw the body, we saw the man who put it there. He came down your walk and drove off in a car. And the car had Maryland tags—109698."

Old Tucker Patterson turned white and gasped.

I spun around in my chair and looked quickly at him. Bones half got to his feet. Dimly, out of the corners of my eyes, I saw Katherine Kraft's fingers leap to her lips.

The doorbell rang.

KATHERINE KRAFT sprang up from the settee, her face alert, and I noticed a quick glance exchanged between her and Skrontch. That was something that was hard to figure. She went out into the hall, I heard the door open, and then heard her voice and Hearn's, talking quietly. I glanced over at Bones, and he looked puzzled. Skrontch wiggled the peaks in his pockets again and licked his teeth.

He whispered very softly: "You will not make any noise, please."

I sat down in a chair and stared at him, then could feel my eyes bulge just a little. He had taken one of his hands out of a coat pocket. The gun he held was not big and blue, but big and black and flat, an automatic. There was a compact silencer fattening the muzzle. It was an automatic with a fixed carriage—other types won't take silencers.

I was staring at it and swallowing hard when Hearn walked briskly into the room.

He had discarded his beautifully fitted light gray suit, but still had not lost his sleek movie-star look. He was dressed now for the very late morning lounge. You've seen a million of those outfits in the fan magazines—loud shaggy sports coats, scarfs knotted at throats, soft white flannels and buckskin sports shoes with thick soles. He looked ready to tell any interviewer the soul secrets of his love life. Then he saw Skrontch and stopped so quickly it startled me.

Skrontch merely levelled the silenced automatic and said very quietly: "So long, Wes, the handsome. Hope they have good tailors in hell."

The automatic leaped in his thin hand three jerky times, and there was a slight wisp of lazy smoke and three hollow sounds like a popgun.

Hearn put his hand to his breast pocket and his eyes rolled around glassily. I think he was dead after the first shot. He took two steps, sat down heavily, then keeled over on his right side and stayed quite still. The three overlapping triangles of his breast pocket handkerchief seeped up blood very slowly, almost like a blotter.

Skrontch showed his teeth again and said quite sadly: "Poor old Wes. I ruined his coat."

My mouth was dry as a prohibition platform, and I squirmed around in the chair and tried not to be scared. On my right, Bones was gaping wide-eyed. Old Tucker Patterson had his hands over his eyes, and Reynal's skin now looked like white sand. But Katherine Kraft stood at the doorway, her close-set eyes glittering scornfully.

She said in a low throaty voice: "I always did hate that guy."

I looked up at her but didn't say anything, and she stepped over the body as if it was a gutter of trash. Her own body, large and rounded and breathlessly shaped, moved liquidly under the emerald-and-gold housecoat, and it was hard to connect it with her nasty mind. She walked over in front of Reynal, got a cigarette off the chow-bench, and lit up casually.

She said through smoke to Skrontch: "Give it to the others. Let's get it over with."

I was squirming before because I was scared—but now I couldn't squirm; I was paralyzed. But Bones just stuck out his tongue and licked his lips. I managed to get my gaze around and see old Tucker Patterson, and there was that shadow again behind his eyes. I gathered that he thought he was to be included among what Katherine Kraft termed the "others." Somehow I found what was left of my voice, and it felt as if I was lifting it way up from my knees.

I growled at him: "109698 doesn't happen to be your license number, does it?"

He nodded slowly. "Y-yes."

I snapped: "But you didn't use that car last night."

This time he shook his head. "No." His deep voice was very strained. "I have two cars. I used the other one."

"And Reynal used the one with 109698?"

Old Tucker Patterson nodded again. "He must have. When I went out to the garage after Kitty phoned me, the other car wasn't in."

I looked at Katherine Kraft and said: "Don't be a sap, lady. Don't be so anxious for Skrontch to kill us—because after he finishes that job, he's going to kill you. Why do you think he came in the kitchen last night?"

Katherine Kraft's eyes hated me. "Why?" she snapped.

I grinned at her. I don't know where I got the grin—it must have looked like a petrified skeleton's. And now it seemed like I had to lift my voice all the way up from my ankles. I said:

"Why? Look, lady. Reynal Patterson owns that dog track, but he was worried because his dad might close down on it. So he came to you—his dad's your sweetie—and offered you dough if you'd keep him from raiding it. And you not only kept him from raiding it, you even coaxed him into buying you some dogs. Am I right on that?"

BUT I didn't look at Katherine Kraft. I wasn't bothered about her reaction or answer; I knew I was right, and I was worried about Skrontch. My eyes moved sideways, and I looked quickly at him. He was holding the automatic loosely down by his thigh.

His face showed nothing, and I went on: "You see, lady"—I was looking at Katherine Kraft again—"Margaret lammed out of town because Hearn had threatened her; she wouldn't tell him who owned the track, because she was engaged to Reynal and wanted to protect him.

"But when she got to Baltimore, Reynal didn't stand by her. He either didn't send her much money, or didn't send her any, because pretty soon she was broke and had to come to our company and borrow some. And finally she got sore at Reynal, and came back to blackmail him. You see, I know everything about this mess."

Katherine Kraft snapped: "Then get around to Skrontch and the kitchen."

Somehow I got another grin on my face and waved a hand at her. But out of the corners of my eyes I was still watching Skrontch. He was fondling the automatic and playing with the safety. It made sharp ominous clicks as he pushed it on and off.

I gulped and said to Katherine Kraft: "I'll give that part to you in just a minute… Listen. Reynal's dog track was making all the money in this town because it was taking everything that had formerly been bet in Hearn's horse joints. So Reynal had more dough to offer Skrontch than Hearn, so Skrontch came over and started working for Reynal. So—" I stopped and looked hard at her. "Or did you know that?"

Kitty Kraft said angrily: "I just found it out today."

I hadn't stopped looking at Skrontch from out of my eye-corners, and now for the first time in almost two minutes, I looked over at Reynal Patterson. He was sitting forward on the edge of the settee, his lean hands tightly gripping his knees. His cold blue eyes glittered behind his glasses. His mouth tightened and he said quietly:

"Don't you think he's talked enough, Skrontch?"

Skrontch showed his teeth once more. "Any time you want to stop him, Reynal, all you have to do is give the word."

I didn't say anything, and I could barely breathe. The base of my spine was beginning to feel like a big hunk of dry ice. Skrontch was still fondling the gun, and his bloodshot eyes were looking at me. I got my voice up—this time from around my heels. I said:

"What I'm telling Katherine Kraft now is all mailed in a separate envelope with my daily report. If I don't show up at the office sometime tomorrow, then that envelope'll be opened, and you know what that'll bring. If you want to stop me from talking, just go ahead. My death warrant is yours too, and don't you forget it."

Reynal Patterson's cold eyes were hard to read. They were fastened steadily on me, and they didn't even flicker, and I couldn't tell whether my bluff had gone over or not. I just sat there and tried to outstare him. My hands felt cold and clammy like a dead man's hands, and I kept imagining that all sorts of guilt was showing up in my face. I know my mouth was drier than a toasted cracker. My tongue felt like it was four sizes too big.

Then Reynal Patterson nodded his head at Skrontch.

CHAPTER VI

HEAD FIRST TO HELL

I BOUNCED out of my chair just as Skrontch's eyes swung toward me, and went into a dive that any fullback would have been proud of. But successfully jumping a gun on a guy as experienced as Skrontch was about as likely as hopping to Mars on a cheap pogo stick.

He skipped backward just about ten miles from my hands and ripped a slug past me that scorched the hair off my left ear. But his second slug merely scooped plaster from the ceiling.

Lying on my belly with my chin dug into green carpet, I wasn't in position to give her much help. I swung up to my knees as Skrontch whirled on her, watched him chop his left fist down savagely across her cheek. She went stumbling backward and smacked squarely into Reynal, then turned on him and rammed him back on the settee.

He hit on the side of his hip, bounced off stiffly to the floor, rolled against the chow-bench and sent that toppling. By that time Katherine Kraft was charging back at Skrontch.

This short bit of by-play had occupied only a few seconds, and over my shoulder I saw Bones with his jaw sagging almost to his chest. Then he heaved out of his chair with a bellow, skimmed over my back like a low hurdle, and drew a slug from Skrontch that kicked carpet lint up at me.

Skrontch was between two charges and I think he almost went cockeyed. Anyway, by the time he decided which way to shoot next, Bones and the girl had him sandwiched.

I got to my feet just as he gun-whipped Bones with the silencer, and Bones staggered back into me, blocking my progress. I remember thinking that this was probably the end, and wondering if our company would send us flowers.

But I knocked Bones out of the way for one more effort, and he stumbled around crazily but stayed on his feet. Skrontch shoved Katherine Kraft away but only at arms' length, and then dimly, like from a distance, I could hear her yelling.

She screamed: "Don't stick all our heads in a noose, Skrontch!"

The fat end of the automatic was swinging up toward me, and I think for once in my life I played smart. One move from me in any direction would have sealed my doom tighter than a mummy's mouth.

I didn't see anybody else's reaction but Skrontch's, and he blinked his bloodshot eyes very slowly, twice. After another moment that was long enough to sink four shafts through to China, he blinked once more—and then suddenly frowned.

He said slowly: "Hell, Reynal, how do we know whether he's bluffing or not? The girl's right; why take a chance on sticking our heads in a noose?"

I tried to get a grip on myself and not relax too fast, but I might as well have tried to get a grip on some mercury. I found my chair and collapsed in it like a guy caught up by the heat. I rolled around in the chair, wiped my mouth with my sleeve, then found I barely had enough strength to sit up again.

I blew out some breath and looked around at Reynal Patterson.

He was just getting up from the floor and his breath was flaring angrily from his nostrils. His cold eyes were looking swiftly from Skrontch to me. He snapped suddenly at Skrontch:

"Just what would you suggest?"

FOR ONCE Skrontch didn't show his broken teeth. He shrugged and said: "I'd let Roberts talk, and then we'll see how much he does know. If he knows it all and can prove it, then we can talk compromise with him. If he doesn't know it all and can't prove it—well, what the hell, why worry?"

Reynal Patterson turned to me and said tightly: "All right, talk ahead—and be sure to include your proof."

I suppose you can only be scared just so long. After a while you get to the point when you feel like yelling that whatever somebody's going to do to you—well, for cripes sake do it. That was the way I felt, and my voice came out with a snap.

"Okay. You'll get it, and you'll get it with proof." I scowled. "Just listen.

"You killed Margaret Kraft because she was trying to blackmail you. And you planted Skrontch outside this house with orders to kill Paul Geisler when he showed up last night. And here's why.

"You knew Paul Geisler and Katherine Kraft were planning to sell your name to Hearn. You knew it because Katherine Kraft—always looking for some extra profit—told you they were going to sell out. You knew it because Katherine said that she and Geisler wouldn't sell if you'd pay them *not* to sell more than Hearn would pay them *to* sell. Is that straight?"

I saw Reynal Patterson glance swiftly at Skrontch. He frowned before he turned back to me. Then he snapped: "Keep right on."

"Remember, bud," I said. "You asked for it… Now." I wiggled my finger. "After Skrontch shot Geisler, Skrontch went to a phone and called you. He told you exactly what time he was going in Katherine Kraft's kitchen, and you were to phone Katherine Kraft at that time. Skrontch also told you about Bones and me being in the house, but"—I wiggled my finger again—"you decided to go through with your plan, anyway. And your plan was for Skrontch to plant a bottle of poisoned gin in the kitchen, so you could kill Katherine Kraft, too.

"So Skrontch came in the kitchen but he made a lot of noise, and we ran in, and he ran out. But just before we ran in the kitchen, you called Katherine Kraft; I heard the phone ring. Then she told you what had happened and you had to change your plans.

"You'd originally called Katherine to keep her busy while Skrontch was in the kitchen, and also because you were reasonably sure she'd tell you about Geisler's murder. That would have given you a chance to come over—apparently to help Katherine. You wanted to bring Margaret's body with you, leave it in the car, come in and persuade Katherine to have a drink as a bracer, which would've killed her.

"Then things would've been dandy. You could plant the bottle of poison itself and make it look like suicide, like Katherine killed herself in remorse after killing Margaret and Paul Geisler. And everybody would think she killed them in one of her terrible tempers. You were going to make her the fall guy—and try to get out of that."

Reynal Patterson said coldly: "You're doing the talking."

Out of my eye-corners, I was watching Skrontch again, watching him still fiddling with the gun's safety.

"Well, you had to change your plans. So you told Katherine Kraft over the phone that you'd help her if she'd get rid of us, and for her to meet you on the corner whether you got rid of us or not. And it was right here you took your long chance. You came right over, dumped Margaret's body on the porch—you knew Katherine couldn't see you; that she'd be on the corner waiting—and trusted to luck that Bones and I wouldn't be around to see you, either. But we did, and we got the license number of the car. It was your dad's—you'd lent yours to Skrontch.

"So then you met Katherine on the corner, and she told you she'd called your dad—Katherine was getting all the help she could get. And that made it necessary for you to change plans again. Your dad would see Katherine drink the gin and die, and know damned well she didn't commit suicide.

"But you came back to the house with Katherine, anyway. You didn't care whether or not Bones and I saw you then—you'd told Katherine you cared before just as a stall. So you came back, registered the proper surprise when you saw Margaret's body, then helped your dad move both bodies, and pretended helpfulness all around." I scowled at him. "How'm I doing?"

Reynal Patterson's eyes were glittering again. He snapped: "You haven't finished—and you haven't showed any proof."

I grinned at him just a little. The grin was easier now, because Bones and I had one chance to live—a chance slim as a grass blade, but still a chance. Then I took one more look at the nasty-eyed Skrontch. He was caressing the gun as though it was something he loved very dearly.

I swallowed hard and said: "Well, here's the rest of it. This morning you came down to see us because we'd seen Skrontch get away in your car, and you were afraid that we'd gotten the license number. You wanted to find out just what we knew. And you planted Skrontch out in the corridor in case we got tough with you and you needed help. Which"—I grinned again—"you happened to need.

"So then you pretended that Skrontch was still working for Hearn because we'd seen him at the house, and seen him in the kitchen. Then when you left the hotel, you realized you were in a spot. We knew you had moved those bodies. So you came over here to see Katherine Kraft and cooked up another scheme with her. You promised her dough if she'd lure Hearn over here, where you could kill him in a nice safe spot. Then you planned to kill Katherine, then Bones and me, and leave the town all to yourself.

"You had a strong hold over your dad because he had helped move Margaret's and Geisler's bodies, and you could make him go light on the police investigation. Which would have made everything ducky for you." I spread my hands. "And that's the crop."

Reynal Patterson snapped: "But not the proof."

I moved my shoulders. "The proofs in the kitchen," I said. "Just lead me to it I'm rarin' to go."

REYNAL PATTERSON frowned very darkly, then looked over at Skrontch and nodded his head. Skrontch pushed himself away from the wall. He walked to the kitchen door, swung it open, and we all filed through it, moving noiselessly.

I stood and looked around thoughtfully for a moment, then walked over to the kitchen shelves.

They were built like they are in the majority of kitchens, in reality one very large kitchen cupboard with drawers at the bottom and shelves at the top. In front of it, the porcelain-top kitchen table had been set upright again.

I reached up to the frosted glass doors, swung them open, and showed Katherine Kraft's gin cache. All the bottles that had fallen had been put back. I said, looking at Katherine Kraft:

"When we heard Skrontch out here in the kitchen, we heard a devil of a clatter, didn't we? All right. That was the gin bottles falling—you'd opened the frosted glass doors, remember? We were out here and you took a switch-hitch.

"Well, this porcelain-top table is kept almost up against the bottom of these shelves. And half of your gin bottles are directly over it. So when the bottles fell, they landed on the table and made a racket like a lot of scrap iron on a tin roof. I know darned well you remember that.

"So here's what happened. Skrontch came in here with a bottle of poisoned gin, put it on the table—in place of the one you had open. I suppose you always have one open, and that would be the easiest way for him to do it. You seem to use one brand of gin, and Reynal could simply have bought a bottle of that, poisoned it, and told Skrontch to leave it. You see, the bottle that you had open could just be dumped. I hope I'm making myself nice and clear."

Katherine Kraft's face was blotched and mottled.

"Just go on."

"Okay." I took a long, deep breath. "But how did those bottles happen to fall if Skrontch merely put your poisoned gin on the table?" I looked slyly over near the door at Skrontch. He was still caressing the gun. I gritted my teeth hard; this was the payoff. I added huskily:

"Well, I'll show you."

This time I didn't bother to look at Skrontch. I just pointed at two large drawers beneath the shelves. Then I bent down quickly and grabbed the handles of the top one. I yanked and the drawer stuck, and the shelves above shimmied. There was a rain of gin bottles down on the porcelain-top table.

A lot of sweat was standing out all over my hands, and I found the handles of the drawer hard to grip. But I kept tugging at that drawer with all the strength that was in me. More gin bottles fell, making more clatter, then the drawer pulled open, and I glanced inside of it. I didn't stop to look around. I couldn't afford to do that; I had to take a chance.

My hand plunged down into the drawer and my fingers folded around the smooth butt of a revolver. The gun was a long-barrelled .45 and weighed half a ton. But I jerked it out and spun with it, praying as I moved. I was praying that all those gin bottles had caused lots of confusion.

MAYBE I figured right; I don't know. When I spun, Skrontch's big automatic was swinging up, the muzzle following me like Uncle Sam's finger on a poster. I remember at that instant I tried to catalogue the room. Katherine Kraft was staring at me, old Tucker was wide-eyed, and Bones was charging across the floor at Skrontch. I squeezed the trigger of the long-barrelled gun.

My first shot must have missed Skrontch a good ten feet. I saw his gun jounce, saw a small jet of blue flame, didn't hear any noise, but felt something nick my neck. The nick felt like a fly bite.

I fired again and my wrist felt numb, but the slug keeled over Skrontch as though he'd been hit by a truck.

Then I slid my gaze around, saw Katherine Kraft dig a small automatic out of her housecoat pocket.

You hardly heard the noise the little gun made, but the smoke floated away lazily and I law her flinch from the recoil. Then I saw Reynal put his hands to his belly. A little blood came out over his fingers, and he seemed faintly surprised, then he folded up like a jack-knife.

And at that moment, old Tucker Patterson stepped up to Katherine Kraft. He socked her squarely on the button with the prettiest right you've ever seen.

I stood and watched her stagger back across the floor, step on one of her gin bottles, and spill sideways to her hip. But she wasn't out, and she suddenly went crazy. She threw the gun away, picked up the gin bottle, smashed it on the floor and began rubbing her hands into the broken glass. Her shrieks sounded like something horrible out of a medieval torture chamber.

She took her hands, cut and streaming with blood, and rubbed them back and forth across her cheeks, as if the blood was a face cream. Then she rolled on the floor, making sure she rolled on the glass, and screamed with delight, clenching her bloody hands and waving them.

Bones stood up and just gaped at Katherine Kraft. I gaped, too; I knew this was one tantrum she'd never get out of. I said to Bones: "For cripes sake, let's get her off that glass."

Bones nodded and we both swallowed hard, then reached down and got good grips on her. It took all our strength to carry her into the living room. Finally we found a clothes line and tied her down on the sofa. Back in the kitchen, we could hear her babbling.

Then old Tucker Patterson came back, his face looking gray.

Bones looked around and wagged his head. He said: "I don't know what you think about it, Shag, but I'm going to cover these bodies and go out for a drink. I wouldn't touch that gin with a ten-foot pole." He shuddered. "You game?"

"I said: "Wait a minute." I looked at old Tucker Patterson. He was leaning against the kitchen sink, his fine gray eyes closed wearily. I went over and touched his arm. I added: "Not to bring up an unpleasant subject, but are you going to call the cops, or do you want us to?"

But he just said in a tired voice: "You call them. I'm done—I'm through. I'm going to admit my part and take what's coming to me."

A HALF hour later, waiting for the cops, Bones and I sat on the porch over beer that he'd gone out and gotten. Old Tucker Patterson sat moodily in a swing. It was still not quite noon.

Bones grinned cheerfully at me. He said: "Aw, Swami, it wasn't so tough to figure. That is, all except that gun-in-the-drawer action." He wiped some foam off his lips with the back of his hand. "Me no able to figure that, Swami."

I looked at him over my glass. I said: "This isn't bad beer, son… Look. That gun *had* to be in there—it was the one right thing. If they had planned to poison Katherine Kraft and make it look like she killed Geisler, they had to plant the murder gun here in the house on her, didn't they? And I couldn't figure why those gin bottles fell. So when I let the two thoughts bang around in my mind together, I got the idea that maybe one of those drawers was the place.

"Nine out of ten of the damned things stick—try your own house some time. And Skrontch would be in a hurry—he'd pull like the devil on it. So that would bring the gin bottles down, and I figured that added up. The thing that worried me was that I might pull the wrong drawer."

Bones growled: "What the hell? It'd be natural for him to use the top one, wouldn't it?"

I said: "Well, that's the way I figured it It'd be closest and easiest, and so most natural. But—"

I broke off and stared at him.

He blinked. "What's the matter?"

I said: "What's the *matter?* Do you know we haven't collected our dough? Do you want to be getting Unemployment Compensation this time next week?"

Bones grinned and waved a hand. "Hell, we can collect our dough from Margaret Kraft's insurance. I wouldn't let a little thing like that worry me."

I looked suspiciously at him. He looked a little too smug, a little too complacent, I growled: "How do you know she's got insurance?"

He waved a freckled hand again. "Look, Swami. You're not the only guy who sees all, hears all, knows all, and tells all."

He grinned. "I'll lay a week-end in Ocean City to a short bus ride that Katherine Kraft took out insurance on Margaret as soon as she was threatened. Like to bet that that money-grabbing dame didn't?"

I just scowled at him.

He laughed and pushed a bottle at me. "Refresh yourself, boy, and ask the new Swami questions. Come on, Shaggie, have a little beer."

ALIBI AND THE FORTY THIEVES

When Shag and Bones played knight errants on a crime crusade, they challenged a murder myth. For there were forty reasons that pointed to a tinsel-baited trap—a trap with jaws that dripped with the venom of vengeance.

CHAPTER I
CRIME CRUSADERS

SHE WAS a tall, lean, hungry-looking woman—and the automatic pistol she held belonged to me. She pointed it at me across about three yards of hotel carpet, and said:

"From this distance, Mr. Roberts, no gun would leave powder marks."

Bones blinked his green eyes. He probably hasn't a peer as a small-loan investigator, and our company—though this wasn't a company job—usually has us work together. He bounced halfway out of his chair and yelled at the woman:

"Hey, there! Watch how you fool with that safety!"

I wiggled a finger at him. "Never mind, son. I haven't got any shells in it." I stood up out of the chair and pinched my lower lip. "Look, Mrs. Weston. You're right. No gun would leave powder marks at about three yards, and no *revolver* would ever leave a bad powder burn that was twice as large as a silver dollar.

"In a revolver, most of the noise and powder smoke escape at the breech. Incidentally, that's why a silencer—which is screwed on a muzzle and does its work there—won't work on any sort of revolver. So a revolver—most of the smoke escaping at the breech—*couldn't* make that large burn, and it's doubtful that even an automatic would.

"And so if Hubbell's forehead had that large a burn, something *is* screwy—you can count on that. You said he was found with a revolver in his hand, didn't you?"

Mrs. Weston looked thoughtfully at me. "Yes."

"Okay. Then you're right. He didn't commit suicide, he was murdered, and Bones and I might be able to find his murderer. But we take ten days of our vacation in the winter so we can have a nice trip to Florida—"

Mrs. Weston said quietly: "We've been through all that."

I was polite. I said: "Yes, we have. But—if you'll pardon the impertinence, Mrs. Weston—to *your* satisfaction, not to ours. In the first place, we're not private detectives like Andy Hubbell, and you can't just hire us—we don't play that way. And in the second place, even if we were private detectives—"

I BROKE off as the hotel door opened, and I'm not sure, but I think my eyes bulged. A girl stood in the doorway, except that she was not merely a girl; this was one of those blonde visions that you generally see only in dreams.

She had hair that was soft and exactly the color of ivory, and it fell to her shoulders with the ends slightly curled. The wind had disarranged it, and she was busy brushing it back; one hand tapped a riding-crop absently on her knee. She burst into the room, saw Bones and me and stopped, then said to Mrs. Weston:

"Why, mother! For goodness sake!"

I know I stood up straighter. Bones hopped out of his chair and grinned.

Behind the girl, a young man appeared in the doorway—a young man as tall, lean, and hungry-looking as Mrs. Weston, but without her young, clear, and very bright eyes. I think he lacked what predominated in her—a restless, nervous, driving energy that gave her a vitality that nothing had ever licked.

She had iron-gray hair, and his was soft and golden; you felt that was the tip-off to the difference between them. They looked a lot alike, but you knew she'd give battle; you knew the young man would quit cold when the going got rough.

The young man stopped in the doorway and stared at my little gun.

Mrs. Weston waved it at him very casually. She said: "It's all right, darling. These are the young men I was expecting." And to her daughter: "Lane—Mr. Roberts and Mr. McPherson."

I muttered something and barely heard Lane's acknowledgement. I was trying hard to look her over and not stare like a rube at a burlesque show. And I did see that she wore jodhpurs that cost enough to pay my rent for a few months, and a canary-yellow sweater, and a soft camel's hair coat.

But then I heard Mrs. Weston talking, and had to look away.

"And my son, Tommy," she said.

I shook hands with Tommy and got my first gander at his lips. Shaped like a cupid's-bow and bright red and moist, they were the kind of lips some of the movie glamour girls try to have.

He smiled with them and said: "Not the famous murder investigators, Shag and Bones?"

I couldn't hold back a scowl. Across from me, Bones' eyes began to look angry. There was enough sarcasm in young Tommy's voice to shrivel the hide of a hangman's son.

Mrs. Weston said quickly: "Now, Tommy, don't be childish." She turned to us and added: "Will you please accept *my* apology?"

Then Tommy sulked and trudged across the room. He went into another room of the suite, slamming the door hard.

Mrs. Weston added softly: "Lately, he resents my"—she hesitated, and smiled a little—"my crusade against crime, as the newspapers seem to call it. Lane, I don't think these young gentlemen are going to help us."

I didn't say anything. I stared hard at Mrs. Weston and thought back over her proposition. The entire business amounted to this:

Mrs. Weston had been the state's ace crime crusader for about the last twenty years. A big shot on the School Board, and a widow of a politician who people *swear* was honest, she had a bug in her brain to rid the state of lice. And she had just about succeeded.

In the underworld she was known as Mary, the Terrible; and in the newspapers they simply used her initials in headlines, such as Mrs. W. says this or Mrs. W. does that. It was said that in her annual speech before election, her recommendation controlled a hundred thousand votes.

But Calvert City, in the western part of the state, had so far been harder to crack than a headwaiter's poise. She had sent Andy Hubbell, her ace private dick down there, and now Andy Hubbell had been charged off as a suicide.

According to Mrs. W., there was a kind of committee in Calvert City—forty men who ruled the roost and divided all the swag. This included slot-machines, horse rooms, dog tracks, and gambling rooms—and in Andy Hubbell's case, evidently bribing the coroner's jury. At any rate, the coroner's jury had officially pronounced Andy Hubbell a suicide by the time Mrs. W. had found out he was dead.

BUT OVER these forty men—still according to Mrs. W.—was the big cheese, the smart brains, a guy who was known as Alibi. Mrs. W. claimed that she knew the names of the forty men, but that this Alibi was as secretive as a girl with her first beau. It was rumored that only one of the forty men knew who he was, and that only the other thirty-nine knew which of them *that* was.

And all Mrs. W. wanted Bones and me to do was: first, prove Hubbell had been murdered and find his murderer; second, pin conspiracy for murder on the forty nice men;

and third, find Alibi and pin conspiracy on him. Which latter, of course, made it a little complicated.

Mrs. W. further claimed that while she knew the names of the forty, she had no evidence against them and so could do nothing. And she also said that due to connections in the police department, the murder room had been untouched and was waiting for our visit. She had had her eye on Bones and me, she said, since we cracked our first murder case, and had come up from Calvert City in a plane when she found we were getting a vacation.

And we had now been on that vacation exactly thirty-four minutes.

I checked this by my watch and said politely: "Mrs. Weston, you're right—we're not going to help. As I said before, even if we *were* private dicks, we wouldn't poke around in any hornet's nest like Calvert City. After they polished off Andy Hubbell like I might swat a fly? Why, no amount of money—"

Mrs. Weston said quietly: "But no money's involved, Mr. Roberts."

I said: "Huh?"

She smiled at me. "I said no money is involved—but it was for Mr. Hubbell, of course. From what I've read of you two, you have sound and admirable ideals—and I think you would do better work if you believed in your objective. However, of course, I would pay all expenses, and do it gladly.

"Besides, one reason I chose you was precisely the same reason I chose Mr. Hubbell—you're a very handsome young man and there's a charming woman in this case. I think she may be the key—"

Bones groaned. He said: "Holy jeepers."

Mrs. Weston looked quickly at him.

He spread his long, flat-boned hands. No crime crusader, not even a queen, would ever begin to awe that guy. I chewed anxiously at my lower lip. He said:

"Look, lady. Don't go dragging charming gals into this—I got enough trouble keeping this mug straight as it is. We're headed for Florida, and I want to go—I don't want to have to be running to Calvert City, taking care of him. We've told you how we stand. Now let it go, will you?"

Mrs. Weston smiled. "You'd ask me to do that, Mr. McPherson?"

Bones said: "Would I!"

Mrs. Weston smiled again. She said softly: "Suppose you and Mr. Roberts talk it over for an hour?"

DOWNSTAIRS, THERE was an electric clock over the bar, and Bones and I took a table across from it. We ordered rye and drank them neat. The bar was empty save for some guy playing a slot-machine, and the barman had his elbows pinning down a scratch sheet.

We had the darky waiter bring us another rye, dumped in our water chasers and sat looking at each other. Finally I grinned and said:

"Look. I want to go to Florida as much as you do, and if our heads aren't too big to stick out a window in the morning, then tomorrow we'll be sunning ourselves on a luxury liner's deck. Why should we stick out our necks and practically commit suicide?"

Bones grunted. "Like Andy Hubbell?"

"Yeah. Like Andy Hubbell. And he was one damned good private dick."

Bones said: "One of the best." He looked thoughtful. His face screwed up just a little, running all of his freckles close together. He added: "If those forty thieves could take Andy Hubbell, what the hell kind of chance would a couple of punks like us have?"

He grinned. "Alibi and the Forty Thieves. Let's go back and tell Mrs. W. off."

I shook my head. That was when I made my mistake. Being polite, or soft—whichever you like—was probably the thing that ran us into trouble. I said:

"Hell, I sort of like the old dame—let's kid her along a little and make her happy. Let's let her think we used her hour for arguing. And don't sit there and nurse that rye. This is vacation, boy. Let's get started."

We drank that rye—to Mrs. W.—then had another one and didn't nurse that one, either. But the next one we sat and dawdled and gassed over. The hands on the electric clock seemed to crawl like a snail.

We'd been there exactly twenty-one minutes—I remember looking at the clock and calling the time—when this pale-faced guy came through the doorway. He was about medium height and even thinner than Bones; his narrow shoulders even looked bony under the padded shoulders of his coat.

But what I didn't like was the bulge under his left shoulder; he looked like he might be carrying a baby howitzer. And inside the doorway, he hesitated a moment until his shiny black eyes spotted us.

Then he came over to our table and put his hands on the edge.

He said in a nasty but level voice: "Roberts and McPherson?"

I pushed back my chair and stared up at the guy. But Bones beat me to the answer. He growled:

"That's right, bud. It mean something to you?"

Mr. Pale-face swiveled his shiny black eyes away from me. I noticed that he wore a narrow-brimmed green felt hat, with a small red feather peeping out of the band. I think they call them Alpine hats.

He snarled: "Keep your pants on, gate. It means plenty."

I said: "Yeah?"

His head jerked toward me again, and I grinned a little; it seemed a good idea to keep his gaze hopping back and forth between us. But four ryes in my belly made almost anything seem like a good idea, except the thought of that baby howitzer swinging under his shoulder.

He snapped: "Yeah. And I'll give it to you. You two are staying out of Calvert City—you get that, gate?"

With that, he spun around and headed for the door, got halfway to it and then came back. He put his hands on the table edge again.

"You—get—that—gates?"

I looked at Bones. "You get it, boy?"

Bones looked up at the guy. He said: "Nuts to you."

I don't think the guy started, but he went so tense he looked stiffer and more sinister than a Turkish sword. I came up out of my chair, my right shooting out, caught his right wrist and jerked him around. Bones kicked back his chair and hopped to his feet; he grinned nastily at me and stared at the guy.

He said: "Just let him loose, son. I can handle him."

But I kept my grip on that baby's wrist; I didn't think he'd try to draw with his left hand. I said, and I kept my voice in a whisper: "Listen, fella. We're hanging on to you, and you're going upstairs. Maybe Mrs. W. might have a few words to say."

There was a screech behind me that was almost a woman's screech; my gaze swiveled quickly and I saw the darky waiter's eyes. They were bulging out so they seemed nothing but whites, and then he screeched again and dropped to his knees. He crawled under a table; the man at the slot-machine stopped playing; the barman crumpled his scratch sheet tightly in his hands.

But I held hard to Pale-face's thin wrist—then saw a man in the doorway gripping a big blue-black gun.

I had my little automatic that Mrs. Weston had given back to me, but even if I'd reloaded it, I wouldn't have gone for it then. I just held on to that wrist, and kept myself still.

THE MAN with the gun was in shadow and I couldn't see much of him; he looked big and bulky, but that was all I could tell. He snapped: "Turn that wrist loose, handsome. And don't try any funnybones. And you, frecklepuss—stop edging toward that glass."

Bones was standing by the table, and his hand had been crawling along its edge. He stopped his hand, looked questioningly at me.

I gasped: "For Pete's sake, son! Not in the face of a gun-muzzle!"

He growled: "What the hell, don't you think I can throw?"

I exhaled some air. Nothing scared Bones just like nothing ever worried him. I snapped angrily at the man in the door:

"All right. Say your piece and get it over with. I suppose you're going to tell us to stay out of Calvert City, too?"

The man snarled: "What are you, baby-face—a broadcasting station?"

I had some lip for that but choked it back. The guy was right. The barman and man at the slot-machine didn't need to know what this was all about. I growled instead:

"Look, fella. Take your advance guard and pound your heels out of here." I shoved Pale-face halfway across the floor just for emphasis. "We're not hired, and we're not taking any propositions—we're bustling down to Florida for the beach and the dames. So go back where you came from and cool off a little. Leave your address and maybe I'll even send you a postcard."

The guy laughed—but the laugh had a sneer a mile broad in it. He said: "Ain't you tough!"

Bones snapped: "We can be tough. Try sticking around, fella." He moved his hand deliberately toward the glass.

The man said softly: "Hold it, lug." The back of my neck began to feel like dry ice. He added, still in the same soft voice: "Come on, Jitter. Pick up your feet. You don't want me to plug that freckle-puss, do you?"

Pale-face stared toward the man and looked sullen. His little shiny eyes switched for a moment, and ran over me. He said: "Plug this gate if you plug one—he's the wise-acre." Then he stamped past the man and out the door, his heels rapping echoes around the room.

The man faded away behind him, and I sank down on my chair.

Bones said through his teeth: "Those lice."

Then he gaped.

I swung around in my chair and stared across the room. In the other entrance to the bar. Lane Weston, still in sweater, jodhpurs, and camel's-hair coat, stood holding her riding-crop and staring hard at us.

I hopped to my feet again.

She said coolly: "Never mind, Mr. Roberts. I came down to talk to you and explain what a nice thing you might help to do. But I didn't know about Florida and"—she hesitated and seemed to wince—"the 'dames.' Is that more important to you than doing something worth while?"

I was still a little excited. I growled: "Do you think practically committing suicide is something worth while?"

She flared: "All right!" Her eyes, blue as any china you ever saw under her ivory hair, flashed like blue-steel glinting in the sun. But then she grew quieter. She added in an almost level voice: "I got to the entrance, Mr. Roberts, just in time to hear you. And I'm glad I did. I'm sorry mother and I misjudged you and Mr. McPherson so."

I was getting control of myself. I said: "Misjudged?"

She looked slightly pale. Her hands, gripping the riding-crop, pressed it tightly across her thighs. She said in an odd sing-song voice: "Yes—misjudged. Newspaper publicity is not always authentic, is it? You and Mr. McPherson must have had a lot of lucky breaks—to get where you've gotten on so cheap an attitude."

I gaped. "Huh?"

She kept the strained sing-song voice: "It seems odd to be told you're small, cheap, and common, doesn't it? Well, I'm glad you're not working for Mother, and I hope you like Florida and all of its *dames.*"

Then before I could even bat one eyelash, she spun on her heel and strode out of the bar.

I turned fast on Bones. "Did you hear that?"

He grinned. "Yep. And let's rye again. The last for a long time."

I said: "Have you gone nuts?"

Bones smacked down on the table with his fist. "Gone nuts? We're going to work on this crusade, aren't we? That dame can't talk to us like that!"

CHAPTER II

HELL-BENT FOR HELL

CALVERT CITY, sprawling tangent to Chesa-
peake Bay, had, even during my high school days,
a reputation that made Paris sound like a Quaker town.
Bones and I came in on a train, registered at the *Marti-
nique Hotel*—and ran a gauntlet of beauties in the lobby
who didn't hide their eyes behind newspapers.

All the way up in the elevator Bones whistled cheerfully,
and up in our double room he broke into song. I could tell
he hadn't cared much about the *beach* in Florida; he showered and put on his pin-striped English-drape best.

I showered, too, and while I was doing it, a bellhop came
with an envelope. There proved to be a hotel master key
inside that Mrs. W. had pulled strings for; that woman
could have gotten passes to a closed session of the U.S.
Supreme Court.

The object of the master key was that we had to *sneak*
in the murder-room; we weren't letting Calvert City
know that we were honoring it with a visit. For instance,
our names on the hotel register were Mr. Smith and Mr.
Boom-Twaddle, which last was Bones' idea of a swell sense
of humor.

We ate a dinner of fried oysters down in the hotel grill
and got to the Tip-Top Club exactly at ten. I fiddled
around at the curb, paying off the cab driver, and Bones

waited at the entrance, rubbernecking at the tinted photos of the chorus. But when I came up to him, he'd stopped his rubbernecking. His green eyes were staring intently down the street.

He reached out and gripped my arm. "Remember Jitter? The guy with the pale face?"

I said: "Huh? I got a memory, haven't I?"

He scowled at me. "Well, I just saw him—shiny eyes, pale face, green Alpine hat and all." He jerked a thumb toward the corner. "He got out of a big sedan about half a block behind us."

I said: "Tailing us?"

"Well, what does it look like?"

I whistled. "And after all the trouble you took thinking up that name Boom-Twaddle."

He grinned at me, but the grin looked a little taut, and we pushed through the double doors and went into the club. I was beginning to feel worried; I didn't like the idea of being spotted. If those guys would brace us outside their town, what would they do to us now that we were in?

A blonde with arched eyebrows took our hats and coats, and a headwaiter bowed to us, then looked arrogantly down his long nose. I ranged the club with my eyes and chewed my lip a moment.

"Mr. Weston here yet?"

The headwaiter had an accent. "Meester Tomme Weston? Yes. Thees way, please."

We followed the headwaiter, and as we moved, I tried ranging the club again with my eyes. But the lights were dim, and I couldn't see much. The club was large and square with a circular dance floor, and on the band-shell, a brunette tinkled a miniature piano. The tables were done in black and silver, and the chromium legs of the chairs gleamed dully in the light.

Tommy Weston stood up from his chair at the edge of the dance floor; we shook hands and sat him down again. Over champagne—it had a purpose—I bent forward and looked hard at him.

I said: "Got it straight?"

He stared back at me. Even in the gloom, his cupid's-bow lips looked moist. His eyes, dark and dull and red-streaked at the corners, were more sullen than they'd ever been.

He said: "In a way."

"Look." I tapped his shoulder. "This might not mean your neck, but it might mean *ours,* and I don't crave any bungling. Now get this: You're to introduce us to this Joyce Isbell as Johnny Smith and"—I groaned—"Quentin Boom-Twaddle. She'll know that's a fake—if she doesn't heaven help her... or rather, heaven help us—we want her to know it's a fake."

"But, anyway, we're supposed to be here on a toot—we're drinking champagne, and we'll buy it for her as long as your mother's five hundred bucks holds out. Now that's all you have to do."

He looked even more sullen and asked: "Why pick on Joyce?"

I GROANED again. "Look, fella. If you hate to do something as much as you're hating to do this, why do you let yourself be talked into it?" I sipped at the champagne. "Get the setup? This Joyce Isbell is supposed to be the warmest thing on this side of the country since Hedy Lamarr passed through New York.

"According to your mother, la Joyce has half of the men in this town standing lopsided on their ears, and the other half crazy to get the opportunity. Now, wait. Don't get your dander up. You're nuts about her, aren't you?"

His eyes lost their sullenness and began to show life. You could almost see some defiance in them. He said: "I'm *wild* about her."

I bobbed my head. "Okay. You're wild about her. You probably mean it—most of the others might be looking for glamour." I tried the champagne again. "Now one of the peculiar things about this Joyce Isbell is that this group of forty men didn't seem to exist until after she'd been in this town about two months.

"And your mother thinks that was no coincidence. She says crime and glamour girls go hand in hand, and that this Joyce is enough glamour girl to rate a big boy like Alibi. So that's the hunch we're trying to play—hoping she'll lead us straight to Alibi. We—"

I broke off as Tommy hopped to his feet; he almost tipped the table over. Some of my champagne spilled, but then I grabbed the glass, stared with bulging eyes at Tommy's distorted, hawklike face.

He bent close to me and whispered: "I won't do it."

I screwed my eyes around, didn't see that he'd drawn much attention, stretched out a leg and clamped my foot on his. Then, with apparent playfulness, I pushed him, and he sat down again, hard. I rapped through my teeth:

"Get up and I'll ruin you."

He didn't get up. He sat so still he might have been a rock pile, except for the dull glow of anger in his eyes. But he whispered again:

"*I won't do it.*"

I drank some champagne. There were a few curious glances in our direction, but when nothing further happened, the glances went away. I drank more champagne. I said:

"Oh, yes, you will. There's a leak somewhere close to your mother, and I've got an idea that leak is you. Who else could it be—your sister, Lane? How did those two mugs find out"—I snapped my fingers—"like that, that your mother had called us in to see her? How much did they pay you—about fifty lousy bucks?"

For a moment he didn't speak. His eyes popped out so far they looked like they might drop in his drink—but then his face simply went to pieces.

"I didn't," he whispered. "I tell you I didn't."

I growled: "In your hat. How much?"

He wouldn't look at me. He lowered his gaze down to the table, then slid it farther down to his lap. He said: "Two hundred dollars."

Bones had his elbow on the table and his chin perched on a fist. He said incredulously: "You sit there and admit it?"

The boy said nothing. He just dabbed fast at his lips.

I sipped more champagne. "Listen, Tommy lad. This is all for now because there's a dame heading for us, and if it isn't Joyce Isbell, I'll take her, instead. Because they don't make 'em any nicer than this one. Remember your part?"

He still said nothing.

Bones and I got up politely as the girl reached the table.

She was all her advance notice had promised her to be—even to looks, which is a small part of a battle. She had the sleekest blue-black hair you ever saw, worn in the new upswept fashion and piled on the top of her beautifully made head. Her eyes were a dark blue, almost a smoky blue—with a look that seemed to take you right smack inside of them.

That was as far as I got before I took her hand; she held it longer than was necessary and my back enjoyed chills.

I yanked out a chair for her and reached for the champagne, but a waiter beat me to it, and I substituted cigarettes. She blew out my match with her first deep inhale.

Then she said: "How do you do, Mr. Shaughnessy Roberts? How do you like our fair little town?"

I almost tumbled out of my chair.

She patted my hand and added: "And don't look so surprised. Your newspaper pictures don't do you justice." She smiled. "Nor do yours, Mr. McPherson. How do *you* like our town?"

BONES HAD his hand stopped in midair. He didn't drink from his glass; he didn't do anything but practically dislocate his jaw. But he recovered quickly. Always fast on the cracks, he came back at her with:

"You actually get city newspapers down in this burg?"

An immensely tall, dark-visaged and savage-eyed man appeared at Bones' shoulder and looked down at us. He had enough dignity to make a queen blush like a schoolgirl. His dinner jacket fitted him like you always hope a tailor might fit you. He wore steel-rimmed spectacles over his savage eyes; but his mustache was more prominent than a horn on a bull and looked like a swathe of black ribbon across his upper lip.

He fixed his eyes on Joyce and said: "Not too long at one table, my dear."

She sipped at the champagne, and without moving the glass from her soft mouth, said: "Be right along, Anton, darling. Mr. Roberts, Mr. Zwieg."

I stood up, and as Joyce Isbell introduced Bones, I gave Anton Zwieg as stiff a bow as he handed me. Evidently, nobody had ever taught the guy how to shake hands.

Then after a few polite formalities, Joyce started away. I stepped over in front of her, and she swerved simply from reflex. But I shifted after her, blocked her again. I grinned and said:

"Not without a dance. You don't mind?"

She didn't even look at Zwieg. She smiled and said softly: "Should I mind?"

I led her slowly out on the floor. I could almost feel Zwieg's savage eyes knifing me in the back. I said: "Well, I hope this turns out to be a beginning. Maybe you'll even let me carry your books home from school."

She came close to me but didn't speak, and I put my arm around her—and then stood still. Those chills had begun steeplechasing up and down my spine. Maybe a few times in your life you've run into that; you just touch a girl and she gives you the shivers. There was music, and I kept my arm around her, but we didn't dance.

My voice came out huskily. "There some place we can talk?"

Her face sobered. Her smile went away entirely and our gazes locked; it seemed like everything around us just fell away. We were standing there in a world of our own.

She whispered softly: "There's my office."

My voice was huskier. "Office—here?"

Her hand closed tightly on my arm. "Well, my dressing room—more or less."

I breathed deeply. I was still trying to think. I said: "Whatever brought you to a town like this?"

Our gazes were still locked; her eyes didn't change. She said in the same soft throbbing voice: "You wouldn't believe it. Nobody ever does. I was a novelist—and a pretty good one, too. I was an intelligent novelist—but they don't make much money. And writing intelligently is such terribly hard work."

My voice was still husky. I said: "Yes?"

"It was so really hard—and I didn't need to work that way. I had a face and figure to trade in—for something soft like this."

I drew in breath. I said: "And so?"

"And so then I met Anton, and traded them in. When he told me he was opening a club here, I used them for barter."

I stared at her. Her words were used like I'd always imagined a novelist would use them; her meaning was commonplace but her manner of putting it was picturesque. Then my stare seemed to break our spell—and Zwieg loomed, towered beside us.

I looked up quickly. His dark face was swollen, congested with angry blood. He said low through his teeth:

"The music's stopped."

It was then I gawked. I must have looked like a farm boy at his first country fair; I stared around with my arms loose at my sides. And up on the bandshell the brunette had stopped playing. People were grinning at us.

But Joyce merely smiled and looked up in my eyes again. "Later?"

I stared at Anton Zwieg. I said, not moving my eyes from his face: "Sure, later. A dozen or so times."

I WATCHED Joyce move away beside the immensely tall man, then drew in breath and went back to our table. Bones had a grin on his face that you could have driven a truck into. But Tommy's chair was empty, and I didn't see him nearby.

I sat down and scowled. I didn't like that. I said: "Where's the young louse?"

Bones kept grinning. He said: "Where were you—up in the moon?"

Our champagne bottle was empty. I sent the waiter scurrying. "Look," I said. "Whenever you see me making a play for a gal, you know it's business—I don't sail for 'em like you do." But that was weak, and I knew it, and I could see Bones knew it. I added: "I was getting some information. What do you think I was doing?"

Bones said: "Boy, I'd hate to tell you. You might mow me down." He kept grinning. "Our young louse went to the washroom. Here he comes back."

I screwed my eyes around and watched Tommy trudge through the gloom; I noticed for the first time that he was wearing sports clothes. He had on a shaggy brown sport coat and odd tan slacks; that's the rich young man's idea of café society dress. But nobody was formal at the club, anyway—except Zwieg, the owner, who didn't count.

Tommy came up to us noiselessly on shoes with thick yellow crepe soles, slid into his chair and just glared sullenly.

I wiggled a finger at him. "Look, fella. To get back—"

Bones gripped my arm. "Shag! Take a gander—quick!"

I spun around in the chair and followed his gaze. There was a large foyer out by the checkroom, and standing in the entrance was our pale-faced Jitter. He had his green Alpine hat in his hand and was stabbing sharp glances swiftly around the club.

I shouldn't have hopped to my feet. It was a sap's play, but I couldn't draw sitting down—not as fast as I could with no chairs or tables to hinder me. And it was when

I got up, knocking my chair spinning, that the pale-face Jitter laid eyes on me.

But he didn't do what I expected him to do; he didn't yank a gun and blast at me through the gloom. He spun around and scampered across the foyer, plunged through the double doors and slammed them behind him. And then Bones shot up beside me. He yelled in my ear:

"After that mug!"

I wasn't doing a lot of thinking that night; I suppose it's natural to follow a guy when he turns and runs away. Anyway, I let some reefs out of my legs. We burst out into the street as a sedan groaned away from the curb, and saw Mr. Jitter peering out of the front window. There was a cab parked at the curb just behind the sedan, and we made for that.

I got some bills out of my pocket and waved them at the driver. "Stick behind that tan car! There's a fin in it for you!"

The cab bounced away with a jerk that smacked me back on the leather cushions, and by the time I got set again, we were twisting through traffic. Ahead of us, the tan sedan streaked down the boulevard. Its twin tail-lights, like bloodshot eyes in the dark, slowly but surely grew dimmer and dimmer.

I tapped on the glass and the driver slid it open. I shoved the five at him and yelled: "Take the brake off, for Pete's sake!"

He took the five off my fingers, then yelled something back at me; I gathered his company's cabs were quite hampered by governors. I sat back and groaned. The twin tail-lights ahead got even dimmer, then flicked around a corner and just disappeared.

I groaned again and snapped at Bones: "Son, they stack all the cards against you in this town."

We sat and fretted until our cab reached that corner, then craned our necks forward as it leaned on the turn. But there were no twin tail-lights ahead of us as far as we could see; the street dipped down a hill after two or three blocks.

The cab lined along until we reached the top of the hill, then the driver slowed it a few feet beyond the crest. He yelled at us without sliding back the glass:

"Think I've got a flat! Hold everything a minute!"

He hopped out on the running board, yanked down the hand-throttle, and before I realized it, had jumped off and was running away. The cab leaped forward, and almost bounced us through the top; I got my balance in a few moments and stared ahead helplessly.

We were charging down a steep grade with nobody at the wheel; were already doing forty and gaining speed fast. And you could tell we were headed down a dead-end street; there was a red reflector ahead of us, winking warningly in the dark.

CHAPTER III

MURDER-ROOM AMBUSH

I **'D KNOWN** a lot of bad moments up to that one, but none that seemed actually to petrify and paralyze me. Whatever was beyond that reflector, I didn't know; it might be a stone wall, it might be a drop. But I just sat like a Sphinx and watched that red light rush toward us—until Bones leaped for a door and pure reflex drove me after him.

I grabbed his arms and hauled him back on the seat. I yelled in his ear:

"You'll break your neck, you fool! Try the front glass!"

I jerked off his hat and stuck it over his hand; he got the idea and went to work. He threw a punch at the glass directly behind the wheel almost before I got off my own hat. But it was like hitting concrete; he nearly broke his wrist.

That glass was bullet-proof, like in a lot of these new cabs; they want to protect their drivers from holdup guys and their gats. And the handle for the panel is outside, where only the driver can reach it. Bones was stymied. He just stared hopelessly at me.

I got my fist balled in the crown of my own hat and socked the glass on my door and found that wasn't bullet-proof. Then I hauled out my little gun, elbowed glass out of the way, leaned out and shot a hole in the cab's right front tire. The car swerved so quickly I was thrown halfway out; I got back in as we bounced half a mile over the curb.

But I was hurled back in through no effort of my own; I landed on Bones as a tree swiped one of our fenders. Then we skimmed over a yard, lost a lot of speed through a hedge, shot up somebody's porch steps before we tipped over. We carried a porch railing with us and the engine kept roaring; I could barely hear Bones yelling at me over it.

Then I got it. It was: "Shag! For cripes sake! Get off my belly!"

I rolled off his belly and got to my hands and knees; the cab was plunked on its left side with my broken window yawning over me. Bones sat up beside me and gingerly felt his ribs. I could hear excited voices and running feet.

I scowled at Bones and rubbed the seat of my pants. I said: "You skinny mutt. I thought I was sitting on broken glass."

I got out of the cab by simply opening the door and crawling out; Bones crawled out beside me, and I turned around and stared. There was a brick wall of a factory a few feet beyond that reflector; if we'd cracked that wall, the ambulance boys would have had to syphon us from the cab.

And there was a small knot of people gathering on the sidewalk, some more gathering in the next yard; a few came running up. But I didn't answer any questions; I just memorized the cab's license number. Then I whipped out my little gun, and Bones and I walked.

When we reached the sidewalk and nobody said anything, I knew we were all right, and kept walking fast. After two blocks, I pocketed my gun and we started to jog. But we'd barely covered two more blocks before there was a shrill screech of a police siren. A prowl car, doing seventy, shot past us at the next corner, and when we reached the main boulevard, two more rocked by.

Somebody had evidently called in about my shot.

We caught a cab a few blocks farther and drew some stares from the driver; we were mussed up and cut a little from all the broken glass. At the hotel we drew more stares, but I didn't care; it was those prowl cars that mattered. We didn't want to get mixed up with any cops at this point. Not in a town where the police commissioner might be one of our quarry.

Bones keyed open the door—and we were staring at Lane Weston.

SHE WORE a woolly-looking green dress and had taken her hat off. She was reading Bones' copy of *Esquire*— he keeps up with the styles—and was lying on her tummy on my twin bed with an apple in her mouth. She didn't take the apple out, either; she just waved a hand. I slammed the door and snapped at her:

"How did *you* get in?"

This time she removed the apple and smiled over it at us. "I played flirt with a bellboy. Where did you get the blood?"

I snorted. I didn't see any reason why I shouldn't tell her, and I let her have it all, even making it more dangerous than it really had been. But she just lay there coolly, taking it all in; she didn't show any more excitement than when she'd asked me about the blood.

I figured here was a lady who could even keep her wits in a shopping jam. Then I said: "Well, that's the crop. Now why are you here?"

She just smiled again. "I'm supposed to help you."

I stared. "You're what?"

"Help you. It's mother's idea. In case you want to examine the murder room, I can act as decoy. The room has a police detective on guard."

I said: "Decoy? Look, Miss Westen. Do you mean to tell me your mother'll let you mix up in this mess? Tommy, yeah—all he had to do was introduce us, anyway—but—" I broke off and wagged my head.

She sat up and dropped an apple seed carefully in the wastebasket. "Mother doesn't even have a bodyguard, Mr. Roberts. She knows she won't ever be harmed, and she knows neither Tommy nor I will be. With her reputation as a crime crusader, everybody decent in the state would take up arms. You see, the criminals know that—they're not so dumb. Besides, mother doesn't trust anybody down here to help you."

I wagged my head again. I had to admit it; Mrs. W. didn't overlook any angles. I growled: "Well, okay. You're just another *dame* in my young life." But that didn't seem to get an effect and I scowled at her. "Well, here's something else you can do before you turn decoy. Run down to the lobby and use a pay phone and tell police headquarters who you are.

"Then tell 'em your mother's interested in that cab that just smashed up—the license number's nine-six-o-eight. Ask 'em if it was reported stolen—before the smashup. They ought to tell you—and by the time you get back we'll be cleaned up." I looked around. "You got another apple?"

She said: "What you need is some iodine. I'll bring some back."

Lane left very briskly and returned in about twenty minutes, bringing not only iodine, but apples, and plenty of information. It seemed that the cab had been reported stolen over two hours before the smash; but I'd expected that, anyway, because otherwise The Forty Thieves might have left a trail.

Still, there was something about the whole mess that had a distinctly rotten odor, and although I had ideas on it, none of them made much sense. So Bones and I sat and munched apples while Lane touched up our cuts. Then we began to get down to the nice business of sneaking into that murder room.

It was exactly eleven forty-three when we had a bottle of whisky sent up, and it was twelve minutes later when I finished my work on the phone. This latter consisted of six calls, one each to rooms that were on the same corridor with the murder room. And it was on the sixth call that the hotel operator said that room was unoccupied; by this time she was boiling and thought I was fried.

I thanked her and hung up, and Bones sprayed whisky on Lane's clothes. She took a drink just for courage, and then we were off.

I slipped her the master key her mother had sent us, when we left the elevator at the third floor. She walked on ahead of us like the best-natured drunk in the world. When she turned into the murder-room corridor, Bones and I put on some speed. I got down on my hands and knees and peeped around the corner.

Lane was reeling like a sailor, and the cop was looking up from his magazine; he was in plainclothes by the murder-room door. He kept staring in Lane's direction even after she keyed her way into the empty room. Then her scream bounced him out of his chair like he had springs a mile thick in his pants.

I hopped up and whispered: "Son, get set. The marlin just struck."

I could hear Bones take in breath when I poked my head out again, and I was just in time to see the cop's coattail whisk through Lane's open door. I waited for a moment, made sure she'd left the key on the outside, then sneaked down and snatched it with the hair crawling on my neck.

Like we'd planned, Lane's noise drowned out mine; she was telling the cop, but not too loudly, that there had been a man in her room.

BONES AND I scooted past the open door while the detective was peeping under the bed. The master key let us into the murder room without any trouble. Then we hauled out flashlights and went to work. We had half an hour to make our canvass in—if Lane could hold that cop that long.

The first five minutes seemed like five years, and I didn't get anything out of it but a good idea of the setup. There was a chair in the center of the room, facing the door—and that was the chair Hubbell had been found in. And I had a good idea why he had been using that chair. A private dick who knew his racket—and Andy Hubbell was one of the best—would sleep sitting up, if he had those Forty Thieves after him.

Bones whispered at me: "Boy, just take a look at this."

His light was hurling a cone of brilliance on the desk-top of a secretary, and I moved over there, stared down at his hands. He was holding what proved to be two steam-ship tickets for a trip to Bermuda on a luxury liner. Bones waved his light and growled:

"We want to take one to Florida—he buys tickets for one to Bermuda. And he's deader than a fried egg—and we're working on his job."

I was peering at the tickets. "Both for the same state-room and dated for no less than yesterday." I shaped my mouth to whistle, then caught myself. "Looks like he was going picnicking with some dame."

Bones grunted. He said: "And *what* a dame, son. Wipe the cobwebs out of your eyes and take a peek at these."

He shoved a handful of snapshots of Joyce Isbell at me, and I stood there in the dark gripping the flashlight tight enough to crack it. The yellow envelope they'd been in was dated just four days back, and there were plenty of negatives inside it that matched with the snapshots.

It looked like I wasn't the only guy Joyce gave the shivers to. And Andy Hubbell had evidently given the shivers to her.

Bones nudged me and said: "I won't look at your face, son. But when you don't talk, something's bad."

I scowled and went back to my prowling; I felt like my chest had been filled up with lead. Maybe that doesn't make much sense, but then those things never do; you never know when Lord Romance is going to pin back your ears. Here I'd just seen a girl once and talked to her five minutes, and I felt like I'd caught my first girl in grade-school pitching woo with the janitor.

But I just kept moving and worked on my prowling; that seemed like the best way to laugh the thing off.

And then I poked my light down in the wastebasket.

It wasn't much that I found. Just a long strip of paste-board that had been ripped from the rim of an ordinary box-top. But I stage-whispered to Bones:

"Hold everything, boy."

Before he could answer me, I turned and scooted across the room, put the beam of my light down at the bottom of the door. There was about three feet of bare floor between the door and the carpet, and I dropped down on my knees, placed my light beam closer. In the cracks between the floorboards, tiny particles glittered at me; I didn't have to look twice to know they were glass. I hopped to my foot and said:

"Boy, this is it. Now we got something."

Bones said: "Huh?"

I started to explain—and then a noise in the hall held me rigid. But it didn't come again, and I exhaled some air. Pivoting, I slipped quietly to the door, opened it and shoved out my nose. I didn't see anybody, but the corridor seemed strangely quiet.

Then there was a loud report, and lead zoomed past me. The door jamb splintered just an inch above my head.

CHAPTER IV

CLUES TO A KILLER

SO FAR I hadn't used much sense in this entire mess—and right then was when I made my prize bright move. I dropped on my belly on the threshold instead of ducking back inside, and the second volley of shots took off my hat. I was lying half in the corridor and guns were blazing from both ends, and my chances of paying the next installment on my life insurance were about eight thousand to one.

But then Bones grabbed my feet and hauled me back inside—just in time for me to see two furrows scooped from the floor at the spot where my head had been.

Bones leaned over and yelled: "You ninny! Get that gun out! You think you're playing cops-and-robbers?"

I hauled out my little gun as we had sudden quiet, smoked my hat in from the threshold, put it on my gun-muzzle and shoved it out again. The volley of shots that greeted it didn't make me feel any better. The enemy wasn't shooting and then running; it looked as if we were in for a siege.

Then a single shot rapped down the corridor, and somebody screamed. Bones nudged me and said gleefully:

"Lane's cop, I bet, son. Preserving law and order—our ally."

The scream was followed by another volley, but none of the slugs hit around our door. And I was able to count two guns, whereas before I knew there had been at least three. So I risked my neck again and shoved out my nose. Two shots crashed at me from one direction, but the corridor's other end was quiet.

This time I didn't duck back, but instead poked out my gun and fired at an arm that was training an automatic my way. But I didn't expect to hit and just chipped paint a yard below it; my idea was to give warning that the sides were now even.

Then I saw that the door of the room Lane had gone in was over halfway open; flame belched from there and paint chipped a foot above my hit. Then—too, *too* suddenly—everything was very quiet.

I stood still and ranged my eyes up and down that corridor. The automatic disappeared and no other guns showed, but down at the other end of the corridor I could see the head of a man. It was a small head and too far away to be recognizable; the head was down on the carpet with the eyes staring at the ceiling. It looked as though the enemy had left a casualty behind.

Then feet pounded in the distance, going away.

I stiffened and yelled: "Get back, you fool!"

The police detective had poked his head out the open door and was stepping out after it, gripping his gun. Evidently, he figured that the enemy was lamming. But then a small blur of color at the corridor end shot into view—and became a green Alpine hat on the head of a man.

An automatic was thrust around the corner and flame forked from it; a big bulky man also stepped into view. He fired twice, but the detective was already going down. I shot the bulky man three times in the belly.

Then the hat disappeared and more feet pounded in the distance; I hopped out into the open and legged it toward the corner. I reached it in time to see Jitter make the stairs at the other end, but I didn't follow because there was more important work to be done.

Eyes at door cracks watched me all the way back to the battle scene, but I didn't pay any attention to them. I stopped long enough at the bulky man to discover he wouldn't do any more shooting—or any more threatening in anybody's hotel bar.

Bones was bending over the police detective, and Lane Weston stood beside him, her face as white as the whitest flour. But she had a lot of courage and plenty of cool brain, that girl did. She said to me huskily:

"Don't you think we ought to go?"

I stared. After a baby war like we'd just had—particularly with bodies lying around—you don't expect a blonde vision to do your thinking for you. I just said: "Huh?"

She bit her lip, hard. "The police—or at least, the house detective—will be here any second. Don't you think we really ought to leave?"

I wagged my head, then grinned at Bones. Eyes were still at cracks in doors, but nobody had come out; he was looking down reflectively at the police detective. I said:

"Is he dead?"

Bones grunted. "One went in under his chin and came out behind his left ear."

I just nodded at him.

Then we collected our clues in the murder room, bustled down the side stairs, found a side entrance and left that hotel, fast.

IT WAS exactly five minutes of one when we piled out of a cab at the Tip-Top club. The long-nosed headwaiter spied us from up near the bandshell—where a colored band had replaced the brunette—made a bee-line for us, but we reached Tommy's table ahead of him. Tommy, however, wasn't at his table, and I didn't sec Joyce or Anton Zwieg. Bones signaled the waiter.

I said to Bones: "You two stay here, boy. I got things to do."

The waiter was pouring us champagne. When he left, Bones scowled at me. "Such as finishing that dance with the glamour girl—and getting Zwieg's shiv in your ribs?"

I said: "Nix. Such as walking up to the person who knocked off Andy Hubbell and accusing them of it." I wiggled a finger at him. "Let's have the tickets and snapshots. I've got the pasteboard."

Bones just goggled at me. "You going screwy on me again?"

I grinned. "Not me, laddie." Then I watched Lane Weston sip champagne. Her eyes watched *me* over the glass. I took the tickets and snapshots from Bones and asked: "Did you phone anywhere besides police headquarters when you went downstairs at the hotel?"

Her sleek brows climbed. "Why, yes. Tommy."

I said: "Here at the club?"

"Uh-huh. He was worried. He made me promise to keep in touch with him." She put her glass down. "You should have heard the instructions he gave me about how to be a careful decoy."

I said: "You should hear the instructions I'm going to give somebody about how *not* to try to kill Bones and me." I stuffed the tickets and snapshots in my pocket. "And don't drink too much of that champagne. If you do, you get the check."

I spun on my heel and hiked through the tables, thinking hard. At the other side of the club I stopped and slid my gaze around. I still didn't see either Joyce or Anton Zwieg.

I stopped a cigarette girl in beige opera stockings. "Where's—"

"That way," she said, and jerked a thumb toward the foyer.

I grinned at her. "Hear a guy out, lady. Why should I wash my hands? I mean Miss Isbell's dressing room."

She gave me a bored scrutiny—but a scrutiny, nevertheless. Evidently, she decided that somehow I rated an answer. She said, "That way," and pointed with her chin at a door beside the band-shell.

The door was unlocked, and when I pushed it open I stopped on the threshold and stood there grinning. Joyce was leaning against a very large flat-topped desk, and Tommy was pacing the floor, muttering furiously. His dull dark eyes held a nasty glow of anger. But he stopped pacing when he saw me, stopped muttering.

I hadn't caught any of his words. But I didn't need to. I said: "What's the matter, Thomas? Doesn't she love you any more?"

His face sulked. "Where do you get the right—"

I interrupted him: "To bust in here without knocking, just like I own her?" I wiggled a finger. "Shucks, Thomas. I'm one of her victims—just like you, Zwieg, and our pal, Andy Hubbell. We're all brothers in the great Sucker Lodge of Romance."

I hadn't looked at Joyce since I'd come in, and now I placed my eyes on her and tried to keep my grin. But I couldn't do it; she was already too deep under my skin. I didn't look cow-eyed, but I got serious, all right. Her dark blue eyes were still strange, boldly inviting worlds.

But I kept remembering that Andy Hubbell had tried to live in them. That made things different, but I still couldn't grin.

I just wrenched my eyes from hers and said: "The great Sucker Lodge of Romance. It makes murderers out of people."

SHE STARED at me. It was the first time I'd ever seen her when she showed any surprise, but the effect didn't injure her beauty a bit. She leaned forward and said: "You know who killed Andy!"

"Yeah," I said, and pointed a finger. "And I know who's been trying to kill Bones and little me."

Tommy Weston stood as still as the sky, watching my finger swivel slowly toward him. Then his face sagged and turned the color of sand. He cowered back and screamed:

"You're a liar! You're mad!"

"Am I?" I whipped at him. I yanked the tickets and snapshots from my pocket and waved them in his face. "Look at these, bright boy! Andy Hubbell and Joyce were going away together. You couldn't stand anybody having her, could you?"

He kept cowering away from me. "Don't believe him, Joyce! I tell you he's mad!"

I growled: "I'll show you how mad I am, youngster." I pulled the pasteboard from my pocket and waved that at him. "Andy Hubbell slept sitting up. The old trick is to have newspaper spread around on the floor, so if anybody gets into the room, the rattle of them stepping on it will wake you up.

"But the new trick is about ten hundred per cent better. You take the top of a pasteboard box, rip off half of the rim, then stick the rest of it on the top of the door when you close it. And that leaves you a shelf that'll fall if the door's opened—and you put an electric bulb up on that shelf.

"Ever hear a bulb hit the floor from that distance? It sounds like a shot, and not only wakes up the guy who planted it—it scares the hell out of the guy who's coining in." I threw the paste board at him. "Didn't it scare *you?*"

But he just screamed again: "I tell you, Joyce, he's mad!"

I snapped: "You're going to say that once too often, Thomas." I pointed my finger again. "Where were you the night Hubbell was killed?"

He cowered back against the wall, his face twisted and distorted, and his moist lips drooling. He screamed: "I was here! Tell him, Joyce!"

I didn't look at her. She said slowly: "He was here. He was here, that is, for two or three hours."

I growled: "And wearing that outfit?"

Her voice was very quiet. "I'm not sure it was that one, but it was some sort of sports clothes. And now I think of it, I've never seen him here in anything else."

I still didn't look at Joyce. I just moved. It took three long steps to get me across that big office; then I grabbed Tommy Weston's wrist and yanked him toward me. He didn't struggle; he was too surprised. I slammed him down and bent over him, and felt the crepe soles of his shoes.

I straightened up and rapped: "So I'm mad, am I? Well, there's bits of *glass* stuck in those crepe soles. Glass that you stepped on when Andy Hubbell's light bulb smashed at your feet. And do you think you can get out of that?"

He said: "What?" And then clawed like a crazy man at his thick crepe soles.

I laughed at him. I reached down, caught his coat lapels, hauled him to his feet and shook him, hard. "So you'll try to kill Bones and me, will you? You'll hire Jitter and his pal to scare us up in the hotel bar so we won't come down and investigate your little murder, will you? And you'll send Jitter in the club here with instructions to beat it when we spot him—knowing the natural thing for us to do is beat it out after him like saps."

I shook him harder. "Well, your cab trick flunked, but your murder-room ambush almost worked. There was just one of those gunmen who was a little too impatient. If he'd've waited two minutes longer, we'd both have been out in the corridor. As it was, that gunman missed me by the width of an ant's leg.

"And *you* ran away, making lots of noise, trying to make us think the coast was clear, didn't you? Oh, you're clever, all right—you tricked our cop ally. But you hadn't planned on him helping us—you overlooked that."

I shook him some more, so hard that his teeth rattled. "Well, the next time you be just a little cleverer—and don't pretend you're worried about your sister and have her phone so you can get information. And don't fake big powder burns on your victim—although I don't know how you did it—and then leave him with a revolver. Revolvers don't make big powder burns.

"And when you clean up the glass from a light bulb, be sure and get down between the floorboards—and you might also remember to take the glass out of your crepe soles. Incidentally, where did you get the key to Hubbell's room?"

He wouldn't look at me. He raised his eyes pleadingly to Joyce. He said: "I—stole it from Lane."

I was stunned. "Lane!" I yelled.

He didn't answer me. He hung his head and stared miserably at the floor, then put his face in his hands and began to blubber like a baby.

And it was at that instant that the door of the office slammed open. Anton Zwieg, staring over a big blue gun, said coldly:

"You will please put up your hands and make no attempts to do otherwise. Hold your palms upward and outward, and do not move or speak."

CHAPTER V

THE DEATH VOTE

T<small>**HE PRECISE**</small> voice of the man, so assured and confident, didn't leave any doubt in my mind just what to do. I shoved my hands up, followed directions about my palms, stood motionless as a granite tomb, and even choked back some lip.

Zwieg stepped to one side of the doorway and gestured toward it with the gun. "Now you will please go through the door and turn to your right. You will put your hands down, of course, and will walk naturally. Please follow the wall until you reach the next door, then enter that room and walk to the desk in its center.

"And I need not tell you that I shall be a yard behind you. Any false move on your part, and I shall certainly shoot you like a rat."

I shrugged and started forward—but then Joyce touched my arm.

I peered sideways at her. But she wasn't looking at me. Her eyes were on Zwieg, and she said: "Anton!"

His voice didn't change. "Mr. Roberts, my dear, is wanted by the police. He has been identified as one of the participants in a shooting at his hotel." He gestured with the gun again. "It is most unfortunate, but we must observe our duties."

I knew he was lying in his teeth about observing any duties, but I just looked at Joyce and grinned, and breezed out the door. Zwieg came out behind me—and then I slowed down. The door we were heading for wasn't hard to see, and it was far enough past the band-shell so I could see our table a few seconds. And that would give Bones a chance to see me.

I put my brain on extra shift trying to figure a way to signal him. But this Anton Zwieg was nobody's fool. When I slowed, he stepped close to me and whispered softly:

"You will walk a good deal faster, and not look either to the right or left. You will make no attempts to signal, and continue to conduct yourself naturally."

I noticed out of my eye-corners that he had his gun in his right pocket, and that he kept me to the right of him, which kept his left side to the club. When we reached the door, I shoved it open and went in, walked to the desk like he had told me to do. I didn't know whether or not Bones had even seen us.

Zwieg shut the door behind him and called: "Nemo!"

A door that looked twice as thick as the one behind Zwieg opened to admit a small-boned, marcelled Filipino dandy. Zwieg inclined his head that way, and said:

"Please, Mr. Roberts."

I've had quite a lot of shocks on going through doors, but the one I got then drove me back on my heels. The horseshoe desk in one corner was the size of a newspaper copy desk. In front of it, two blue leather chairs looked large enough to play ball in, and under it, a blue Chinese rug looked thick enough to weigh tons.

I just stood and gaped at the room—until the Filipino's hand in my back knocked the gape off my face.

He pushed me from a foot over the threshold to the middle of that Chinese rug.

I swung around, grinning a little, but he was too far away for a punch to reach him.

Zwieg wiggled the gun and said: "Be seated, please, Mr. Roberts."

I chose one of the blue leather chairs in front of the huge desk, and Zwieg went around behind the desk and seated himself in the curve of the horseshoe. But he kept the blue gun carefully trained on my chin.

He picked up a telephone, then put it down and said: "How careless of us, Nemo. Have you searched Mr. Roberts?"

I didn't hear the Filipino say anything.

But Zwieg smiled coldly and said: "Well, do so. Oh, yes. Please do so—by all means."

I didn't hear the dandy behind me, but I did feel his breath on my neck. At Zwieg's word I stood up, and Nemo whisked away my little gun; I sat down again and scowled across the desk. Nemo shoved my gun in his coat pocket and walked off to one side, watching me with small, bright black eyes. He looked like he wouldn't mind sawing me in half.

Zwieg put his gun down and picked up the telephone again. He said into it: "I'm not in for any outside calls."

THEN HE re-cradled that phone and opened a large drawer beside him.

He took out a telephone head-set, and clapped it on. There was a dial beside him, attached to the desk-edge, and he picked up a metal-topped pencil, dragged a long sheet of paper near him. He began dialing with the pencil's metal top, his savage eyes not leaving me.

But before he got his first number, he said softly: "Our organization, Mr. Roberts, has a private telephone system. It is one of the few independently operated systems in the country."

I just gawked at him.

He said into his head-set mouthpiece: "Yes... No. We're voting on Mr. Roberts and Mr. McPherson, and our man, Jitter Mack.... No. Please let me explain... What?"

He laughed—a cold, bitter laugh—and kept staring at me. "No. Please, Gordon, have patience, and hear me out. You see—"

I was already gripping the chair arm so tight my muscles ached, and I leaned forward and drank in every word. I'd thought that stuff about the police wanting me was just an excuse to Joyce and Tommy, but I hadn't expected to step into Alibi's private lair.

At that point, I would have bet my coupé against a baby's G-man scooter that the sheet of paper he had beside him had forty names on it. I watched the guy when he finished talking to his Gordon, and he made a check mark in a column opposite a name.

I tugged at my collar. "You say you're voting on something?"

Zwieg's broad mustache twitched. "The telephone system saves us considerable time and the inconvenience of a meeting. Yes, we are."

I grinned—but probably the grin was a little taut. I didn't like sitting there listening to him talk; I particularly didn't like listening to the election returns roll in. There was about as much doubt in my mind as to what the voting was for as there is in a bridegroom's when he struts up the aisle.

I was listening to forty guys, probably calm and comfortable in their homes, knit their placid brows over whether or not I should *live.*

And the first ten votes all went in one column.

I squirmed a good deal in my chair and said: "I can see it's a landslide, but would you mind saying which way?"

Zwieg looked up from the paper. "Why, certainly. The trend seems to be against you."

I said: *"Trend?"* I tugged at my collar again. "Brother, that's a masterpiece of understatement, and I still don't know why. We didn't have any more on you guys than a hoochie dancer at an old men's stag."

Zwieg took off his steel-rimmed spectacles, polished them, and then put them back on his nose. He said: "My dear Mr. Roberts. Unfortunately for you, I was informed immediately of the shooting in your hotel. And of the three men who died, two were our men—they were not, however, working for us at the hotel. Still, it's possible that those men talked before dying, and we have no way to ascertain this correctly.

"If we tortured you, it would undoubtedly be useless— you certainly would not incriminate yourself. We credit you with sufficient intelligence to realize that if you admitted the men talked, we would certainly kill you, for there would be no alternative. We couldn't afford to let you go with the information you'd possess."

I said nastily: "Or let me go now that I've been in your den."

He gave me that cold smile. "The voting on *you,* Mr. Roberts, is merely a formality. Your reputation in itself sufficiently assures us that we would be guilty of foolhardiness to allow you lo go free. However, we are against killings"—he said that as calmly as if they were against salt in your beer—"and we try to avoid them whenever it's possible.

"Mr. McPherson, we feel, would not endanger us without you—unless he has learned valuable information from our men before they died. Consequently, we—"

I said: "Don't be a ninny."

His savage eyes seemed to jump at me.

"Look," I growled. "Your men talked and they talked plenty, and we've relayed it all to Mrs. W. Why do you think we came back here? Because those men hadn't died when we left, and we figured some of your forty thieves were on the cops. And suppose those wounded guys talked to them? We weren't taking a chance on them warning you, and you slipping away, my mustachioed friend. Do you think Bones and I would be saps enough for that?"

I WAS working hard on my bluff, and was half out of my chair, and I got to him enough to bounce him clean out of his. I had one chance to live, and nobody was going to say I didn't try it; but the chance was as slim as a molecule's waist.

If I could prod him into action, he might forget me for a moment: I wanted just one moment—so I could get that dandy by the throat. With that situation, I knew I could get my gun back, and with my gun in my fist—well, I'd *like* the odds even with Zwieg.

Zwieg, still standing, bent and whipped furiously at the dial.

I rapped through my teeth: "Call brother. Call any one, or all of 'em. Mrs. W.'s got the *state* cops—a whole damned batallion."

I was still half out of my chair and I got my legs set under me; Zwieg straightened with a jerk and stood so motionless he seemed frozen. But this was only for an instant. Before I'd hardly had time to bat my eyes, he had abandoned his dial and was leaning across the desk.

He slapped open an annunciator and buzzed it three times.

When there was no answering buzz, his lips thinned to a grim line. He snapped at the dandy: "Wait here, Nemo. I'll be back in a moment."

I got my legs set a little more firmly under me, watched him take off his head-set and stride out of the mouth of that horseshoe. His big blue gun still lay on the desk near the dial. I watched its barrel gleam in the light, realized it was too far away for me to get it before Nemo could draw.

I waited until Zwieg was halfway across the room.

Maybe it was a sap's way for anybody to jump a gun, but I didn't know Nemo had one in his hand. The last time I'd looked at him, he had just been standing off hating me—but when I pivoted and leaped, I saw the glint of gun-metal in front of him.

But at that point there wasn't anything I could do about it; I was in the air and the gun was pointing at my face. But Nemo didn't shoot, and anyway, I misjudged the distance. I landed a yard short on all fours, and he stepped forward and gun-whipped me.

It felt like shrapnel was banging around inside my skull.

Then, later on, I was crawling around, not knowing exactly where I was going. I saw five or six of Nemo, and then three of Zwieg; I must have been out no more than a few seconds, because he hadn't left the room. I heard his precise voice say to the Filipino:

"Admirably done, Nemo. Admirably done."

Then Nemo said: "I thought it unwise to shoot him here, sir."

"Splendid thinking, Nemo. It will be far better else-where."

Zwieg placed his savage eyes on me a moment, then pivoted toward the room's thick door. I watched three of him dwindle into two, and wondered if my head would ever stop aching. Then, oddly, I saw two of Bones.

Maybe the condition of my head would have made anybody wonder; I thought I'd simply gone batty, and that was that. But there Bones was, standing in the doorway, leering over a very small gun.

Zwieg had just opened the thick door, and now he jerked back like he'd been hit, and Bones' gaze swiveled as Nemo spun. For one awful instant I thought Nemo was winning, but then Bones shot him twice before the dandy's gun even went off. Nemo fell at my feet and his gun banged at nothing.

Then Bones pointed his small gun at Zwieg and growled: "Try some funnybones, hot shot. I've got special slugs for you."

Zwieg backed up slowly into the middle of the room, and I looked at Bones and still saw two of him. I wanted to say something, but couldn't find words; then when I did find them I couldn't find my voice. It was down somewhere around my toes, and by the time it crawled through me it came out with a peculiar, choked-like sound:

"Why, you old skinny freckled son-of-a-gun."

He grinned. He didn't hear me because he didn't come back at me; he just winked merrily and said: "Take a guess."

This time my voice eased out in a faint whisper. I said: "Take a guess at what?"

His grin broadened. He winked again and said: "How I knew something smelled."

I didn't say anything, and he chuckled to himself. He said: "Look, son. I saw you marching across the club with this Zwieg guy, and I saw him step up close to you and whisper almost in your ear. And you didn't open your trap. So I said to Lane, 'When that guy doesn't talk, especially when somebody talks to him, something is bad, and no mistake.'"

He patted the small pearl-handled revolver he held. "And so finally, when you seemed to be here too long, I started over and Lane loaned me this little gun."

I said: "You mean you just got here?"

HE GRINNED again. "Hell, no. That door was locked and I wasn't fool enough to play with it, and maybe tip ten thousand guys that I was out there. But I could hear your voice through it, and you didn't sound happy, although I couldn't catch any of your words."

He laughed and moved his skinny shoulders. "So—well, I just stuck around."

I was still on the floor and I got to my feet. My head was throbbing like a motor was inside it, and my stomach felt like it was upside down. I gritted my teeth and choked back the nausea, but when I looked down at Nemo, it came shooting back up at me. He had a hole over his left eye and another in a nostril; the little slug had torn half his nose away.

I turned away, but then leaned on the desk and just succeeded in not ruining that nice Chinese rug. But then I heard footsteps and looked toward the doorway and saw the cigarette girl and headwaiter staring with bulging eyes.

The headwaiter's gaze jerked to Zwieg. He said: "But, sir! These shots! We hear them inside!"

I said: "Then come in and be comfortable."

He gaped. "Pardon."

My voice was beginning to come back to normal. I growled: "Look, bud. I don't know whether you're mixed up in this or not, but—"

I broke off as feet pounded heavily through the outer office, and Tommy appeared in the doorway, breathless and shaking. He thrust the headwaiter aside, almost bowled over the girl, burst in and didn't even stop at sight of Nemo. He just waved his arms and screamed:

"They've got Lane!"

Bones said: "Huh?"

Tommy didn't even look at him. He waved his arms at me. "Well, do something! Don't just stand there like an idiot! They've got Lane, I tell you! Jitter's got her!"

CHAPTER VI

BULLET BUSINESS

A **NYBODY'S FIRST** reaction after getting a
shock like that would have been to charge out in
that club like a plenty piqued bull. I know that was my
first reaction—and I carried my bum head and all as far as
the door. But there an idea squirmed into my bean, and I
stopped just short of the cigarette girl. I swung around and
snapped at Tommy:

"Jitter's got her? Has he made off with her?"

Tommy was still waving his arms. "Of course, he has,
you fool! I saw him take her!"

All through my body my blood felt funny. It was as if it
was all simmering and about to break out and boil. I said
through my teeth: "You *saw* him take her?"

He screamed hysterically: "Didn't I tell you I did? I
followed her out! We were afraid it might be some sort
of trap!"

My fingernails were raising hell with my palms. I opened
my fists—and then they jerked closed again. I snapped:
"Damn you, Tommy. Tell it all and tell it straight, or I'll
smack those moist lips until they're dry as a cracker. Tell
it, you oaf!"

He cried wildly: "I'm trying to tell it! Joyce and Lane and
I were at the table. The doorman came in and said some-

298

body wanted to see Lane—said it was a message to her from mother. So I went out with her—and it was Jitter. He flashed a gun on me, and made Lane get in a car."

I snapped, "Did you get the license number?"

He stopped waving his hands long enough to shake his head furiously. He screamed at me: "No! No! It never occurred to me!"

I just stared at him. I could see that it wouldn't have occurred to him; he had probably stood like an idiot and merely wrung his hands. But there was something about this that nagged at my brain, and I walked around behind the desk. That long sheet of paper was still beside the dial, and I picked it up, scowled at it.

I put it down and said: "The votes on this paper are for Roberts and McPherson, and *Jitter Mack.* Did you suddenly put him back in good graces, Zwieg?"

But Zwieg said nothing. His savage eyes glittered at Tommy.

I turned to Tommy and snapped: "Or did you hire Jitter to kidnap Lane?"

That got to him. You could see the shock as it spread up into his face, loosening those moist lips, bulging out his eyes. But then his face tightened and he murmured huskily:

"Oh, my God, no. Oh, no—not...."

I leaned across the desk and pointed a finger at him. "No?" I wiggled the finger. "Look, fella. *Jitter Mack* was on this list because he worked for you. The Forty Thieves couldn't afford to trust a man who'd work for somebody else. He might get jammed up on another job, and spill his guts to get clear. And those Forty Thieves aren't the kind who take any chances."

I brought my hand down and smacked the desk. "So if they were just voting to kill him, why would they have him snatch Lane?"

Tommy just cringed away from me, and murmured slowly: "I—don't—know."

All of the blood in my body was still at that simmering point, and for a moment I felt like going after his throat. But then I got over it—and I kept my eyes away from him. I didn't want any temptation in front of me.

But Bones took one step and shoved him halfway across the room. His green eyes danced, and he rapped: "No decent sewer would even let you be buried in it."

Then under a paperweight on the desk I spotted another long sheet. I said quickly: "Wait a moment, son."

I picked up the sheet and as I looked at the name that had been voted on, I could feel my jaw drop almost to my chest. There were forty votes in a column headed by DEATH—in red letters; there were forty names on the sheet and a check-mark in that column by each one. I put the paper down on the desk again and trusted myself to stare at Tommy.

I growled: "Fella, the Forty Thieves had the finger on *you*."

I THINK I'd already handed him the biggest shock I could ever hand him when I'd accused him of kidnapping Lane. Everything I said now was just anti-climax; he cringed a little, but his eyes almost met mine.

He said slowly: "I sort of expected that."

Bones stuck out his jaw. "Huh?"

Tommy didn't look at him. He said to me: "I needed money, Mr. Roberts. I needed it to buy Joyce drinks, to take her places on her night off, to give her gifts, to—"

I snapped: "Get to the point."

He dabbed at his moist lips. "Well, anyway, I needed it, and mother wouldn't give me any—she said she had spoiled me enough already." He hesitated. "And so then I got an offer from these 'Forty Thieves,' as you call 'em.

"Mother was beginning to try to put pressure on them, and they wanted to know how and when she'd really strike. So I took the offer, and they paid me a hundred dollars a week, and—"

He stopped and looked pleadingly at me.

I said: "And you kept them informed—but then you went a little too far. It—"

I broke off as I caught a trace of movement a little beyond the cigarette girl. Joyce appeared in the doorway, stopped suddenly and stared at Nemo with wide blue eyes. When she raised her head, her face was lax from shock and you could see her lips quivering gently.

She breathed in a low voice: "Oh, my heavens...."

I waved an arm around the room. "Nice guys you pick to work for."

She followed the wave of my arm with her gaze and then stared hard at Zwieg. She said, almost whispering: "He's not—"

She broke off, and I scowled. "And how he is, lady."

Joyce slowly closed her eyes. She said, as if talking at all was a wrench: "Several people heard the shots, but I've quieted them." She braced herself by putting a hand against the doorjamb. "And Lane?"

I said grimly: "We've got to find her."

Joyce took her hand from the doorjamb, opened her eyes and breathed deeply. She said gently: "I think I can help you a little. I think I know where Jitter took her."

Bones said: "What?"

Joyce smiled slightly at him. "You see, Jitter used to hang around here quite a lot, and occasionally he chauffeured for Anton and drove me home. He used to point out an old deserted house where he said he sometimes ran a dice game."

Her gaze slowly came back to me. "Don't you think it's worth a try?"

I yelled: *"Worth* a try? For Pete's sake, what are we waiting for?"

We found a couple of prisons in the outer office—a large closet almost filled with Zwieg's dress clothes and a private washroom with a high window not over a foot square. Bones and I herded Zwieg and the headwaiter into the closet and gave the washroom to the cigarette girl.

Then I locked both doors, shoved the keys in my pocket, and Bones got my little gun from Nemo for me. My head still throbbed and my stomach still wasn't normal; I wasn't going to take any chances and bend over that dandy again.

We filed out into the club and I locked the outer office door.

At my side, Tommy said: "Not me?"

I dropped that key in my pocket and turned a scowl on him. "Listen, youngster. After all, I'm working for your mother. Personally, I think you ought to hang by your neck, and I think she'll say so, too. Maybe she won't like it, but she's got what it takes. You're not staying here, no. Bones is going to turn you over to her."

Bones said: "Hey!"

I rapped at him: "You can get her on long distance, and she can be down here on a train in three hours. You don't think I trust that monkey enough to take him along, do you?"

Joyce had evidently done a nice job of explaining about those shots. Nobody had given us more than a few stares—that is, up to that moment, when Tommy moved. He just leaped forward, shoved Bones out of the way, and legged it furiously toward the club's rear exit. And he screamed wildly, just once:

"You're not going to hang *me!*"

I was too startled to move until Tommy was almost to the exit, and then I stretched my own legs and struck out after him. I reached the back door in time to see him tearing across the back lot, and Bones burst out of the door behind me.

THEN I saw Tommy was heading toward a sleek, chromium-trimmed convertible that was parked among a group of cars along a high wire-mesh fence. I was angling that way when Tommy reached the car; he hopped in—and then the world blew up in my face.

It was a bomb—although I didn't realize it then—and when he toed the starter, the thing went to town. There was a blast—the force of it hurled me back against Bones—then a blaze of green, red and yellow light that flashed for an instant against the background of sky.

Bones said: "Good jeepers!"

I jerked my head up and looked away, but the nausea caught up to me for just a few moments. I staggered away, and Bones walked along beside me; he was wagging his head back and forth and whistling through his teeth. And that's more than I've ever seen anything affect him.

Then Joyce came out of the back door, saw us, and ran up to us, looking breathless.

She caught my arm. "My goodness! What was it?"

I said through my teeth: "A bomb. Attached to Tommy's car."

Her hand tightened, and for a moment her lips moved wordlessly. Then: "He was—"

Bones said: "It didn't go off until he touched the starter."

Joyce swayed a little. I caught her and gripped her arms, but she fought me away and stood rigid. She said: "Do you still—"

A surge of people out of the club's back door made her break off in the middle of her sentence. Some of them rushed toward us, shouting questions wildly; most of them rushed toward the knot of cars near the fence. A sedan was burning and there was the smell of scorched paint.

Two cops charging around the corner of the club brought me a little back to my senses.

I gripped Joyce's arms again. "If you mean do we still want to go find Lane—hell, yes. You got a car?"

She nodded woodenly. Her body was still rigid. "Around in front of the club. It's my roadster."

I said grimly: "Then lead us to it."

Joyce led the way, and nobody tried to stop us. She climbed in behind the wheel, got her keys in the ignition and then really drove. The car whipped through town, shot out into country, then zoomed along for about three miles before Joyce slowed.

We topped a small hill and I heard her breath catch. She flicked off her headlights and pulled to the side of the road.

We had plenty of moonlight, and she didn't have to speak. The night was cold, bright and clear, and you could have seen the house a mile or so off. Bones and I climbed out and ducked into bushes. We pushed through them to their edge, poked our noses into a yard.

We were about halfway down the hill, and the house was some ninety feet from our shelter. It was a huge old frame house with half of the roof caved in—and without one light in any of the windows. It was so quiet and dark and downright sinister that a sudden scream from it would have ripped you right out of your skin.

Bones gripped my arm. "Let's try it, son. Which one you want?"

I said: "I'll take the front."

He growled: "Like hell you will." He poked a fist at me. "I mean which *straw* you want. Why should you take all the danger?"

I drew and won, and he crept off muttering, and I took a good long breath and stepped out in that yard. I figured the best thing to do was to take it boldly, so I just set sail for the front porch, not moving too fast.

After all, if I crept or ran, Jitter might shoot without talking; this way he might not recognize me and call out for what I wanted. And that might give me a chance to make that front porch, or at least make one of the few trees scattered around near it.

This, of course, provided Jitter was here.

Then, when I hadn't covered over a third of that ninety feet, a sub-machine gun broke loose from a second floor window.

I knew where he'd gotten that name Jitter then.

I flopped on my belly and felt like laughing in his face—that was twice his nervousness had saved my skin. At twenty yards you can't hit a battleship with a sub-machine gun—unless you're Hercules, Houdini, and Annie Oakley combined. That burst must have gone over my head about fifteen yards and the second one was more than that.

I hopped to my feet and hauled out my little gun, zigzagged in close to that porch—then stopped and let him have it.

I emptied my little gun into that window, and the sub-machine gun bounced on the porch roof.

Upstairs we found Lane bound and gagged in a room, and Jitter hanging half over the window sill.

Bones leaned out over him, took a look and came back in. He said: "Well, I'll be a dirty name. One of your slugs bored the center of his forehead, but he's still got on that Alpine hat."

CHAPTER VII

BROKEN ALIBI

I SHOVED away my empty breakfast plate, drank some coffee, and scowled darkly. On the other side of the table, Mrs. Weston sipped coffee, and to her right, Bones smoked and grinned. Over in a corner of the small restaurant, a porter hovered around our bags. It was nine o'clock and our train was due.

I said: "And that's the story, Mrs. Weston—loose ends or no loose ends. You've got the forty men rounded up; you've Zwieg as Alibi, and you've got those sheets. You can surely pin Tommy's death on them, and in this state that'll be enough. Everyone'll hang—they ought to hang Zwieg twice—and yet you sit here and tell me something's wrong." I scowled again. "What's wrong?"

Our train's whistle, not far down the track, got us all up out of our chairs. I left a bill on the table, shrugged into my coat, and we all filed toward the door, Mrs. W. at my side.

Outside on the platform, a battery of flash bulbs blazed, but Mrs. Weston spurned reporters. When they had backed off to a distance, she said:

"That Joyce Isbell for one thing—where is she? And Andy Hubbell wasn't in love with her. He simply took those snapshots to send to me, because I wanted to show them to some help I was planning to send him.

"And something's wrong about Tommy killing Andy. The boy hadn't the ingenuity for it—you forget the size of those powder burns. Do you know how they were made?"

Our train was pulling in. I said: "Pardon me, Mrs. Weston, but I do know that. Bones and I experimented this morning and found that loose gunpowder can be dropped around a wound, and a match then applied to it. That's easy for anybody to do."

She said stubbornly: "But Tommy hadn't that ingenuity."

The train wheezed to a stop, and I shrugged my shoulders, told Mrs. Weston I'd see her at the trial, and followed our porter. When I reached the car steps and looked back at her, she was watching me with angry eyes.

Then Lane slipped out of the crowd and touched my arm. "Would you mind if I talked to you a moment?"

We wedged through half a dozen newspaper men, then got off to ourselves, and I grunted and stared at her.

She said in a soft voice: "I was terribly nasty at first and I want to apologize because I think you did a splendid job. But there's just one thing that's worrying me, and I think I should tell you."

We were in a passageway not far from our drawing-room, and I saw Bones stop the porter at the door. He tipped him and carried in the bags himself.

I rubbed my chin. "Yes?"

"You won't tell mother?"

I laughed. "Why should I?"

She said: "Well, it's important that you shouldn't because I couldn't bear her to know." She looked cool, but her light blue eyes shone. "Andy Hubbell wasn't taking Joyce Isbell to Bermuda. Those tickets were for Andy and me."

I just went crazy. A conductor, breezing through the passageway, was warning all non-passengers to get off, and I grabbed him. I yelled in his face:

"Hold this train!"

He gaped. "What?"

I bellowed: "Hold this train, damn you! Don't ask questions! Hold it!"

He just kept gaping, and I shoved him aside, made the door of our drawing-room in four good leaps. I burst in and slammed the door behind me.

JOYCE LOOKED up from the green settee. "We made it, darling." She put down a scotch and soda. "I got on at Cranston like you said, and I've—" She broke off and said anxiously: "What in the world's the matter with you?"

I said through my teeth: "You louse."

Her eyes sprang wide. "What?"

I said again: "You louse. Andy Hubbell was a pretty good-looking guy, wasn't he? When he spurned you for Lane Weston, it wasn't a bad idea to have him killed, was it?"

She didn't move.

I growled: "You and your sweet novelist's mind. You couldn't stand losing Hubbell to some other girl, so you goaded her brother into killing him for you. Why? Because—if the sheer drama of it isn't enough—your Forty Thieves wouldn't kill him; they wouldn't even try to touch us until after they thought some of their men talked before they died.

"You see, you're really Alibi, my sweet beautiful louse— why, when I bluffed Zwieg in his office, he didn't know what to do.

"And do you know *what* he did? He slapped open an annunciator that ran to your office, buzzed you before he spoke, because he didn't know who might be there. But you weren't there—you were with Tommy and Lane at the table—and Zwieg even started out to ask your advice.

"Why, all of Tommy's tricks were ideas out of your sweet novelist's mind. The cab trick, the powder-mark trick—they're fancy things he didn't have the ingenuity for. But I couldn't see it because I was nuts about you—I couldn't even realize Lane's kidnapping had a double motive. You wanted to get rid of her and at the same time bait a trap for us—I *should've* seen it; it was all there in front of us.

"You had to get Lane out of the way before I talked to her, because when I asked her about having a key to Hubbell's room—which you knew damned well I would ask her—she'd probably tell me about Hubbell and herself. And that would make it seem queer as hell that Tommy practically *admitted* killing him because he—Tommy—thought Hubbell was running away with *you*.

"And so then you knew I'd question Tommy again, and find out *you* had told him you were running away with Hubbell. Or that, in other words, you had deliberately goaded him to the kill.

"But Jitter—well, the Forty Thieves were planning to kill him, and I thought *Tommy* had hired him. And Lane and her key.... Well, her mother had had her help us and I thought her mother might've had her help Hubbell, too."

I stopped for breath. I didn't take my eyes off Joyce, but I could see a glint of surprise in Bones' eyes. I went on:

"Oh, I was blind all right, beautiful, and I still don't see some of this business. For instance, I can guess how you goaded Tommy into killing Hubbell, but how you got him to do the rest, I don't know. As far as Hubbell was concerned, you—"

She said: "As far as Andy Hubbell was concerned, that was easy. I told Tommy I was running away with Andy—and told him ten minutes later how I could make a murder look like suicide. But you and—" She hesitated, looked at Bones, and smiled gently. "But you two were far easier. Tommy was worried, and he'd put questions to me, like: 'Suppose you were in this position, what would you do?' And I just told him. Don't you see?"

I yelled: "*See?*" I was stunned. She was sitting there coolly, smiling, admitting things.

SHE SMILED again and said: "And you, Shag. You're the kind of man I'd either love or kill, and when I touched you, shivers ran through me. It was delicious—but then it would be horrifying. I'd want to love you one moment and mangle you the next."

She drank slowly from her scotch and soda. "So when I couldn't kill you, I decided to love you, and now you've decided that you'll *hang* me."

I didn't say anything. I couldn't. I couldn't breathe.

She drank more scotch and said: "Well, that's all of it—or is there something else? Oh, yes. I simply hired Jitter to get Lane and you, and Tommy didn't know I was Alibi. That's the reason Anton told me, Shag—in front of Tommy—that you were wanted by the police.

"And the whole setup—the telephone system and that nice room—was all conceived by my novelist's mind." She put down her glass and quickly raised it again. "Oh, yes. A little more.

"You see, *nobody* knew I was Alibi, Shag—except Anton, and he'll talk now. He's a very cold, self-centered person, and he'll talk to try to save his skin. But if I'd succeeded in going away with you, *you* couldn't have testified against me. Because a husband can't testify against his wife."

She smiled once more and sipped her scotch. "So I think you might have defended me, Shag—anyway, that was the only chance I had to go free. But now that you've turned against me.... Well, what's the use? What chance have I got against you both? Besides, I'll like the courtroom and all its drama—and do you think a jury would hang a beautiful girl who can act so innocent she almost fooled *you?* Why, if I get life, I'll be paroled in ten years—and think of all the books I can write with no men to bother me!"

She put her glass down again and laughed. "Now would you like to call the police?"

I gritted my teeth and reached for the knob.

Bones yelled: "Hey!"

I looked over my shoulder at him.

He grinned broadly. He said: "Don't leave me alone with this dame. I don't want to be loved and then mangled."

Joyce smiled over her glass. "You wouldn't be in any danger."

Bones just said: "Ah...." A dreamy look got into his green eyes, and he lifted his right hand, licked his knuckles. He added: "I've just been waiting for a good excuse."

Joyce said nothing. Bones grinned at me, reached in a vest pocket and took out the wedding ring I'd bought that morning. He tossed it my way, saying cheerfully:

"You won't need that any more, Shaggle."

Then he strolled across the floor, his green eyes dreamy again, and socked her squarely on the chin with the prettiest right you've ever seen.

ME—CORPSE!

*Shag and Bones—those musketeers of murder—become
the open sesame to homicide when they tangle with a
sinister marriage mart.*

CHAPTER I
STRAY DEATH

THE REDHEADED waitress didn't like the picture of George Washington on my money. I showed her a bill with Jefferson on it. "A five," I said. "Five pairs of good hose and maybe a dime over for a powder puff. Is this Keith guy making time, and if he really is, since when?"

The waitress lowered her mascaraed lashes. "I wouldn't know, handsome."

Bones wiggled a finger at her. He's probably the country's ace small-loan investigator, and when our company works investigators in pairs, we generally find ourselves nosing around together. But we were nosing around now—although I didn't like it—for a brunette vision with a honeyed Southern voice who had cooed in our ears that her hubby had a foot loose.

And we had tailed hubby—a guy named Waldo Keith—to this night club, where he now sat with a blonde. The blonde had just wound up the floor show with *My Heart Belongs to Daddy*, only her blonde hair was light orange and she didn't look like she had a heart. Bones steadied the finger and said:

"Don't work the lashes overtime, honey. Look. My handsome friend—Shag Roberts to you—goes along with the ace, and also the fin. But if you want more dough, *I* go with it."

He let his skinny hands dangle loosely and his freckled face sag like an idiot's. His eyes rolled up into his head until you merely saw tiny crescents of the irises. It didn't make him a very lovely sight. He added: "We could jitterbug at the nut-house ball."

The redhead shuddered but cast a look at the five. I had it down below table where the surrounding customers couldn't see it, but a couple of girls nearby were staring pop-eyed at Bones. I kicked him on the ankle and he almost hopped out of the chair. The redhead jumped back like I'd kicked her, and said:

"See here, handsome! Five bucks is still chicken feed, but I ain't going to get fired for twenty. Understand?"

I grinned. "Sure, I do."

"So?"

"So you just run along now and get us a couple more bottles of beer."

She looked suspiciously at me. "Okay," she said in a moment.

She turned and went off among the tables, and disappeared into the bar. The bar was behind a seedy-looking lattice-work that looked as if a puff of cigar smoke would blow it over. From behind the lattice-work came the clatter of various slot- and pin-machines.

I said to Bones: "Swell joint."

He growled: "What did you expect of a guy who'd two-time Peggy Anne?"

I grinned again. Besides a honeyed Southern voice, Peggy Anne Keith had a way with her that you never quite forgot. Back in the old days when she used to trot the

proms, you'd have thought the stag line behind her was at a World Series' ticket window. Small, slender, nicely made, she looked like a baby, acted like a baby, and never knew a man who wouldn't break his neck to protect her. I never knew exactly why this included me.

Bones snapped: "Well, what *would* you expect?"

I said: "Listen, son. Peggy Anne may be all right—I used to drag her to proms myself. But being with her too much is like living on chocolate creams for a month. And if I'd—" I broke off and rapped:

"Hold tight a minute. Here comes our informer."

THE REDHEAD had come out of the bar, lugging two bottles of beer by their necks, but when she was about four tables away from us, she veered sharply to her left. She went over to a table where a girl sat alone and in shadow, and for a moment I didn't breathe.

The girl's table was next to Waldo Keith and the blonde, and it had looked momentarily as if the redhead was going to *them*. But when she stopped at the other table, I breathed again, and when she finally started our way, I mopped my brow mentally and relaxed. She came up and plunked down the beer bottles in front of us.

She said: "Do you slay 'em, handsome!"

I said: "Huh?"

She put a folded piece of paper down in front of me and took my thirty cents. She looked at the change and demanded: "What—no tip?"

I pointed at the paper. "What's this thing?"

The redhead placed a hand on a plump hip and shrugged. "A girl called me over and told me to give it to you. She's at the fourth table from the dance floor entrance."

I said: "Okay. Just freeze a second." I unfolded the paper and spread it out in front of me. There was no salutation and no signature on it. It was simply these lines, written in a girl's handwriting, and in what I took to be fancy eyebrow pencil:

You're too beautiful to be sitting with nothing but a man. Why not come over and chat for a moment?

I scowled at the redhead. "Is this a rib?"

She shrugged her other shoulder. "Why don't you ask the girl?"

I folded the paper before Bones could get a gander at it, got up and left him gaping in his chair. I went over to the table, but the girl was still in shadow. I didn't get a good look at her until I sat down.

I shoved the note at her. "What's the joke?"

She said: "It's no joke to be lonely, is it?"

I was staring at her as if my eyes were lying to me; she wasn't beautiful but there was something about her. She had a narrow, high cheekboned face, and swollen slant eyes that looked Eurasian. Her mouth was large, full-lipped, and painted scarlet, and her teeth were slightly pointed with spaces between them. Her clothes might have been worn by a Southern deb, but her face belonged to the mistress of a Chinese pirate king off Singapore.

I fumbled over cigarettes, stalling for time, because I wasn't sure whose move it was next.

She said softly: "Well, you'll agree loneliness is no joke, won't you?" And added in a moment: "Don't you really *talk?*"

Waldo Keith sat about two yards behind me, but he was bent intently toward his orange blonde. I doubted if he would recognize me, anyway. After all, I'd only met the guy once and that was about a year and a half before.

But even if he had recognized me, he wouldn't have known I was tailing him for Peggy Anne. I said to the girl: "Only to strangers, never to friends." I grinned. "But this is the Swing Club and a jitterbug stronghold. I didn't expect to find a girl like you here."

A massive man in a topcoat with a bright red face came out of the bar and walked over to us. A small man with a sharp dark face came up behind him, but stopped a few feet away. The massive man reached out a hand that was as big as a ham, got a handful of my lapels and jerked me to my feet. He had very small, bright, hard blue eyes. He looked at my chin, sneered and said:

"You like slapping ropes around people's necks, don't you, Roberts?"

Then he shook me like I was a cellophane bag and slammed me down so hard I think I rocked the building.

I LANDED flat on my back, my shoulders crashing into some chair legs, and spilled Waldo Keith down on top of me. He stood up and I sat up, bewildered. I *had* slapped ropes around a few murderers' necks, but I hadn't expected any backfire like this.

But the massive man was standing there, still sneering at me, and now there was a big black revolver gripped in his huge hand. He threw back his big head, laughed harshly, and said:

"The great murder investigator gets fresh air into his guts."

I didn't have any time to be scared; the huge hand squeezed the gun and flame tongued at me. Something punched my side, as if I'd been touched solidly with a foil, but I didn't notice any particular pain. But the gun kept exploding, the sound of it deafening.

I counted three more shots but didn't feel any more punches. I noticed that the small man with the sharp dark face gripped a gun, too, but wasn't using it.

Pandemonium had broken loose in the club, and people were scampering wildly for the doors. Then, even over the screams and the pound of running feet, I heard a yell it wasn't hard to recognize. Bones appeared to my left, gripping both our beer bottles; his freckled face was twisted furiously, and his green eyes were wild.

He chucked one of the beer bottles and caught the small man in the chest; the small man was knocked off balance and stumbled haphazardly in my direction. Bones cocked his arm and chucked the other bottle. But this one missed the big man by a couple of yards and brought down a section of the lattice-work about twenty feet behind him.

The big man grinned loosely and pointed the revolver at Bones. A cop appeared in the front entrance, barked:

"You! Drop the rod!"

He was a young harness bull, probably not long on the force, or he would have fired instead of barking a lot of crazy orders. The big man just looked at him and chuckled and shot him twice in the forehead. The cop fell sprawling and twitched a little, and the big man sucked a tooth. He spat in the cop's general direction and said:

"Them kids, Harry. Are they gettin' 'em from grade school these days?"

He kept sucking his tooth and cocked his gaze toward me again, but I was getting up and looking around for something to club. I found a beer bottle near my right foot and stood up with that. The man called Harry swung his gun up toward me, but Bones charged in and drew his gaze, and I swatted the guy across the temple.

He folded up as if his spine had cracked in pieces, and I was left standing there with the neck of a broken bottle in my hand. But I spun around and slammed that at the big man. It bounced off his belly as if it had smacked the side of a tent, and the big man just sneered and wiggled the gun at us. He said through the sneer:

"Well, well, boys. How you like this ending, hey?"

That punch in my side still hadn't begun to hurt. I growled: "Nuts to you, fella. That's a Colt you're holding. Since when did they make one that holds over six slugs?"

The big man widened his small hard eyes. He said, still sneering: "So you ain't overrated, hey, pretty boy?" He twirled the cylinder and slipped the gun in a coat pocket. "Sorry I ain't got time to reload."

I was standing there like a goon swapping lip with the guy, but Bones had a different and better idea. He swooped down for the fallen Harry's gun, but the big man moved as if he had springs inside him. He got over to us in two long sliding steps, kicked the gun out of Bones' reach, then got hold of my lapels again.

He picked me up and threw me at least ten feet, kicked Bones expertly on the chin, and scooped up Harry. He slung him over his shoulder and stretched legs for the back entrance, and the few people huddled in the corners didn't try to stop him.

I got out from under a table in time to see him vanish down a dim corridor and hear the back door slam very faintly in the distance.

Bones sat up and rubbed his chin. He said anxiously: "You all right?"

I opened my coat and peered at my side. The bullet had scraped away about six inches of my flesh, but the gutter wasn't bleeding too freely and didn't look bad. I said: "Yeah."

Bones came over and peered at the wound, still anxious. "You better get something on that, boy." He rubbed his chin again. "Jeepers! What a guy!"

I grinned. "Something, wasn't he?"

Bones wagged his head. "They don't make 'em any tougher than that ox." He looked at me curiously. "What was it all about? You spit in his soup?"

I was looking around. The girl with the slant Eurasian eyes had simply disappeared. I said: "It looks like the past is beginning to catch up with us, son. The guy said something about ropes around people's necks." I stopped, then added: "Who's that over there?"

"Huh?"

"Over there—bleeding, I think."

Bones turned and looked. Near the edge of the dance floor, a man lay sprawled on his back, his right arm twisted under him, his eyes staring glassily at the ceiling. There was a small round hole in the center of his forehead.

I caught my breath, and Bones said: "Bleeding, hell!"

He scowled quite fiercely and walked toward the man, but I stayed where I was. Nothing in the world can make any effect on that guy's stomach. He kneeled and felt the man's pulse and then stood up.

"Dead?" I asked.

Bones said: "Yeah. Waldo Keith."

I yelled: "Huh?"

Bones scowled again. "Yeah. But don't look like you're being sawed in half."

I didn't know how I looked. I only knew how I felt. I said bitterly: "Now, isn't this something. We tail Waldo Keith to a night club, some hoods try to knock off me, and a stray bullet knocks off *him*. At least, that's the way it *looks*."

Bones said: "Have you gone batty?"

I didn't answer him for a moment. I took a few short steps to my left until I could get a glimpse of the cop. There were two bullet holes in the center of *his* forehead. I said: "Son, you can bet on it—I'm gol-blamed sane."

CHAPTER II

BULLET TARGET

I WALKED to one of the broad high windows of the Central Police Station, looked out at the street— it was Fallsway—and fingered the bandage on my side. I turned around presently and went over to Michael Canavan, placed my hands on his desk and glared at him. We were in the homicide squadroom, and nobody was in there with us but Bones.

"Listen," I said. "Bones and I have been mixed up in just five murder cases. Count 'em up. In all of 'em, everybody who was off-side with the law is either dead or taking their exercise in a nice yard. And none of them has been paroled or none of 'em has come back from the dead. So where does your revenge motive come in?"

Canavan said: "The doc said for you to rest."

I kept leaning heavily on my hands. "Let's just skip the doc a moment. Look, lieutenant. How many times do I have to tell you that little Shag was just a blind? I'm telling you that big egg could *shoot*. That young harness bull comes in, barks an order, and the big guy just chuckles and shoots him *twice* in the forehead."

I snapped my fingers. "Like that—and in the center of his forehead. You could cover both bullet holes with the ball of your thumb. Yet when the guy shoots at me—and

I'm almost close enough to kiss him—all he does to me is drill a hunk out of my side."

I snorted. "But Waldo Keith gets it in the center of his forehead, and two shots *miss* me altogether. If that makes sense, you tell me how."

Canavan said: "That could be coincidence."

I groaned and took my hands off the desk. Bones was sitting on an oak bench, smoking and grinning at me. I said: "Sure, it *could* be coincidence. It could be coincidence that we had marines at Argonne Forest, but I got an idea the history books won't call it that. What would be a better way to bump Waldo Keith off?"

Canavan said softly: "You're talking like a kid now, Shag."

I groaned again and made fists out of my hands. I jabbed my fists on my hips and said: "Okay. I'm talking like a kid. I suppose you think that girl fingered me for the killers, huh?"

Canavan nodded. "What else?"

I said angrily: "Remember, I'm still talking like a kid… Now: The girl sent the note, not to put the finger on me, but to get me over at her table *in front* of Waldo Keith."

Canavan stiffened slightly. It was the first time since I'd started hammering at him—at eleven-thirty and now it was ten minutes of twelve—that he had shown any possibility of believing me. His clear blue eyes, startling under heavy black brows, stared fixedly at me, and then he frowned.

I said: "Yeah, *in front of* Waldo Keith. That way it would look natural for a bullet to go wild and lodge in his skull. And people would think that some of the murderers—or murderesses—I've had a hand in convicting had decided to have some revenge on me.

"Yeah, lieutenant—like *you* think. And you can beat out your brains if you want to trying to solve this thing by thinking the motive was just to get sweet little *me*. But I'm going to pry for another motive, and already I've got a nice idea to start with."

Canavan was still frowning. He said: "Some relatives or friends of the murderers could have hired the killers, Shag."

I growled: "Sure, they could."

CANAVAN'S EXPRESSION didn't change. He said softly: "You're not open to much speculation, are you?" He laced his fingers together and looked questioningly at me. "What have you got to be so sore about?"

I said: *"What?"* I was almost yelling. "Listen, lieutenant. Just because we were tailing Waldo Keith, a lot of people already think we were responsible for his death. Do you think we like *that?* And furthermore, one of these days our company's going to fire us just because we're getting too damned notorious. They're the world's biggest loan company; they don't want us typing *them*."

Canavan was grave. "But you want to help crack this case, don't you?"

I said: *"Want* to?" I was still almost yelling at him. "Look. Get this. I want the case busted wide open by *somebody;* I don't care who—but I don't want any more murder case publicity. And if I bust it myself, I want to lay it right in your lap, have you take all the credit and get all the medals. But"—I snorted angrily—"you've been assigned to the case and you sit here and argue about revenge, and—"

I broke off as the door to the squadroom popped open and a homicide patrolman stuck his head inside. "The Keiths are out here," he said.

Canavan lifted his heavy black brows. "Yes?" he said. He seemed surprised. Then to me: "Hold it a minute, Shag." And to the patrolman: "Send them in."

I blinked. "The *Keiths.* Both of them?"

The patrolman wagged his head. "Mrs. Peggy Anne and Mrs. Roxanne. A couple of glamour gals about twenty years apart." He grinned. "Now, lieutenant?"

Canavan nodded. "Now."

Peggy Anne, wearing a light gray Spahi coat and a white Spahi turban, came into the room and stared at me with brown eyes. She couldn't have looked more beautiful at her first dance. But I was more interested in Roxanne Keith. She was a woman over thirty-five and less than fifty, and I guessed she was nearer the latter. And she looked as smart as Peggy Anne.

Her clothes were tailored—by somebody who knew how—and she wore a sort of shako hat, tilted smartly over her right eye. She was a tall, slender, rawboned woman with a cool Indian-like beauty that wears like marble. She looked like maybe she had a marble heart.

She didn't even glance at me. She said: "Lieutenant Canavan?"

Canavan stood up politely. "Yes?"

Roxanne Keith looked him over as if she was considering buying him for her racing stable. She said calmly: "I'm Waldo Keith's step-mother. I'd like to make some arrangements about his body." She might have been making arrangements with a grocer for a quart of peas. "Have you finished the autopsy?"

Canavan frowned. "Yes."

Roxanne Keith said stiffly: "I'll have some undertakers stop by at once."

She was turning arrogantly away from Canavan when her black eyes fell on me. She gave me that same horse-buying scrutiny she had handed out to the lieutenant. She said: "Your newspaper pictures don't flatter you, Mr. Roberts." Then: "You were following Waldo for Peggy Anne tonight, weren't you?"

I said softly: "Did you let *that* out?"

Roxanne Keith looked sharply at me. "I've talked to the newspapers and given them the entire story. I feel you're responsible for Waldo's death."

I just goggled at her. I hadn't expected her to brace me like that, and for a few moments, I felt like I was going to tear her in half. This was going a little too far.

But she didn't say anything else. She turned arrogantly on a heel and stalked out of the room, and Peggy Anne gave me a frightened glance as she tagged along. Bones hopped to his feet and stared at me incredulously.

He yelled: "Are you going to stand there and take a thing like that?"

MAYBE THAT'S where I made my mistake. Up to then I was plenty sore, but not sore enough to go off my nut. Bones had prodded me just enough. I snapped: "You know better than to have that idea, son. Take the weight off your heels and follow baby."

I swiveled and breezed out before Canavan could stop me, and strode fast down the long dim corridor. Reporters and photographers were lining both sides of it, but I just pushed through them like they were so many store dummies.

Behind me Bones was almost walking in lock-step, and I could feel his breath on my neck. I got to the Fallsway entrance of the big gray building just as Roxanne Keith was going through it.

I went down three steps and got around in front of her. She stopped and hated me with those cold black eyes.

"Listen, Mrs. Keith," I said. "I haven't any quarrel with you, except with what you just said. You still think I'm responsible for Waldo's death?"

About six flash bulbs blazed light around us.

This didn't make Roxanne Keith's eyes soften any. She said coldly: "Naturally, I do. Please move aside."

"Wait a minute," I said. I stared at Peggy Anne. "Do *you* think I'm responsible?"

Peggy Anne still looked frightened. She shrank away a little, looked imploringly at Bones.

"Look," I growled. "Up until two weeks ago I hadn't seen you for about a year and a half. Then after all that publicity on that last murder case, you called me up and said you'd read it And you told me you were in a jam and asked me if I could fix you up with a loan. You remember that?"

Peggy Anne said tremulously: "Yes."

I ground on: "Okay. So I told you that we could send a representative out to your house, but you insisted that you'd rather not have the loan than deal with a stranger. So your home was in Bones' territory, and we *both* went out. The boss sent us both. He was anxious for the business.

"And so we made you the loan all right, but you wanted to see *me* to get me to follow Waldo. And you wanted the loan to pay an insurance policy. You were the beneficiary and Waldo had let it lapse, and if you didn't pay soon, the policy was going to lapse altogether. How much was that insurance policy, Peggy Anne?"

Peggy Anne cried in that Southern voice: "Shag! Don't *look* at me that way!"

I didn't pay any attention to that. I scowled at her and wiggled a finger in her face. All around us more flash bulbs blazed. I snapped: "Listen, beautiful. That insurance policy was for thirty-five thousand bucks, double indemnity—which makes it seventy thousand. Seventy thousand bananas you get because somebody killed Waldo Keith."

I shoved my face in close to hers. "How much did you pay that somebody?"

Peggy Anne put a hand to her mouth and screamed.

Canavan pushed through the edge of the crowd, came up to me and put his hand on my arm. He was taller than I was, anyway—which made him over six feet one—but on the step above me he loomed like a monument. I noticed that he had put on his black derby, his black fly-front overcoat, and carried his black gloves, which he never wore. But there was nothing in his clear eyes that I could read. He said softly:

"This is a sap's play, Shag."

STILL MORE flash bulbs were exploding around us, and I hesitated but didn't think. I took his hand off my arm gently.

"Maybe it is," I said through my teeth. "But I've made it now. I'm sticking to it."

Peggy Anne had put both hands to her mouth. She screamed again, very piercingly.

I turned around and with Bones at my side, trotted down the marble steps to the sidewalk. My cheeks felt like a couple of branding irons. I stopped on the sidewalk and looked back at Canavan.

"Listen, lieutenant," I said. "Little Shag was just a blind, and nobody tried to *kill* me." I was so sore my words sounded blurred. I didn't even hear the sedan.

Bones told me later it was parked at the curb, and that when we reached the sidewalk, the motor began to hum. It was probably idling up to then—but not that *that* makes much difference. The next thing I knew after I spoke, a skinny shoulder slammed into my hip. I went down on the sidewalk with Bones on top of me, and gunfire roared at us from the curb.

My chin said hello to some nice hard concrete and a lead slug chipped some of it inches from my nose. Bones rolled off me, but I kept flat. Another slug dipped my hat over my eye, and then there was more gunfire, but from the steps. I heard lead slam metallically into tin, heard a motor race and then gears mesh.

I turned in time to see a black sedan angle from the curb, jump a red light at the corner and run like hell. The twin tail-lights curved into Baltimore Street, and then Canavan's hard heels smacked the sidewalk.

He yelled: "Riority, put it on the air! Black sedan, four doors, whitewalled tires!" He yelled the make and the license number. There wasn't much that got by that guy. Then: "Schnure, get your prowl car rolling!" In another moment, he was helping me.

He got me up to a sitting position. I could hear his breath come irregularly and hard. "Nip you, Shag?"

I shook my head and peered around for Bones. He was squatting Turkish fashion in the center of the sidewalk, very carefully re-blocking his hat. You couldn't make him forget his clothes with anything less than chloroform. He looked over at me and grinned. "Tackle you too hard, boy?"

I grinned back at him. "Who'd you play for—Vassar?"

Then a reporter towered over me and said: "Nobody tried to kill *you*, Mr. Roberts?"

I looked up at him—and lost my grin. He just chuckled ironically and strode away.

CHAPTER III

BLOOD MONEY

TWELVE REPORTERS sneered at us when we left the police station, and I knew the rewrite boys were going to have fun blasting me. I had gone out on a limb and the limb had busted in forty places, and I didn't even know how hard I was going to fall.

We walked down to Baltimore Street and Bones flagged a cab, and we rode north along St. Paul, not talking very much. My side had begun to ache—Bones' tackle had started some fresh bleeding—and my head throbbed from the smack of my chin on the concrete. We stopped at Tommy Regan's and had two ryes apiece, then rode another cab for about ten blocks to find out if we were being tailed.

We were—and by what looked to be an independent cab, although whoever was paying the fare didn't seem to bother to get close to us. I directed our cab over to my apartment, sent Bones up for my little gun, and peeped out the back window.

The independent cab stopped about three blocks behind us.

When Bones came back, our driver's eyes were bulging. He was a little dandy of a man with a lot of gold in his mouth.

I took the gun and made sure it was loaded. I told the driver: "Go up about four blocks. At Thirtieth and Charles, turn right and stop quick. I'm getting out and doing a little ambushing."

The driver fidgeted and licked nervously at his lips. He swallowed and said: "Hey! You know what you're doin'?"

I pointed the gun at him. "In a way. Do you?"

His small eyes got wide and bright. He said: "Yeah, bo." He swung around, yanked the cab into gear and made time up Charles Street.

I turned around and tried the back window again. The independent cab was still after us, still about three blocks behind.

Our cab leaned hard on the right turn into Thirtieth, but stopped about thirty feet from the corner and I piled out. Bones rolled down the window and looked anxiously at me. A bright yellow moon overhead showed the freckles on his nose.

He said: "Shag, if it turns out to be that tough ox, you're nuts. That guy can shoot enough rings around you to make you look like a rajah's best gal. I'm not kidding."

I said: "You hold this cab here." I turned away and walked down to the corner, then very cautiously poked out my nose.

The independent cab had just crossed Twenty-ninth Street and was clipping along at a pretty steep rate. I couldn't see who was riding inside of it. Charles Street was quiet and deserted, and directly opposite me, the trees shadowed the grass in Wyman's Park.

I didn't realize until then how scared I was.

The back of my neck was cold as a seal's nose and the gun shook in my hand like it had the d.t.'s. I thumbed the hammer, and then the independent cab turned the corner.

I fired at the right front tire and put out a headlight, but my second shot found rubber, and the cab swerved toward the curb.

It bounced up on the sidewalk and jolted to a stop, and I sprinted over to it, yanked open a door.

My side ached like a sore tooth, but it was my party now. The ox would be getting his bearings; he wouldn't be prepared for a gun.

I pointed mine at the middle of a back and snapped: "Outside, you sweet gentle little hippo. How you like *this* ending, hey?"

But when the back turned around, a girl's face was attached to it. The face stared at me, and the girl's gasp was loud as a wind storm. She said: "What *is* this?"

I gaped at her. "Huh?"

She was on her knees on the floor where the bounce of the cab had thrown her, and her slant Eurasian eyes still stared at me incredulously. She said: "Oh—*you.*"

I growled: "Who'd you expect—J. Edgar Hoover and staff?"

THE GIRL seemed to think this was funny, but I didn't laugh. She got up on the seat and straightened her Miles Standish hat, and I stepped back and took a look around. Nobody in the neighborhood seemed very curious.

I went to the front of the cab and peered in at the driver. He was sitting behind the wheel, rubbing gently at his chin. I poked the gun at him with one hand and ten bucks with the other.

I said: "This is for the bum lamp and bum tire you got, fella."

He gaped at me. "This ain't on the level!"

I dropped the two fives in his lap. "And if the cops come before you get away, I was a pretty little fat man with a carnation in his buttonhole."

He picked up the money but just sat there gaping, and I went back to the girl and pointed toward our cab with the gun. She didn't even hesitate, simply smiled at me, and got going. We walked up to the cab, piled in, and the driver's eyes bulged.

He swallowed and said hoarsely: "Good Judas—not no snatch!"

I wiggled the gun at him. "Your job, baby, is to drive."

He jerked around and gave the cab the juice. I yelled, "South on Calvert!" and slid my gaze sideways. The girl sat calmly between Bones and me and he stared at her slant eyes.

Then, after a moment, a great light seemed to dawn on him. "Holy jeepers!"

I grinned. "Yeah."

He scowled at me. "Do we wring her pretty neck here, or do we wait and find a torture chamber?"

I turned my grin on the girl. I said pleasantly: "Well, there you are, beautiful. Either you talk and talk pretty or you're going to think a medieval torture rack is like dozing on the sand at Miami. Make up your mind."

She said: "Oh, I'm going to talk to you."

I blinked. "Huh?"

She smiled at me. She looked very cool. She said: "The reason I followed you was so I could talk to you, but"—she turned the smile on Bones—"I wanted to see you alone because I hear *he's* excitable." She turned back to me. "Well?"

I had to grin. Over her shoulder I caught Bones' eye, but he was scowling. She wasn't wrong about him being excitable. You wouldn't even *consider* giving him a hot-foot unless you knew him well enough to borrow his shirt.

But I didn't say anything and tried to do a little thinking. The girl seemed to have plenty of poise and spirit, but I still would have bet that her note was just a come-on to put me in front of Waldo Keith.

I wondered if she'd talk about *that* little trick.

I had the driver turn right at North Avenue and ride over to Charles, and when we pulled in at the curb there, she just looked at me quizzically. She didn't seem any more afraid that we'd turn her over to the cops than she had about the two of us getting very tough with her.

I shoved my little gun into my right-hand coat pocket—and then reached out and grabbed her slender wrist.

I said: "It's a nice spiel, beautiful—but we'll look in the handbag. You haven't told us anything yet."

She smiled coolly. "You think of everything, don't you?"

I growled, "About you I do," and opened her bag.

It was big enough to have held a long-barreled Colt, but I didn't even find a pea-shooter inside of it. It held the usual compact, lipstick, handkerchief and so on, and a small pink envelope addressed to Caroline Grady.

"How do you do," I said pleasantly.

She was still cool. "Charmed, I'm sure."

I found a hundred and two dollars—five twenties and two ones—folded neatly in a small silk change purse. "You play the horses?"

She shook her head. "Nope. But I play pretty good guitar and piano, and my voice's got a throb in it. Look at some old papers. You'll see me billed in the cocktail lounges."

I was looking at the money. *"Old* papers, you say?"

SHE LAUGHED a little, but the laugh had a bitter edge. "Old papers—say about two months ago. You know how it is. My Dream Man came along one night, and— well, after a while, almost every night. He was tall, dark, almost as beautiful as you, and he bought champagne and dressed like Fredric March. Well, we were one of the last couples to make the deadline out at Elkton."

I said: "Too much champagne?"

She shook her head. "Cold sober. I happened to be in *love* with him, mind you, and married him with the eyes wide open. It was just a darned dirty pity that his wife finally had to show up."

I blinked. "Huh?"

She laughed again, and this time the laugh held more edge. "Well, she *did* give us about a month together—it took her that long to find the rat. But don't look so shocked, because it happens every day and you know it and little Caroline was just a plain damned fool. I've always had a weakness for beautiful men—like you."

She saw me still looking at the money. "This isn't a holdup, is it?"

I scowled. "It might be. You carry a lot of reason for it."

She said: "You interested in that reason?"

I looked up at her. "Huh?"

"The money—the five twenty-dollar bills you see. Well, if you're not interested in it, you ought to be."

I said: "You wouldn't kid a guy, would you, beautiful?"

"Well, that money was paid to get you over to my table. It was the huge red-faced man who gave it to me."

I don't think I did more than actually jump a foot off the seat. It wasn't the information that surprised me; I just hadn't expected her to give it. I grabbed her shoulders and looked hard into her slant eyes. She looked back at me steadily; you could tell she wasn't lying.

I put pressure on her shoulders and shook her, hard. "Who gave it to *him?*" I growled.

She put her hands on my hands and pried furiously at my fingers. "Stop it, ninny! Stop it, darn you! You're hurting me!"

I took my hands away. "Sorry," I said.

She rubbed her shoulders slowly with her fingers. Her face had thickened and her mouth looked drawn. She said angrily: "You don't care who you knock around, do you?" She looked directly at me. "I don't know who gave it to him."

I said: "I didn't mean to hurt you."

She flared: "Do you think I wouldn't tell you because of a little thing like that?" Even in the darkness of the cab, I could see her eyes flash. "What kind of cheap people are you used to dealing with? I tell you, I don't know, and that's all there is to it!"

For a few moments, I didn't speak. I just sat there staring at her. Then I said, "Okay," and climbed out of the cab. Bones climbed out after me, his green eyes looking a little puzzled, and the girl followed him.

I paid the driver and leaned in close to him. I growled: "Now dust, baby. Out of this neighborhood—fast."

The cab ground away with a rough clash of gears, and I waved an arm at another one parked near the North Inn. This one zoomed into a U-turn around the ends of the safety zones, skidded into the curb, and I opened the door.

Bones helped the girl in, stopped with his foot on the running board. "Where to?"

"Peggy Anne's," I said.

His eyes bulged. "Peggy Anne's!"

I growled: "Listen, son. Every paper in town's laughing down my neck, and if things don't happen by tomorrow, *I'm* going to be out of work. What do you think the company's going to do—kiss me for *that* kind of publicity? Son, this gal knows things—and we're taking her to Peggy Anne's."

CHAPTER IV

CANAVAN CRASHES IN

A **SMALL** hedge, not much higher than a good-sized duck, hemmed in the lawn in front of Peggy Anne's home. But I just sat and stared stupidly at it. All the way out there my head had been spinning, and when we pulled jerkily into the curb I knew I had a wound again. In fact, the pain and the light-headedness were doing things to my eyes. The maroon roadster parked in front of us looked like about six fleets of battleships.

I managed to reach out and grab Bones' arm. "Hey," I said.

He was climbing out, and in the darkness couldn't see my face. It was probably a few shades whiter than a major-domo's teeth. He stopped and looked quizzically at me. "Huh?"

Most of the dizziness went away, but my voice sounded strange. I said: "When we investigated Peggy Anne for the loan, Waldo didn't have a car. If she's having visitors—anyway, at this time of night—we ought to be sort of cautious, son. Hold everything."

He said; "You got a frog in your throat?"

I tried to grin. "Sure. Two of 'em."

He scowled. "Then damned if they haven't fought each other till they're dying. That voice of yours don't sound like it comes from anything alive."

I decided not to try to answer that, and before he could switch on the dome-light, I scrambled over him and climbed out. But once on the sidewalk, I didn't feel so bad.

I cat-footed up on the porch, took off my hat and peeped in the lighted window. In the center of the living-room, both of them standing, Peggy Anne and a tall guy were in each other's arms.

I shaped my mouth to form a whistle but didn't let any sound out of it. This might add up and make a little sense.

I had to stand there at the window and watch a few kisses, and you could tell as they went on that at least Peggy Anne wasn't kidding. Then they broke finally and she stood with her hands clenched. The man—his back was to me and I couldn't see much of him—shoved his hands into his pockets and stood watching her with his shoulders hunched.

Then, after a little of this, he turned and went into the hall. Peggy Anne closed her eyes and stood motionless, and you could see she was barely breathing.

The door to the porch opened and the man stepped outside. I went in on his left side and shoved my gun into his kidneys.

"Ever been a soldier?" I asked.

The man blinked. "What?"

I stepped back and let him see my little gun. I growled: "Well, whether you have or not, let's see an about face. This thing, brother, doesn't hold cigarettes."

I couldn't see his expression in the porch shadows, but for a few moments he stood stiffly, like he might try to take me. So I backed away another step, and after another moment he turned and I followed him inside.

We went into the living room and I grinned at Peggy Anne.

She said: "Shag!"

I wiggled the gun. "So Waldo had a foot loose, and you wanted him tailed, huh? Just the little innocent, wronged, baby-eyed wife."

She said again: "Shag!"

I growled: "That's twice, honey. Now try *his* name." I stepped around so I could see him. "We haven't met formally."

Peggy Anne bit her lip but didn't say anything. The man turned black eyes directly on me.

He looked like the type Peggy Anne might go for. He was about as tall as I was and he had soft smooth brown skin like a Mexican's, black curly hair, and big glistening teeth. But that skin didn't deceive you; he was just a young American boy—only those black eyes didn't look at me like they had a young boy's innocence. They were the hot, sullen, nasty eyes of a guy who had probably pawned the gold spoon his old man had poked in his mouth.

But right now his eyes looked as if there was tumult and shouting behind them, and if you poked a spoon at him, he'd bite it in half. They swept over me and then darted to Peggy Anne. He growled low in his throat: "A tricky slut, aren't you?"

Peggy Anne's face just fell apart. *"What?"*

He took a long swift sliding step, lifted a lean hand and slapped her viciously across the mouth, twice. His hands clenched and he whispered fiercely:

"So you asked us both out for a party, did you?"

I was staring at him. I yelled: "Hey!"

HE LIFTED one of his clenched hands, opened it before he struck. Peggy Anne tried to duck this time and the fingers caught her cheekbone; the heel of the hand struck her jaw and sent her staggering into a coffee table. The coffee table tipped over, and I swore and closed in. I didn't know this was what he wanted until I got over next to him.

I didn't handle it like a bright guy, anyway. I jabbed the gun into his ribs again, which is always a sucker's play; they even show the young cops in their first school tricks to handle that one. And he was expecting it, which made it even nicer.

He simply pivoted, swinging his left arm hard behind him, and his left forearm hit my wrist and I didn't have the gun on him any more. And this put my right arm off to one side and left my chin as wide open as the torso of a bubble dancer. He hit me once, his fist fairly whistling through the opening. I did a cute Corrigan to the other side of the room.

I landed on the small of my back, which practically ruined my side, and when my senses began working I could feel blood crawling on my thigh. But by this time he had booted the gun out of my hand and stood staring down hard at me, the gun gripped firmly in his. Peggy Anne stood in the center of the room and stared hard at both of us.

I wondered how much noise we'd made. The coffee table had hit the floor along with a few books and bookends, but a rug with a deep nap had cushioned that into practically nothing. Bones was probably still sitting in the cab, chinning comfortably with Caroline Grady.

I didn't even know if he'd seen me pull my gun on the porch.

The hot black eyes of the guy shifted from me to Peggy Anne. He leered at her and his lips pulled down nastily at the corners. "Tell it," he snarled.

I managed to sit up, but the room crawled dizzily in front of my eyes.

Peggy Anne had taken off both the Spahi turban and coat and had taken off whatever went under it in a transformation of personality. She wore a print dress slashed in a long V almost to her waist, and a broad crocheted belt molded it smoothly to her figure. There was a white posy tucked neatly over her left ear. With her dark skin and brown eyes, the effect was terrific.

She touched the white marks on her lips and didn't say anything.

The dark guy poked the gun at her. "I said tell it," he snapped.

She looked coyly at him. Her weapons were what she had and what she had on, and I remembered that she'd known this way back in high school. That look was supposed to make him a repentant ardent lover. He sneered and said:

"Save the charm for the next chump. Me, I'm fed up with it."

That got to her. She didn't get sore because that had never worked with her; she pouted and got a couple bucketfuls of tears up in her eyes. These she released slowly as if she knew each drop's weight.

She sobbed and said: "Teddy...."

Names seemed to be the limit of her vocabulary that night.

Teddy snarled: "Do I have to come over there and slap it out of you?"

Peggy Anne made sure the divan was behind her, jockeyed for position momentarily, and then fainted dead away on it.

Teddy looked at me angrily as if to say: "Lamp that, fella. That's what *I* got to put up with."

He brought her to by slapping her roughly, just once, and she turned over and buried her face deep into a pillow. He stood sneering down at her, and then strode over to me. When he spoke his voice was a rough snarl deep in his chest:

"Get this, Roberts, You were pulled into this like you think, but nobody had any murders in their minds. Mrs. Keith got a threat a little while ago."

The room was still crawling in front of me like something alive. I braced myself by putting my palms on the floor. "Mrs. Keith?"

He snapped: "Mrs. Roxanne Keith."

"You're telling it," I said.

THE SNARL stayed in his chest: "A sea captain came to her a few days ago—last Wednesday—and showed her proof that old Roger Keith had never been divorced from his second wife. Old Roger Keith was her husband—and Waldo's old man. Waldo was the child of his first wife, a Marion Wintes."

"You're still telling it," I said.

His lower lip flicked up and licked at the upper. "Well, this sea captain had a long story to tell. It seemed that when old Roger's first wife died—a fall from a horse did it—he was pretty broken up and took a trip around the world. Well, being lonely and all that—you know how a guy gets—when he got down in Mexico, he fell for a young girl.

"She was nothing but a peon, and illiterate as hell—the captain says—but one of those pretty flowers that flourish in the muck. So old Roger sailed for her—he was a young guy then—stored her away on a ship and married her out to sea. But he was society and she was a peon, so naturally he couldn't bring her home. He had the Keith family honor to uphold.

"He just smuggled her into the country and lived up in Philly with her for about six months. He got tired of her then, so he just up and shipped her back."

I said: "Wasn't he afraid she'd talk?"

"This captain claims she was too damned dumb."

I scowled. "How does he know?"

"He took her back," Teddy said.

My voice sounded like a soprano with laryngitis. I tried to growl: "What's the proof he married her in the first place?"

The guy was examining the safety on my little gun. He had found how to work it and I didn't like that. "Tricky," he said. "Well, both parties signed the captain's log, and so did the witnesses—half of the whole damned crew. He always kept records of marriages that way."

"And he's still got the log?"

"He kept it as sort of a keepsake when the ship was scuttled."

Peggy Anne was sitting bolt upright on the divan. Her palms were pressed flat on the tops of her thighs, and her lower lip was caught tightly between her teeth. I tried not to show that I'd noticed her at all.

There was a faint scraping sound from the direction of the dining-room and then the drapes across the entrance—an archway—moved as though a breeze had billowed them. There was another faint sound that might have been a foot-step. Then there was silence and no sound at all.

I looked up at Teddy and tried to look like a guy who'd asked a question. That first scraping sound could have been a window going up.

He didn't look like my act was going over. His lower lip had inched up, snagging the upper; it stayed there, not moving and his eyeballs crawled.

A very faint but distinct step sounded in the hall.

Canavan—tall, grim-faced, straight as a rifle barrel—appeared in the door to the hallway with Bones wedged in beside him. I didn't even get a chance to yell. Canavan gripped a big police positive and Teddy whirled, and at that moment a big black gun poked through the drapes at the archway.

Canavan clipped, "Drop it, fella!" to Teddy, but the black gun was already booming. It went off three times in rapid succession, as fast as a machine gun, only louder.

CHAPTER V

TERRIBLE TEDDY

I'M QUITE sure Peggy Anne didn't move. She sat with her palms still pressed flat on her thighs, and her slender body was rigid from shock. I know I didn't move. I was so weak I couldn't flutter an eyelash and I just sat and stared blankly around. But Bones and Canavan both moved instantly. Bones went down, a leg shot from under him, and Canavan reeled against the doorjamb, his arm dripping blood. The police positive hit the rug and skidded noiselessly. My friend Teddy just froze and stared. Nobody showed any momentum but the huge red-faced man.

He pushed the drapes aside and stepped into the room, sneered at Teddy and thrust the big black gun at him. Teddy dropped my little gun and stared at him stupidly. The big man covered Canavan casually with the black gun, sidled over to Teddy and used a left hand.

It was a nice hook that didn't travel eight inches, and Teddy dropped like a man who didn't have any bones in him. Then the big man leered down at me. He spat at my feet and said:

"You can wait, pretty boy."

Then running feet drummed up the walk in the yard.

The big man contemptuously sucked a tooth. He sidestepped to the window, knocked out a hole with the gun-barrel, leveled his thick arm and fired twice. That left him one slug in his Colt. A slug from outside must have missed him by inches.

The big man grinned loosely and scratched his chin with the gun-muzzle. A flock of bullets nipped the windows and put holes in the far walls.

The big man used the front sight of his Colt to scratch at his right ear. He said: "One slug ain't goin' to stop three of 'em, hey, friend?"

He seemed to be addressing me and I was trying to keep my eyes on him. I was putting a lot of effort into it, too. Bones was crawling across the rug, dragging a limp and bloody leg, his green eyes fastened on Canavan's gun. It looked for a moment like he might make it. Then the big man saw him and wagged his head.

He sucked a tooth and growled at me: "Don't this freckle-puss know when it's quittin' time?"

Bones leered up nastily and just kept crawling. The big man kicked him behind an ear.

More bullets nipped glass out of the windows. Two of them brought down a glazed Chinese print that had hung near the archway.

The big man spat again. He leered my way, saying nastily: "Well, when you gotta go, bud, you gotta go."

He hopped over Bones, scampered out through the drapes and his big feet pounded across the dining-room. A swing-door swished in the sudden quiet. Then the back door slammed and feet ran away from us.

Another volley of bullets poured through the windows.

Canavan muttered: "They put guns in their hands and that makes 'em policemen." His lips were drawn back slightly, his mouth-corners turned down. "I wish to heaven they could put brains into their heads."

He walked boldly to a window and cupped his good hand to his mouth. "Riority! He's back-doored you, damn you!"

A car started up and hummed away down the alley.

A voice from the yard yelled: "Gotcha, lieutenant!"

Canavan stood straight and motionless at the window and stared pensively out at the yard.

IT WAS a good two hours before we got down to head-quarters again, and nobody had had a chance to ask many questions. There had been a succession of cops and ambulances, reporters and photographers; even the D.A. himself who had been dragged out of bed.

Canavan and Bones had both been bandaged up, and I had had a fresh bandage put neatly on my side. Peggy Anne—according to the M.E.—was suffering pretty badly from shock. She was in bed at Union Memorial Hospital. Teddy—his last name turned out to be Warren—was simply watching everything sullenly with the hot coal-black eyes.

But Caroline Grady wasn't around. The cops had left her in the taxi when the shooting started, and when the shooting ended, she just wasn't there any more. It seemed that nobody had bothered to put any cuffs on her. The D.A. raised merry hell about this.

It seemed that Canavan had put an eye out at Peggy Anne's house, and when I hopped out of the cab the eye had lamped me and recognized me. He had been behind a tall hedge on the opposite side of the street and had simply beat it back through an areaway and made tracks to a call-box.

So Canavan had come out right away, found Bones and the girl in the taxi, recognized the girl from my description and left the three cops to hang on to her. This was because Bones hadn't known what I was up to in the house and because Canavan had decided they should come in and find out. The lieutenant argued that nothing had happened up to that time and he saw no reason to drag policemen into Peggy Anne's home.

But when he and Bones reached the porch, they saw Teddy through the windows, and Teddy was standing there gripping a gun. The door was open—I remembered this; I'd left it open—and so they naturally came in as quietly as they could. Then they reached the living room and the big black gun boomed.

The D.A. hemmed and hawed over this.

He had the taxi driver brought in but this didn't help, because the driver had no idea where Caroline Grady had gone. He had scuttled out of the cab for safer places when the first gun went off, and he wasn't ashamed to tell anyone, he said.

The D.A. was quite dry about this.

He shooed all the overflow out of the office until just Bones, Canavan, Teddy and I were left. He lighted a thin cigar, studied the coal for a few moments, then placed bright dark eyes directly on me. He was a dapper little man, round and soft like a chestnut worm, with a short thin neck that made his head look overbalanced. He put it to one side, mocked me with bright eyes and said:

"Well, Mr. Roberts?"

I looked at Canavan and said exactly nothing.

The lieutenant's arm—two bullets had gone into it— was resting in a sling, but he didn't seem to be aware of it. He stood as straight as ever, met my gaze but as usual showed me nothing. He said: "It's all up to Mr. Cornwell now, Shag."

Cornwell chuckled. He kept his head to one side, tapped the cigar, said cheerfully: "Now there's something for us, Mr. Roberts. Now we know the lieutenant's on our side." I didn't like his sense of humor. He chuckled again. "Could we start with the Grady girl?".

I looked at him levelly. "Could we?"

He waved a plump hand. "I'm sure, Mr. Roberts, that could be arranged. Now: Is there any particular reason why, after you—uh—apprehended the Grady girl that you didn't turn her directly over to the police?"

I said: "Is there?"

The bright eyes twinkled. "It's no fun, Mr. Roberts, when you ask the questions."

I spread my hands. "And it's no fun sitting here with you trying to make a monkey out of me. Listen, Mr. Cornwell. I took the Grady girl out to Peg—to Mrs. Keith's—because I had gone out on a limb once and nobody around here had listened to me."

I kept my eyes carefully away from Canavan. "I had a theory about this case and I got sore and yelled it, and then somebody shot at me and I was in the dog-house. And with that publicity, my company will sure as hell fire me, and I wanted to have a comeback when that publicity came out.

"And I figured that if Peg—if Mrs. Keith—had hired the Grady girl, it wouldn't be a bad idea to get them together. Maybe I could break them down and get a couple of admissions. But when I got out there, this Warren guy was in the way."

The D.A. put his head on the other side. "Was that any reason to brace him with a gun?"

I growled: "There'd been too many people shooting at me all night *not* to brace him with a gun, Mr. Cornwell. There wasn't any way I could tell his angle—then."

CORNWELL'S MOUTH shaped a small perfect O. Then he looked at the coal of his cigar, leaned back in the swivel chair, chuckled briefly, and said: "Ah…" Teddy Warren fiddled with the knot in his tie.

I shifted position in my leather chair, made my side more comfortable and looked at Bones. He was sitting in a big chair across the room with his leg in a splint and a crutch beside him. He nodded to me and winked merrily.

I looked directly at Cornwell and said: "When I got out to Peggy Anne Keith's tonight, she and this Warren were in a clinch. I spotted it through the windows. Does that tell you anything?"

Cornwell looked cheerfully over his cigar and said: "No."

"All right." I didn't look at Warren. "But it told me something. When Peggy Anne Keith came to us for a loan, we investigated the family pretty thoroughly. We couldn't understand *why* she'd need a loan. When Roger Keith died about two years ago he left a pretty good-sized fortune—that was common knowledge. And he died without a will.

"That meant that Waldo—the only child—Was entitled to two-thirds of the fortune, and the wife—Roxanne—the rest. But we found out that Waldo had been kicked out of the house by his old man because the boy liked his likker too much. He'd get drunk and play the horses, get mixed up with women and end up in all sorts of a mess.

"Well, he did it once too often and old Roger gave him the boot. And because of this—his being so damned irresponsible—Roxanne Keith took the case to court and got all of the dough but a hundred grand. This went into a trust fund for Waldo—to revert to the estate in case of his death. Do you get any tie-up now?"

Cornwell said pleasantly: "The floor's still yours."

"Okay." I still didn't look at Warren. "Well, here you are. Waldo was out too many nights, and Peggy Anne, restless and finally fed up, went into a tailspin for Teddy here. But Teddy didn't care anything about her; you should have seen him slap her around tonight. He had his eye cocked on the Keith dough. Do you know what he told me out at Peggy Anne's?"

Cornwell chuckled deep in his throat. The swivel chair creaked as he leaned backward and his plump little body shook all over. He said cheerfully: "Now just how would I know that, Mr. Roberts?"

I growled: "Have your fun. Look." I gave him Teddy Warren's story just as Warren gave it to me. "Do you think there's really a sea captain and that the old bird kept his log as a keepsake?"

Cornwell shook with another chuckle. "It's quite possible, Mr. Roberts."

I glowered at him. "You guys and your possibilities. Why don't you question him about it?"

Teddy Warren said nastily: "Why don't *you* question me, Roberts?"

For the first time since I'd started talking, I looked him over. There was even more fierceness in the black eyes than he'd shown before, and there was madness in the ugly down-twist to his face. If this guy got any kind of a chance, he'd break me in two and play ball with the halves.

I growled: "Why should I question you? Hell, I know. You got the family history some way—maybe from Peggy Anne—saw your chance, and put the business to Roxanne Keith. You got yourself a fake captain—and probably a fake log—and had him go to Roxanne Keith and put the bee on her for some dough.

"But she wouldn't pay, and so you had your captain threaten her about Waldo. Why not? You knew she didn't care much about Waldo—he isn't even her son—but there wasn't anybody else unless you threatened Roxanne herself, or Peggy Anne. But Waldo fitted nicely.

"You could have him bumped, apparently because Roxanne wouldn't pay—and that would give Peggy Anne the insurance, seventy thousand bucks. And you had Peggy Anne tied up—maybe you wouldn't even have had to marry her—and with Roxanne thinking the blackmailers meant business, maybe you could even have tapped *her* wad. Which—"

Teddy Warren made no separate movements. He charged at me, a snarling human windmill, his breathing almost as loud as the quick scuffle of his feet. I didn't even have time to get up out of my chair. Fists flailed at me—cuffing my nose, chin, forehead, and eyes; and the force of his charge tipped my chair over backwards.

I landed spread-eagled with Teddy Warren's knees in my belly; and the lash of pain through my side was like ribs torn out by the roots. I yelled and found strength somewhere to roll him off me. He came scrambling back on his knees, his big glistening teeth bared horribly, and I hiked my right shoulder and hit him on the chin.

It wasn't as nice a punch as he'd given me at Peggy Anne's, but it floored him without pulling too many more ribs out of my side.

It had all happened so quickly nobody else had moved.

The door of the office popped open and a harness bull stuck his head inside. He leered at the two of us but spoke to the D.A.:

"I thought mebbe a maniac had gotten loose, Mr. Cornwell."

Cornwell chuckled softly. "So did I, Schnure."

The harness bull waited a moment, shifted awkwardly on big feet; and when nobody else spoke, went out and shut the door.

Teddy Warren lay panting on his belly and didn't take his eyes from my throat.

CHAPTER VI

H.Q. GETAWAY

A **DESK** telephone rang. I put my chair back on its feet and sat down in it and watched Cornwell answer the phone. Bones was looking anxiously at me. Nothing—as usual—showed in Canavan's face.

Cornwell said: "Yes…. Yes." The little body shook slightly with the now familiar chuckle. "If he's not incapacitated, Mrs. Keith."

There could have been a cactus bush sprouting in my side. I took my teeth out of my lower lip and said: "Huh?"

Cornwell said into the phone: "Chiefly because he and another young man had sort of a disagreement…. Yes." Another chuckle bubbled and he held the phone out toward me. "Roxanne Keith."

I scowled. "Some other time."

He wiggled the phone at me. "It's so much nicer to have you talk to her from here." His eyes were twinkling. "Now, Mr. Roberts, you wouldn't keep a lady waiting."

There was no sense arguing. I was still in the middle of this mess, and D.A.'s never make nice enemies.

I took the phone and Cornwell punched a button. He picked up another phone and clapped his hand over the mouthpiece. He told me: "Now, Mr. Roberts."

I scowled and said: "Yes?"

The voice was cool and unhurried: "Mr. Roberts? Could you meet me on the corner of Broadway and Fayette in about two hours, say at six o'clock?"

I said: "Huh?"

The voice became brisk: "It's very important, I assure you, to both of us. Could you?"

I looked across the desk at Cornwell. Of course, the button he'd punched had rung in the other phone on our line, and he was smoking his cigar and eavesdropping cheerfully. I said: "Maybe."

Cornwell nodded at me.

I said: "If it's important, I *will* make it. You can count on me, Mrs. Keith."

The voice became more brisk: "That's splendid. But one important thing. If you don't come without the police, there's simply no sense in coming at all. Can you do that?"

I scowled at Cornwall. "Yeah."

"Then I'll see you—"

There was a flurry of movement off to my right and I lost interest in the telephone conversation. I jerked my head around as Teddy Warren got up off the floor; he took two long steps and got past Canavan and behind him. I couldn't tell what Teddy was up to at first.

Canavan swung around, but he had moved too late; Teddy darted in from the rear and wrapped long arms around his waist. And with his right arm in a sling, Canavan had too great a handicap. Teddy pulled back the lieutenant's coat, unbuttoned his holster, and yanked out the police positive before I could even get close to him.

Across the room Bones was helpless with his leg in the splint, and Cornwell didn't even try to move. You could tell that any personal action was beneath his dignity. That was for cops; he wasn't going to soil his hands.

He calmly pressed an ivory button on the desk. He said: "You probably won't live to regret this, Warren."

I had stopped only about a yard from Canavan. The telephone—I still had it in my hands—shook slightly as I listened to a "Number, please." I clipped it together and put it back on the desk.

Teddy was holding the police positive loosely, and it seemed to point at no one in particular. He was a little to the right of Canavan—if you were facing him, which I was—and the hot black eyes were abnormally bright. He said to the D.A.:

"When the copper comes in, give him an errand to go on. A good errand, mister, or somebody gets hurt."

The rest of us looked at Cornwell, but he didn't speak. For once he didn't chuckle, either, but the bright eyes looked calm.

Teddy got behind Canavan again, which hid the police positive nicely from the doorway. Then the door opened and the harness bull came in.

MY SPINE felt like a stiff breeze was chilling it. I glanced at the harness bull—as casually as I could—and leaned against the desk edge. I had an idea that if Teddy did any shooting, one of the first slugs might have *my* label. Bones stirred in his chair and played with his crutch and Canavan calmly smoothed out his sling. But the D.A. blew a nice fat smoke ring and sent the harness bull after coffee.

The cop went out and shut the door. The D.A. chuckled softly and looked at Warren. "You'd have cut him down and probably spat on him, wouldn't you?"

Teddy leered contemptuously. "What do you think?" He stepped out into the middle of the room.

"Look, mister," he said. "You're not going to drag me in here and make me a fall-guy and have me take it lying down. I'm wise to you coppers; you don't shove me around. I got a record on the Coast as long as your left leg. Why do you think I talked to this Roberts?"

I said: "You want me to tell you?"

Teddy's black eyes swiveled, almost seemed to jump at me.

My spine still felt a trifle chilled. But I wasn't going to let him back me down. I growled: "Look, guy. When we investigated the Keith finances, we found out Roxanne Keith was almost broke. She'd just piddled away her share of the dough.

"But she had enough left to pay Waldo's insurance for Peggy Anne—although why she didn't I don't know, nor did that happen to be any of my business. But why Waldo himself didn't pay *was* my business—and he was spending all of his dough on the horses and his orange blonde. How much blackmail did that captain want?"

Teddy snarled: "A hundred grand."

"Okay." I watched his eyes. "But Roxanne Keith didn't pay because that would have cleaned her out—which was pretty tough for you. But then Peggy Anne gave you an idea. There was plenty publicity about Bones and me in the papers and she saw it—she told us she saw it. And she also told *you* she saw it. She would; she thinks I'm a celebrity, and she's just the kind of cluck who always claims to know celebrities.

"So you got her to come to us for a nice double purpose. First, because you wanted the dough for the insurance—if it lapsed, it wasn't any good to you—and second, because you wanted to use us as a blind and kill Waldo and get that insurance."

Teddy stood absolutely motionless. He said softly: "And why did I talk to you?"

That chill in my spine had crept up to my neck. I flexed my shoulders a little and then sat very still. I growled:

"Because I'd caught you in Peggy Anne's arms, and her hubby had been knocked off with too much insurance. Add to that your record out on the Coast— It made you look innocent as hell, didn't it—all the pretense at blowing your top?"

Bones yelled: "Shag!"

I heard him, but I was watching Teddy, too. And I didn't wait for that guy to move. I got a glimpse of his face thickening through the cheeks, of his lower lip crawling skyward and licking the upper. His whole body stiffened slightly, and his black eyes bounced. I went off the desk—backward—twisting for balance and swearing.

Teddy put four slugs into the desk.

I didn't get a chance to draw my little gun. Teddy leaped for the windows and yanked one up; and both Canavan and Bones were too sensible to try to stop him. He climbed up on the sill and jumped to the sidewalk, and we could hear the pound of his heels, running away.

I got up on my feet again and hurried to the open window. We were on the ground floor facing Fallsway, and there was about an eight-foot drop.

Cops swarmed into the office at both entrances.

I pulled my head and shoulders out of the window before one of them got the idea I was taking a sneak. Bones was up on his crutch and wagging his head merrily at me. Canavan—looking grim and implacable—was already barking into a phone, putting the dragnet into action.

I could feel that cactus bush sprouting in my side again. I went over to the desk and sat down on the edge.

The D.A. chuckled and puffed at his cigar. He said: "You're certainly popular with our friend, Mr. Warren. By the way, if your reconstruction is true—and I hope it is for *your* sake, Mr. Roberts—why did the big gunman sock our friend on the chin?"

I grinned. "Maybe Teddy forgot to pay him."

He waved the cigar. "That's a little disappointing. Think you're equal to your date with Mrs. Keith?"

He was smiling now and I found the smile too bright. I was wondering if he knew Caroline Grady had imitated Roxanne Keith's voice. I said: "Would it make any difference?"

For the first time he laughed aloud. He said: "Roberts, you're a son-of-a-gun."

CHAPTER VII

DISASTER— WHOLESALE

A DULL gray dawn pressing over the tops of the houses made the corners of Broadway and Fayette bleak and dim. I paid off my cab and stood huddled in a doorway. A block down Fayette a black sedan was parked at the curb, and a block up Broadway another sedan had its motor idling. Directly across the street a newsboy hawked papers and looked impish.

I decided six o'clock was much too early for a newsboy.

I went across the street and looked down at him. He was an Italian boy, about fifteen, with large dark eyes and plenty-of teeth. He grinned—this was meant to disarm me—while the big eyes looked me over carefully. After a moment, he put his eyes into the grin.

He said: "It's a *Sun* you want, mister."

I said: "Where'd she pick you up?" He whipped a paper off the back of his pack, folded it, and shoved it at me. He winked one of the big eyes. "I sell in front of *Horn & Horn's*—you know, it's open all night. She give me a deuce and said you'd do better." He held out one of his grimy palms.

I let him hold it there and looked at the paper. Penciled across the margin along the top was a message in a familiar feminine hand. It was short, concise and to the point:

366

The door's open at—Broadway. Go straight thru and out to the alley. I'll be waiting in a car. Love.

I tucked the paper under my arm and dug down into a pant's pocket. The boy still held out a grimy palm. I said casually: "A big red-faced fellow still with her?"

He didn't hesitate. "Nobody's been with her."

I put two dollars into the palm. "She didn't tell you I'd better a deuce, either."

He started, but then his dark face flushed sheepishly. I just grinned and walked across the street.

My number on Broadway was an old square red-brick house. I went through a narrow hall and opened the back door. Through the crack made at the hinges, I saw a small back yard littered with paper and tin cans. The yard was bounded by a high wooden fence. At an opening in the fence—the gate had probably been lifted for firewood— the rear end of a sedan showed me a battered spare tire.

It was a red sedan and didn't look like a police car. I got out my little gun and went out and across the yard.

Caroline Grady was behind the wheel of the sedan.

I climbed in beside her and exhaled some breath. "Let's get away from two carloads of policemen. We don't want them in our hair."

She kicked life into the motor but didn't say anything. We rolled for several minutes and went up past Fayette. She parked in the middle of this block and smiled at me mysteriously. Again I noticed the sharp pointed teeth, spaced slightly.

She said: "Don't look at them."

I blinked. "What?"

"My teeth—or these slanting eyes. They always give a man the wrong impression."

I grinned. "Listen, beautiful. I just put my life in your hands. Let's talk about why I'm here and forget all about the sex appeal."

She patted my hand. "I knew I liked you. Well, I couldn't get in touch with you any other way, and I thought the police would probably listen in. So I used the other name and got the newsboy. I gave him a lovely description of you. He spotted you all right?"

I said: "I spotted him."

SHE LIFTED her brows. "Well, anyway, I thought maybe you were in a jam because you hadn't turned me over to the police. So I decided to use the other name"— she smiled—"principally because if they knew you were meeting *me,* I knew they'd pick me up some way. And next because—this is a nicer reason—I didn't want them to think you were too chummy with me. That might not have been nice for you. Am I clear?"

I said: "Too frank. But go ahead."

She smiled. "You always look behind people's words, don't you? Well, anyway, how'd you like to pick up Gunter?" She saw me hesitate and added softly: "The big red-faced man. Do I have to go further?"

I realized I was gaping at her.

She patted my hand again. "Please listen to me. Please believe my frankness. You see, I've bought this car. I got it at an all-night garage for fifty dollars, and I'm going to"— she hesitated—"get out of town in it."

She frowned sharply, her brow creasing, and then laughed. The laugh had a harsh metallic ring. "I was going to say 'make my getaway in it.' That sounds awfully criminal, doesn't it?"

My tongue felt thick. I wasn't even looking at her. My voice didn't sound at all like my voice: "Where is this Gunter?"

Her eyes had darkened. Her hands—one on the wheel and one still on my hand—tightened. She gave me a number on Broadway, adding huskily: "Second floor rear. Roxanne Keith's with him."

She just couldn't surprise me any more. I said: "Doing what?"

She looked levelly at me. Her eyes had cleared until they were normal, but her voice still held low-pitched huskiness. I could believe this girl could put over a torch song now. She said: "She's buying the fake log Gunter had made up to fool her. Or don't you know anything about that?"

I didn't answer her. A shaft of sunlight was splitting the dull gray dawn, and a milk-wagon clippity-clopped up the street. A guy in dungarees went by and wiggled a finger at us.

"He thinks we've been out carousing," I said.

I was watching Caroline Grady stare up at me. Then I leaned over and kissed her, but she didn't stop staring. Her eyes stayed wide open and her lips were cold.

I got out of the car and stood with my hat in my hands.

She said: "Some other time."

I was watching her eyes. "Yeah."

"Some time when there's no nastiness, ugliness, policemen, or murders."

I said: "I can believe you now."

Her eyes looked calm, but she didn't speak.

I said: "If you'd have polished off things by going to work on that kiss, you'd already be on your way to headquarters.

There hasn't been a come-on girl yet who wouldn't have burned my lips off."

She said: "I know. That's what stopped me."

I just stood slack-jawed. I couldn't find an answer to that.

"Some other time," she told me softly.

The car started quickly, and she drove away....

My new number on Broadway was three and a half blocks above Fayette, and the walk didn't do my side any good. There was a small knot of blue uniforms far down the street, but much too far for anybody to be recognized. I went up the white wooden steps and pressed a bell. I had to press three of them before the door buzzed.

I went in and an old woman poked her head out of a flat entrance. I said, "Sorry, lady. Forgot my key," and left her looking sullen as I headed toward the stairs. I went up to the second floor and walked toward the rear flat.

I wondered why I was taking such chances.

Voices sounded soft and muffled behind the door. I banged on it and yelled: "Cut down on the racket, will ya? What're you gonna do with that broad—chin all night?"

I had my little gun in my fist when the big guy opened the door. His small blue eyes were dark and nasty with anger. I just wiggled my little gun and went in, fast. The eyes got smaller, wary, and his neck muscles thickened.

I flattened my back against the wall.

ROXANNE KEITH stood up out of an old dusty rocker, held herself very rigidly and just stared at me. Her cool Indian-like face told me nothing. She wore the same sort of shako hat—dipped over her right eye—the same tailored clothes. On a table close to her—we were in a living room—lay her gloves, purse and a thick black book.

I kept the gun on the big man. "Turn around."

His mouth twisted contemptuously, but he turned around, stood with his shoulder muscles bunched and his huge hands half raised. Next I had him take off his coat. After this came the shoulder-rig—his big black gun was in it—and when it thumped to the floor, he made thick snarling noises. But Roxanne Keith looked on inscrutably. Nothing about her changed at all.

I pointed my gun at the shoulder-rig. "Would you mind getting it, Mrs. Keith?"

She showed some expression this time—like I'd asked her to shine my shoes—but went over and got it, carried it to the table and put it down. Light from a nearby floor-lamp glittered on the gun butt. When Roxanne Keith turned toward me, her black eyes looked dull.

I turned back to the big man. "All right. Spill it."

He said: "Huh?"

I growled: "Your pal Teddy blew his top to the coppers." This was a shot in the dark, but I had to take chances. When I laid the big boy in Cornwell's lap, I had to have a story to lay alongside of him. I got more bark into my voice and snapped:

"But it didn't include your try at burning me down in front of the police station. That doesn't add with the rest of it, fella."

He didn't fly at me, but he almost did. Flesh bunched around the small hard eyes, and craftiness and suspicion glittered in them coldly. His jaw knotted, and his huge hands clenched.

"Listen, handsome," he said hoarsely. "There ain't no rubber hose made that'd get talk out of Teddy. And as for me— Well, I tried to burn you down in front of that station because that beer bottle you swung killed my pal, see? Nobody kills Gunter's pals and gets away with it. That ain't the way I do business."

I said: "No?"

He leered. "No. And if you want to know why I let you live out at that house— Well, I'd cooled off some then, handsome, and had time to think a little. I figured just plain killing was too good for you. I wanted to let you know why you were dying; put the screws on you; watch you squirm and kick a little. But Teddy never did no talking, pretty boy."

I said: "You weren't there, were you, Charlie?"

His eyes were gleaming cold blue discs. "It ain't no wise crack without the accent, handsome." His shoulder muscles bulged against his shirt. "Look, fella. Teddy never blew his top. Teddy's tough and Teddy's got brains, see?"

He tapped his forehead with a huge blunt forefinger. "Teddy wouldn't rat. He's my pal."

I growled: "You always treat your pals so nice?"

He said: "Huh?"

"Cocking 'em on the chin so they're out for ten minutes?"

He sneered at me. "Look, handsome. Teddy ain't got all the brains in our tie-up. Me, I carry a few, too, see?" He sucked a tooth and spat on the carpet. "Well, I was waitin' for Teddy a few blocks away, and when he didn't show when he said he would, I went to see why. So I find coppers outside, but I don't see Teddy, so I drive past and around back and go in the window. Then I see he's really in a spot.

"The coppers are comin' in; Teddy's holding a gun. And if I know Teddy, he's goin' to use that gun. But the coppers'll have the drop on 'im, see? Teddy's in a fair way to have his guts blown out. Well, I give it to the coppers to give Teddy a break, and then sock 'im so it won't look like he's tied in with me, see?

"The dame out there could've put the finger on Teddy, and I figure it's better for him to look on the side of the law. There ain't no sense in him lammin' with me and so have the coppers lookin' for both of us. Me, I use the brains, too. See, handsome?"

THAT GUY must have had a lot of faith in my nerves. Before I could even bat one eyelash, he turned on his heel and strode across the room. One step toward his gun, and I'd have emptied mine into him. But he didn't even lean in that direction.

There was a large overstuffed sofa between the room's two windows, and he lifted an end of it like I might lift a toothpick. He carried the end to the center of the room where the sofa was almost at a right angle to the wall.

Behind the sofa, something was covered with a sheet, and the big man ripped this off in a hurry. I saw a dead man with a sharp dark face and dull brown eyes that were mercilessly open. There was a large bruise across the temple where my beer bottle had landed so nicely. I shuffled my feet again and looked at Roxanne Keith.

I should have known better than that.

Roxanne Keith merely looked quizzical, as though somebody she didn't know had stepped into the room. I looked quickly toward the big man again. He was already bending over the body, scooping it up by the armpits; and by the time I got what he was doing, he had it in front of him as a shield. He sneered at me and said mockingly:

"Me, I use the brains, too. See, pretty boy?"

He charged at me across the room, holding the corpse in front of him, and making snarling noises. I tried to side-step and get a shot. Then he rammed into me, the corpse between us, and I went down on my back, hard.

He threw the corpse away and kicked my gun arm. He kicked it again and the gun went spinning.

His small hard eyes looked at my throat. His lips grinned satanically, and his red face looked swollen. I saw the big hands start towards my throat.

Roxanne Keith shot him four times in the back.

He fell forward, across the body of his pal, twitched a little, and then didn't move. I got up on my hands and knees. Roxanne Keith was gripping his big black gun.

Bits of tar rattled against a window.

She turned coolly, glancing toward the window, and then more bits of tar rattled the panes. She walked over to it and looked out curiously. Half of hell crashed in over her head.

There was a blinding flash—a mixture of reds and yellows—and the building rocked and we didn't have panes any more. Plaster—in hunks as long as your arm—came off the walls with such force that it pitted the woodwork. The table somersaulted and swept into the door, and I went along with it, not enjoying the ride. I don't remember hitting the door. I woke up beside it—very bloody and stone-deaf.

I wiped some blood out of my eyes, got up on my feet, weaved around for a bit. The room was filled with the gray dust from the plaster. Flames licked around the hole that had once been a window.

I stumbled over to the other window—now just a sill.

Directly below me there was a garage with a peaked roof that almost spanned the small narrow yard. Across the yard, there was another red-brick house and somebody familiar was up on the roof. His legs were hidden by a kind of parapet, but I didn't need to see his legs to recognize him. The same evidently held true for him. He saw me and yelled something savagely.

I couldn't hear him and I'm no lip reader. I saw Teddy Warren draw back his right arm.

I didn't wait for the arm to sweep forward. I got myself up on the sill—and then went out the window.

CORPSE FOR PLEASURE

IT SEEMED I was dropping down a dim shaft with a lot of bombs going off around me, only I didn't hear the bombs and just saw the reds and yellows in the flashes. Then I was in bottomless darkness, just hanging there for no reason, and millions of peaked roof-tops were taking turns bumping my side.

Then after that—still making no sense at all—I was peaceful and quiet, and there was a face up above me. I was doing my best to recognize the face. It even talked to me several times, but only once did I hear words. They were something like this:

"There... there, darling.... There, now.... Be quiet."

Three centuries passed.

I opened my eyes.

Caroline Grady was sitting by my bed. She put a hand on my forehead. Then she got up and went out and, after a year or so, came back. There was a man with her, and he was wearing a gray suit. He put a stethoscope on my chest and looked vaguely worried.

That sort of thing went on for quite a while.

Then one morning everything was different. There was a lot of bright sunlight making patterns on the floor, and I could smell the flowers by my bed and hear noises outside.

I could remember Roxanne Keith, Teddy Warren, and the big man, the bomb going off, and even me going out the window.

I wondered if Teddy's second bomb had missed me very much. I checked all my parts gingerly, found them battered but still there.

Bandages covered my side, shoulder and head.

It was two or three days before anybody would talk to me. Nobody came in the room but Caroline Grady and the doctor, and both of them would wiggle fingers and warn me to rest. Then one morning the doctor gave me a clean bill of health, and Caroline Grady came in when he left and sat down by the bed. She had a bundle of newspapers with her and put them on her knees.

"Almost dead with curiosity?" she asked.

I grunted. "Yeah."

She selected a paper and pushed it at me. "According to this, you *are* dead."

I blinked my eyes—the bandages on my head didn't cover them—got hold of the paper and turned it around. Scareheads an inch thick blazed up at me.

ROBERTS KILLED IN BOMBING
MRS. KEITH MAIMED

I found I was gaping at Caroline Grady.

She said: "One of the roomers on the floor dragged her out of the fire. She was horribly mutilated, but still alive. She's lived, too. They took her home two days ago."

I looked at the date on the paper. It was three weeks old.

Caroline Grady said: "Gunter's body was recovered by firemen, but they found hardly anything of his friend's. Everybody was sure *that* was you."

I just stared at her. I didn't even like to listen. I could remember Gunter, carrying his shield.

She said: "Now about you—"

I released some breath. "Sweet cripes!"

She patted my hand. "Anyway about you: You see, after I left you I realized you were going after Gunter because of me, and— Well, I realized you could have turned me into the police and cleared yourself, but that instead, you were letting me go and going after Gunter to make *him* clear you. So I felt pretty badly, and thought maybe I could help, and—" She flushed.

I grinned. "Is that why I did it?"

HER FLUSH went away, and she smiled at me. "You know it is.... Now wait. You see, I drove up the alley behind the house, and it seemed like I hadn't been there a second when shooting started upstairs. And then I saw Teddy up on the roof of the other house. He threw the first bomb, and then I saw you at the other window, all bloody.

"And then Teddy threw the second bomb, but you dived out before it hit. You landed on the garage roof, rolled off and fell between the garage and the house. The house you dived out of, I mean. And I— Well, I ran in the yard and dragged you out to the alley to my car."

I said: "Huh?"

She laughed. "Here. Look." She doubled her arm and made a muscle. "I'm no sissy."

I shook my head, grinning. "I didn't mean that. Maybe you could even carry me." I watched her slant eyes. "I meant why."

She said: "Oh." She saw me watching her and frowned, drawing her sleek brows together. "Sometimes I think you don't know what it is to trust people."

Her eyes darkened and she stiffened slightly. "Teddy was shooting at you. He missed twice and then I didn't see him any more. I guessed he was coming down to finish you, and"—her eyes flashed at me—"he was—we just got away in time."

I said: "Where'd you get the doctor?"

Her hands were tight fists, resting on top of the pile of papers. But then she smiled. It was a slight smile, but her eyes were in it. "Darn you," she said. "He's a police doctor. Mr. Cornwell and Lieutenant Canavan both know you're here."

That froze me. I just gawked at her.

She smiled, and went on: "You see, my first thought was to get you away from Teddy. But then you were in such bad shape, and—" She paused, bit her lip. "Well, I phoned your friend, Mr. Bones, but it seems he doesn't trust people, either. He brought Mr. Cornwell and the lieutenant with him."

I grinned. "He would."

She smiled ruefully. "And it was a pretty good thing for me he did. He didn't believe me, and— Well, he *is* excitable, isn't he? Anyhow, the other two believed me, and then Mr. Bones said you were in a spot. Your company had almost fired him, and he said they'd be sure to fire you.

"But my story cleared you with Mr. Cornwell, so he decided to let you stay dead for a while. You see, there was already an extra out, announcing your death."

I scowled. "And where am I now—down at the morgue?"

She nodded. "Naturally, Mr. Cornwell isn't going to *bury* the other man as you."

"Nice of him," I growled. "And what about Teddy?"

Her eyes looked dull. "Teddy stayed at the scene of his crime too long. The two carloads of policemen—still looking for you—heard both of the explosions, came running and trapped him. And Teddy made the mistake of trying to shoot his way clear. They put eighteen bullets in him. He's been buried."

I said: "What are you holding back on me?"

She started and then smiled. But the smile was slow and very strained. When she spoke her voice was a lifeless monotone:

"Teddy happens to be the beautiful boy I married. I think that'll be enough for today...."

It was three weeks later—which made it six weeks from the actual bombing—when I climbed into a U-Drive-It beside Bones and we drove north along darkened streets. The night was bright, warm, with just a slight breeze from the Bay. We pulled in a block from Peggy Anne's house and sat watching our cigarette ends glow in the dark. Canavan came out of a tall boxwood hedge, opened our door, and said:

"All ready, Shag."

He went away, tall and erect in the gloom, and I felt Bones' fingers touch my arm. He said: "I still don't trust her, boy."

I scowled. "Look, son. Caroline Grady broke her singing contract when she married Teddy, and after she left him, the circuit wouldn't take her back. No other circuit would book her, either. So she didn't have a buffalo nickel, and the girl had to live *some* way. Besides, Gunter told her that the business in the club wasn't anything but a publicity stunt."

Bones said: "Yeah. But she's a smart dame. That'd be a tough item to shove down her throat."

I GROWLED: "Maybe it was. But suppose you were broke and almost down and out—how much would you swallow for a hundred bucks? Besides, we were all over the front pages on that other case and that made Gunter's story pretty logical. Anyway, Gunter was Teddy's best friend, and he'd always been nice as hell to her.

"Incidentally, Gunter gave her the proposition when she went to him to borrow money to get out to the Coast. She was going to try the movies. And she didn't know there was going to be shooting—Gunter told her I was just to get a public lacing. And besides that, she didn't know Gunter and Teddy had records."

Bones snapped angrily: "But she took the dough *after* Waldo's shooting, boy. That don't quite add up in my book."

I groaned. "Look, son. What the hell else could she do? She was in it then up to her neck, and if she'd turned down the money, they'd have gotten suspicious of her. And if they'd have thought she was going to turn them up to the cops, her life wouldn't have been worth the skin off a pickle. And if she *had* turned them up to the cops, the publicity would've ruined her singing career. So she did the next best thing and tried to come to me."

Bones said stubbornly: "I still don't trust her."

I flipped my cigarette and got out of the car. My arm was in a sling, but my side had healed, and I felt pretty good. But officially I was still pretty dead. Bones, Canavan, and Cornwell had all played it pretty safe, none of them coming to see me until the last couple of days. My tag—with my name beautifully typewritten—was still on a mangled stiff down at the morgue.

There wasn't any sense in arguing with Bones. I went up the street and turned in at Peggy Anne's. There was a yellow bloom of light on the second-floor sleeping porch.

I went up the porch steps and tried the front door. It was open, of course—my path all cleared for me—and I went in and walked silently up the steep narrow stairs. At the top, a long dim corridor led to the door of the sleeping porch, and I went on tiptoes to the doorway, opened the door, and stepped out.

Roxanne Keith was reading a magazine under the bright bloom of yellow light. I went over and stood in front of her.

"Hello, Mrs. Keith," I said.

She didn't look up right away. She was sitting in a wheel-chair and almost completely swathed in blankets, but what the blankets didn't cover, it seemed that bandages did. Her head, neck, and shoulders were bound like a mummy's, but there wasn't even a strip of adhesive On her face. By one of Fate's little tricks—if you want to call it that—the cool Indian-like features had been left unmarked.

She tucked a blotter in the magazine to mark her place, then shut it coolly and laid it aside.

She looked up at me and her lips twitched and drew taut.

I said: "I made two mistakes concerning motive, Mrs. Keith. First, I thought the real motive was Waldo's insurance—with Peggy Anne after it body, tooth and nail. But Peggy Anne was only a pawn that Teddy used; she didn't have anything to do with the murder. Then I thought Teddy himself was after the insurance—which he was, but only as part of *his* scheme.

"The real motive was Waldo's trust fund, which *reverted to the estate* at his death. You were almost broke and you needed that trust fund to pay the hundred grand blackmail Gunter—the fake captain—demanded. Don't you see it's all clear now, Mrs. Keith?"

She sat as motionless as a stone woman, staring dully at me. Her dark skin had paled until it looked ugly and soiled, like the buff paint of a freighter that badly needs washing down. But then her jaw jutted a little, and she made low guttural noises.

I leaned forward slightly. "You see, Teddy Warren had his eye cocked on the Keith dough, and he was playing around with both *you* and Peggy Anne. He even piddled away almost all of your money—and used part of it to *marry* another girl. That was a Miss Caroline Grady; but you found it out in about a month—a thing like that is hard to keep from a sweetie.

"And so you went to the Grady girl and said *you* were Teddy's wife; and she didn't bother to wait for Teddy to verify it. By then she'd realized anyway that she'd made a mistake. So when you told her that morning, she was out—bag and baggage—by noon.

"BUT YOU'D made the mistake of telling Teddy the family history and he began to crack down on you. He got Gunter—you were society; he naturally hadn't introduced him to you—to act as the captain and trick you with a fake log. And you agreed to pay Gunter if he'd kill Waldo—you could turn the cash from Waldo's trust fund over to him pronto.

"But then you killed Gunter—not just to save *my* life, as it looked—but simply because you had the opportunity to kill him from a justifiable standpoint by law. Which left you the hundred grand from the trust fund—you couldn't have turned it over to him that quickly—and only Teddy to deal with—who you now had something on.

"You knew from Gunter's talk in the room that Teddy was an accomplice in Waldo's murder. And with that against him, Teddy couldn't put any pressure on you."

Roxanne Keith put the back of her hand to her mouth and screamed. Then her teeth dug fiercely into the flesh, choking off sound, twisting her face violently.

I gritted my own teeth. I said: "But in the meantime, Teddy had been pulled in by the cops, and I'd given the cops a pretty good slant on *his* angle. But he broke loose and decided to get clear—the only way he knew how, by wiping out the proof, you and Gunter. Which didn't leave much evidence against you, except from Caroline Grady, who can verify your pose as Teddy's wife.

"You see, fortunately for you, the Grady girl didn't know much. She didn't know that you'd gotten Gunter to kill Waldo; Gunter told her Waldo was killed just to carry out the threat made to you. Which is the crop, Mrs. Keith, and maybe you've paid enough. Teddy made a foul of you—and left you like *this*."

For a few moments she just sat; but her teeth didn't leave her hand. Then she took her hand away and screamed at me—horribly. She tried to get out of the chair, and kept screaming. Her cool Indian-like face became blotched and hideously mottled.

There was a torrent of invectives and a lot of guttural swearing.

She wound up with this, repeated half a dozen times: "And I'll make a fool of you—like I made one of Waldo! I had him killed and I'll have you hanged!"

That was an admission, and I stepped away from her. A window to the sleeping porch opened, and Cornwell put his head out. Peggy Anne showed behind him, looking pale and very frightened.

Cornwell waved one of his cigars and said: "All right, Roberts. And say hello to the girl for me."

Back at the car I gave Bones results. "You still doubt Caroline now, son?"

He scowled at me in the darkness. "Hell, if that Keith woman didn't implicate her, I suppose she's in the clear. Anyway, the company'll welcome you back with open arms now. Canavan and Cornwell'll get all the case-busting publicity—you were just drawn into it because you were used as a blind. Hey! How long you going to stay dead?"

I grinned. "For a few days, anyway. Caroline and I get more privacy with me as a corpse."

CORPSES WITH WINGS

*This corpse took the high road to heaven on the wings
of a rifle bullet. And when Shag and Bones—those
devil demons of homicide—followed the trigger trail
skyward, they found themselves at the mercy of mob
fury that drove them on the low road to hell.*

CHAPTER I

MURDER MESSAGE

S **HE RODE** a sleek black stallion—no kidding now,
either—and a midnight blue mask covered her face.
Her hat was of the ten-gallon variety, and also midnight
blue; and she wore the same color whipcord breeches and
gleaming black boots. She pulled the stallion in front of
my coupé and fired two shots in the air.

I stopped the coupé.

Bones held up the bottle of beer he'd been drinking and
inspected the label and sniffed at the neck. He said: "It
smells like it, Shaggie."

"Smells like what?"

"Beer."

I squeezed my eyes shut—not at the crack—but when I
opened them again, the girl on the stallion was still there.
I grunted and poked my nose out the window. We were
on one of the new dual highways, about five miles out of
Lambville, and I didn't see any circuses around. In fact, I
didn't see anything but a lot of woods and fields.

The girl had galloped the stallion out of a clump of
nearby pines that overlooked the highway from the top of
a small knoll. Sunlight—hot midmorning sun—gleamed
on her stirrups and poured sweat down my face.

Bones finished the bottle of beer he'd inspected and snatched another one out of the galvanized tub at his feet. He sampled it and grinned. "This one's beer, too."

I was watching the girl ride up to my side of the car. The stallion was pawing and snorting. She called: "Aren't you Shag Roberts?"

I said: "Huh?"

The girl's eyes, a deep shimmering green behind the mask, scrutinized me carefully, and then switched to Bones. She said, panting a little: "You *are* Shag Roberts. I recognize you from your newspaper pictures. And that's Bones McPherson—I recognize him." She fished a small envelope out of her bosom. "This is for you."

I squinted at her. "Twentieth century pony express, huh?"

The eyes were cool. "This is for you."

I took the envelope, wagging my head a little, ripped it open. There was a letter with a check clipped to it. The check was made out to the Home Aid Finance Company,

in the amount of three hundred bucks, and signed William Hill. The letter was brief and to the point:

Messrs. Roberts and McPherson,

Investigators, Home Aid Finance Co.

Dear Sirs:

Enclosed please find check for three hundred dollars to cover payment of Jerome Watt's account in full. I regret that Mr. Watt did not settle long ago. However, now that the account is settled, I trust you will not find it necessary to come to Lambville. There has been considerable antagonism stirred up toward you throughout our town, and we do not want any trouble. Please give my messenger your receipt.

There was a sincerely yours, and the letter was on the stationery of the Lambville Baseball Club. Under the signature, which looked like a few chicken tracks, was William Hill, President and Manager.

I grinned. "He owns the club, doesn't he?"

The ten-gallon hat nodded. "He owns it, runs it, manages—everything."

"And who are you?"

"Never mind who I am."

I STUFFED the check and letter back into the envelope. "Okay. But take this back to him and tell him no can do, because there's a year's interest due on that three hundred bucks. Also tell Mr. William Hill that we're sorry but we don't take checks on an open road—not when we'd have to ride back forty miles to Parkersburg to find out whether or not the thing would stretch. You get it—we get a lot of rubber ones in this business. Nothing personal against Mr. Hill. We just have to be careful."

The eyes stayed cool. "How much is the interest?"

I shrugged. "Not much. It's the principle of the thing."

The eyes flashed this time. "You're just trying to make trouble for us!"

"Listen, lady," I said. "We don't want to make trouble for anybody. We're just a couple of guys with a job to do, but we like to do it as well as we can. Now if this check was certified and the right amount, we might take it and breeze away from here.

"But I don't like Mr. Hill's idea of bringing up that antagonism, hoping *that'll* help his idea of getting us to take the check. We don't scare that easy, lady. What are they going to do in this town—ride us out on a rail?"

She flared: "You won't get in the town!"

"And you won't get there whole and healthy, either, if you don't stop waving that gun around." I opened the door of the coupé and slid out. The stallion r'ared back, whinnied, and shook in his harness. The girl patted his neck again, and he quieted down. I said: "Put that thing up, or I'll haul you off of there."

She blazed: "It's only loaded with blanks, you ninny! I had to make sure you'd stop for me, didn't I?"

I growled: "Well, don't ever tell a guy a thing like that. Just wait till he wrings your lovely neck." I mopped my face with a handkerchief, and the perspiration wasn't all from the sun, either. "Now beat it. Tell Mr. Hill we're not trying to make trouble. We'll go to see him and try to settle things."

She said angrily: "I tell you, you won't ever get into town!"

Bones snapped: "Who's going to stop us—a couple divisions of marines?"

I groaned, and looked anxiously at him. His freckled face was sticking out the window on my side, and one of his skinny hands waved a beer bottle. He's excitable, and I didn't want to get him started. His own green eyes already had a dance to them.

I said hastily: "Now wait a minute, son." And to the girl: "What makes you think we won't get in?"

She said: "There's about thirty men just outside of town, blocking this road to make sure you won't. Can you handle thirty men?"

I whipped the palm of my hand against the stallion's flank. He bucked, r'ared up again, then plunged away down the road, his shoes ringing on the concrete. I got back in the car and kicked some life into the motor. We ran away from there, hitting close to sixty, and it only took us a couple of minutes to leave the girl far behind.

I stopped the car as soon as we lost sight of her, yanked open the glove compartment, and hauled out a map. Bones was scowling. "What's this?"

"If there's any ice left in the tub, a bottle of beer for daddy," I said. "We're going into town by some other route."

He growled: "What? And miss all the fun?"

"Listen, son," I said. "It's not even noon. Personally, I always make it a rule not to argue with thirty guys before lunch. What the hell are they there for, anyway?"

Bones grinned. "You tell me, Sherlock."

"Well, I've got an idea the word's gotten around that we can stop Jerry Watt from pitching ball. These farmers take their baseball seriously. But why didn't this Billy Hill loosen up before?"

Bones said: "Why didn't he send that girl to us before?"

I groaned. "There you go."

"Well, I suppose *you* weren't lamping her? Say! She could stop a girl show with a walk-on part, even if she came on with a pumpkin on her head. And don't ask me how I know it, even if she was sitting down."

I said: "She's just a kid."

"Huh?"

"Her neck was small, like she hasn't finished growing—I'd say she was seventeen or eighteen, maybe less. And that outfit of hers helps that idea along. Anyway, what I liked was her eyes."

Bones gaped. "You liked her *eyes?*" He leaned back and threw up his hands. "I know, Shag. You're the baby who liked Lady Godiva because of her voice."

WE BLEW into Lambville—it's a town of about fifty thousand—by the shortest by-road we could find on the map. It took up about two minutes to find the *Hotel Traill.* It was a fat red-brick building facing the city's main square, and there were eight or ten loafers scattered around on its big, old-fashioned porch.

The loafers stared at us bleakly when we got out of the coupé, but we didn't pay any attention to them. I noticed out of my eye-corners that they began to group together, and the darky who took our bags didn't seem to like it. The desk clerk in the lobby looked positively sick.

He took our names and let us register without fainting dead away, and we went up to our room and dumped our bags. The room faced the square, only it was not really a square, but a traffic circle with a monument to Joshua Lamb in its center. I never did find out exactly who *he* was, but I did notice two more hotels almost directly across the circle from us.

I didn't realize that was important then. I didn't know bullets were going to be flying around.

We took showers—the thing was a ring hung over the tub—got into fresh clothes and I called the desk. The clerk still sounded like he might have a stomach ailment. Finally I got put through to Mike Martinez' room.

"So you're here," Mike said.

"All in one piece," I told him.

"Come on down or up. Two-seventeen."

We were on the fourth floor, so we went out and took the rickety cage elevator down. Mike met us at the door, smiling all over his broad face, his big teeth against his bronzed skin glistening like white tile. He was a man of medium height, bowlegged and deep-chested, and he'd coached our ball club in high school after he drank himself out of the big leagues.

But he soon drank himself out of the high school job, too, and he'd been down here for the last eight seasons. He was only thirty-nine—he'd reached the big leagues at twenty—and I knew he still caught an occasional game. He *always* caught when Jerry Watt pitched, and once in a while handled another kid pitcher. Mike wasn't a perpetual drinker. He rode the wagon for long stretches and then went on sprees.

I introduced Bones—natty in a double-breasted gabardine—and we went inside and Mike looked us over. We gabbed for a little while and then Mike asked: "How did you get past the mob waiting on the road for you?"

I told him.

He grinned. "The girl'll be Marcia Daly—she's kind of the club mascot. Our club's called the Cowboys—heaven knows why—and she wears that outfit at games. It's Billy Hill's idea—he's a showman—and it sort of lets him keep her around. Billy's forty-five and married, but that don't stop him."

"How old is the girl?" I asked.

Marcia? Just seventeen—but you'd swear she was a woman once you talked to her for ten minutes or so." He tapped his forehead. "She's got a head, that girl has. You'll see her leading the parade."

I wiggled a finger at Bones. Mike lifted his brows and I said: "He was about to say a head wasn't all she has. What's this about a parade?"

Mike squinted at me. "Hell, you wouldn't know, would you? Well, look. Our club won the Valley League, and Parkersburg won the Mountain League. This is the play-off for the section championship—five games, or first team to win three.

"Well, we've won two behind Jerry Watt and lost one and we're gonna lose today. Nobody can stop those Parkersburg boys but Jerry Watt and this town knows it. We played in Parkersburg yesterday and the day before, and this is a homecoming, and so the parade."

I said: "Why didn't you phone us about the guys on the road?"

MIKE GRINNED. "Hell, I didn't know they were *out* on the road until just about half an hour ago. Anyway, every penny in this town's bet on the Cowboys, Shag. And if I'd gone down and tried to stop that mob, people might've thought I was trying to help you collect. And ball fans around here are tough."

I growled: "But we're not going to stop Jerry Watt from playing."

"You can," Mike pointed out.

I tapped my breast pocket. "Look, Mike. This Lambville ball club isn't in organized baseball. But it's a well organized league just the same, and its president says its players got to pay their bills and act right or else they just don't play ball. And Jerry Watt's got to pay his loan, or else I've got a letter here that'll stop him from pitching. That's all.

"The letter's just a collection lever, but when the money's paid, that's the end of it. But because a sports writer ran the story of us being after Jerry Watt, everybody's got the thing all twisted up. As soon as we get our money we'll breeze out of here."

Mike held up a gnarled hand. "There's the parade."

He strode for a window with Bones and me at his heels, and the three of us squeezed in at the sill for a look. But the parade hadn't reached the traffic circle yet. From the distance, we could hear drums pounding away and an occasional shot ringing out in the air. People began appearing in doorways, windows, and out on the sidewalks. We were a trifle crowded at our window, so Bones left us and took another.

The girl was first into the square, still astride the stallion and still wearing the mask. Behind her came a troop of cowboys, firing blanks up in the air. Behind them, cowboys walked, carrying streamers between them, and behind all this came a cowboy-dressed band. The girl's stallion strutted magnificently. Spectators applauded, and the din was terrific.

I held my ears and turned to Mike. "Who's sponsoring this—a headache powder company?"

Mike didn't say anything. He was slumped across the window sill, hanging on his chest, and his arms dangled loosely at his sides. I said, "Hey! This is no time to pass out," and then almost bit off my tongue.

I'd touched his arm and it didn't feel right. I started to speak again, but my tongue felt thick.

I got my hands under his armpits and lifted him until I could see his face. It was blank and expressionless and the eyes were open, only the eyes weren't seeing anything. On his chest, just above his heart, there were two small holes in his shirt and blood was spreading around them.

I don't remember exactly what I did at that moment. But in the next one I was peering across the square.

In one of the hotels opposite, on the second floor, a window went down very fast. I wouldn't have noticed it probably, except that it was to the west, and the early sun struck silver against the glass. I counted quickly in from the corner of the building; it was the fourth window and none were occupied near it.

I laid Mike gently on the floor. Bones turned from his window and goggled at me.

I said: "Yeah. From one of the hotels across the way."

His face tightened. We both sprinted for the door.

CHAPTER II

RIFLE WITH WINGS

WE SCORNED the rickety elevator and leaped down the stairs, and were halfway through the lobby when the desk clerk ran up to us. He still looked a trifle ill. He grabbed my sleeve and panted: "Mr. Hill to see you, Mr. Roberts."

I stared at him. It's funny; I didn't feel much then, maybe because I was just too shocked to feel anything, but as I stared into his face, my blood began to boil. I shoved him a quarter of the way across the lobby. I snarled: "Keep the paws off me, fella. Some other time."

A tall, distinguished-looking man got up from a nearby chair, strolled casually in front of me, and blocked my way. He said: "Now just a moment, Mr. Roberts."

I said: "Are you Hill?"

He nodded. "Of course."

I snapped: "Did you know Mike Martinez has just been murdered?"

He put his iron-gray head to one side. "I beg your pardon?"

"Look," I growled. I gave it to him straight. "What do you want to do—let the killer get to China?"

Hill said: "Sweet heaven!"

I didn't say anything else. The lobby was deserted—everybody out on the big porch for the parade—and we ran out and sprinted across the square. The parade was just passing but we didn't let that bother us. I went straight through the band with Bones and Hill at my heels and climbed the steps of a porch almost identical to that of the *Hotel Traill's*. The porch was crowded and people stared at us in amazement. We ran through the lobby and I bounded up the stairs.

At the second floor, Bones and Hill were still behind me, and most of the crowd on the porch had begun to stream along behind them. Hill was yelling information over his shoulder. The corridor was deserted, and I yanked out my .32, and ran down to the second door from the end.

I figured each room would probably have two windows, and that the fourth window from the corner would be in the second one. I tried the knob and found the door locked. The three of us put our shoulders against it, and on the third heave, it gave.

We plunged in and I threw myself flat, but no gunfire lanced out at us. I got to my feet and saw the room was empty. It contained a bed, dresser, highboy and an easy-chair, and the easy-chair was in front of the fourth window. It was *facing* the window, its seat touching the wall, which put its back about four feet from the window sill. I scowled and went over to the door. An ordinary spring-lock had locked us out.

An excited crowd had gathered out in the corridor, and a man pushed through it, and leaned in the doorway. He was a thin, gaunt man wearing a black linen coat. Hill looked up at him and said:

"Hello, Hank."

I looked at him, too. "You the clerk?"

He said haughtily: "The owner, sir."

Hill introduced us, but the guy's manner didn't change. He had small black eyes, and the eyes didn't like me.

I gave it to him straight, like I'd given it to Hill. "From this room," I added. "You didn't see a guy with a rifle, did you?"

He kept leaning in the doorway. "I saw a man."

I said: "Huh?"

"I was in the back, inspecting the kitchen and the garbage, and when I went out in the—"

"The garbage?"

"Naturally, sir. Some darkies are quite wasteful."

I grinned. "Go on."

"Well, when I went out in the alley to look at the garbage, a man jumped behind a telephone pole. It seemed strange to me, but I'm a man who tries to attend to his own business."

"How long ago was this?"

"I came in when I heard the rumpus, sir."

I yelled: *"What?"*

"I just this minute came inside, sir."

I didn't wait for anything else. I thrust past him into the corridor and began slamming people out of my way. Behind me, Bones' feet pounded heavily, and pretty soon the whole mob was in our wake. I went downstairs and sprinted through the lobby and burst out the back entrance into the alley. There was the main back entrance—the one I went out through—and another one to the kitchen about fifty feet away.

THE ALLEY was long and narrow and completely walled on one side by the rear walls of the two hotels. The hotels were jammed together with not even an areaway in between; these were the two I'd noticed directly across the square from the *Traill.*

On the other side, like in a lot of small cities, the alley was walled by the back yards of a block of residences. These backyards were bounded by a high wooden fence, each with its own private gate. Out in the square, the parade still went on; I found out later it strutted around the circle three times.

One of the gates in the alley opened a crack, and then, very slowly and gently, closed.

I whispered to Bones: "See it, son?"

He yelled: "What?"

People were spilling out the back entrance and crowding around us, and he couldn't have heard my whisper if I'd had my lips in his ear. Everybody was chattering and looking around wildly.

I yelled, "Hold everything!" and went across the alley.

My gate was one about twenty yards away, but I opened the first one I came to and slipped inside. An English bulldog, his jaws dripping and yammering, banged the end of his chain and missed my pants leg an inch. I circled him carefully, saying "Nice boy, nice boy," and shinnied up the high wooden fence that bound the yard on its south side.

Then I went across the next yard and shimmied another fence. When I poked my nose over the next one, my heart almost popped out of my mouth.

As my head went up, a head went up on the other side, so close we almost touched our cheeks. That should have been funny, but at the time it wasn't. The head dropped out of sight, but I was so startled, I clung.

No shots banged out so I poked my nose up again, and a rock bounced off the fence an inch below my chin. I shoved my little gun over and fired a shot into the ground. I yelled: "One more rock and I'll aim it, mister!"

A tall gangling fellow dropped a handful of stones and stepped out into the center of the yard. I swung my legs over and dropped down in front of him.

He was young, not over twenty-two, with a huge width of shoulder and long whiplike arms. His face was clear-skinned and burnished gold by the sun; he was probably as nice a looking guy as I've ever seen. He had teeth like you see in the dental ads.

I squinted at him. "Where's your rifle?"

He was watching my little gun. "What?"

I growled: "If you ditched it, brother, we'll find it. Why would a guy like you kill old Mike, anyway?"

He cocked his head slightly. "What the hell are you raving about?"

I peered at him. He didn't look like a murderer. His crack hadn't been made sullenly, either; he seemed like a guy who had some spirit. I scowled. I told him: "Walk, mister. You'll find out."

The gate at the end of the yard banged, and a couple of men looked inside. One went away, shouting, "Here, Captain Quackenbush!" and the other two stood holding the gate. Presently, a lean rawboned man in his early thirties came in flanked by uniformed cops. Bones and Billy Hill hustled in behind them. Bones thrust aside the rawboned man and yelped:

"You all right, Shag?"

I grinned. "Okay, son."

Quackenbush spat a stream of tobacco juice that looked like it might have spurted from a six-inch hose. He cocked his chin at Bones. "Watch the pushing, freckles." He came striding up to my walking dental ad, spat on the ground at his feet, contemptuously. He said: "Hi, Jerry."

I yelled: *"Huh?"*

Jerry Watt hipped his big hands. "Have you guys gone nuts?"

Billy Hill's blunt jaw dropped. He looked like death itself had smacked him in the face.

I LEFT the room we'd broken into—where Quackenbush was questioning Jerry Watt—and climbed five flights of stairs to the top floor of the hotel. There was a large skylight in the roof with a circular staircase winding up to it, and I reached the bottom step as Bones was coming down. He stuck his head over the rail and wiggled a finger at me.

"The skylight's open, boy. The janitor says it's always open—no cause to lock it, he claims. You still think the guy went *up?*"

I climbed the iron stairs and lifted the steel-framed skylight. "Providing Jerry Watt isn't the guy who did the shooting, yeah. But Quackenbush seems dead certain that he did."

"Huh?"

I lifted the skylight higher and stepped out on the roof. The two six-story hotels dwarfed the buildings around them, and there was a vast sweep of roof-tops, and beyond it, low rolling hills. I said: "Son, Captain Quackenbush doesn't like Mr. Jerry Watt. What does that tell you?"

Bones looked pained. "Now, look. Don't go hemming and hawing and being Mr. Mysterious Detective on me. There are certain things a guy can take from another guy, but if you start doing *that* to me, you gotta smile." He straightened up and swelled out his skinny chest. "Dammit, suh. I still have my pride, suh."

"Nuts," I said. I grunted and prowled around.

The roof was an old-time heavily tarred job with a kind of parapet along the front of the hotel. It fell away from the parapet in a slight slope—for drainage—and there was a wide tin rain-gutter along its rear rim. I walked the length of the rim, peering down into the gutter, and got down on my hands and knees where the gutter met its perpendicular pipe.

There was no elbow in the joint—the gutter and pipe met at right angles—and the mouth of the pipe was a wide, flat rectangle. But about ten feet below the rim there was a bend in the pipe, where it swung to the right to get past a ledge. I stood up and looked at the chimney. There was about twelve feet of sheer brick between the roof and its mouth.

I began prowling again, not missing anything, and finally came to the other hotel. Its roof was about a foot higher, through somebody's different idea of architecture, and I stepped up and went over it slowly. It was peaked slightly in the middle with drainage grates at each corner, and the pipes under them were small and round. There was a skylight, but it was built into the roof, making a kind of glass vestibule which boasted a regular size glass door.

I opened this and examined its lock. It was an ordinary tumbler lock, but no key was in it.

I said: "It looks like this one's always open, too, son."

Bones looked at me suspiciously and I grinned at him, and we went back over the two roofs and then downstairs. He didn't speak until we got off the elevator. Then he grinned sheepishly and said:

"I catch, boy."

I wiggled a finger. "Well, hold on to it. I got a hunch the time isn't ripe, son."

We were on the second floor and voices ripped through the doorway, its shattered door propped haphazardly across it. I squeezed in and Bones slipped through after me. Quackenbush stood in the center of the floor, his thumbs hooked in his waistband, and occasionally swiveled his head and spat heavily in the wastebasket.

Billy Hill, no longer pale, but his shrewd eyes darkly troubled, sat on the bed and listened intently. There were two uniformed cops in the room. You could barely see the windows through the smoke.

Quackenbush was saying: "The hell you didn't."

JERRY WATT jumped up from the edge of the bed, and his gaze leaped wildly around the room. "Won't one of you guys stop him? You know damned well I wouldn't kill Mike. He was like a father to me—he found me, signed me, coached me.... Listen, Billy. Stop him before I get my hands on him."

Quackenbush spat viciously. "Come ahead, beautiful. I'm waiting."

"Then wait another minute," I said.

Quackenbush's head swiveled. He didn't spit this time, but he almost did. He made a guttural noise deep in his throat. "Who the hell let you in?"

I grinned. "A little bird. Now don't get your pants in an uproar. Listen. We know how Mike was killed. Somebody shoved that chair over under the window and used the back of it to rest his rifle on. With the back about four feet away from the window, the rifle barrel wouldn't have to be shoved *outside*. That means nobody would see it.

"And then the guy shot Mike and pulled the window down. He went out and locked the door—there's a spring lock on it—and any fool could've jimmied his way in. And also the room's occupied. But the guy who lives in it was in the parade."

Quackenbush said: "So what?"

"So whoever shot Mike knew the guy was going to be in the parade. But that's something anybody could find out. Where does Watt live?"

Quackenbush jerked a thumb over his shoulder. "Two rooms down."

I growled: "So you think that instead of going to his room, he went out in the alley to ditch the rifle, huh? But you haven't found the rifle. Now, listen. Suppose he *didn't* go out to ditch it? Has he said *why* he went out?"

Quackenbush's face turned a dull bleached gray. I thought for a moment he was going to jump at me. Flesh bunched around his small dark eyes, and the muscles in his neck bulged, thickened. But then he whirled on Jerry Watt. His voice whipped at him:

"*Why*, beautiful?"

Jerry Watt looked at me. He didn't cower, didn't look sullen. He faced Quackenbush squarely and said: "That's none of your damned business."

Which one of them moved first, I don't know. They collided in the center of the room like a couple of freight trains; they stood toe-to-toe and flailed at each other. But Jerry Watt was younger, bigger and stronger. He forced Quackenbush back, then slid in close to him, and almost tore his head off with a short right hook.

Quackenbush slammed into a corner with a force that shook the walls, and a uniformed copper brought his nightstick down on Jerry Watt's head. Bones yelped, "Hey, flat-foot! That ain't fair!" and knocked the copper flat with a looping right swing. Then the second copper leaped at Bones, lifting his nightstick, and I tripped him and sent him reeling into the bed.

Quackenbush came out of the corner with a gun in his fist. "Okay, beautiful. If that's the way you want to play,"

Jerry Watt was down on one knee on the floor, holding his head and looking bewildered. I yelled, "Hey!" and stamped my foot. It was enough to draw Quackenbush's eyes momentarily, and in that instant, I got around in front of Watt. I shouted:

"He's not resisting arrest now, you ninny! You can't just burn him down!"

Quackenbush's eyes glowed with a dark fire, but he clipped the gun back in its shoulder holster. He said: "All right, beautiful. Stand up." And to me: "You're a smart guy."

I growled: "Look, fella. Don't think I'm doing any favors for Jerry Watt—it's just that I'd like a little justice around here. What would be his motive for killing Mike?"

Quackenbush snapped: "He ain't got one."

I just gawked. "Huh?"

Quackenbush said: "You and your buddy been chasing him around for months, and he was just fed up with it. He didn't try to kill Mike. He just tried to kill you and missed."

Bones said: "Have you gone bats?"

Quackenbush got the range of the wastebasket and spat. "*You* might think so, but I don't, brother. And seeing as how your coming here kind of forced beautiful's hand, if I was you I'd start thinking about them ball fans."

I looked questioningly at Billy Hill. "*Is* he bats?"

Hill looked haggard, weary, almost worn out. He said: "Mobs are terrific in this part of the country, Mr. Roberts.

And Jerry can't pitch if he's in a cell. When this gets out, there's going to be trouble, and I'd advise you to get out of town."

I scowled. "No can do, mister."

Quackenbush lifted his gaze to me sourly. "Okay. You're tough, and we know it. But I warned you. I done my bit."

CHAPTER III

ONE-MAN STRONGARM SQUAD

IT **WAS** a quarter of six when Billy Hill telephoned me to tell me that Lambville had lost the ball game. "It was terrible. Fourteen to two. Nobody can stop those Parkersburg boys but Jerry."

I said: "There's a guy named Ruffing with the Yanks who's supposed to be pretty good. Look. How about that check?"

"I've had one made up to the right amount and certified. I'll bring it right up to you." He hesitated. "Have you been bothered yet?"

"Not yet."

He sounded worried. "I think it'll probably begin now. The licking left it all up to Jerry."

"Well, you hustle up here with that check," I growled.

I rang off and faced Bones. We'd been in all afternoon—not because we took any stock in that mob business—but because we'd been out late the night before, and because something told me we might be out late again. We'd had our galvanized tub chocked with ice and beer, and between naps had kept ourselves cool.

Bones, in a pair of striped silk shorts, was squatting in the center of the floor tossing cards at my hat. He said: "So they lost?"

"Yeah."

"Shall we call the papers?"

"There's only one of them," I said. "But look. These guys may be all wet about this mob stuff, but I've got a weak hunch they *might* be right. We're not going to let old Mike down, are we?"

Bones grinned. "He was your friend, boy."

"Okay," I said. "And maybe somebody tried to kill me and missed, but I like the other way better. *Two* slugs in Mike sort of makes me feel that way. You get your pants on."

"I got my pants on."

"Well, strut through the dining-room without your others. *I* can take it," I said. "We'll call the *Chronicle*, and then we eat."

We were in a corner of the dining-room—where we could watch the square through a window—and working on our ice-cream when a bellhop led Billy Hill in. He breezed through the tables, his face a grim tight mask, came up to us breathlessly, and put a hand on the table edge. The other hand slapped a copy of the *Chronicle* down on the table in front of us. It was still damp and limp from the presses, and the headlines screamed:

MYSTERIOUS TIPSTER CLAIMS MURDER SOLUTION

"Well, I'll be dawg-goned," I said.

Hill looked at me. I got it over, all right, putting on a poker face, went back to my ice-cream, but didn't look at Bones, he did a little coughing into his handkerchief. Hill frowned sharply at us.

"You know anything about this?"

I shook my head. "Not a thing."

He still watched us suspiciously. "It's evidently from a crank of some kind. Whoever it is claims they've gone over the hotel from top to bottom, and that tomorrow they're going to put the solution in Quackenbush's lap. But in the meantime Jerry's still in jail, and anyway, there's something I want to see you about."

I looked up at him. "Oh. The check."

He said tightly: "Not the check." He slipped it out of an inside pocket and handed it to me. It was the right amount and certified, and I put it in my own pocket. He leaned forward slightly. "Something else."

"Yeah?" I said.

He nodded slowly. "The mob's already started to form. The police have got their hands full now; they've broken up two small mobs downtown a little bit. Marcia's at head-quarters and keeping me posted."

"Who is?"

"Marcia Daly. She's the sister of Quackenbush's wife. You met her on the road this morning."

I stood up slowly. "She's the sister of Quackenbush's *wife?*"

His shrewd eyes looked puzzled. "Yes. Why?"

I scowled. Nobody had told me Quackenbush had a wife. I said: "You and Bones stick here a while. I got a few things to do."

I left the hotel by the rear entrance and went across a graveled lot to the hotel's garage. A darky in a blue jumper brought my coupé, and I climbed in and rolled it out to the square. It was as if that was a signal of some kind.

While I waited for the traffic light to change, a crowd of men came swinging into the square. They were big men, rough men, and none of them were grinning; and their eyes were fixed on the *Hotel Traill*. The back of my neck began to feel chilled. I was in a narrow alleyway between them and the hotel, and if they used the sidewalk, they'd pass in front of my nose.

I looked anxiously out at the traffic. It was moving fast and in a solid line and I didn't see any place to bully my way in. Even if I jumped the red light, I'd only pile up on somebody out in the square.

THE CROWD was moving along, and growing, and it kept to the sidewalk because of the traffic. I slammed the coupé into reverse. It leaped back, as a car will when you jerk it, and then stopped with a crash that shook me half out of the seat. I'd been too excited to look in the rear-view mirror. A car had come out behind me, and I'd practically smashed in its front end.

By the time I got my wits together, a red-faced guy was shaking his fist under my nose.

I didn't get out. I yelled: "Are we hooked?"

He told me with a stream of profanity just what kind of a Sunday driver I was.

The first platoon of the crowd had arrived by this time, and they stopped and stared curiously at the coupé. Or maybe they stopped to listen to my friend. Anyway, I put a hand in his face and pushed him away, and then kicked life into my motor and yanked it in gear. It was right at this time that somebody yelled.

My name banged around the circle in a rising echo, and I leaned on the horn and put weight on the gas. For one sickening moment—it seemed long enough to grow a tree—the car bucked and clanked and didn't move a foot. Then it shot forward like it had been blown from a tube, and the crowd parted magically and the center of the square was in front of me. I wrenched the wheel over hard and made the circle on one wheel.

I'd gotten one break, though—the traffic light had switched—and I leaned the coupé into the first street and swept into the outside traffic lane. There was a red light at the next corner, but I jumped that, and then a traffic whistle blasted shrilly behind me.

I glanced in the rear-view mirror—long enough to see a fat copper on foot—turned a couple of blocks farther and crisscrossed around town. By the time I drew up in front of police headquarters, I'd used up twenty minutes and the streets were almost dark.

The cop at the desk looked me over carefully. "Miss Daly? She just went home to supper."

I said: "She still live on Jefferson Street?"

He scowled at me. "Jefferson Street? Two-twelve Parkway Place. She's—" His scowl deepened, and his eyes grew suspicious.

"Thanks," I said, and breezed out in a hurry before he realized I'd bluffed it out of him.

I telephoned Bones from a drug store a couple of blocks away. "How's the mob?"

He cackled. "What did you do to 'em?"

I explained my bit of fun. "They bothering you, son?"

He said: "Your mess brought some cops running, and now they're down in front of the hotel, although they don't seem to like their job so much. Hey! What's that dame look like without the mask?"

I grinned. "What's it to you? You didn't care about her face, did you?"

I hung up and got directions to Parkway Place from the druggist, drove down there in about five minutes and nosed the coupé into the curb. Darkness had settled everywhere now. I got out and prowled along the sidewalk.

Number two-twelve had a light in its middle room, and a dark-haired girl was gathering up dishes from a table. I opened a small gate, went up a narrow walk between flower-beds, climbed to the porch and pressed a bell.

The door was opened by a big thick-shouldered man who peered hard at me in the gloom.

I said: "May I see Miss Daly, please?"

He kept peering at me. "Who will I say is calling?"

I hesitated. "Mr. Roberts."

The man started visibly, even in the darkness, and then a big hand shot out and gripped my shirt front and tie. Before I even knew what was happening, I was being hauled bodily into the hall.

MAYBE IT was just the surprise that knocked the props out from under me, but by the time I got my wits I was under the drop-light near the stairs. The big man still had hold of my shirt-front. He had a bright red face with solidly padded cheeks, and the general look of a guy who does his work outdoors. His eyes were small, clear, and very bright and crow's feet were etched at their corners. I sized him up as a fellow who'd make a good friend, and who'd drum up a lot of respect even from guys who were enemies.

He yelled: "Marcia!" And then said to me: "This is the best break that's come my way since the flood."

I got hold of his biceps, just under his shoulder, socked a hit into him and tried to throw him over my back. I might as well have tried to bend the Washington Monument. He laughed and straightened me up by hooking a big hand under my chin.

Marcia Daly appeared in the doorway to the living room.

The big man had forced my chin back until my neck was at right angles to my spine, so naturally I couldn't see her very well. He chuckled and said cheerfully:

"Friend of yours, isn't he?"

I heard her gasp slightly. "Uncle Trix! You'll kill him!"

Uncle Trix chuckled again. He said: "Honsy-wonsy, you give me an idea." But he released some pressure on my neck and I could swallow again. He added: "That mob downtown would pay good dough for this chance, and here he walks right into old Trixie's mitts. Maybe I ought to take out my dollar's worth. Maybe after that I ought to turn him over to 'em."

Marcia said coldly: "You know you wouldn't do it."

Uncle Trix answered her by turning me loose and ramming a hand in my back that drove me stumbling against the wall. He said lightly: "Put 'em up, friend." He came in with his fists clenched.

This was a little more in my line. I feinted with a left and piled a right at his chin that must have missed by a quarter of a mile. This baby was not only tough; he was fast as a greased whippet. He hit me three times in the belly and twice on the chin, and I wound up in the corner on the back of my neck.

Marcia said "Oo-oh!"

Uncle Trix chewed his lip and stuffed in his shirt-tail. He said speculatively: "That a buck's worth?"

I pushed my chin around for a little while until it felt normal again. "You wouldn't take bargain prices," I said.

"Holy horse! It's got life in it, honey!"

I got up on my feet, seeing two Uncle Trixie's, both coming in standing straight up, and both having two fists.

Naturally, I piled my hooks at the wrong one. I wound up in another corner on the small of my back.

Uncle Trix said: "It grows monotonous, honey."

"You're still getting bargain prices," I gritted.

I waited this time until I saw one Uncle Trix and got up with my gaze fixed on his dun. I didn't try any feints or hooks, either. He came in again, standing straight up, and I remembered there's such a thing as a straight left.

I let him have it, feeling the jar all the way to my shoulder, and a couple of streams of blood jumped out of his nose. He rocked back on his heels and wiped it away with a forefinger. Then he looked at the forefinger ruefully and grinned.

"I'm kind of beginning to like you," he said.

I grinned back at him. "Hell, I'm just getting the kinks out of my arms."

He came in again, weaving around my straight left, and my head snapped back like it had springs in it. Short right hooks rained on my chin. The next thing I knew I was slung over his shoulder—firemen's carry—and we were shoving through the door to the porch.

He carried me out and dumped me down on the grass and stood chewing his lip and regarding me speculatively. Then he attended to his shirt-tail again. He scratched his head and said:

"What would that mob do to you?"

He was see-sawing dizzily in front of my eyes. "Not much more," I said a little vaguely.

HE SQUATTED on his heels and broke off a blade of grass. "Now, look." He pointed the blade at me. "You don't seem like a bad fellow and so I'm giving you a break, but I'm warning you—don't fool around with Marcia. She's only a kid and I don't want her mixed up in any murder business, so anything you want to ask her, you just ask elsewhere. And I'm not playing duck-on-the-rock with you now; I'm giving it to you straight, and buddy, I mean it."

"Were you a good friend of Mike's?" I asked.

He frowned. "Mike and I were pretty good pals. He taught me all I know, and I caught when he didn't!"

I shook my head trying to clear it and peered at him in the darkness. He didn't look much over thirty. I said: "Well, you're certainly being screwy about the kid."

He cocked his head to one side. "Hey?"

"Listen," I snapped. "Mike was murdered. You know, murdered—there's a law against it. In this state, the law hangs people who murder other people. You follow me?"

He grinned. "They ought to call you Lippy."

"They do. Now, look. Mike told me Marcia had a brain in her head, and I think she'll have sense enough to talk to me. Maybe if she does, I can clear Jerry Watt. Maybe if I do that, I can nab the bird who killed Mike. But you go screwy and pitch me out on my ear. I can take a licking but stupidity riles me. Understand?"

He growled: "Meaning what?"

My head was beginning to clear. I said: "Meaning—tactfully—will you please let me talk to her?"

"No," he snapped.

"Then meaning I'm going to talk to her, anyway."

He chewed his lip and looked me over a moment, and then got out of his squat and tightened his belt. He said: "I meant what I said, buddy."

"Okay," I growled. "I'll shoot some light into that thick head."

He didn't say anything, just kept chewing his lips, and then turned on his heel and went into the house. I stood up and took stock of my face. It felt skinned and bruised around my nose and mouth, so I went back to the coupé and scouted for a drug store. A little flesh-colored adhesive fixed me up satisfactorily, and I slipped in a booth and telephoned Bones.

"You still breathing, son?"

He didn't sound quite so cheerful. "Say! There's about three hundred guys out in that square. Not doing much, mind you, but it's not going to take much to set 'em off. Half of the police force is down on the porch."

I said: "How'd you like to be rescued by a girl—minus her mask?"

"Huh?" he almost yelled.

"Put on your Sunday best," I said. "She'll be around."

I hung up and went back out in the drug store and killed a little over an hour reading detective magazines. Then I went out to the coupé and drove around aimlessly. It was a nice clear night and pretty good for thinking, but it took me another half an hour to get things straight in my mind. Which made it just a few minutes short of nine when I curbed the coupé again on Parkway Place.

CHAPTER IV

ESCAPE

I USED the alley this time instead of the sidewalk, and counted off numbers until I reached two-twelve. The house was quiet, but far from dark. There was a light in the front room—the living room—where Uncle Trixie was reading newspapers; the kitchen door was propped open for summer ventilation and I could see him through the kitchen window. There was an archway and no door between the dining room and living room. Trixie's wife—at least, that's who I guessed it was—was cutting out dress patterns on the dining-room table.

The only other light that I could see was directly above me—second floor rear.

There was a small back porch, with lattice-work that was a second-story man's dream. I went up it and catfooted across the roof, peeped in the lighted window, and then tapped gently on the screen. I was putting a whole lot of faith in Mike's judgment of Marcia Daly. If she lost her head and went schoolgirl and screamed, I was going to have bullets nipping at my ears.

But she didn't scream.

She was reading something, which isn't for schoolgirls by a long shot, and she sat up sharply on the bed and laid the book aside. She wore a white cotton beach robe and a chartreuse nightgown. Somehow the outfit seemed to pronounce rather than cover, and Bones would probably have fallen off the roof.

I didn't stand there so steadily, either.

She came to the window and peered out through the screen. Her green eyes weren't scared; they were just pretty curious.

I said: "Mike told me you had a darned good head on you."

She gasped. "You must be insane!"

I said anxiously: "Okay. Maybe you're right. I won't argue with you. But you don't have to tell people out in Oklahoma, do you?"

She lowered her voice. "What do you want?"

"In," I said. "I got a lot to ask you."

She regarded me dubiously for a moment, and then tiptoed to her door and listened for a while. Presently she closed the door and turned on the radio. She had a head on her, all right. She opened the screen and I slid in.

Then she wrapped the book in a face towel and hid it in a small fireplace in the room. "You're taking awful chances," she said.

I grinned. "How about you?"

"Well, Uncle Trix gave me an Elsie Dinsmore last Christmas. That'll give you an idea of what *he* thinks I should read." Her eyes brightened. "I didn't think you had the ordinary stupid look."

"Listen," I said. "You're making it easy for me. Your sister is Quackenbush's wife, isn't she?"

She nodded. "Yes."

"And she and Jerry Watt are nuts, about each other?"

She looked at me sharply. She was in the center of the room where the light fell flush across her face, and it was the first time I had gotten a good look at her. She had dark skin, almost dusky, and her face was a little wide through the jaws. She was no doll-faced Hollywood type. I liked the jaws and the high curved forehead.

Her mouth was wide and soft, and she nibbled at it reflectively. "Why do you ask that?"

I said: "Quackenbush hates Jerry Watt enough to goad him into action so he—Quackie—might get a legitimate excuse to kill him. He tried it over at the hotel. Next to that he's set on seeing Jerry hang."

Her face paled. "He would be," she whispered.

"Huh?"

"Walter Quackenbush would, I mean. Lila should never have married him. It's—true about she and Jerry. But they're keeping it—well"—she hesitated—"honorable."

"Is that where Jerry was this morning?"

She nodded slowly. "That's the reason he lives at the hotel. Walter and Lila live in the block of houses behind it, and Jerry sneaks over in the mornings to see her. And Walter knows—he *must* know, Lila says. Not that Jerry goes there in the mornings, but that she and Jerry are crazy about each other. He's often made a lot of veiled hints."

"But nobody else suspects?" I asked.

SHE FROWNED. "No. That is, nobody but me. Lila confides in me—she says she *has* to confide in somebody— You see, she's afraid that if she ask's Walter for a divorce, he'll kill Jerry. But nobody else suspects; she and Jerry have hidden it beautifully. When he gets to the big leagues and has money, he thinks he'll be able to do something about it."

I said: "Look, lady. I'm beginning to like Jerry Watt a little, but there's something about his character that doesn't add up. Why would a guy like that—who'll face a murder rap rather than pull his girl into a scandal—give us the runaround on a lousy three hundred dollar loan?"

She seemed surprised. "You don't know?"

I growled: "I'm just in here, risking getting my ears shot off, to ask you a lot of questions I already know the answers to."

She laughed aloud—one peal—and then smothered it, and chills steeple-chased up and down my spine. The house, all at once, seemed still as a tomb. I tiptoed over to the door and listened a few moments, and an owl hooting outside almost tore me out of my skin. But no sounds came from the stairs. I whispered:

"For gossakes! Don't do *that* again."

Her eyes shone, excitement and laughter mixed up in them. You could see the child in her then, because it made her look mischievous. She said: "Uncle Trix told me you had enough lip for ten men."

"Let's get back to Jerry Watt," I growled.

Footsteps clattered on the stairs, and my mouth snapped shut so quickly I almost nipped my tongue. Marcia Daly didn't hesitate an instant. She stepped over to the screen and slid it up, and I went swiftly across the room. I slid over the sill and stepped out on the roof, and for a moment, I was silhouetted against the window.

That was evidently what somebody was waiting for. A shot banged out and flame tongued at me from the alley.

The slug kicked splinters out of a shingle about six inches from my left ear and I threw myself flat on the roof. By that time, two more shots had thundered. But I never knew just where they landed because I had thrown myself down too hard. I skidded over the edge of the roof and somersaulted down into the yard.

I landed on a rose bush and skewered off into a flower-bed, rolled over and pulled my little gun. Out in the alley somewhere a motor started up and then faded in the distance. Up on the second floor, the screen banged up. A head poked out and Uncle Trixie's voice bellowed:

"I'm coming down after you, bud!"

I got to my feet and ran quickly up on the back porch. I opened the kitchen door and ran to the doorway of the living room. The woman at the dining-room table screeched at sight of me and fled.

I waited until she was out of sight, and then went back on the porch again. Uncle Trix, I figured, would now be getting his gun. I could hear the woman hustling up the stairs, screaming I was in the dining room, so I went up the lattice-work again and poked my nose over the roof.

The screen was still up and nobody was at the window, and I climbed to the roof and went across it noiselessly. Marcia Daly stood in the doorway. She whirled as I stepped in, her lower lip caught between her teeth, and I ran across and clapped a hand over her mouth. In a room nearby, the woman was still screaming. A door banged in the hall and heavy footsteps ran toward the stairs.

I pressed myself flat against the wall and watched Uncle Trixie's back plough past the doorway. I went out after him, fast, but I wasn't quite cat-like enough. My feet scuffled loudly and he spun, crouching, and I think I'll always hear his big Colt go off. It blasted in front of me as I whipped my gun-butt at his forehead, but the slug whistled past my shoulder and I felt the gun-butt land.

Uncle Trix crumpled and I bent anxiously over him. But he was breathing steadily and his skull still felt whole.

Marcia Daly watched us from the doorway. Her dark skin was almost white. "You haven't—?" She bit her lips.

"He'll be all right," I said. I felt limp inside. I didn't like battling with good guys I didn't want to hurt.

She steadied herself by gripping the doorjamb. But even the excitement hadn't affected her brain. She said: "You better—get out. People'll come running. Everybody isn't exactly—well, friendly toward you, you know."

I nodded. The other woman was still screaming. I stood up and said: "How about going along?"

She looked startled. "What?"

"Listen, little lady. I can't leave Bones to the mercy of that mob—not while I got any strength inside of me. And I think you've got the brains and courage to sneak him out. Why not take a crack at it for me?"

She blinked. "Me?"

"Sure. And Billy Hill's sweet on you, isn't he?"

She flushed slightly. "How in the world did you find *that* out?"

I looked anxiously at Uncle Trix. He didn't show any signs of coming out of it. I said: "From Mike. But never mind. Billy Hill'll help you, and I think you can do it."

She said dubiously: "I might try."

The doorbell began ringing, insistently. I said: "Swell. Grab yourself some clothes."

WE USED the stairs and the rear entrance, and by the time we got to the coupé, the whole neighborhood seemed to be awake. We could see a crowd on the porch and hear voices yelling to Trix to open up, and then a prowl car leaned into the street. The coupé was parked about fifty yards from the house and I slipped it in reverse and backed to the corner.

After that, we didn't have any worries. I drove out of the neighborhood and through town to the outskirts, and went about half a mile out the new dual highway. Then I stopped the car and got out on the road.

"How long will it take to climb into those clothes?" I asked.

She smiled a little. "About umpteen seconds."

The night was clouding up slightly and a thin moon wasn't giving much light, and I walked down the road and went through a cigarette thoughtfully. I didn't like being pressed for time like I was. That mob wouldn't really get nasty unless something else happened to aggravate it, but I had a hunch Uncle Trixie's story would. He'd made a lot of me being up in Marcia's bedroom, and he'd make more about her disappearing with me.

It wasn't a nice spot, but I was already in up to my neck, and there wasn't anything left but to see the thing through. I was wondering just how I'd better go about it when Marcia leaned out of the coupé and called to me.

I went back and climbed in beside her. She wore a crisp white blouse and dark skirt, and had even remembered to powder her nose. She said brightly:

"How do I look?"

I wiggled a finger at her. "Fine. But let's get back to Jerry Watt."

She laughed. "You don't forget very easily, do you? Well, Jerry got that loan when he was working—not playing ball—and when Mike discovered him and gave him a contract, he naturally quit the job. That was a year ago, the early part of last summer. And because Jerry had hood-winked your company when he got the loan from you, he was afraid to tell Mike he had gotten it.

"You see, Jerry really wanted the money to pay a gambling debt—he liked playing the horses and had run up a big debt to a bookie—but he told your company he

wanted it to pay his tuition in night school. He was studying law at night."

I grunted. "Yeah. But he didn't pay the tuition."

"That's right—that is, not *that* summer. You see, he—
Well, knowing Mike you'll be able to understand. Mike
had ruined his own baseball life by his drinking, and he
knew how important morals were to a young ballplayer's
success. So when he found some boy who looked like he
had a future, Mike always found out about his morals first
before he signed him. You see—or probably you already
know—outside of his one weakness, Mike was pretty
shrewd.

"He signed Jerry to a personal contract with him—
Mike—and then hired out Jerry to Billy Hill, by the season.
You see, Lambville's not in organized baseball and so Mike
could do that. Mike believed Jerry has a real future, and
he wanted to go on working with him and coaching him.
That's the reason Mike always caught when Jerry pitched.

"And— Well, Jerry knew how Mike was on young
ballplayer's morals—Mike used to preach *that*—and so
Jerry was afraid to tell him about the gambling and about
getting the loan to pay the debt. But you knew Mike and
you contacted him while investigating Jerry, and Mike
confronted Jerry with your story, and Jerry admitted it."

"That was the first of this summer," I growled.

SHE NODDED. "Certainly. And Mike told Jerry he'd
better pay. You see, Mike didn't think too much money
was good for young ballplayers so he told Jerry he was
only getting half of what he really got. The rest Mike put
in the bank for him. So Mike told Jerry he'd gotten a raise
from Billy Hill for him, and gave him enough extra money
to make payments to you. But Jerry was so sore at your

company because of some hard-boiled letters he got from Mr. McPherson—"

I laughed. "Bones is a little excitable. He believes people should pay their loans on time. Anyway, Jerry was only sending enough for some of the back interest, nothing for the principal."

She looked sharply at me. "Well, whatever it was, Jerry got sore. He decided he'd pay the tuition he hadn't paid instead of the loan, and nothing Mike could say could convince him otherwise. And Mike couldn't take the supposed raise away from him—"

"Huh?" I said.

She frowned. "Oh. You see, Mike hadn't told Jerry he was putting money away in the bank for him—Mike told Jerry he'd sold his contract to Billy Hill. Because Mike was afraid that if Jerry knew, he'd rebel and demand all his money. Nobody knew Jerry was under personal contract to Mike but Billy Hill and myself. Mike told me on one of his sprees."

I stared at her. "Sure of that?"

She nodded. "Positively. That was a secret Mike and Billy pleaded with me to keep."

I whistled softly. "And Uncle Trixie didn't want you mixed up in this! Look. Where do you think I can find Quackenbush now?"

She looked startled. "Why—why, at the hotel probably, on account of the mob."

I started the car, sent it roaring back towards town. "Now, listen," I said. "You get hold of Mr. Quackenbush and send him to the hotel those shots were fired from. I'll go in the back way and be on the top floor. Tell him Mike's murderer'll be up the roof tonight."

She stared incredulously at me. "What?"

We had reached Lambville's sparsely settled outskirts. We roared through, and cut into the main boulevard. I said: "He will. At least, I'm counting on it. Try to sneak Bones over there, too, because I think I'm going to need him. If Billy Hill's there, bring him along."

She was pale. "I'll try."

"Good girl. Now remember, I'm counting on you."

I let her out two blocks from the square and sat listening to a distant rumble of voices and watching her nicely made figure moving away from me. The street was almost deserted where I was parked. At the next corner, cops were diverting traffic from the square, and I could see the edge of the crowd beyond them.

I wondered, feeling the pit of my stomach crawl, what that crowd might do if they heard Uncle Trixie's story. The worst part of it was that something told me they would; I didn't think Trix would take his rebuff lying down. I climbed out of the coupé and went into a near-by confectionery, found a booth and telephoned Bones.

He said: "Jumping jeepers!"

"What is it, son?"

"Well, there was a little nastiness about half an hour ago, but the cops were able to handle it okay. Now, though, a maniac just got here. I'm tipping a bellboy to keep me wise to what's going on, and *he* says this guy claimed you kidnaped his niece. Now, look, Shaggie, this ain't the time for amours or crime, whichever one you got in that pretty bean of yours. And just between you and me—"

I was already gripping the phone. It hadn't taken Uncle Trix long. I said through my teeth: "She's on her way to sneak you out, dope."

"Huh?"

"When she gets you out, breeze over to the hotel the shooting came from and maybe we can get at the bottom of this business. Son, we've just *got* to now."

Bones snapped: "You're telling me? Look, boy. There's even some irony in this. A little while ago a guy comes up to the room and says he's a scout for a big-league ball club. He shows me papers to prove it and goes on to say that his club is ready to buy Jerry Watt for a cool thirty grand. He offers us dough if we'll prove Watt innocent—Watt can't pitch ball when he's behind bars for murder. How do you like those apples, huh?"

I held my breath. "Is the guy staying over there at the *Hotel Traill?*"

Bones said: "Just down the hall. What's the matter? You got asthma?"

I was breathing hard now. "Listen, son. When the girl sneaks you out, you bring that big-league scout along. Understand?"

Bones groaned. "Now, listen, Shaggie. One kidnaping is enough for one night, and besides—"

"Bring him along," I almost yelled. I banged up the phone.

OUTSIDE ON the sidewalk again, I didn't go to the coupé, but walked to the end of the block—away from the square—turned left and walked two blocks east. The alley that ran behind the two hotels was in the center of the next block, and I turned into it and strode rapidly to their rear entrances.

I went in the hotel the shooting had come from and peeped cautiously into the lobby. The night clerk was at a window, peering out into the square, and nobody else was in the lobby at all. I sneaked carefully over to the stairs and went up.

Nobody joined me on the top floor for ten minutes.

Quackenbush and Billy Hill were the first ones to arrive, and both of them were breathing heavily from excitement. Quackenbush splattered the hall runner disdainfully with tobacco juice.

"Was that a trick of yours?" he snapped.

I blinked. "What?"

Quackenbush bit off fresh tobacco from a plug. "Listen," he growled.

I frowned at him, and listened. There was a lot of noise going on down in the square, but the hotel walls muffled it. Then, all at once, I got it. The noise was growing fainter, moving away.

Quackenbush said: "Marcia came up and said you were over here, and told Billy and me you wanted to see us. Then, no more than we got here, we hear a yell. She's run out on the *Traill's* porch—she come in the back way—and she's yelling to Trix that you and McPherson are down on Walton Street. That's about four blocks away, and the crowd goes hell-bent for it. Did you put her up to that, too?"

I grinned. "In a way, yeah. In a couple of minutes, she ought to be over here with Bones."

It actually didn't seem to take a couple of minutes—before Quackenbush could corner me into answering any more questions, the elevator doors rattled open and three people stepped out. There was Marcia, who led, with a short, thick-set man behind her, and Bones' freckled face showed over his shoulder. The thick-set man was smiling blandly. He came up and said:

"Hello, Billy."

Hill frowned. "Hello, Mac." Then, grinning: "Mac, this is the Shag Roberts you've been hearing about. And Captain Quackenbush. This is Tom McGowan." The grin went away and the frown returned. "What in heaven's name brings you over here, fella?"

McGowan jerked a fat thumb at Bones. "Him, Billy. He's not the type of man I like to argue with." He chuckled quietly and shook hands with me. "I believe I've met Captain Quackenbush."

Quackenbush growled: "Yeah. You're from the big leagues, down to scout Jerry Watt, ain't you?" He looked suspiciously at McGowan. Marcia was nodding to Hill, but Hill didn't seem to see her. Quackenbush's pale brows bent toward me. "This another of your tricks?"

I grinned. "Listen, captain. Whoever killed Mike is going to be up on this roof in a little while, so he can get the rifle he shot Mike with. The rifle's hidden up there in the drainpipe—it won't go down all the way because there's a bend in the pipe about ten feet below the roof—and the killer's going to be frightened by those headlines tonight. Did you see 'em?

"It said a mysterious tipster claimed a solution to the murder—claimed he'd been over the hotel from *top to bottom*. Well, that's going to scare him enough to see if the rifle's still there, and if it *is* there, to fish it out. You know why I think so?"

QUACKENBUSH LOOKED dumbstruck. He stretched his chin, shifted his chew temporarily, then slipped it back into place and spat again. He said darkly: "How the hell would I?"

I wiggled a finger. "Don't ask me. Now, look. If that rifle can't be traced to its owner, the guy who used it wouldn't have bothered to hide it, he'd have simply tossed it over the edge of the roof. Or he might have even left it in the room he used it in—that would've been a whole lot safer, because he wouldn't've had to carry it upstairs. Somebody might have accidentally seen him carrying it up, you know.

But the rifle evidently *can* be traced to him, so he hid it in the drain-pipe—a pretty darned good place—probably planning just to leave it there for a while. Then when all this trouble blew over in a few weeks, he could fish it out in comparative safety, take it out in the country and bury it some place. But those headlines'll scare him, and he'll be after it."

Quackenbush growled: "Did you see it in there?"

I grinned. "Hell, no. You can't get me *that* way, Mr. Quackenbush. This is just a *theory* of mine; I haven't seen it, and so I haven't been concealing evidence. But when the guy escaped down through the hotel next door, I hardly think he carried the rifle with him. Or if he had a room in that hotel—which he probably did—he wouldn't take the rifle *there*.

"So he had to get rid of it, and that looks like the only place to hide it, because the chimney is too tall for a guy to reach the top of it, and too sheer to climb. You follow me?"

Quackenbush's eyes shimmered. "How do you know he hasn't fished it out already?"

I shrugged. "Maybe he has. But believe me if *I* was fishing it out, I'd wait till pretty late when there wasn't so much chance of being seen. I wouldn't do it before ten o'clock, when hotel corridors are still pretty full of life."

Quackenbush growled deep in his throat. He yanked out a big gold watch, looked at it, and snapped: "It's ten-fifteen. We'll go up and watch for a few hours and if nobody shows by then, we'll tear the pipe apart and see if you're right. Maybe Jerry Watt put it in there."

I didn't say anything. I wasn't paying very much attention to him right then. In the distance there was a roar, growing steadily in volume; there wasn't any doubt about it; the crowd was coming back. Bones and I looked quickly at each other.

Marcia said quietly: "Some people might have seen us come in, too. And I don't think the marines could stop that mob now."

CHAPTER V

SKYWAY TO HELL

BONES AND I lay on our bellies on the roof of the adjoining hotel. We were off to the left of the skylight that was kind of a vestibule, at just about a forty-five degree angle from its door. Overhead, the clouds had grown heavy, almost blotting out the moon, and you could barely see over two yards in front of you.

From the square, there were noises of the crowd milling about, and somewhere a tower clock sonorously tolled the half hour. That meant it was half past ten. We heard scuffling noises a little in front of us, and Billy Hill crept out of the darkness.

We made room for him on the blanket Bones had snitched from a room to protect his natty double-breasted gabardine.

"Is there a good word?" I said.

Hill flattened himself down beside me. "By some miracle, the crowd hasn't found we're here yet, but they're questioning anybody who comes along. Quackenbush stopped the night clerk and the elevator boy—they tried to run out and snitch—and he's over by the other skylight now, waiting like we are. There're cops with him and he has others downstairs. They're watching the clerk and the boy and protecting Marcia and McGowan."

"That's not such a bad word," I said. "You just come up from downstairs?"

"Yes."

"Got a gun?"

He said grimly: "My .38 and plenty of cartridges."

Bones grabbed my arm. "Hold everything," he whispered.

The light from inside the hotel came dimly through the glass skylight, placing a rectangular yellow patch on the dark surface of the roof. As we watched, a shadow bulked ominously in the midst of the patch—the shadow of a man's head, his shoulders, and then his torso. I could feel the hair rise on the back of my neck. There was a faint footstep, and then the glass door squeaked open.

The man stood motionless momentarily, and then a flashlight winked on and he swung the beam slowly from side to side. Presently he walked across the roof. He stepped to the other roof, wheeling the beam about, and finally stopped in front of the drain-pipe. Then he clamped the flashlight under an arm and snatched out a length of cord with a loop on the end of it.

He put the beam directly over the wide mouth of the pipe and fed cord into it with the other hand. Then—for about three full minutes—he fished around and swore intermittently. Finally, the rifle came up, the loop pulled tight over the front sight—and the beam of another flashlight sliced through the darkness.

Quackenbush's voice roared: "Put up your hands!"

The man cringed suddenly, pinned in the beam of the police light, and Billy Hill's gun banged out beside me. The man threw down the rifle and clawed a pistol from his coat pocket. He fired at the police light, which winked out instantly, only to wink on again as shots flashed beside it. But the man had turned and was sprinting toward us. Hill's gun banged again and the man swerved toward the chimney, ducked behind it and poured bullets our way.

The police light splashed on the chimney, and slugs kicked dust out of the bricks, and then the man was in the open again. The upper half of his body was silhouetted over the top of the parapet against the glow of light from the square. Then Hill's gun and the police guns banged together. The man fell against the parapet, balanced against it momentarily, and then a second volley of bullets drove him over it.

He wasn't dead when he disappeared over the edge. We heard his wild screeching yell on his way down.

I got up and ran across the roofs into the glare of Quackenbush's light. "Anybody hurt?" I yelled.

Quackenbush sprayed the beam on himself. There was a round hole just below his breastbone and his lean face was a ghastly yellow. His gun had dropped to the roof and he had the flashlight gripped in both hands. But he wouldn't be gripping it for very long.

Bones and Hill came running up behind me.

One of the cops stood up from examining Quackenbush's wound. He wagged his head slowly and said: "He hasn't got over five minutes. Who was it, Roberts?"

I scowled. "How do I know?"

"Huh?"

"I'm going down and find out," I growled.

I LIFTED the skylight and went down the circular iron staircase with Bones and Billy Hill close behind me. The elevator was propped open with a stool. We got on and I shot it down, got off at the lobby and strode through it to the porch. The porch itself was almost deserted, but the blast of sound from the sidewalk was deafening.

The mob—hundreds now; it jammed the square—were gabbing excitedly among themselves. On the sidewalk, a small circle was cleared around a man's crushed body, and Uncle Trix was standing over it. I stopped abruptly at the top of the porch steps, looked out over the mob, and scarcely breathed.

Then I yelled: "Trix!"

A couple of hundred pairs of eyes swiveled toward me and a hush settled over the square. I could feel the blood beating at my temples and my arms seemed to have no strength.

Trix whirled, catlike for a big man, and stood crouching a little, his eyes fixed on my face. I didn't see a gun in his hand.

We were only about fifteen yards apart. The porch was lined with lights and a huge sign hung outside; it winked on and off and hurled white and yellow light over the crowd. Then somebody hooted, and the mob surged forward savagely.

I yelled again: "Trix!"

The surge hadn't blotted out the small circle. Trix cupped his hands to his mouth and shouted:

"Like to shoot it out, rat?"

Our voices banged over the sudden shuffle of the crowd, and almost instantly another hush settled. The circle around Trix began to grow larger. It widened slowly, and then there was a wild stampede, men stumbling and falling trying to get out of bullet range. I kept my hands carefully still. Trix' hand was clawed over a baggy coat pocket.

I yelled: "Listen to me, Trix! Who's the dead man?"

"Don't go stalling on me, rat!"

"You dumb-head!" I shouted. "He's the guy who sniped off Mike! He's the guy who was hired for the job by a guy here behind me, Billy Hill! You know why?" I didn't wait for an answer. "A big-league ball club was going to buy Jerry Watt, and Jerry was signed up to Mike Martinez personally! Only nobody knew it but Billy Hill and Marcia! Hill stood to make thirty grand out of the kill!"

There was one paralyzed moment of absolute stillness, the sign blinking over doubtful sinister faces. My chest felt like it had collapsed. This was my ace, my last opportunity; I didn't have much else to give out. If this flunked on me, I'd have to try to shoot a man, and if I shot him, I'd be trampled to death. And Bones would be trampled along with me. He'd be back of me, trying to help, as long as there was a single breath in his body.

Then the door of the hotel banged and Marcia ran breathlessly out on the porch. She screamed: "Uncle Trix! Mike *did* own Jerry's contract! And the big-league scout is right inside!"

I twisted suddenly and shot a look at Hill, and saw his lower teeth climb and snag his lip. He stood stiffly, his shoulders hunched, and his eyes, for the first time, lost their shrewdness. They darted from side to side, then settled on Marcia, and she faced him with her chin lifted defiantly. Hill's eyes had darkened, and now they looked murderous.

I yelled: "Marcia! Look out!"

Hill's hand struck for his coat pocket, and I leaped forward and slammed my shoulder against the girl. Hill's gun went off, the sound of it deafening, but by that time we were down on the porch floor. Then Bones' yell rose over the sound of the shot and the crowd, and he charged in from the side and grabbed Hill's gun wrist.

I was down on my belly in front of them and I reached out and grabbed Hill's leg. He fell backward, Bones falling on top of him, but when Bones rolled off, he had Hill's gun. He yelled down at him:

"You gonna get up?"

HILL STRUGGLED to his knees and Bones slammed the butt of his gun on his forehead. Then he winked at me, picked up Hill on his shoulder, and walked over to the top of the porch steps.

His green eyes danced and he grinned wickedly. He yelled: "You boys want him out there?"

The crowd surged, and a roar went up.

Bones lifted a skinny hand. "Okay! Step right up! How much are you gonna bid?"

The luminius clock on my dashboard said twelve after two when I curbed the coupé for the third time on Parkway Place. I said: "Glad you finally saw it my way, Trix."

Trixie opened the door and grinned. "I'd've shot you—or anyway, tried to've shot you—sure'n hell if you'd've gone for the gun." He scratched his head. "You want to linger awhile, honey?"

Marcia said: "For a minute. If you don't mind."

Trix chuckled. "Well, I still got the gun. All you got to do is yell out, honey." He extended a hand. "See you after the ball game tomorrow, I hope, fella."

We shook hands. I said: "You'll play, huh?"

"We put it up to Mrs. Hill, and she said okay. Billy himself don't give a hoot, and we wired the league president, and he said okay. You know, that mob would probably have torn Billy apart if that pal of yours hadn't conked him so hard. Somehow you don't feel like working on an unconscious guy."

I said: "Go along, will you?"

He grinned broadly. "Okay. But remember, I still got the gun, fella."

He closed the door and walked away into the darkness, and Marcia closed her eyes and put her head back against the seat. Outside, a whippoorwill called. This was her idea; I waited for her to move.

She said: "Who shot at you?"

I blinked. "Huh?"

"I mean, at the house here. Billy or his hireling?"

I said: "The hireling. Billy wasn't taking any chances; he was at the hotel with a good alibi. He naturally guessed where I was headed when he told me you were Mrs. Quackenbush's sister, and he was afraid you'd spill the beans about the contract, like you did. So he wanted me killed, in case I'd gotten that information, because he knew it wouldn't be tough to fix a motive on him then.

"Besides, I think he knew Bones and I'd phoned in that mysterious tip to the *Chronicle*, and he knew if we found the rifle we could trace it to the hireling. He was Charley Smiley, a Lambville product, and Hill was afraid he'd squeal if pressed. That's the reason Hill shot before the guy even reached for a gun up there on the roof tonight. He tried to kill Smiley, and he'd've gotten away with it, too. He could've sworn *he* saw Smiley reach for a gun."

I frowned. "And I think he would've had *you* killed if he hadn't been gone on you. But just your knowing about the contract didn't condemn him anyway—that didn't hurt until I happened to tie it up. Anyway, he probably had hopes of making more time with you with that thirty grand stuffed in his pockets."

Now I was grinning at her. "You see, he was the sole owner of the club, president, manager, and everything, and he could've easily faked his papers to make it look like he owned Jerry. Then he could've sold him to the big leagues, pocketed the cash…"

I chewed my lip. "Oh, yes. The reason he sent you out to stop us on the road was that he didn't want any guys with reputations for cracking murders in town. And he was always trying to get Bones and me to scram. Pretty sly about it, too. I think the guy was clever."

Marcia said: "And I think you were clever, too. I didn't even think of Billy until I heard you out on the porch." She opened her eyes and looked sideways at me. "Do you know how old I am?"

I nodded. "Seventeen."

"And is that the reason you're not going to kiss me good-night?"

I said: "Huh?"

She laughed gently. "Is it?"

She had me there. I said: "I'll be darned if I know."

"Well, then, will you come back, say when I'm eighteen, and find out exactly, certainly, and for sure?"

I grinned. "I'll come with bells on."

She said: "Then you scout all around town tomorrow and see if you can find any bells that aren't being used. Then sling 'em over your shoulders—providing you find some— and come around tomorrow night jingling 'em cheerfully."

I said: "Don't tell me—"

She laughed and got out of the car. "That's right— tomorrow's my birthday. And don't bring me the bells for a present, either."